I0838750

WOLF LAND

TURBO-9308

ISBN 978-1-957220-85-7 (paperback)
ISBN 978-1-957220-86-4 (digital)

Copyright © 2022 by Turbo-9308

All rights reserved. No part of this publication may be reproduced, distributed, or transmitted in any form or by any means, including photocopying, recording, or other electronic or mechanical methods without the prior written permission of the publisher. For permission requests, solicit the publisher via the address below.

Rushmore Press LLC
1 800 460 9188
www.rushmorepress.com

Printed in the United States of America

PROLOGUE

SOME SAY THAT THESE wolves or aliens came from another planet by traveling in some sort of spacecraft. Others say that a team of scientists opened up a portal to another world. Then, other sources state that the same group of scientists created a few of the wolves and everything went out of control. Either way, the majority of us, like me, don't really give a shit because we've got jobs to do and money to make.

Man, could I be completely *wrong* about that.

CHAPTER ONE
Location: Ottawa, Kansas
Date: September 12, 2014
Time: 10:30 PM

I JUST PULLED INTO a Shell gas station here in Ottawa to fill up my truck. Even though I've got half a tank left, it feels just right to top her off since I'm delivering a load to Nashville, Tennessee. I also pulled into this fine establishment to stretch my legs and check my load. Allow me to introduce myself. My name is Will Young. I'm 21 years old and I'm an asphalt cowboy, also known as a truck driver. My handle is Lonesome Cowboy. Let me guess, y'all are thinking that I should be attending college at this age instead of driving a truck. Well, let me tell you something. When you move into a town that you weren't born in and the education system started to challenge you in elementary school and treated you like shit from middle school to high school, it really shows that they don't give a damn about the self-esteem of minor, learning, disabled kids. During that time, picking up a job halfway through high school that only pays $7.25 ain't a good way to live off. Adding on top of that is when your home becomes a broken home halfway through high school and all you got is your buddies from the auto shop that really treat you like a family. All in all, I did graduate from high school with good grades, but I wanted to get out of that town as soon as possible. And here I am.

I've been an asphalt cowboy for three years, so yeah, after a month after graduating from high school, I went into a truck driving school, got my CDL, and right off the bat, I got employed. Aside from that, what you guys just read on the previous page is true. During this past summer, everything was smooth sailing until the beginning of September when all of the news media outlets were reporting that an alien species crash-landed or were created in some secret lap up in Montana, decided to break out, and started taking over the state in good and horrible ways. Some other news reports state that they have the species well-contained within the state lines, but who knows how long that's going to last? So far, up to this date, the insanity has been holding, but for me, I'm a little bit uneasy. So, I carry a hunting knife strapped to my belt and a Colt 1911 45ACP locked and hidden in my truck. Don't worry, I have the proper paperwork and license to carry it.

Anyway, I put the nozzle in my tank, let it fill up, and walk around my "parking garage" which is a CB term for hauling brand new cars and trucks on a trailer to the dealership. Now, this type of parking garage that I'm hauling to Nashville is a "traitor parking garage" which means I'm hauling Toyotas to the city of country music and all of the cars are new Priuses. Every time that I check them in person or even see them in my mirrors, I just feel disgusted and shake my head from what this country has come to. Oh well, it's America and any person has the right to purchase and drive any vehicle that they want. Overall, it's my duty to inspect and make sure that the products are in great condition and they stay that way when they are delivered—safe and on time. I have been highly recommended by my manager due to the fact I've created a great reputation of delivering loads on time and sometimes early. So, maybe that's why I was chosen for this load.

Sigh. It looks like all of these "green" cars are in good condition and that makes me happy.

Then, the diesel pump shuts off, revealing a total of $400.78.

"Perfect," I say to myself.

I head inside to pay the cashier. Looking around in the store, a newspaper stand catches my eye with the latest newspaper on the top shelf yelling in bold words on the front page. I reach for it, unfold it, and read, *"Border Containment Units Having Trouble Holding Back Alien Race!"*

I keep on reading the article, *"Authorities have stated that the border containment units are beginning to fail because of the great force of the alien race. There have been times where the alien race has attacked officials in order to break free. Of course, officials have used deadly fire a few times to keep them at bay, but there is great confusion among them and civilians that live in the area. Reports have shown that there is one group that's bigger than the other, shows that they are good, and mean no harm to the public. Other reports say that the second group is deadly and shows no mercy, but these two groups look identical and the authorities have told every civilian to pack up whatever they can carry and immediately leave the area at once, and do not trust any of the aliens."*

I stop to look at the picture in the middle of the front page. The image is a bit blurry, but it looks like the cameraman was able to get a decent shot of one of the aliens. Examining the image, I can make out the head. It looks a bit canine and it seems to be standing upright while wearing normal clothes.

I keep on scrutinizing the image until the cashier talks to me, "Some messed up shit, ain't it?"

I look right back up to him to acknowledge his question, then back down, and reply, "Yeah, it seems pretty messed up."

With that being said, I fold the newspaper back up and put it away. I pay the cashier, thank him for his service, and head back out to my rig. Approaching the pump to remove the nozzle, the lights above me begin to flicker for some strange reason, and after a couple of minutes, they remain solid and continue their normal buzzing sound. I keep my fear at bay and calmly reach for my knife. I hear a howl in the distant darkness that sounds like a wolf for about a minute and it stops. I calmly check my surroundings, then I remove the nozzle, holster it, and I calmly walk back to the driver door, opening it, getting in, and immediately shutting it. To further my protection, I lock my cabin and start the engine of my Kenworth. I pull out of the refueling station and get my rig back on the highway as if nothing has happened.

I'm still on edge for a little bit from what I just experienced. To steady my nerves once more, I grab my CB and make a call into it, "Breaker 1-9, breaker 1-9, this the Lonesome Cowboy doing a radio check."

I wait for a few seconds and then a male voice comes out of the speaker, "Lonesome Cowboy, this is Pig Stew and your radio sounds real good."

I smile to myself thinking that whatever happened was made up and it's going to be fine.

I reply back, "10-4. Thanks for the comeback."

"10-4," says Pig Stew.

With that out of the way, I get my rig up to 70 miles per hour, put on cruise control, turn on my iPod, and select my country mix that my auto shop teacher made and gave to me. I hit the play button for the first track and I don't settle into my seat until I hear the lyrics of "Semis Together" by W.C. Caller come through the speakers. Once they do, I settle down, and right at that moment, it hits me that it's still gonna be a long, ass drive to Nashville, Tennessee and a long, ass night.

CHAPTER TWO
Location: I-35, Three Miles
West of Kansas City
Date: September 13, 2014
Time: 12:05 AM

MY GOAL TONIGHT IS to get through Kansas City which I think is going to be impossible because I am really exhausted and I've been up since 5:30 AM yesterday morning. I keep on driving, hoping there's a rest stop of some sort that I can just pull over and hit the hay. As minutes go by, I've seen no rest stop and I am already in the city limits. So, screw it. Luckily, all the roadways in this great city are clear, but of course, there are some eighteen-wheelers and other vehicles cruising along the highways.

Aw man, I'm so tired.

For some reason, I don't know if I should try to reach my mini frig and try to grab a Nos energy drink, so I look back for a few seconds and, nope. The frig is too far away to reach because the sleeper cabin of my Kenworth T680 is pretty damn big, plus, I'm traveling at seventy miles per hour, and I should be more responsible with my rig and my load. To scrub away the stupid idea, I glance in my driver-side mirror.

"Ugh, they're so disgusting," I say to myself.

Then the CB comes alive, "Breaker, breaker, to any soul on this here channel, I have a Smokey update to tell."

My eyes burst open and I grab the mic, replying, "Yes, sir, there's a soul on this channel. Let me hear your Smokey update."

The person on the other side asks, "Is this the famous Lonesome Cowboy I hear?"

I smile again, "Yes, sir, it is, and who's this I'm hearing on my end?"

"Well, Lonesome Cowboy, this here is The Hillbilly and the Smokey update I've got for you is not a good one."

"Well, let's hear it."

"Well, my friend, I've come to a complete stop and haven't moved since because I'm here at a search checkpoint. And these smokies, they're armed to the teeth and they ain't messin' around. They're searchin' every car, pick-up, SUV, and semi for those wolf-like aliens. Well, lucky me, I'm up next."

"Thanks for the update, Hillbilly."

"10-4 Cowboy."

Great, this alien race has broken through the secured borders of Montana and they've made their way this far south.

Other than that, I still cruise along the almost empty highway, preparing myself to be heavily questioned and searched—both man and machine. For a while, everything still looks pretty normal until I start to notice a repeating light source that's strobing fast, changing between red and blue. Ahead of me for almost a mile, I take notice that cars of all types are coming to a stop. I just easily turn off the cruise control and gently press down on the brake pedal. Approaching the line of stopped cars, I am truly amazed by the size of this checkpoint.

There's got to be at least thirty or so vehicles in total, about fifteen are patrol cars, ten are heavily armed SWAT trucks and vans, and five are Hazard Control vans with special tents set up. With these vehicles added together, there's got to be well over a hundred officials here. I come to a stop, put on the air emergency brake, lean back in my seat, and take in the view.

The traffic is being divided into three columns: the one in the far left is for cars, the one in the middle is for pick-up trucks, vans, and SUVs, and the one on the far right is for semis. I also see that there are more K-9 units that are sniffing around every inch of every semi. This column would take a lot longer than the other two. I decide to pull out my papers for the load that I'm hauling to and from, my driver's license, and permit for my gun. With that done, I calmly pull out my gun, the magazines, and my knife and I spread them all out on the dashboard. I know it would be a matter of time when they see them and cops throw my door open and drag me out to the ground. The traffic slowly starts to move again and I'm up next. I slowly approach the checkpoint and I calmly raise my hands saying that I mean no harm and I'm willing to cooperate with them. It's not long until the officers take notice of the weapons I placed on the dash and start to point their guns at me. Almost all of them are yelling at me to keep my hands up in their sights and get out of my truck.

While descending out of the cab, I'm immediately shoved up against a cop car, have handcuffs placed on me, and immediately turned around to be hammered by fast, impatient questions. The officer that I am facing is almost as tall as me, medium-sized built, and looks like to be in his thirties.

"Why do you have a gun and a knife in your possession?" the officer asked furiously.

"For protection," I answer without a pause.

"Do you have a permit for that gun?"

"Yes, yes I do. It's on the passenger seat along with the documents from what type of load that I'm hauling to and from and my driver's license."

"Protection from what?"

"From the alien race that has broken through the Montana state lines. Is that why you guys set up this checkpoint?"

He scrutinizes my face to check if I was telling the truth. He looks back at his comrades and orders them to grab the documents and run a computer scan on them to make sure they're legit. Then he looks back at me, finally recognizing that I am telling the truth, so he backs off and eases his voice to ask me further questions.

"Where are you coming from?"

"Salt Lake City, Utah, sir."

"Where are you going?"

"Nashville, Tennessee, sir."

He soon asks one of his comrades if those documents are legit and he replies back saying that everything checks out from my load to my gun to my driver's license. Then he orders the K-9 group to sniff out my truck and trailer.

He looks at my load for a moment, back at me, and asks, "Are you carrying any illegal drugs, people, or aliens on this vehicle?"

"No, sir."

"May we take a look to make sure?"

"Hey, you got me in handcuffs, I'm not going anywhere, and all of you are armed with heavy-duty machine guns and dogs."

The officer chuckles a little and nods his head in saying that's true. As the minutes go by, the other officers and K-9 units complete the search, giving the okay that I'm clean, and I should be released. The officer takes off the cuffs and gives back my documents, but watches me with his flashlight to make sure I don't pull anything out to surprise him or the dogs while I put my documents away. When I turn around, the same officer has my gun in his hand, handing it back to me butt first.

As I grab it, he places his free hand firmly on my shoulder, and tells me, "You use this weapon wisely, son. Do you understand me?"

I nod. He hands back the magazines and my knife. When I put everything away, I thank all the officers for doing their job, and as I am about to shake a few of their hands, some of the dogs start to bark furiously down the empty highway where the North-East bound traffic is coming from. Then down below the highway where we stand, a building suddenly explodes in a great ball of fire and smoke and begins to crumble down to earth. A few of the cars in the columns that were half through being checked, the drivers and passengers, push back the officers to get back in their rides, and they peel out of the checkpoint. The other vehicles behind them follow and break through the barricades. All of the officer's radios start to sound off with mixed screaming voices for backup and all sorts of things. Every officer starts to run to their stations, but they come to an abrupt halt when we all hear a loud, echoing howl. Then the highway lights give out when the same crumbling building takes down some heavy-duty power lines. Soon, the entire city of Kansas City goes black. I'm in so much shock that I don't climb up into my rig and start burning rubber from what is happening here.

The dogs keep on barking in the same direction at something, but all of us can't tell what it is. When a few minutes pass, we all started seeing blood-red eyes with black slits in the middle and dark, menacing growls coming from them. The search checkpoint dogs growl back but are whining and start to back up. The only lights that illuminate the area are the flashing LEDs on the official vehicles and they reveal what lurks in the darkness ahead of us. We are all completely in shock at the menacing creatures that start walking toward us. To describe them, they walk on their hind legs, like humans, and have fully muscular torsos, arms, and legs. At the end of their hands are long, sharp claws that can slice through anything. Then, those creatures come to stop to intimidate us, and immediately, the one that is at the head of this large pack starts to sprint at us, bearing its fangs. His troops also follow at full speed. The cops open fire at them and they start going down like flies.

As for me, *I'm gettin' the fuckin' hell outta here!*

I leap into my rig. Starting it up and burning rubber, the momentum throws me into my seat as I slam the hammer straight down to the metal. I look in my driver's mirror and oh, the horror. Every police officer and hazard worker is attacked and slaughtered within seconds. I don't stop. I just keep on trucking, saving my own ass and skin. Some of the wolves jump onto my rig in a swift movement and start clawing at the body. In reaction, I thrash the steering left and right, ramming the truck up against the concrete dividers. The loud noise of grinding metal up against the concrete echoes all around me with sparks flying. The wolves who clawed on scream and howl in pain as they are peeled away by the walls, leaving long streaks of blood and organs that are immediately flattened and torn to bits. Returning into the cruising lane, I think I'm in the clear. All is quiet for a few minutes until one more breaks the window on the passenger door and thrashes its claws at me.

Holy fucking shit!

Again, I ram the right side of my truck against the wall, but the bastard still hangs on. I reach for my pistol, still grinding my rig along the wall at 65 MPH. I pull it out just in time before the monster gets in and shoot him dead straight in the head. The corpse slumps over in the broken window and again, jerking the steering wheel to the right once more. It flies out, falls onto the road, and gets run over by the wheels on the trailer, finishing the job.

Now, I am torn between two choices: one, should I keep on delivering these "green" cars to the city that is the heart of country music and pretend everything is under control (yet my truck is scraped up and down to hell)? Or two, should I drive for a couple of miles until I pull off onto a frontage road, unhitch the trailer, leave it, and head to the nearest gun store?

I ponder on these choices for a long time. I look in the mirror at those ugly cars and back at the road. I look back and forth. The more time I spend thinking about my options, the more frustrating it gets.

I look down at the clock which is reading 1:00 AM. With one long draw of my breath, I shout this, "Ah, the hell with it! I'm delivering these pieces of crap and getting my *money*!" After that, I keep the needle of my speedometer at eighty-five and push through the rest of the night.

CHAPTER THREE
Location: Truck Stop Diner Just Off I-25, Nashville, Tennessee
Date: September 15, 2014
Time: 9:00 AM

LAST NIGHT, I PULLED into this truck stop and spent the night in my truck. During that night, I dreamt about those humanoid-like wolves that annihilated the police at that checkpoint back in Kansas City, and instead of fleeing, I too was attacked, and was murdered within seconds. I woke a couple of times and it took me a while to fall back to sleep. But now, I wake up, exhausted, but I'm relieved that I finally made it to Nashville, Tennessee. The weather outside is clear and the sun is shining nice and bright. I roll out of my bed and straight onto the floor which really wakes me up. I stumble around the cabin putting on fresh clothes and getting them all straightened out. Within minutes, it looks decent enough for me, so I grab my cowboy hat, boots, shades, and leave my rig to get some breakfast.

Walking across the parking lot, I take notice of other asphalt cowboys climbing out of their rigs, also exhausted due to a long drive or lack of sleep. Yet, as I look back at my rig, the damage I gave looks worse in daylight than it did during the night.

Shit, that's gonna cost me a crapload of cash to repair.

Nonetheless, my stomach growls and it focuses my attention to keep on walking to the diner. A few of the guys heading in the same direction wave at me and I wave back with a smile on my face. Entering the diner, there's not a lot of people in here, but man, the food smells really good. I take a seat at the bar that neighbors the kitchen and I'm handed a menu. After a few minutes of ordering what I want, I drink my coffee, and the volume on the TV is loud enough to grab my attention, but I keep on ignoring it until another trucker asks one of the employees to turn it up.

Turning my eyes up to the monitor, I see a news reporter standing in front of some building that seemed to have exploded because of the state that it's in. It looks terrible, and the male news reporter says, "I'm at the main site where a top-secret lab facility was housed, but it was a made-up building to appear as an abandoned warehouse. In this lab facility, top-secret information that has been leaked shows that the scientists found a UFO that crash-landed weeks ago and was located just five miles to the south of us. The crash site was investigated, brought the aliens to this facility, revived them, and performed multiple tests on them to see how they function. That's why a few days ago, this area was thrown into chaos because the alien species revolted and broke out from this facility to seek better refuge. However, the spaceship that the scientists discovered turned out to be a prisoner transporter of some kind and that is why there is great confusion amongst the entire nation to differ between the good aliens and the bad ones. Reports have also shown that both of these races have indeed broken through the secured lines here in Montana and have run into the woods in this nation. Back to you, John."

The camera changes locations to newsroom and the head news reporter, John, says, "Thank you, Mike. Again, none of the American people should trust these aliens."

The TV screen splits into two views of the reporters. Mike replies, "Yes, John, that is indeed correct. No American should trust these aliens and we both should now be more careful of our surroundings."

After that, one of the diner's cooks turns the TV off and everybody that's in here bursts into loud murmuring conversations. For me, I still drink my coffee while I wait for my food. To tell you the truth, I am now scared and I think I should head to the nearest gun store to arm myself after I deliver my load. When my food arrives, I immediately chow down on it and after that, I pay my bill and head back to my rig. Every time that I arrive in a new location that I don't know, I just punch in my destination on my GPS and follow the confusing thing through the heavy traffic. Within thirty minutes, I arrive at the Toyota dealership with the brand new "green" cars. I back my rig in the delivery drop-off zone and guess what kind of person that comes walking over with a very pissed-off look on her face.

Sigh. I don't have the time to do this nor the energy, but this could be another test from God.

Descending out of my rig, this woman starts yelling at me, "How dare you pollute our beautiful planet with your gas-guzzling piece of shit!"

Sighing once more, I pull out my knife, pointing it right at her face, and answering, "How dare I pollute this planet? The question should be, how dare *you* people buy these cars that use more energy to accommodate to the speed limits in this nation? Listen, lady, I had a very long drive, hauling your precious new Priuses to this location. I'm tired and in case you didn't notice, we have a crazy alien race taking over our nation. My truck has suffered a lot of damage from some sort of attack, and overall, I think that those two are more important than this matter. Now, how 'bout you fuck off, let me do my job, and leave me alone?"

Right after that, she takes off like a little dog that thought it was tough but realized I was the bigger dog, and I shouldn't be messed around with. Listen, I know it's wrong to pull out a knife on an unarmed civilian, but I'm doing my job, plus, the truth is these Priuses don't receive a good gas mileage that they promote in their commercials. They use more energy to perform with normal gasoline and diesel engines, and producing those cars pollutes the planet more than my Kenworth. Especially, they have special metals that are mined out and are combined with other materials that create the battery and cannot be properly disposed of. Anyway, I put my knife back, grab my paperwork, and walk into the dealership to complete this journey.

An hour or so has passed, everything is checked out, and I get my paycheck of $800.00, plus a bonus for delivering the cargo four hours early than the designated time. I'm a happy man as I climb back into my rig, fire up my laptop, and begin to locate the nearest gun store. Within minutes, I find one and leave the dealership. What's interesting about this gun store is that it has an ATM where I can cash my check and immediately purchase my items. The next three miles roll by and I have to say there's a lot of military trucks and machinery being transported across these highways here in Nashville. But not just here, from the past few days, I've noticed a lot of those vehicles on the highways just halfway through my journey when I was transporting those Priuses.

Ah, it's so nice not to see those things lingering behind me.

While I'm getting off the highway and onto the street that would lead me to the gun store, for some odd reason, the traffic starts backing up. I reach for the CB to see if I could get some answers, "Breaker, breaker, this is the Lonesome Cowboy. Does anybody up ahead got an idea what's holding up the traffic?"

Within seconds, I get my answer, "Lonesome Cowboy, this is Foxy, and the reason why the traffic is held up here is that there's a car wreck. More like a fender bender, but those people are making a huge fight about it."

"10-4, Foxy," I reply.

"10-4."

Great, a simple fender bender and it's going to take a very long, ass time to get this mess all cleared up. I know I could just turn on my normal radio and tune in to one of the multiple stations to hear the traffic report, but CB radios are better. I put my truck in park and unbuckle myself to grab something from my mini-fridge. After I grab my soda, I decide to browse through my country CDs. I pick one, slide back into the seat, and pop the disk in my radio. While looking out from all three of my windows, another semi catches my attention. When it comes to a stop, I wave at the person. The person has his or her hood up, but when he turns his head in my direction, instead of expecting to see another human, this person has a head shaped like a canine. It has the mouth, nose, eyes, and ears of the creature. What's interesting is that the eyes are navy blue instead of blood-red, but in the end, it still scares the hell out of me. I snap my head to look in the opposite direction, trying to calm myself down that whatever I just saw wasn't real.

After a few seconds have ticked away, I gather enough courage to look at the same person. Shockingly, the canine is not there, but a real human face. The man waves at me with a smile and I am absolutely horrified. Now, my heart is racing. My blood feels ice cold. I pray to God to have the traffic in my lane start moving and so it does. I calmly disengage the parking brake and gently press down on the gas pedal. To my surprise, which annoys me, the fender bender took place at the next intersection, not far from where I was. Driving through the intersection, I spot the two people that caused the backup and I simply shake my head as they see me coming through. They just give dirty looks, but I don't care.

Business people getting all upset over the littlest things. We asphalt cowboys, we have a "real" job to do. We're one of the important backbones of this great nation. I find that "our" job is more important.

Anyway, we don't matter in the public's eye. Besides, I see the gun store on the right and I pull in. I grab my check and walk straight up to the ATM that's right next to the entrance to change that little piece of paper into multiple pieces of paper.

Walking in through the front door, coincidentally, a song called "This Honkey Tonk" by Keith Tobes starts playing, and I take a few steps in just to take in all the different types of guns. Also, there are bows and crossbows being sold, too. At times like these where I am simply amazed by a new sight of cars, weapons, or anything else, I just simply stick my hands in my pockets and just browse the store. This time, I'm trying to figure out which weapon I should purchase.

The man behind the counter comes around and greets me, "Hello, sir. Is there something I can help you with?"

I look at him and reply, "Um, yeah. Are you aware of what the hell is happening out there?"

"Oh, hell yeah. What type of weapon are you interested in?"

Looking around a couple of times, two weapons seem to pop out and I tell the clerk, "I want to check out that crossbow and that hunting rifle."

The clerk turns toward the direction where I'm pointing and walks back behind the counter to grab the two weapons. Soon, he places them down in front of me and asks, "So, what are you going to use the weapons for?"

The weapons that I picked out are a Barnett Red Dot Crossbow Package priced at $199.99 and a Savage Axis XP Rifle Combo priced at $150.99. Both of these weapons are on sale and that makes me happy.

Before the clerk hands them to me, he states, "Listen, sir, you and I both know that these are crazy times, but I still need to run a background check on you."

"That's cool. I've done it before."

Soon, the clerk walks toward his computer and asks me for my name, date of birth, and my current age. After he punched the information in, he looks back up at me and tells me that it's all good but asks me if I've committed any crime, like a felony, that would prevent me from purchasing any other weapons. I look at him seriously and truthfully in the face and tell him "no." He still researches my criminal record and remains silent for a moment. Scrutinizing at the information laid out on the screen before him, he looks back at me, smiles, and tells me that I'm clear.

I look back at him and answer his previous question, "For two things. One: hunting, and two: better protection."

He asks if there's anything else, so pick out a couple of boxes of arrows and rifle bullets. With that done, I tell him that's everything and he rings me up. While I'm leaving the store, more people pull into the parking lot and hustle in. The way that they move, they seem to be scared, but they have the reason to be. Climbing into my rig, I set my weapons aside and fire it up; immediately, the CB comes alive with horrified, frantic voices.

"They've taken over the city! I repeat, this is Blue Jay, the crazy alien race is taking over the city!"

More horrified voices come through.

"Breaker, breaker, this is Bulldog. These bastards are swarming in from the northeast!"

Then the sound of a shotgun sounds off through the small, CB speaker.

"This is Northwind, I see them coming from the west! Holy shit, they're swarming my truck! *Shit*!"

More and more voices keep on screeching through the CB until it cuts out. I reach for the mic, letting it fall. I scramble my hands around to get a firm grip. Pushing the button, I say this, "This is the Lonesome Cowboy. Is there anybody on this channel?" Static.

I switch stations, saying the same thing. More static. I change it again, saying the same thing. Same result. I am beginning to really freak out. I hear car horns down the road, some speed down the asphalt, dodging other cars. I can see them, the alien race, just appearing on the horizon. I don't even hesitate. I pop my truck-in drive and slam the gas pedal down to the floor. Again, I burn rubber and the momentum throws me into my seat. This time, I'm not buckled in. I dodge every car and truck on the road, run through every intersection, causing a few wrecks behind me. At the same time, I'm blowing my horn. Out of the blue, an SUV in front of me blows a tire and spins out, but I jerk the wheel to the right, hopping the curb right onto the sidewalk while mowing down street signs and lamps, still blowing my horn. Later on, I see that the street is beginning to clear. I move my truck back onto the road. Still not slowing down, I glance down at my compass on the cup holder and it turns out I'm heading south. But I don't care. I have to get the hell out of dodge.

As the miles roll by, the buildings are getting smaller and smaller, and between the buildings, I start to notice the wolf-like aliens in small groups. They're jogging right toward me and other vehicles with their paws up telling us to slow down. I keep on flying, blowing my horn to keep them away. Another thing that catches my eyes behind these groups is a very large, thick fog following them, covering up everything between it and the wolves. Moving my eyes back to the road, I see the fog about to take form and thicken. This phenomenon scares the hell out of me, but I keep the hammer down driving right into the mist, not knowing what the fucking hell lies ahead of me.

CHAPTER FOUR
Location: Highway 218, Iowa
Date: September 18, 2014
Time: 3:35 PM

IT'S BEEN THREE DAYS since I peeled out of Nashville. Three days since the humanoid-wolf aliens took over that city. Three days since the mist started to form, thicken, and cover every square mile of this nation wherever those aliens traveled. Three days of *radio silence*. For the past three days, I've traveled through Mississippi, Arkansas, and Missouri. Where am I heading? I'm heading back to my birthplace, Green Bay, Wisconsin. Why? To see if any of my relatives are still alive and save them. So, I've been traveling in a big "U" just by taking country roads and avoiding the big cities. Now here I am, traveling on the state highway 218 in Iowa almost about to run out of fuel.

Run out of fuel?

I look down at the fuel gage and sure enough, it's on "E." Thirty minutes fly by so fast, my truck gives out, and I coax it to the side of the road.

I put it in park and turn everything off. I look around the cabin, knowing that this place might only be, no, this is only the true place that was my home. The weather this past day has been gray and nothing else but for the thick mist. I look out my windshield, only to see just half a mile of road before it's covered up by the mist. Again, I look around the cabin and above me are a few pictures of my friends from high school and my family that are taped to the upper compartments. Looking at them, I begin to cry silently because I am truly afraid that I do believe I would be immediately slaughtered once I step out of this truck. I exhale a heavy breath, unbuckle, grab my backpack, and began packing clothes, my iPod, some food, water, sunglasses, and my weapons. I breathe in and out before I open my door.

What if I die? What if there's nothing out there? What if?

I think for a moment and I finally open my door.

In mere moments that I open the door, a huge amount of fresh air that smells like pine and many other full-grown trees in the woods come sweeping in. The air is so fresh and clean like never was before. It's so . . . inviting. I still take caution of the dangers that lie out there as I descend down the steps and put on my cowboy hat. With one last look at the cabin, I toss the keys inside, press the lock button, and shut the door.

"Here goes nothing."

With that being said, earbuds go in, music cranked up to 17 percent with bass, and I press play on this one song. As it starts to play, I take my first step when the lyrics come alive. What's interesting is that this song seems to be my only companion ever since middle school. This song only sounded like an ordinary song that wasn't relevant to my life until halfway through high school. But now, it is because it's so true that I *do* walk alone on the road of no hope and broken dreams, and I don't have a damn clue where it goes. For some odd reason, there's this feeling inside of me that is telling me to turn around and look back of what is left of my life. I keep on walking, ignoring the urge, but it keeps on getting bigger and bigger. At this point, I'm getting annoyed at it, so I immediately come to a halt and turn around. I can see my semi, but barely because the mist is circulating around it and thickening. Time goes on like usual and in minutes, my semi is covered by the mist completely, and I can't even make out the bright, racing red paint job.

On the flip side, out of the corner of my eye, the mist is dissipating, revealing trees. No, more like a full grown, healthy forest. The trees are fully dark green with no brown spots indicating that it's dying or losing its strength. Their branches, trunks, leaves, and pine needles are so thick that I can only see a few yards which gives a gut feeling to turn off my iPod and bring around my rifle so that I can hear and be prepared if anything comes from those trees and attacks me. I take another deep breath of the fresh, clean air, and keep on walking away from my truck, if it's still there. During this new part of my journey, the only noises that I hear are the critters in the thick forest that hug the road and my footsteps walking upon it.

Hours pass and the day is becoming dark and I find that it would be a good time to stop and create a fire near the road. Moving to the edge of the road, it begins to rain. Not in a harsh pour, but like in a soft tone. I unpack my Swiss Army knife and start to pull in lower branches to create a decent roof. It takes some time yet I complete it and start working on building a fire. I struggle trying to find dry timber and igniting it on the wet ground. I groan and pray that it ignites, and so that I can be warm for the first night of my survival trip back to Green Bay. Match after match, each one fails. Seconds later, there's one match left; taking it out of the box, I scrutinize it, hoping and praying that this would be the one to ignite.

"Please, God. Please. Let this be the one that works."

I strike it and the little flame appears. Carefully moving it to the dry timber, holding my breath for this final moment, the tiny little flame ignites and grows throughout the timber. I am so happy that it works and I pick it up to blow more oxygen into it. Finally, I place the burning timber in the logs and the fire increases, burning greatly. Yet again, after my short celebration, I hear a howl in the dark night. More join in and I growl in annoyance and anger.

I stand up fast, pulling out my Colt, and firing rounds in random directions. After emptying the entire magazine, I yell out, *"Fuck off!"*

The howling stops. I hear nothing. After an hour, nothing. After two hours, nothing. Then a branch snaps behind me. I immediately swing my rifle around my chest and shoot four rounds. *"Fuck off!"*

I still wait for any sudden weird noises before eating, hell, forget about eating. I am exhausted and I just want to get some sleep. I spin in circles a couple of times to check my surroundings and guarantee that it's okay to sleep on the ground and close my eyes. All is clear and I go to sleep.

CHAPTER FIVE
Location: The Same
Date: September 19, 2014
Time: Don't Know, Don't Care

I WAKE UP COLD and hungry. I have no more matches to burn. I grab a can of beans, crack it open, and eat in silence. This whole area is dead quiet. There's no critter making any noise of the sort. The noises that I hear are my chewing and a small breeze, rustling through the trees. Today, it's overcast and it looks like it might rain again; the mist has begun to dissipate and revealing more of the fully thick green forest. While sitting on the ground, I am completely amazed by the sight. I look up to see where I tore off the branches and instead of seeing the stubs where branches were, brand-new-like branches are there, fully green and swaying in the breeze. I get up to inspect them and to check if I'm hallucinating. I touch, smell, and even taste them.

This can't be real. Did these branches just suddenly grow back last night?

I look around if there's any creature or person that might've camped close to me or somewhere else in the area. I do remember that I didn't see any other fires blazing in the dark. I'm still all alone.

I look at the branches one more time before packing up my things and stirring up the dirt to make sure the fire is out.

I walk back onto the road, reloading my Colt, but I holster it. I shoulder my rifle, but I notch an arrow into the crossbow and hold it in my hands. I turn around every ten minutes to check if there's nothing behind or is following me.

Man, this journey is going to be long.

TWO MILES

FOUR MILES

EIGHT MILES

TEN MILES

After ten miles, this road has been completely empty and this includes any sort of car and person. Although, during the last ten miles, the mist has been dissipating at a quicker pace, revealing more of the forest which is becoming more and more beautiful. This sight makes me come to a stop and take in the landscape. The last time I could remember, all this land was dairy farms, crop fields, etc. How the hell were they all completely changed into a fully grown forest? For the question that seems to have no answer, I just shrug and keep on moving. Pretty soon, my stomach growls and the feeling of being hungry rolls over me like a huge wave. I search every pocket to see if there's any match or lighter I could use to start another fire, but after a couple of minutes, it's unsuccessful. My stomach growls louder than the first time. I realize that day is slowly turning into night, and I suddenly drop to my knees with the feeling that there is no more hope left for me nor within me.

Tears start rolling down my face and there's still a slight breeze in the air. For some odd reason, my mind tells me that something is or was behind me and is now gone. I turn around in a flash and find nothing except the same road and trees. My eyes and head dash from left to right, up and down. Then something catches my eyes. I look back down at the ground again to find a matchbox. I pick it up; it has a note strung around it. While I inspect it, the paper itself is not like an ordinary paper. It's a bit heavier with a shade of bright gold and with a fancy curve border on the corners that seem to look medieval.

I read the note, "These matches will last a very long time. With one strike, they would burn long and bright until you extinguish them. Also, turn around."

I turn around and find a strange mechanical device. I pick it up and find the same, exact paper strung to it. This object is circular, about two inches thick, with three, knobble protection squares that are equally spaced around the object, and the object itself is black. I flip the object over and over in my hands to find anything strange about it. Yet, it still looks the same.

I open the note, "The directions are very simple. Place the object on the ground and press the power button. When the machine fully reveals itself, a keypad will appear for you to punch in your destination, and step through the portal."

I look back at the device, not feeling that I truly believe the directions or that I should trust it. The main thing that catches my attention is that night is approaching and my stomach growls louder. About the same time, a pack of deer comes through the trees on my left. They approach the road and all stop to look at me if I make any sudden moves. After a few, intense moments go by, they keep on walking to the other side. I calmly and slowly set down the so-called magical box of matches and the strange mechanical device. Next, I slowly pull out my Colt, raising it to my eyes. As the sight is aligned with one of the deer, I immediately open fire and it drops down fast. The rest of the pack sprint away into the forest. I walk over to the animal to make sure it's dead and sure enough, it is. Soon after, I begin to set up camp for another cold and lonely night. I turn on my LED flashlight and begin skinning my meal while giving thanks to God for this meal and for providing the two strange objects. I look back at the matchbox, debating if I should use those matches. I decide to give it a try. I dig a pit, build a pyramid of wood, and grab a match. I eye that little piece of wood in the LED light and I struck it against the sandpaper. Within a split second, it combusts into a large ocean blue flame.

I am completely amazed by the size and light of the flame on that little piece of wood, and as I make the flame contact with the dry timber, within a second, the dry timber ignites good and strong and I place it near the wood. The ocean blue flames interact and spread throughout the wood. The light from the fire gives enough light that I don't need to use my flashlight. The heat is very strong that makes me feel instantly warm. I throw the burning match into the pit and continue on skinning my meal. With the best meat, I impale the protein on a stick and set it above the fire. Slowly turning the stick, my mind begins to slip away from all the worries and fear from what has been happening these past few weeks. I don't give a damn anymore. As long as this fire keeps on burning and roasting the meat, I am totally calm. Sliding up against a tree, I open my backpack, pull out my iPod and external speakers, and start playing my country music. Then I look at the strange, circular device, trying to figure out how to open it or even activate it. It hasn't been ten minutes when there's a howl that comes out through the night. My mind snaps back into defense and offense mode. My hand grabs my crossbow, but something stops me from getting up. I listen closely to the howl. The tone sounds like a harmonic hymn rather than the tone of wild wolves that just found their prey. I ease off the tension in my arms and legs and lean back onto the tree listening to the howl.

Soon, more chime in. The whole night lights up with the sound of a wolf choir. Again, I listen closely, trying to figure out what they're howling at. Then it hits me. These wolves are howling to the music I'm playing. To make sure this theory is true, I pause it, and the howling stops.

Suddenly, I hear a male voice in the distance, "Oh, c'mon, cowboy! Why did you stop it? That was a great song!"

Then another, "Yeah, that country singer sounds really cool. Who is it?"

This scares the shit out of me. I scramble around in the dirt, immediately throwing the iPod and speakers back into the backpack, stomping and kicking the soil into the fire. I throw everything back on my shoulders, sprint back onto the road, and run away from the campsite.

I hear another voice, "Wait! Come back! We didn't mean to scare you, cowboy! We just wanna talk!"

This sounded like a female, but I don't stop. I keep on sprinting down the road, putting as much distance as I could between me and those voices.

Great, I didn't get to eat this time!

CHAPTER SIX
Location: Unknown
Date: September 20, 2014
Time: Seems to Be Eight or Nine O'Clock

AFTER A FEW HOURS passed, the sky is clear, and the sun is beating down onto the road. I can feel the temperature and the humidity slowly rising. I've hiked all night. I am so hungry and exhausted. I want to stop and rest for a moment, but the more I hike, the more distance I lay down between me and those voices. This time, the only sound that I hear are my boots hitting the pavement and then the sound becomes more like rocks and soil. This makes me stop and look down. Sure enough, the highway is becoming a dirt road or more like a path. And the forest is edging closer and getting thicker near the road. My knees begin trembling, struggling to keep my weight upright. Within seconds, they give out and I collapse. My mouth is dry, I have no more water, and there is little or no strength left in my arms and legs, nor the strength to keep on traveling. Through the haze of the air, there's a mileage sign off to my right. Squinting my eyes to make out the letters, it says, "Madison, WI 300."

"Argh!"

I throw my weapons forward and rip my backpack off, also throwing it forward in frustration.

"*Just* end my life, Lord! Right here, right *now*!"

Then I fall forward, landing flat on my stomach. Crying in desperation, there's no hope for me, but something pulls me to look forward through my water-filled eyes. My eyes refocus back onto my backpack. I see the flat, round, black device. I begin dragging my body across the ground, getting closer to the bag while stretching out my hand to grab it; I finally reach it. Pulling myself together, I eye the device much closer, trying to find if there's an "on" button. Again, I flip this object several times in my hands. Then I come to the conclusion that the side facing up would be the right side. I do remember what the directions told me to do. Before I get down to business, I slowly gather my strength and pick up the backpack and weapons. I struggle for a moment to get up on my feet and I succeed. I place the device onto the ground and press the center, hoping that the power button would be there. Sure enough, it is; it begins to glow lime green, spreading from the power symbol from the top and from the bottom. As the two lines met their ends, one line goes to the right, while the other goes to the left. When they complete the circumference of the device, the green begins to glow brighter and brighter.

At this moment, clouds begin to thicken in the sky, blocking out the sun, making the morning turn back to night. However, returning my attention back at the device, the glowing green appears at the crease line that's in the middle of the device on its side and it, too, glows brighter and brighter. Suddenly, it pops open with three mechanical arms stretching outward. I take a few more steps back for safety but still watching this amazing transformation. Then the upper half pulls itself upright, making a mechanical sound that you hear from the Transformers movies. When the three legs have full-grown and impale the ground with spikes, the top, right, and left square edges separate themselves only putting a half-inch gap between them and the raised upper half of the device. Later, the top half circle evolves from a six-inch diameter circle to a circle that's six feet in diameter. After the transformation is complete, I can still see the road and trees on the other side, although a liquid state spontaneously comes alive inside the circle. The only way I can describe the liquid state is that it's like looking at a blank television screen with no snow or the sound of the snow. After a few seconds tick by, a keypad of some kind magically transforms itself from the even left edge of the circle. As it completes assembling itself, I walk toward the machine.

I look down at the keypad. The entire thing looks like a touch screen and at the top of it says, "Type in your destination" in navy blue, computer block font.

Looking back at the machine itself, it finally occurs to me: this device seems to be a teleportation machine that can quickly teleport me anywhere in this country or anywhere in the world. But how could this machine possibly exist? It is so advanced that our technology could never ever create such a fine, sophisticated machine as this one.

I look back down at the keypad and type in my destination, "Lambeau Field, Green Bay, Wisconsin."

Hitting the "Enter" button, the liquid shapes and shows the east parking lot of the Packers stadium. Looking at the screen, it seems to be snowing in that city; it's foggy and cloudy. With caution, I push my entire arm through the liquid screen to wonder if the screen is solid. However, my arm passes through the state and I can clearly see it on the other side. Plus, I can also feel the different temperatures, the wind, and the snow touching my arm.

"This can't be real." At the same time, I step through the portal and sure enough, it is for real.

Stepping through the portal, I begin to feel the wind, the cold, the snow, and right after a few strides away from the portal, it immediately closes up with a bright flash of light. After closing and reopening my eyes, I look around to check if there is another portal device that I just used and as it turns out, there isn't one. So, it looks like this portal just opened up into thin air and immediately disappeared, which absolutely makes no sense to me whatsoever. I should probably put on a thick jacket because it's cold out here. Looking around to get my bearings, I try to remember where my old childhood house was. Yet again, my stomach growls and as I look around, this entire area looks abandoned with no sign of life nor any source of electricity. It also looks like another forest has taken over and has fully grown to adulthood. Again, I fall down to my knees finally knowing that I have no home and that my relatives might be dead or have escaped. Either way, I still shed tears.

I don't know how much time has passed, but the snow begins to pile up on and around me. All I hear is the howling wind and my heavy heaves of breath. Then I hear a voice.

"Hey, are you alright?"

I look up and turn my head to that voice. As soon as I do, that source comes from a humanoid wolf male and he's not alone. Another three more are standing behind him. The first humanoid wolf is male and has brown fur, the other two are also male and have black fur, and the last one is a female and has pure white fur. They're all wearing cloaks with hoods up, and they look like travelers or guardsmen from the medieval time, carrying medium-sized sacks that are purple with faded gold ropes as straps. The colors of their clothes are dark blue, purple, with an outline of silver. None of them are wearing shoes or boots and taking a closer look at their faces, their eyes are light blue, and they're all carrying tall rods that seem to adjust to their heights. All of the rods are blue with an oval, three-dimensional glass orb at the end. I don't know if they're using them for style, or are they weapons? Within a flash, I bolt upright, dropping my crossbow, bringing my rifle around to my chest, lowering my head against the barrel to line up my left eye with the scope, and I load a round in.

The leader of the group raises his arms, "Whoa, whoa. We don't mean any harm unless you pull the trigger. But before you do, we're just a search party, scouting for humans, like you, and take them back to our kingdom."

I don't lower my gun. I still don't trust them. I don't really know if these guys are playing the good guys, or they are the bad guys in reality. I look at all four of them again, throwing the theory around in my head for a while. Still, the leader takes a few more steps closer to me, extending his hand toward me in a friendly gesture. I finally come to the conclusion that these aliens, or people, are really good, and that they show no sort of action of being hostile. I lower my rifle and my stomach growls again, this time much louder than before.

"You must be very hungry and tired. I'm Ulric and this is Althalos, Forthwind, and Ryia. Again, we're one of the many scout groups that have been sent by our great King Borin, King of Sparta."

As soon as Ulric told me why he and his crew were sent out here, it just makes me raise my eyebrows and drop my rifle. I mean, can his story be real, or is it made up? All in all, it sounds ludicrous. I look around at what's left of Green Bay and it seems that I travel all this way for nothing. This entire city looks completely abandoned, with no power and no livelihood of any person. I'm the only human that's out here in this stretch of land. Out of the blue, there's a huge gust of wind that totally brings me back to reality and makes me shiver. Plus, my cowboy hat flies off into the distance. *Sigh.* I look back at Ulric and his crew, building enough confidence to speak.

I take a huge breath of air through my nose and start, "My name is Will Young. I was born here in Wisconsin and moved to New Mexico. I'm 21 and my job was being an asphalt cowboy. My nickname or handle for that job was and still is Lonesome Cowboy."

CHAPTER SEVEN
Location: Green Bay
Time: Don't Know

AFTER THE FIRST TIME that I spoke to Ulric and his crew, I started to spill my guts. I told them everything from what I like to what has happened to me and described my friends and family. By that time, for some odd reason, time flew by so fast that it started to get dark. At that time, Althalos, Forthwind, and Ryia took off their sacks and begun to set up camp for the night. At this very moment, I'm still telling all four of them what my life used to be before their society showed up. What's interesting is that all of them are really interested in me. Ulric took off his sack and pulled out, you wouldn't believe this, a pane of glass, less than an inch thick, and as he swiped his index finger, this pane of glass turns on like an iPod. He opens up like a Word program, starts typing notes, and begins researching anything about me that I might've left out. I am absolutely blown away by that sort of technology. Minutes later, a big tent is set up, representing the colors of their kingdom and a small flag pole is stuck into the ground with a flag flapping in the wind. I try to get a better look at it, but Forthwind ushers me in quickly so that I can warm up.

Once I'm in their big tent, I am again blown away. Instead of being a simple tarp covering the ground, the tarp is covered in plush thick fur, pillows big and small, thick quilts, and a good fire blazing in the middle which makes it really warm. I take off my boots and scurry over to the blaze. It feels so great that I have this feeling that maybe this could be something good. On the opposite side of the fire, Althalos and Ryia pull out food from their packs and begin prepping it. Judging by the size of their sacks, they seem to be small and probably seem to have the capacity to carry *all* of this stuff. I want to ask, but I feel like that would be rude.

"Something on your mind, Will?" Forthwind asks as he sits next to me.

His question throws my thoughts way off track. It takes me a while to gather them back so that I can answer.

"Oh, um, I was just curious about how your sacks can carry *all* of this stuff? I mean, they look pretty small and how do you have that type of technology?"

"What?" He asks.

"When you guys were setting up this awesome tent, Ulric pulled out a glass pane tablet that's a touch screen. Not to be rude, but you look like you're still living in the Medieval Era."

Forthwind sticks out his tongue and begins to laugh, so does everybody else. I don't know if they're laughing at me, at my question, or that I'm hallucinating all of the things because I'm very hungry.

After they're done laughing, Ryia answers the question, "Oh, Will you're so funny. Yes, we do have very advanced technology, but we like to use sorcery most of the time. That's why our sacks can carry all of our equipment because they are created out of a material that can easily store and carry any size of any item."

"And the reason why we dress like we're still in the Medieval Era," Althalos chimes in, "Is that our great ancestors lived this type of lifestyle and as time rolled on, we decided to keep it and we still kept it alive when our technology started to get advanced through time."

At this moment, he impales three different kinds of meat on a skillet and sets it on two stands that hold the meat just directly over the fire. Then Ryia brings over fruits and vegetables on separate platters and lays them on the floor. They soon start to eat while the main course cooks over the color-changing fire. Reaching for an apple, I feel a pair of hands touch my back. I snap my head back to find Ulric putting up his hands.

"Please, let me unarm you. Just relax and enjoy the food. You're gonna need your strength for the journey back to our kingdom." He says in a kind, gentle voice with a bit of plea in it.

I look right into his wolf eyes to see if there are any tricks he is hiding that he, or anybody else, would do to harm me when I'm unarmed. After staring in those eyes, I see nothing but the truth, so I ease off and let him remove my weapons. Once all of them are off, it feels so nice not to feel the extra fifty pounds strapped to my shoulders. I reach for the apple and lean back on the pillows feeling totally relaxed.

"Why do you have all of these weapons?" Ulric asks.

After taking the first bite and swallowing, I reply, "Well, for starters, the Colt and the hunting knife were for my own personal protection when I started trucking and the reason is that some of the teachers from the school district where I grew up in thought I couldn't make it in life. Plus, they wanted to see me fail. So, if they got a word I was driving and the payment is a lot better, I had the paranoia that they might come after me and shut me down. Maybe I was overthinking, but maybe because I'm a really paranoid person. Then, after you guys showed up, I was hearing about these attacks that were happening to my race and that there was much confusion of which humanoid wolf was good and bad. Once chaos broke out in Nashville, I drove to the nearest gun store and hauled my ass out because I feared for my life and that's why I came here, to see if any of my relatives are still here. But I take it as a no."

As Forthwind takes the cooked meat off the fire, he says, "But now you know that we're the good guys, we're saving your planet, and that we're trying to catch or terminate those murderers who only care for the taste of any blood."

I nod my head that I do understand that Ulric, Forthwind, Althalos, and Ryia are the good guys. They're just scouting this land to seek and bring us to their kingdom to keep us safe. But I have to wonder, are there other kingdoms that have been established in the US, or is the Sparta Kingdom the only one? However, I don't have the brain capacity to think it over; the only thing that's on my mind is food. I just keep on eating the fruit and vegetables until I'm handed a plate with a juicy steak on it. I look around the tent to see all four of them just eating with their hands like true wolves and I join in letting my animal side take over.

Man, this steak is so good, no, it's so fucking delicious. It's so freaking great just to eat in a calm environment without worrying about what's out there and not being able to eat in the last three or four days.

I just keep on chowing down until I'm completely satisfied. After swallowing my last bite, I just simply lean back and slowly close my eyes. Before my eyes are completely closed, Ulric has his glass tablet out, activated, and holding it over my body.

"What are you doing?"

"I'm just scanning your body to see how good your health is." Then his tablet makes a noise. "How long has it been since you last ate officially?"

"It's been three or four days."

He nods, "Well, technically five, according to the results. But you seem to be in good health and sleep well. We've got a long journey ahead of us."

I nod in agreement, pulling a blanket over, and within seconds, I fall right to sleep. I can still make out of the noises and I hear the guys chatting in a soft tone. Most of the conversation was about me and what hell I've been through, but one of them points out that I still have the strength to make it back to their castle or fort. After that, I truly fall asleep, and man does it feel good.

CHAPTER EIGHT
Sparta, Here We Come.

I WAKE UP TO the smell of pancakes and bacon.

This can't be real.

Getting up to see, it's real. Forthwind seems to be hunched over a stove doing some cooking. He looks over and says "Morning" to me. Turning my head around, I find Ryia with headphones in her ears only to figure out she's jamming out to my iPod. She sees me and nods to me. Looking around the tent, I don't see Ulric and Althalos, so they must be outside. The pillows and blankets are thick and warm and my body is so relaxed that I have a hard time getting up. Finally making it outside, I'm suddenly blinded by the morning sunlight.

"Here." Althalos hands over my sunglasses. I say "Thank you" to him and to my surprise, the weather seems to be calm, sunny, and warm. Looking around, I don't see a single cloud in the sky nor a single patch of snow in any shade on the ground. It's amazing how bipolar the weather could be this far north, but I don't think it happens that often. Only in New Mexico.

"How'd you sleep last night?" Ulric asks.

"Hmm . . . oh, yeah, I slept really well last night. You guys got really comfy pillows and blankets. It's much better than sleeping on a thin, stiff mattress in a semi."

Both guys laugh, pat me on the back, and keep on looking out at the horizon, which makes me curious about what they're looking out for.

"What are you guys looking for?"

"We're just making sure that the land is safe to cross and that we get you to Sparta all in one piece. Oh yeah, I forgot to give you something," says Althalos as he reaches into his robes and pulls out my camouflage hat with the barbed wire, thread design stretching across from the back of the adjustable strap to the brim of the visor.

My question is, how in the hell did he find it? I try to ask, but Althalos tells me right off the bat that they all knew I drove a Kenworth, found some stuff that I've left behind, and they gave me the matchbox filled with magic matches and the portal device to teleport me from Iowa to Wisconsin. I am in total disbelief and in total shock.

"Please, don't be angry at us. We just wanted to take the time and make a well secure meet and greet." Ulric turns me around with a desperate look in his eyes.

But how can I be angry with him and his crew? They've helped me get this far and after realizing that the entire city of Green Bay is deserted and that my relatives are not here, I am totally willing to travel with them back to their kingdom. And also, to start a new life.

So, I respond, "I am not angry at you, guys. I am surprised, but in my current situation, I have to travel with you guys back to Sparta."

Forthwind calls out that breakfast is ready. We head back into the tent and there's a medium, long table that has pancakes, bacon, fruit, and sausages. We all sit down and begin to eat. Again, the food is really good and it's so nice to feast in a calm environment. I have to say it is quite interesting to feast with humanoid wolves and that this scout group is willing to protect me no matter what the cost. All in all, I just keep on eating and soon, I am full.

Forthwind notices and asks, "Did you have enough or do you want more?"

"Nah, I'm full. Thanks for the breakfast, Forthwind."

"Alright then, guys, time to pack up and head back home," says Ulric.

I rummage around the pillows and quilts to gather my pack and weapons. When that is completed, I toss them outside and stood outside to watch as the four of them begin packing up the entire tent. I stand here in amazement, witnessing how all of that bulky stuff can fit in those medium-sized sacks. Suddenly, Ryia tosses me an extra sack and tells me it would be better for me to carry all of my stuff in that enchanted state. Now, I'm not completely sold on the magic thing because I know that magic is all about illusions and that magicians use all sorts of contraptions to create those illusions, but I take her word for it and I begin to take out all of my clothes and other things and put them in the sack. Surprisingly, the sack feels very light and I press forward putting the other things in. Once my backpack is empty, I grab my rifle and proceed with caution by putting the butt in first.

This ain't gonna work. This ain't gonna work.

Miraculously, the rifle slides into the sack with ease and soon, the entire gun is inside. With enthusiasm, I grab the crossbow, removing the scope to be safe, fold in the collapsible arms of the bow, and put it in. Again, it slides very smoothly into the sack as if there are no other items in there. Within seconds, I toss the boxes of ammo for the rifle in, the scope and arrows for the bow, and the last magazine for my Colt. Next, I attach the holster of my gun to my belt with the gun in it of course and shoulder the sack. Feeling the weight of the sack on my shoulders, it seems to be about ten pounds, a very comfortable weight to have, especially when you're about to travel a great distance.

I look back noticing that the guys are almost done backing up the tent. The last things that are still out are the sleeping items, the tarp, the pole, and the flag. I didn't get a good look at the flag yesterday, but now I take this brisk opportunity. The flag has the same colors, dark blue, purple, and some silver, but how the colors are portrayed is different. Plus, it's the same size as the average American flag you see flying in the wind at every public place. The base color of the flag is purple; in the center is a tribal wolf head designed out in major, thick lines in dark blue to create the shape, and it's outlined with silver. Below the symbol is one word, spelled in Segoe Script writing saying, *"Sparta"* also in silver. Soon, Ulric, Ryia, Forthwind, and Althalos come over and start taking the flag down. Ulric pulls the pole out of the ground and lowers it to Forthwind and Althalos. As the two guys detach the flag from the pole, they fold it up in a ceremonial way as our military folds up our flag after a ceremony. Then Forthwind holds open a box in his hands as Althalos puts the flag into it with the wolf symbol facing upward like it's looking at them. Forthwind closes the box and puts it in his sack, lacing it up. Ulric and Ryia twist the pole in opposite directions and pull it apart. After that, Ryia places the two pole pieces in her sack, also lacing it up. All of them put up their hoods, grab their staffs, and shoulder their sacks.

Ulric looks at me and asks, "Ready to go, Will?"

"Hell, yeah. But with one question, where is your kingdom located?"

"Our kingdom is established in a mountain range that you humans have named the Appalachian."

The Appalachian Mountains? That's roughly five hundred and ninety-six miles away. By car or semi, that takes us humans about a day, but to travel on foot, that'll take us about nineteen days. And fall is about to begin, not to mention winter. Plus, this is a mid-western state, and traveling east to other northern states, the climate is much colder in the fall and winter, and who knows how long this small heatwave will last? The other thing that's bugging me is that there's a small part of my brain that tells me all four of them can sense my emotions, simply because they're a canine species.

"If you're nervous about the cold and long travel, that's ahead of us," as Ulric puts his arm around my shoulders. "We'll give you a boost."

Give me a boost?

From the corner of my eye, I see Althalos bringing down his right fist with an object clenched in his fingers. A split second later, I feel a long, very thin tube being punctured into my left shoulder and feeling a liquid being injected in. Finally knowing that the object in his hand was a syringe, I look up at Ulric and mouth one word, *"Why?"*

He smiles and says to me, "Don't worry, Will, it's nothing lethal. The shot that you just received has a chemical that'll mix into your bloodstream increasing your heart rate, muscles, and senses to react in situations if by any chance they become deadly. So, you're gonna be like us for about five or so days. By that time, we'll be in Sparta and all your senses will return to normal."

I look at him, Forthwind, Ryia, and Althalos for a brief moment and say to them, "So, basically, its steroids mixed in with your DNA." All of them nod in agreement and it is true. All of them are a couple of inches taller than me (5 ft. and 10 in.) and it makes perfect sense that they walk and run faster than I, their body temperatures are higher, and they're stronger.

I look around one last time, especially at Lambeau Field, then up at the sky to where the sun is. It looks like it's eight or nine o'clock.

"C'mon y'all we're burning daylight." While I start walking east, I feel the small changes from the shot inside me; the only way I can put it is that I feel a bit stronger and with my pace quickening, I have this smile on my face getting bigger and bigger.

Inside of my head, I hear a song called "Zeus' Reign" by Diamond Back beginning to play and as soon as the chorus strikes, I burst into a run with lots of energy, excitement, and determination. With my hearing also increasing, I can hear the four of them starting to catch up and telling me to slow down because of the dangers that lay ahead of me. But I don't care, my new life and journey began once I woke up in that tent. The trees of the forest approach fast and I keep on running, almost into a full sprint. Later on, all five of us are in the forest enjoying the run back home.

Within four hours, we make it to Kewaunee (located on the East Shore of Michigan Lake) where it, too, is abandoned; plus, the forest is slowly creeping in and I can literally see it with my own eyes growing at a slow pace. It makes me cringe at the sight and also the thought that this might be happening all over the country. My question is, is all of this happening here in the US or all over the planet? Okay, it's nice to meet a small search party of humanoid wolves that are really friendly and they are helping other humans to be saved and be brought to their kingdom. Forthwind pats my shoulder and reassures me that everything is going to be fine, but without wasting a second, I spill out my first question.

"Why are these trees taking over these towns and cities? Is this happening here in my country or is this happening all over the world?"

All four of them stop and turn toward me except Ulric. He hangs his head and breathes a heavy sigh, then turns to look at me with sympathy on his face and in his eyes.

"Will, the reason the trees are taking over the land is that we conjured that."

"*Why?*"

"Because your planet is or was dying and our race realized that; so that's why we broke up into two major groups taking refuge in the existing forest and start growing them. Plus, we try to find those prisoners so that we can capture them before they murder or even turn your race into one of them, and continue on their raid."

So, it is true that the kingdom of Sparta is not the only kingdom and I blurt out asking who's in charge and where it's located.

"The king that rules that kingdom is Terrin and his kingdom is located in the thick forests in the Rocky Mountains, but that doesn't matter," says Ryia.

Well, it sort of does matter because I want to learn what is happening to my *home* and it might give me some closure. Still, I breathe the fresh clean air and continue on walking.

Leave your past behind. None of that matters. The only thing that does matter is what lies ahead. Just think of these two little words: new life.

We keep on marching through the empty streets until we reach the beach that borders with good ol' Michigan Lake. Looking left as far as my eyes can see, I don't see a boat and the same result when I look right. Turning my head back toward the great lake, I don't know if it's gonna be possible to cross it.

Forthwind steps next to me and says, "Did you look what's right in front of ya?" as he gestures with his hand pointing straight down the cliff where a thick, large bush is just below us.

I can't see what's in there, but all four of them descend down the cliff toward the bush. They all take their positions, lift the bush in one heave, carry it away, and reveal a boat. Well, it's more like a small ship that looks like it could handle the waves and storms on the lake. The ship looks so awesome that I lean too far over the edge that I fall down the steep, sandy slope. Once I reach the bottom, Althalos picks me up and brushes me off while asking if I'm okay. I assure him that I'm good and walk up to the boat to get a better look. Standing right next to it, the ship itself is constructed out of oak wood, and for height-wise, it seems to be twenty feet tall and about fifty yards long. There's a rudder, but no propellers, and there's no ladder that's hanging over nor carved into the hull. Then a shadow flies over me and as I look up, there's Forthwind waving down at me with a big grin on his face. Looking back, both Althalos and Ulric put a certain distance between them and the ship, then they run toward it, and once they're about to run into it, they leap and land on the deck without breaking a sweat.

Surprisingly, Ryia puts her hands around my waist and asks, "You ready?"

"Huh?" Within a flash, she throws me up with great strength like a stuffed animal, and as I fall down back to earth, Althalos catches me with ease and sets me on my feet. Then Ryia jumps up and joins us on deck. As she passes by me, she winks and brushes her hand against my face in a flirty way.

You know when people say that they have that fuzzy warm feeling inside when a good thing is happening or something like that, well I have that feeling. The problem is I've never been really close to any type of girl because I think I'm not good enough for them. On the flip side, I can talk to them and I did have a few girls as friends back in high school, but we didn't go on any dates. If you're asking what stopped me, well there was homework, family issues, and that I was a loner for a long time in the school community. Satisfied? Anyway, looking around at the ship, it seems to be just one, large oak tree that was cut in half and was hollowed out. At the stern of the ship, a small section of the deck is raised up three times with one, wide piece of wood for each step that stretches twenty feet from starboard to port. On the deck that all of us are standing on, it stretches all the way to the bow. Another thing that catches my attention is that there are no poles for the masts.

"How are you guys going to get this ship into the water and how are you going to make it sail?"

Again, all four of them laugh. Forthwind walks to the stern, rolls up his sleeves, and stretches his arms with fingers fully extended as if he's waiting for something or is about to embrace some sort of force. I walk up in curiosity to fully see what he's doing and then I see his eyes are closed. Simultaneously, he breathes in heavily several times and reopens his eyes which makes me stumble backward because his eyes are glowing lime green and the same exact color starts to take form, no, outline his body. He throws back his arms, then forward, and back again with tremendous force over and over again. I look over the starboard rail and my eyes begin to widen because the waves from the lake are increasing in size and are bashing against the hull. Minutes later, water surrounds the ship, rising at a steady pace, and the ship begins to float. Looking back at Forthwind, he smiles at me, but his face turns back into a serious expression as he puts his arms in front of him and bends his elbows fully.

"You might want to grab onto the rail," Ulric tells me as he, Ryia, and Althalos grab the rail.

I take his warning, firmly grabbing the rail with both hands and bending my knees preparing for whatever force is going to hit us. Looking back at Forthwind, he thrusts his arms forward and the entire ship launches with tremendous force forward into the deeper zone of the lake. Then the laws of science begin to no longer exist because the currents of the lake are pushing the ship with ease.

"How the hell did you do that?" I ask in total wonder.

The glow in Forthwind's eyes dies down, turns to me, smiles, and replies, "Like Ulric told you before, we all like doing sorcery. It's one of those things that we kept on when our civilization was developing."

"So, who's controlling the water?" I ask.

"Me," answers Ryia, "I control water and bend to which direction I want it to bend," while she calmly takes hold of the helm like nothing is happening.

"This is pretty cool," I say out loud in amazement.

I look over at Althalos and Ulric curious about what their magical powers are. Of course, Ulric catches me off guard and answers my question like he can read the look on my face.

"Well Will, Althalos is a great fighter, well better than us, and he has the power to conjure any weapon alive that lies nearby and use it against its foe or with its ally. For me, I deal with potions and other sorcery skills."

Well, ain't that something? These guys just keep on getting better and better with every passing minute on our journey to Sparta. I feel like I want to tell them my real nickname, the one I got from the auto shop teacher back when I was in high school, but I'll wait 'til the time is right. For now, I turn my eyes toward the horizon as we sail through the great Lake Michigan.

CHAPTER NINE
Our Journey Comes to an End

WITHIN HOURS, SURPRISINGLY, WE land on a beach which I believe has got to be in Indiana. If y'all are wondering how we traveled so far and covered a lot of distance in a short period of time, it's because of Ryia, and after traveling for about ten or so miles, she thought we were going too slow, so she sped up the currents and I asked how fast we were going. She tells me we traveled at forty knots. I know that sounds crazy, but hey, they all like doing magic.

Anyway, the bow touches the beach with ease, but I feel the entire hull being pulled forward by another source of magic. I walk up to see two more wolf humanoids pulling with full force, with hand-over-hand movements like they're really pulling on a large rope. Then another force comes out of nowhere and pushes me forward. This opposite force was strong enough to knock me off my feet. I look back to see if anyone of them really pushed me or that my mind is making things up.

"Sorry, Will," Ryia says to me, looking over her shoulder as she bends the water to push the boat further up the beach so that it doesn't float away. If it did, I'm pretty sure Ryia would just roll her eyes and force the currents to bring it back.

Getting back up and looking over the rail, almost half of the hull is now beached and there's no way that the waves from Michigan Lake can carry it away.

"You there." The voice from one of the guards catches my attention and points directly at me, "Is Ulric, Ryia, Althalos, and Forthwind with you?"

I begin to respond, yet Ulric walks over, and replies, "Yes, Hawkman, we are all here."

The guard Hawkman gives gestures to his partner that I'm not a threat and replies, "Okay, but you need to come down here and sort out some documents before you proceed east with that human tagging along."

"Of course." He acknowledges with a smile.

Within a moment, all of them just throw themselves over the railing and land perfectly on their feet. I step back in disbelief and start pacing on the deck because the ship is twenty feet tall from the belly of the hull to the top of the railing so it's kind of nerve-racking if you're gonna land with ease or end up with both of your legs broken. In situations like these, my heart begins picking up pace and my adrenaline starts kicking in. The more I pace back and forth and the thought of just throwing myself over the railing starts intensifying in my head which makes me more and more frustrated.

"Are you okay, Will?" Forthwind asks.

I reply by giving him a thumbs-up as I keep on pacing and still becoming more and more frustrated by a simple, stupid choice.

After minutes of pacing, I stop and look real hard at the railing. I tighten the ropes on my sack, ball up my hands, tighten my jaw, and finally scream out loud, "Ah, fuck it!"

I throw my hands upon the railing and thrust my body over the ship. The fall seems to last a second and I land with a loud thud onto the sand with both feet on the ground and my right fist into the sand to stabilize my landing. Breathing in and out heavily, I slowly stand up, looking myself over if I have sustained any injuries, but none to be on me. Amazingly, it seems that the shot that Ulric gave me out of the blue is still activated in my veins and it helped with the landing, which makes me feel happy. Turning around to my friends, they all seem to want to ask me if I'm okay, but before they can ask, I just give them two thumbs up. They just all shrug and Ulric gestures with his arm to the guards that they should get the paperwork of some sort completed so that we can continue on our journey.

Both guards look at each other, shrug, and turn toward the trees signaling that we should follow. Within the trees is a small clearing where the tent is up and a couple of banners that are roped to the poles which are impaled into the ground and all of them have the same color, symbol, and print like on the flag that was flapping in the wind back in Green Bay where my life began anew. Hawkman and his partner usher me into the tent where the same glass pane tablets are activated and ready to transfer information that Ulric has about me and perhaps fill in some blanks.

"Alright, Ulric, you know the drill," says Hawkman.

Ulric nods, pulls out his tablet, turns it on, and with a few silent keys and finger strokes, Ulric sends the information to one of the tablets as it chimes off within a second. Then, Hawkman gestures me with his hand to sit down at three chairs and a table that are set up. As I take my seat, Hawkman and his partner sit on the opposite side. Hawkman swipes his finger across his screen of the information toward his partner's tablet so that they can look over my life without sharing one. They browse through paragraph after paragraph, opening new tabs to research deeply into my life from health to school records. My eyes begin to wander around the tent for a few seconds until Hawkman's partner clears his throat in saying that I should keep my eyes on them.

This is taking forever, I'm not a horrible guy. I'm just an average person who pretty much had an average life and that life had a lot of ups and downs.

After an hour or so, both guards look at one another and nod in agreement that *everything* on me is all clean.

Hawkman looks at me a little bit serious and asks, "Are you sure you're Will Young born in Green Bay, Wisconsin on June 3, 1993?"

"Yes sir."

"Moved to Los Alamos, New Mexico on August 10, 2000, and graduated from Los Alamos High School on May 18?"

"Yes sir."

Hawkman looks at his partner which nods in agreement that I'm totally telling the truth.

Hawkman looks back at me, then at Ulric and his group, and says to them, "You guys may proceed forward. Will Young, I hope you enjoy Sparta." Then he types a few things and presses send.

I'm curious what he just sent, but I don't give rats' ass. I'm clear and I can press forward on this awesome journey. The guards and I get up at the same time and we shake hands. Approaching my traveling group, they all begin to clap, give me pats on the back, and all of them tell me, "Welcome to Sparta."

We begin leaving the security campsite until a chilly breeze blows in, making me shiver. Hawkman sees my body language, snaps his fingers, and walks back into the tent. Moments later, he brings out the same type of robe that all of them are wearing and very good hiking boots.

"Here, Will." He hands them out. "This robe will probably fit you and keep you really warm. Plus, these hiking boots will also match your foot size and be much more comfortable than your cowboy boots."

I grab them, sit on a stump, and put the new boots on. Amazingly, they fit really well, not too big and not too small. After that, I put on the robe. The robe itself feels thick, seems to be made out of fleece inside and out. It has a sturdy gold zipper with a flap of fabric that Velcros the entire length of the zipper as it ends at the waistline. Without wasting another moment, I slip my arms through the sleeves, draping the main part of the robe over my shoulders. Then I pull the zipper up to my chest and put the hood up. In seconds, I feel warm and pretty confident that the rest of this journey is going to be smooth sailing.

"Well," I say to the guys, "Are we going to carry on with our journey?" gesturing with my arm, hand facing upward toward the forest.

All of them smile and Ryia replies, "Yes."

What happens next, which I wasn't ready for, and makes my heart beat a little stronger, is that as Ryia walks toward me, she grabs my other hand with hers, winks, and gently pulls me along. At this point, I am beginning to fall in love, but I have to pace myself to make sure that Ryia is the right one. I don't want to screw anything up, yet my heart and gut are strongly telling me that she might be the one girl I have been looking for. I feel embarrassed in a good way and my skin begins to turn red around my face and on the backside of my neck. Her hand feels soft and warm around mine that I, without even second-guessing, walk closer to her as we hike our way through the trees. I look back casually to see that Ulric, Althalos, and Forthwind shake hands with the checkpoint guards and begin to jog to catch up. Looking up at Ryia's face, right into her eyes, everything that I worry about or has put me on edge just absolutely melts away. She smiles at me and I smile back. I can feel her warm body temperature radiating from her cloak which makes my head fall onto her arm. She laughs and squeezes my hand a little bit tighter.

With my sharpened sense of direction, I can tell that we've traveled for about five miles and it's really nice to hear the sounds of nature which makes me feel like I'm in a fantasy world. However, in the back of my mind, a switch goes off reminding me that this is still the real world and this is still the United States of America. Yet, how can it be the real world? I am hiking with a pack of four humanoid wolves that came from another planet, crash-landed by accident, and are trying to reclaim their enemy before they murder every one of us. I guess this answers the number one question of all: are we alone? No, we are not alone. We are not the only species that are smart and have very advanced technology. Well, their technology is more advanced than ours. However, I believe that they will share it under the right conditions.

We keep on hiking until Ryia interrupts my thoughts, "Hey, Will?"

"Yeah."

"What's your technique name?"

I think about the word technique for a few moments, then realize she means what my nickname is.

"I already told you," as I look at her and the guys, "My nickname is Lonesome Cowboy."

"We all know that, but what's your real technique name?" she still asks.

I stop which makes them stop. I look at each one for a couple of minutes before asking, "Why do you wanna know?"

"Because," she says, "when Ulric transferred the final data to Hawkman's tablet, something on the profile about you when you were in high school said that you went by 'N.O.S.' Now, it's not just me, but the rest of us would like to know what that stands for."

Huffing a laugh with a grin, I reply, "N.O.S. does not stand for anything. It's simply pronounced as Nos."

"How'd you get that name?" Forthwind wraps his arms around his staff in curiosity.

"I got the name Nos from the auto shop teacher when I was a freshman in high school and the purpose of it is that I ran fast because of this huge adrenaline rush that happens. And this adrenaline is always activated and ready to be used whenever. Now, if you guys have sensed that I'm on edge or anxious, it's because of it."

"Really?" Both Uric and Althalos say in unison with a huge grin on their faces.

Then Ulric replies, "But you seem completely calm, at ease, since Ryia took your hand as we were leaving the camp checkpoint."

Looking down, I'm still holding her hand and I look back up into her eyes, "Maybe it's because I've found the girl that truly puts my nerves at ease. Not by a little bit, but by one hundred percent."

Out of the blue, Ryia brushes her free hand against my face, bends down, and kisses me with loads of soft pleasure. While she bends back with a pleasurable smile, my hand slips from hers as I collapse onto one of my knees.

I was trying to keep myself from passing out from one of the awesome moments that just happened in my life that I thought was never, ever going to happen. Ryia immediately grabs me, pulls me up, and firmly grasps my shoulders asking that I'm okay. Shaking my head a couple of times and taking a few breaths I reassure her that I'm okay, and tell her that it was amazing. She throws her head back, laughs, and so does Ulric and Forthwind.

Then Althalos speaks up, "I hate to ruin the moment, but we need to get a move on." We all look up at the sky and notice the position of the sun and seems to be around two o'clock. We break out into a run to reduce the distance between us and Sparta.

We run for miles, jumping over fallen trees, rocks in all shapes and sizes and a couple of creeks, sometimes rivers. My stomach growls and within an instant, we all come to a stop.

Pretty soon, their stomachs growl.

"Lunchtime!" Ryia announces.

The four of them remove their sacks, pulling out tools that are a small shovel, pots, pans, a rotisserie, and food. Ulric hands me the shovel and I begin digging the fire pit. Once that was done, I search for rocks to keep the fire contained. Completing the pit, Ryia brings over wood and builds a small pyramid. She looks at me, I do the same, and we just burst out snickering. Forthwind impales raw meat on the rotisserie and sets it over the pit. Ulric reaches into his sack and it hits me that he's going to pull out his ignition source. I wave him off and tell him that I'll light the fire. Reaching into my own sack, I pull out the small box of the enchanted matches and struck one of them. Tossing it into the pit, the wood is engulfed in dark red flames instead of blue when I used the matches for the first time.

So, these matches vary in multiple colors? Interesting.

We all sit down and wait for the meat to cook. As time goes by, Forthwind passes out a variety of fruit and vegetables.

"You know," says Forthwind, "this would be a great time to play some country music," while he rolls his eyes in my direction.

I swallow the bite I took from peach and look at Forthwind in confusion, "How do you know that I listen to country music?"

"Well, we're just curious about it and we're starting to like you."

I ask, "So, what song do you want to hear?"

"Whatever your heart desires," Althalos replies.

"Plus, can you sing along with it?" Ryia asks.

What? Hear me sing? I don't think my singing is any good because I don't sing out in public, but only near friends and when I'm by myself. Looking back at Ryia, she really wants to hear what I sound like. I turn my attention to the other guys and they also nod in encouragement.

I simply shrug my shoulders, "Alright then, do you have a water bottle or something?"

Ulric nods and tosses me an empty one, then points at the creek that we jumped over before breaking for lunch. I walk over to the creek, fill the bottle up, and come back. Next, I dig around my sack. I pull out my iPod and external speakers. Once everything is set up, I prep myself to be calm and make sure that I don't mess up on any of the lyrics

Sigh. Okay, here goes nothing.

I take a few gulps of water and browse through the albums. I look for a few moments and I finally know what song I can play and sound kinda good while singing along.

"Alright, this song is called 'Lots of Country Out Here' by Tom Joshington." Then I hit play and begin singing along with it.

After the song concluded, everybody applauded and Ryia tells me that she wants more. Scrolling down the list, I pick my country mix album and begin singing along with every song. After a few tracks, they start to jam out and I join them showing off my body gestures and emotions to the lyrics.

After fifteen tracks, the meat is ready, and we all sit down to chow down while leaving the iPod playing. Again, we don't use silverware, we just use our hands to hold the food. I like being tuned in with my animal side. Plus, I do really feel like I'm one of them. I don't know why, but I do. Then something silvery and shiny that's hanging down from Ulric's neck catches my eye.

I swallow. "Hey Ulric, what's that hanging around your neck?"

He looks down, his eyes widen, quickly swallows, and says, "Ah crap, guys we forgot to say grace to bless our food and our journey."

Say what!

Ulric pulls out the necklace revealing it's a cross with a little man impaled on it. I walk over to get a better look and my eyes really widen like never before because the man impaled on the cross is Jesus, but instead of being a normal human being, he's a humanoid wolf like them! The excitement becomes too much that I blackout for some strange reason from the sight that I've just seen.

I don't know how long I was out, but when my eyes open, I realize I'm inside the same tent. Looking left, Ryia is kneeling beside me with the glass tablet activated, monitoring my health. Looking right and over my chest I see Ulric, and he seems to be hunched over something like a pot while messing around with something in his hands. He turns around, in his hands is a wet rag, plus he seems relieved and pleased to see that I'm awake. Same thing with Ryia.

So, Althalos and Forthwind must be outside, guarding.

"How are you feeling?" Ulric says, sitting next to me.

Slowly getting up, looking at both of them, "I'm okay, it's just that I find it amazing that our worlds are almost similar. You see, we humans worship the same person and when I saw your cross, I think it was a bit too much for me."

Both Ulric and Ryia look at one another with some concern in their eyes. He gestures to have the tablet handed to him and Ryia hands it over without any hesitation. He looks over the data to see that I'm fully functioning well. He taps and swipes at the screen for a few more minutes to double and triple-check the data.

"Hmm . . ." He says while putting his index finger to his mouth. Then he turns around to his sack and reaches into it. He pulls out a small vial and a syringe. Turning back around, he inserts the needle into the vial and says to me, "Perhaps you need another boost. This time, your body will slowly morph into our body size."

Ryia's eyes widen, "You can't be serious. That's four times the potent than we gave him when we were in . . ." She looks at me.

"Green Bay," I fill in.

"Exactly."

Ulric replies, "But it needs to be done. We're wasting time. It's not your fault, Nos, but the enemy has picked up on our trail."

Suddenly, Forthwind bursts through the tent entrance looking extremely on edge in his face and eyes. I look at him very closely why he's really uptight and then it hits me. Ulric was telling Ryia that their enemy has finally picked up on our trail and might arrive at any second. I give Ulric one quick nod saying that he can stab that needle right into my arm. I don't care if I become one of them and that it might terminate my body, but I need the strength and agility to fight off the enemy. I'm just a normal human being, so the strength that I have is absolutely worthless compared to what they have. I'll be torn to shreds within a blink of an eye. Without wasting another moment, Ulric thrusts the needle into my arm and pushes the DNA of their kind into my bloodstream.

Again, my heart rate increases and I'm beginning to feel stronger. I get up with ease, opening my sack while grabbing my rifle, pistol, and crossbow. While locking and loading all of the ammo, I look right at Forthwind, right into his eyes.

"How far away?"

"Almost right on top of us," he replies.

CHAPTER TEN
We Fight

ALL FOUR OF US burst out of the tent to meet Althalos positioning his body for the attack while holding his staff in both of his hands and letting out a low and threatening growl. Immediately, Ulric, Forthwind, and Ryia take the same position, aiming their staffs in opposite directions. I bring my rifle toward my chest, raising the sight to my left eye, slowly taking steps, and turning in circles. It's so dark out here that I can't see a thing, but on the other hand, my eyes seem to evolve, giving me the vision to see in the dark. Within seconds, I can see that we're still in the same area, near the creek where we jumped over, with the same trees and rocks. I can see everything now. Then I hear a small pack of running feet west of us and I decide to swing my barrel toward that direction. Then a glowing light appears out of the corner of my eye. Glancing over, the glowing light is coming from the glass oval orbs at the end of their staffs.

Their staffs are weapons. How interesting.

The sound of running feet suddenly stops, which makes my eyes move back to looking down the barrel of the rifle. All is quiet. Too quiet.

"Get ready," says Ulric.

Everything remains quiet until I hear a whoosh sound flying past me, impaling some source that squirts blood onto the left side of my face, then a scream of pain. Looking to where the blood came from, my heart hits rock bottom when I see Ryia on the ground with an arrow in her left shoulder. The branches snap in front of us. I see them, the evil wolves, the ones that tore those poor police officers and government people apart back in Kansas City. With a quick swift of my eyes from left to right, I count around twenty. One of them was holding a bow with an arrow at the ready, pointing it at Ryia to finish her off. He has an evil, sinister grin on his face which makes my blood boil and mentally has me firing off on all cylinders. Without wasting another moment, I immediately pulled the trigger and shot the fucker right in the head. This triggers his remaining nineteen friends to charge right at us.

We all open fire. Three of them come right at me, but I shoot them right in the chest, killing them instantly. I hope this bought me a second to check on Ryia, but very surprisingly, she stands up, holding her weight on her staff in her left hand. With her right hand, she grabs the arrow and tears it right out with a muffling scream. She looks at me and winks that she's fine and she can fight. Suddenly, I hear a burst of a blood-thirsty growl, and one of the evil wolves leaps right on top of me. Before I can shoot, Ryia shoots a round of bursting green light that also kills him. That same burst of light that came from her staff is the same color that's being fired from the other guys' staffs. More come at me, but I keep on firing. Then something is pulling from my waist. Looking down, I see it's my Colt trying to get free. More of the evil wolves come at me, but Ryia takes them down.

I look at Althalos with his left arm and hand stretched out toward me. His eyes are glowing again but also have a pleading look in them. I remember from what the guys told back on the ship when we were sailing across Michigan Lake that Althalos can conjure any weapon nearby. This includes my Colt. I immediately unsnap the leather that holds it and it flies out. The thing begins firing at any nearby enemy like it has a conscience.

Talk about people saying that guns kill people.

I also feel the strap of my crossbow being pulled against my chest. I guess Althalos needs this weapon, too. The same result happens when I unbuckle the clip and the thing goes flying off and shooting with its own conscience. It's just amazing the type of magic I am just witnessing, but I'm immediately brought back to reality when another evil wolf jumps on top of me, knocking me off my feet. The sheer strength of this fucker is so damn strong, not to mention its quick, snapping jaw a few inches from my face, but it makes me find the strength to push it off with my gun. When it gets up, I notice its balls, so that means it's a guy. I take the small window of opportunity by kicking them so hard. He wails in pain and I shoot him right in the head. Looking around, Forthwind is taken down, losing his grip on his staff. I rush over, flipping the rifle in my hands, now holding the hot barrel in my hands. I leap and give one hell of a swing by smacking the wolf in the face with the butt of the gun and immediately flipping it back as it was, shooting my final round.

"Shit. Althalos, I'm out!"

He shoves over another wolf off, thrusts one of his free hands forward at the tent, and within a second, one of the boxes of ammo for the rifle come flying out. I catch it with ease.

"Forthwind, cover me!" I shout to him.

He nods as I crouch to the ground and begin reloading. Once I load the first round into the chamber, I say to Forthwind, "Alright man, I'm good!"

Then a shadow jumps over me and attacks Forthwind. I look up and turn around to see the enemy has already sunk its teeth into his neck. I shoot that asshole in the shoulder to get his attention. He turns toward me, baring his fangs soaked with blood; immediately, three rounds go right into his head. I check him over, but it's too late. Forthwind is dead. Then I hear the same scream from before and see

Ryia being taken down by another one with its jaw. Again, I shoot at that asshole until it's dead. I run over to see where the new injury is.

Getting to her, I hear, "Will," Says Ulric, "Take Ryia inside and save her!"

Grabbing her by her armpits, I drag Ryia inside the tent. Amidst this most terrifying action, I hear Althalos yelling at Ulric that there are too many of them. What seems to take forever, I finally got Ryia inside the tent. I do my best to prop her properly on the pillows. She coughs up some blood and her eyes look a bit glazed over. I try to remain calm, trying to hold back the tears, but it seems that I can't.

"Where's your first aid kit?" Chocking on some air.

She points as she replies, "In my sack, Will," with a confident smile.

Scrambling around the tent, I find her sack, open it, and dump all of the contents out until the first aid kit reveals itself. Instead of being a small kit that you find at your local grocery store or something like that, this kit is a heavy-duty stock with all of the tools that the EMS personally uses on patients during their transport to the hospital. Then I hear Ryia calling my name. Rushing over, throwing open the kit, I look at her in question if it's okay that I open her robe. She nods and I unzip it, hoping that her girl parts are covered and sure enough, they are. Breathing a sigh of relief, I continue on removing the upper half of her robe.

Once the robe was off, I begin wiping and cleaning up the wound. With that done, that new wound is in the same area of her shoulder when she got impaled by that arrow. She coughs some more blood which squirts the blood from her shoulder into my face.

"Please Ryia, try not to move," I beg and she laughs a bit.

A few minutes fly by. I feel one of her hands on my head, I look at her, and she says to me, "Will, I gotta tell you something."

Looking right into her eyes, she continues, "You have been . . . the most interesting . . . person I've ever met."

"You're not going to die, Ryia. You're not going to die!"

She just smiles and keeps on talking, "You're so funny, kind, and cute. From the first time I saw you and spoke to you, I've . . . always," She coughs, "I've always . . . loved . . . you." She gives out her final breath. I begin shedding tears and my mind begins to play "Under the Moonlight" by Adam Brian which makes me cry even more. Closing her eyes, Ulric stumbles and falls into the tent. He's totally wounded and gasping for air. He rolls over onto his back and gestures me to come forward.

I kneel down, still weeping. He grabs my robe, pulls my head toward his mouth, and says, "Will . . . take my staff. Use it, channel all of your energy into it, and it will perform its power." At the same time, he thrusts his staff into my hands.

With his dying breath, he speaks, "Fight, terminate the enemy, and get your ass to Sparta as fast as you can." And then he passes on.

Firmly grasping his staff, I march out of the tent with revenge, hatred, and courage running throughout my body. To my left, I see Althalos dead, and to my right, my enemy. They all turn with the desire to murder me in their eyes. I firmly stand my ground, positioning my body to attack. I point the glass orb right at them and begin to think about hardcore rock songs that signify war by bands starting with the remix of "Near You" by Parking Lincoln. The lyrics come alive in my head. I shout along with the lead singer, *"Come on!"*

I run at them, then leaping into the air, the glass orb begins to glow red instead of green; with one good swing of the staff, a blade-like light comes out and decapitates ten in half. Landing back on my feet, I shoot an unlimited amount of the red light at every evil wolf and it murders them right on the spot. More come charging at me and again, I swing the staff, releasing another blade light that decapitates them. I feel unstoppable and very good that I'm reigning down the hell from what I've experienced in the past. As their numbers begin to go down, the remaining wolves get the idea that they can't stop me, so they plan to retreat.

"Big, fucking mistake," I growl under my breath.

I shoot more of the red lights at the remaining survivors that die in a second. I let out my best howl in enthusiasm and pride, stabbing the ground with the butt of the staff.

I yell out in triumph into the empty wilderness, "My name is Nos! And this is my motherfuckin' land! If there are any of you assholes who want to fuck around with this country boy, bring! It! On!"

Then I hear nothing, except for my voice echoing off the rocks and trees. Looking around to see the death and devastation of the camp, seeing my dead friends brings some sorrow to my heart, though I suck it up. I walk back toward the tent. I gather my strength and will to drag Ulric's and Ryia's corpses out of the tent.

"I'll bury them tomorrow." I close and tie up the flaps, extinguish the fire, and settle in for a very long ass night and day.

CHAPTER ELEVEN
Burial and onto Sparta

I WAKE UP AND try to make some breakfast. I decide to look around my friends' sacks if I could find any cold food. I do find fruits and eat them in silence. The event that took place last night hits me like a rock and a reminder of sadness comes back to my mind. Opening the flap door, the sun shines right into my eyes. I'm blinded by the light for a few minutes, but once my eyes adjust, I am absolutely horrified by the sight that lays out before me.

To give a decent description, I have a question. Have any of you guys seen the movie *War of the Worlds*? Yes? No? If no, oh well. Anyway, for those who have seen that movie, remember the 747 plane crash scene where the main character comes out of the basement and sees the entire neighborhood completely demolished and the aircraft nearly demolished, too? Well, from what I'm seeing, it's sort of like it except there are loads of decapitated and torn corpses of the enemy along with Ulric, Forthwind, Althalos, and . . . Ryia. Just seeing her dead, lifeless, makes my heart crumble, and my heart even crumbles even more for Ulric, Althalos, and Forthwind. I really thought that my future was going to be bright, but as it turns out, everything I come too close to or when some things start becoming good, it immediately goes shit. Walking around the battle sight, there are some fog lying very low, close to the ground, swirling around the corpses. The sight is so gruesome that I can see all organs of all functions spilled and spread out from the waist and from the head where the red blade light I used to slice them had been after my friends were murdered. I can see all the bones that form their bodies. I advert my vision to my friends. The injuries that they died from are less gruesome, although they're still disturbing. Next to the entrance of the tent, I find the shovel that we used to make the fire pit for lunch before *all* of this happened.

I swallow my sadness and began digging graves for my friends. It takes me hours to dig the holes six or so feet long and six feet deep. After I finish digging the fourth hole, I scramble out of it, preparing their bodies in the most suitable way. Laying the arms across Ryia's chest, I see a shiny necklace reflecting the morning sunlight around her neck. Picking it up and examining it, the necklace has a lightweight gold chain securing a small oval, gold plate with the same wolf head symbol carved onto it. Flipping to the back, there's a letter inscribed in an ancient language that I can't understand. Miraculously, the letter morphs into perfect English letters that says, "Ryia Heartfelt."

Hmm, dog tags.

I gently begin searching on the guy's bodies and they have the same necklace with their names on the back.

Holding all four of their tags in my hand, I say out loud, "I should definitely bring these along with me and return them to the king."

I put all four of them deep inside one of the pockets of my jeans. Looking at them, I gently pick them up and lay them in the holes. Putting Ryia in her grave is the hardest thing because I feel like the connection between us was real and it was getting strong. Just thinking about it makes me cry a little; I continue on. Once all four of them are in, I begin filling the holes, then I move on making crosses and whittle their first names into them. Next, I use a small hammer to pound them into the ground at the head of the graves.

Let's hope that I don't have to do this again.

Finally, I stand before them and pray out loud, "Lord up in heaven, I know you and I don't talk very much, but I beg of you that you accept these kind and awesome people up into your kingdom. I know that we all are created in your vision and you accept anybody that's of any different race, religion, and species. I hope that you take really good care of them up there and that you guide me through these woods toward Sparta, and . . ." turning my attention toward the evil wolves' corpses, "that you have smitten the evil bastards to hell and made sure that they're burning severely for their sins. In your son's name I pray. Amen."

Concluding the prayer, I scout for my weapons that Althalos used in the battle last night and within minutes, I find them, then discover that all of them are empty. Quickly, an idea pops into my head. I stack one on top of the other at the center of the camp site, then grabbing Ryia's, Forthwind's, and Althalos' staffs, I impale them into the ground and angle them to make a pyramid shape over my weapons in respect for my dead friends.

Lastly, I move toward the tent and begin throwing the cooking supplies, food, a few pillows, and quilts into my sack. The stronger shot that Ulric gave me is still active and my senses tell me that Sparta is to the east. Nearly departing for my journey, I lower the flag, which got torn up in the battle at half-staff, retrieve Ulric's staff, and continue onto my new home.

CHAPTER TWELVE
I Make It to Sparta, Sort Of

FOR THE PAST TEN days, I've been running. Most of the time, I haven't caught enough hours of sleep. Why? After the fight that occurred and burying my only friends, I've been chased by those evil wolves for miles upon miles, days upon days. There has been a time where I've been able to sit down and catch my breath, and I'll tell you what happened.

After running for about one hundred miles or more, I thought I've outrun my pursuers; I slow down and began walking. I was so out of breath, felt like I was going to pass out, but nonetheless, the strong shot that Ulric gave was still pumping through my veins. On the other hand, my legs were about to give out. I took cover in a shallow cave as I was about to pass. Once inside, I dug around in the sack looking for any leftover meat. My patience for finding any decent food was beginning to get shorter and shorter by the second. In desperation, I started throwing everything out. After all of the contents were thrown out before me, my eyes search over the pile with no luck of finding any food.

Letting my body fall back against the nearest wall of the cave, there was a gut feeling telling me that I wasn't going to make it. I bring my knees toward my chest, put my head in between them, then fold my arms on top. I finally began to weep again. Not even five minutes go by when the sound of snapping twigs catches my attention. The sound makes my head snap right up and my eyes scan the trees. Then a small pack of deer of about five comes strolling past me. Remaining absolutely silent and moving as slow as possible, I move my arm to grab Ulric's staff, well my staff now, slowing wrapping my fingers around it and positioning it to fire some sort of ball of light energy at them. All of a sudden, they stopped and looked at me, which makes me freeze in an instant. They looked at me for a while and decided to continue walking on. Without wasting another second, I quickly point the staff, and without moving my legs to make any sound with the leaves, the glass orb was locked on and I fired. Again, a red light burst out of the orb, impacting and killing one of the deer. At the time, my question was: does the light source that comes out of the orb the type of energy that's circulating inside of me, or is it the type of emotion that I'm feeling? Anyway, I scrabbled toward the deer and dragged it back. With ease and excitement, I set up the rotisserie, impaled the freshly cut meat, and began cooking it. Turning the meat little by little, I took the time putting the rest of the items back in the sack. The smell from the cooking meat was so welcoming that it really made my stomach growl a lot. I moved the rotisserie away from the fire and just ripped off the hot meat with my own bare hands because I couldn't wait any longer.

Just biting, just even sinking my teeth into my food was so intensifying that little did I know the smell would attract other animals. When I mean other animals, I mean the evil wolves catching the scent of the food and beginning to move toward my little camp. I didn't know they were still on my trail. I thought they gave up, but no. These creatures just wanted to murder me and taste and enjoy whatever leftover meat I have left on my bones, including my blood. As they were sprinting toward me, I just kept on eating away like everything is going to be fine. Man was I so wrong. Overall, here are what happened: eating on the second leg of my deer, I was hearing a lot of snapping wood. This makes me stop and take a look around. Shortly peaking my head around one of the corners, I'm rapidly taken down with ease. My senses kick in and I push the bastard off with my staff and shot him. Twirling around, there were six more standing on top of the entrance of the cave. With no hesitation, swinging the staff from right to left, I released another blade light that decapitates them in a second. Grabbing my final bite and throwing whatever things were still left out into the sack, I went back to sprinting east, trying to lose my murderers in the thick woods. Everything was going so well until I'm blindsided by another one which makes me fall off a cliff, tumble down the steep slope, and hit every rock and tree on the way down. During that time, I lose grip of the staff halfway down the cliff.

Landing on the ground below with a loud thud on my back, I felt like I couldn't move, like every bone in my body was broken or even worse, shattered. Lifting my head, my vision was blurry, but I can kind of make out the landscape. My glazed eyes were searching the ground for the staff until it landed about ten feet away from my feet. The same wolf drops down and lands between me and my only weapon. The way he's stood was like he was waiting for me to get up and try to fight. Crawling onto my hands and knees and slowly standing up hurt like hell twenty times over. Yet, the shot was still active and I felt it healing me. The first thing that it healed was my eyes. In seconds, my vision was cleared and I put my fists up, ready to die. The wolf smiles in an evil way and charged at me with great speed. Getting closer, he jumped and was about to take me down. I grabbed the fur around his neck and threw him as hard and as far away as I could. It crashed through the trees, whimpering of pain. Scrabbling through the leaves to grab the staff, I was in hands' reach until I was thrown toward the trees. Crashing into them and then falling back down to the ground added new pain. Again, the monster jumped and this time, it landed on me. Holding me down by my chest, it snaps its jaw and clawed it at my chest. I used enough strength to grab hold of the head, turn it onto one side, and then sink my own teeth in and around the eye. I rolled it onto its back and I pulled my head back, ripping out the eye in my mouth. I grabbed a branch nearby with a sharp, pointed end. Using all of my force, I stabbed the branch right into the hollow eye socket. The monster cried out in tremendous pain and I gave it one hard kick in the face with my right foot.

With achievement the second time, I grabbed the staff firmly in both hands. I began channeling all of my energy into the staff to give the monster the final blow whatever it takes off into the woods. Thinking that I've won the battle, the same monster again tackled me into the ground from behind, and then the unthinkable happened. It grabbed my left leg with both of its hands and twisted it until there was a loud snap. I screamed out in bloody murder and the monster took the moment by giving me one more final slash onto my chest. I tried to gather the remainder of my strength and threw it off to the side with the staff. I thought with all of my might to have a very, very sharp arrowhead taking form around the glass orb, and it did with a pure blood-red color. The evil wolf charged at me with its jaw wide open and I forced the staff right through its mouth, up, and through its head. Lots of its own blood came spewing out from its head, but I rolled away to keep my blood from being contaminated. The spewing lasted for a few seconds and I used the remainder of my strength to pull my staff out. Looking up at the sky, it was turning dark and I felt like I didn't have enough strength to keep on marching to my new home. During that night, I just screamed out in pain over and over again, praying to God out loud to keep me alive and have the medicine or shot work faster.

As the day broke, my chest and leg didn't hurt like a twenty-five; they felt like nearly a ten. I could feel strength returning back in my arms and I took the time to build a splint for my leg. Upon completion, I pulled up my own weight onto the staff and continued east.

So, here I am climbing steep hills and crossing fast-moving rivers and creeks with a broken leg, slowly healing chest, and multiple lacerations on my hands, arms, head, and back. Eating that deer awhile back was my last meal and I am yet again severely hungry and thirsty. Still, there's a small fire burning inside me, igniting the thought to keep on hiking. Mile after mile, the terrain is starting to get rougher and the trees are getting greener and thicker. My senses are beginning to tell me that I must be approaching the Appalachian Mountain Range. I stop to breathe and get my bearings, but I can't get a clear view of where I'm at. Plus, I'm feeling that the shot is wearing out and I could feel my human self coming back. This almost makes me crumble to the ground; I grab hold of my staff to keep myself up.

After breathing for about twenty minutes, managing the strength left in my legs and arms, I use them to climb one of the tallest hills. Now, this hill that I'm climbing is covered in trees that are separated by big boulders and loads of loose rocks, which makes it kind of hard when your left leg is in a splint. The climb itself takes me a while to climb to the top after slipping a couple of times, losing my grip on one of the boulders, and almost falling to my death. In the end, I make it to the top. The view that I see gives my perspective an entire three hundred and sixty degrees. At this moment, I feel like I'm an assassin and that makes me feel awesome on the inside. Naturally, the sun is setting in the west, but something black, puffy, and seems to be moving catches my eye and moves my head back toward the east. Examining the black vapor closely, it turns out to be one big vapor, with several other black vapors arising from the trees. This couldn't be a forest fire; the plumes seem to be more stationary and singular. Studying the black plumes even more closely, the thought hits me like an atomic bomb.

I say my answer out loud, "Sparta. That's Sparta!"

Choosing the same side I climbed, I slide down the hill with great enthusiasm, rounding that same hill, and begin running or limping toward my destination. I feel like nothing can stop me now.

After running for about ten miles, it's already dark as I am getting near the kingdom. I see the same banners and flags with the same color layout and wolf symbol on them. I can hear people talking or singing, possibly both, like some sort of festival is happening. Also,

I can smell food. There are some drawbacks. After running those ten miles, the shot was really wearing out, making me feel like a weak human again, which makes me collapse a couple of times. Still, I keep pressing on. The pain in my chest and leg is getting worse. On top of that, I feel completely famished and thirsty. My robe has been torn up and has been torn since I fell off that cliff and fought with that evil wolf that almost murdered me. To sum it all up, I'm really cold, and thick snowflakes come dwindling down from the sky. Later on, a path forms in front of me and I follow it toward the voices, sound of music, and the smell of food. Rounding a few more trees, I see two tall stone towers with a small bridge across them. Hanging below the bridge is a huge banner being held horizontally with the same colors, icon, and Segoe Script that says, *"Sparta"* in silver.

Looks like I'm approaching the gate to the kingdom.

During my approach, I see four humanoid wolves, two on the bridge, and each one standing at the base of the left and right towers.

The wolf standing at the left tower points his staff at me and shouts, "Halt!"

This makes me collapse to the ground one more time and I have the trouble of finding the strength to get back up.

His buddy standing at the right tower runs toward me and tells the other guy in an Irish accent, "Easy, mate! We've got a hurt one. Marco, make the call for the medical tent." At this moment, I'm lying flat on my stomach, coughing, and about to blackout. Then I hear a horn being blasted.

The Irish accent wolf rolls me over, pats my shoulder, and speaks to me, "Easy lad, easy. Help is on the way. Here, have some water."

I feel my head being picked up and slightly moved forward. Then something circular with a hole touches my lips and the most magical thing happened. I can feel the cold, refreshing water slowly being poured into my dry mouth and as I drink for the first time, the cool liquid soothes my dry throat which feels like I'm in heaven. Moments passed. I hear feet running toward our direction, then I'm being picked up and laid onto a stretcher, I think. Soon, the entire stretcher is lifted and moving at a great pace. There are numerous voices ordering to clear the way over and over again. Through my blurry eyes, I see numerous faces, wolves and humans, as I'm rushed by. I don't care if it's me, but all of those faces have a concerned or worried expression. All in all, I must be in Sparta and that is good enough for me. Moreover, I decide to pass out from exhaustion, thirst, and hunger.

I slowly wake up to a beeping sound that entered my head not too long ago. Slowly opening my eyes, I see a soft, ocean blue tube-like lighting that seems to form a rectangular shape above me. I glance around at the area that I'm in. My human senses tell me that I'm lying on top of something that is really comfy and cushioning to my injured body. This also brings up the thought I'm alive and that I'm in a good, safe haven. Continuing to look around, there are a bed sheet and thick quilt covering my legs and my body up to my shoulders. The beeping still sounds off softly and as I look up and left, there's a glass computer tablet with red, green, and yellow lines going across it horizontally from left to right. Almost where the lines end at the far right of the screen, a blue dot goes off, synchronizing with the beeping sound, making the three lines go up a certain height, and remaining the same height as they go off the screen.

So, I must be in a hospital.

I just keep on exploring with my eyes finding a curtain that's pulled around my bed, then feeling a decent heat source being poured in from some sort of a heater. Next, I find a small, clear tube wrapping underneath my nose with two smaller ones in each nostril supplying air. After that, I feel a tube in my mouth that's stuffed down my throat, possibly a feeding tube or something else. Glancing some more, there are more tubes attached to me from giving blood to removing my urine. I try to speak, but I can't. When I thought the sentence, "So, I must be in a hospital." I did hear a clicking sound nearby. Glancing at my upper right, there's another glass tablet, slightly bigger than the heart monitor, on a stand with a blank, white page with the sentence, "So, I must be in a hospital," in a decent font size colored black. I realize there is some kind of a sticky substance pressed against my forehead.

Looking at the monitor, I say to it, "Hello? Is there somebody there?"

The machine picks up my thought which excites me. Soon, the curtain is pulled back for a moment and a male wolf, with light grey fur and a military haircut in between his ears, wearing an all-white cloak with red crosses on both of his shoulders, enters. On the left side of his cloak seems to have his name, but in the same ancient medieval writing, just like the writing on the back of my friends' dog tags. God, just thinking about them makes me weep a few tears.

His ears perk forward. He walks toward my left side, places one of his hands, and speaks to me in a deep voice, "My name is Tristen Maverick. I'll be your doctor and mentor, showing you how the kingdom of Sparta works. I understand what you've been through, Will."

I reply back, "How do you understand? How do you know what hell I went through just to get here?"

He sighs and replies, "You do understand that our technology is very advanced."

I nod in saying yes.

He continues, "When you passed out, I took charge taking care of you, and by doing that, I used a system that taps into your mind to rewind and replay the events that you went through." Then he grabs a nearby stool and takes a seat, still talking, "The fight scene was very horrific and the saddest part was that you took the time to bury Ulric, Althalos, Ryia, and Forthwind. That's when my associates and I pull out their I.D. tags from your jeans."

I think that over for a moment and try to imagine what that device looks like and how they operate it.

He smiles, "Now, onto your injuries. You've suffered a broken leg, the slash mark on your chest is a little deep, but lucky for you, our enemy didn't break open your rib cage. Furthermore, it seems that the shot that Ulric gave you did some of the healing for both your leg and chest, including multiple lacerations on your arms, torso, and head. But since the shot has finally worn off, your body will heal at its usual pace, so I highly recommend that you really take it easy. However, you have suffered from almost severe dehydration and almost starved to death. Yet, you have a strong spirit and made it here alive. Now, don't worry, you'll be given the finest healthy food and lots of water to drink. Do you any questions?"

I ask him, "Two. Can you take the tube out of my mouth? And how long was I unconscious?"

Tristan gets up, moves the bed slightly forward so that he can stand behind my head, lowers the back part flat, tells me to relax as he opens my mouth as wide as it goes, uses a long narrow, silvery manual mechanical device that has a claw on it, and puts it down into my throat. Now, having two objects in your throat is a very unpleasant thing. Now I can feel the claw grabbing the tube and having it being pulled out. Once Doctor Maverick gets the tube out, I cough a little bit and I'm handed a cup of water. While I drink, Maverick removes the wireless receivers from my head and tells me I've been out for two weeks. Then he asks if I need anything else and I reply to him, "No," in a weak, scratchy voice. As he draws back the curtain, he tells me to get some sleep because it's ten o'clock at night and then he leaves. I finish the cup of water, slowly closing my eyes and letting the heart rate monitor put me to sleep.

The last thought that goes through my mind is, *Wow, two weeks. What day is it going to be tomorrow?*

CHAPTER THIRTEEN
Recovery

I WAKE UP TO the sound of some chatter in a language I don't understand. The chatter seems to be coming from the other side of the curtain. I listen closely to the tone of the voices, wondering if they're happy, sad, concerned, or angry. Listening to the chatter for a few minutes, the tones in the voices are of annoyance. Then the voices fall silent and turn over to English.

"My patient is weak. He needs more time to recover. He nearly . . ."

"I understand and you've told me a hundred times over, but listen to me again and understand what I'm saying. The king, especially his daughter, wants to meet him and thank him for returning the ID's of those four wolves. Also, the king wants to start the relationship between Will and his daughter ASAP. You have one month, Dr. Maverick."

I hear Tristan sighs in aggravation and he comes through the curtain, but puts on a smile once he notices that I'm awake. He walks toward the front of my bed, pulls out a smaller glass tablet, and swipes across the screen, comparing the data to the glass tablet and keeping pace with my heart. He comes over toward my left side and pulls out his stethoscope. He helps me lean forward and proceeds to check my vitals.

After completing the checkup routine, he asks, "How do you feel today?"

"Okay, I guess, but I'm hungry, thirsty, and my leg hurts."

He steps quickly to his left, lifting the covers up to look at my leg. Seeing my leg for the first time in two weeks makes me raise my eyebrows. Why? Because my leg is all black and blue, being held straight in a pair of pure white splints with a board underneath, and three half rings curving over my leg. The center ring, which goes over the knee, has a few needles that are inserted into it and are connected to that ring. I couldn't resist, so I asked away.

"What's with the needles, Doc?"

He looks up and back at the knee, "Your knee was twisted in opposite directions to the point where it was almost torn apart. I had to twist it back and reinsert the bones back together. The needles were put in to keep your leg from not moving so that the knee will heal properly."

Makes perfect sense.

At that point, the smell of beautiful food comes along making me feel really, really hungry.

"Ah, your breakfast has arrived," he says with a big grin on his face.

Tristen turns, pulls back the curtain, and reveals a young female wolf that looks like she's in her late teens or early twenties. Her facial features are very beautiful and her eyes are ice blue but have a calm presence in them. The color of her fur is milk chocolate and on her face is a long, narrow, slit type black line that crosses her left eye straight down. The fur on top of her head takes on a mass and forms real hair, which seems to be cut short from both sides and possibly on the back, leaving longer hair, especially one long strand that's about four inches, that covers her left eye. At the end of that piece of hair, it's dyed in dark purple and only travels up an inch. Also, she's wearing the same cloak as my doctor is wearing. She smiles and I smile back. In front of this lovely woman is a rolling cart that has a silver platter that's covered. The smell coming from that tray is so inviting, but when I look at Tristen, his smile is replaced by the expression of annoyance while he looks down at the woman.

What did she do? She's just bringing me food. Is she not a registered nurse? What's going on?

When I'm about to ask my final question out loud, Tristen grabs her left arm, moves in his head toward her left ear, and whispers in his annoyed tone, "He's. Not. Ready."

The woman jerks her arm away from him, looking very annoyed, but grabs him by his cloak, pulls him back to where I believe would be the hallway, and closes the curtain.

"What are you doing here?" Tristen asks in a little harsh tone.

Then the beautiful wolf female sighs and answers, "In case you forgot, Dr. Maverick, I have the right to be wherever I want and . . ." Then she switches languages to finish her sentence.

Tristen sighs, "Yes, I know that, but please understand that he just woke up and he's been through a lot of shit. Besides, aren't you missing out on some of your classes?"

The female sighs again and answers, "You're such an annoyance."

Tristen sighs again and pulls back the curtain to let himself back in, pressing his thumb and index finger against his nose while he relaxes. Next, he pulls out a bed tray from under my bed, places it above my waist, reveals my food, and sets the silver platter in front of me. On the tray are pancakes covered in syrup, sunny side up eggs, fruits like grapes and apples, bacon, and sausages with two glasses of water and orange juice. Tristen tells me to enjoy my breakfast, but before he vanishes behind the curtain, I have another question.

"Hey, Tristen. What's today's date?"

He looks back, "It's October 15, 2014. Again, enjoy your breakfast. Holler when you're done and we'll begin your recovery." He leaves, but I hear him mutter out loud, "One month, my ass."

My stomach growls really loud and I dive into the food.

When I was done with my meal, I was moved to a huge room, well, more like a gym that's been set up to help patients get their strength back. From my room to this cool-looking place, the hospital seems to be one giant tent with a few hallways that connect between areas made for normal bedrooms, I.C.U. rooms (where I came from), and restrooms. Anyway, once Tristen and I entered the gym, there are a few doctors standing by for some reason, but once we entered, they looked up and greeted Tristen and me. Immediately, all of the doctors start to get down to business by exchanging and sharing data about me on all of their tablets. A few of them and I started talking about certain medical things and onto things I like to do. Right then and there, the recovery section in my life starts to take off.

For the first few days, the doctors have taken X-rays for multiple times in my leg, given me a menu created around the type of food I like to eat, most of which is very organic, and ordered me to drink lots and lots of water. During this entire course, the doctors have been running tests by taking very small doses of my blood.

During that time, the results I have been shown indicates that the shot that Ulric gave me on the night where he and his crew met their deadly fate was a bit too powerful and that was starting to transform my body into their wolf form with the fact that I didn't eat and drink anything for days when I struggled to get my ass to Sparta. In essence, the shot was eating away my body in order to keep me going. I am told not only by Tristen but by the other doctors that I should really take it easy to let my human form heal properly. Still, the conversation that Tristen had with that other person at the time I woke up before this session began makes me want to ask.

"Hey, Tristen, can I ask something?"

He nods in acknowledgment as he takes a bite out of his sandwich and chews.

Breathing in and out, I ask, "Who was that person you were talking to over a week and a half ago?"

He swallows, "That was Cora. She's one of the king's superiors. When you were asleep, she wanted to bring the king in so that he can thank you for bringing back the tags of Ulric, Althalos, Forthwind, and Ryia. Furthermore, his daughter spotted you from her private balcony when you collapsed and were brought in from the West Gate."

"So, is that why you and your co-workers have a month to get me back in working order so that I could be thanked and that I should start bonding with his daughter?"

"Yes." Placing his hand over his eyes and letting his head hang, he brings it back up and continues, "But you're still human. You won't heal as fast as we do and after the hell you've been through, it's really for best that you, Will, take it slow."

So, I get to meet their king and his daughter, but I hardly know what she looks like and she doesn't know anything about me. Likewise, for me about her. Plus, I don't even know if she's going to like me or not.

I look at Tristen and I can tell that he understands what I'm feeling from the vibe of my body and the expression on my face. Out of the blue, he smiles and puts a hand on my shoulder while saying, "You've met her before, and trust me, she definitely likes you."

After he says it, we get back to work on my road to recovery. Hopefully, I'll be back in a working human, an order by the end of this month.

CHAPTER FOURTEEN
Reunited with Old Friends
Date: November 22, 2014

THE TIME LIMIT THAT Tristen was given is about to run out, but as the month comes to a close, I can wiggle my toes and slightly move my foot left and right. Plus, the weird splint that was on my leg when I woke up in the hospital the first time was removed. Still, I'm getting X-rayed and my leg is put into a cast. During the course of my recovery, I've been able to get around the medical tent on crutches which I really don't mind. Getting up this morning, I stumble around my room to find any window to see what's outside because I'm really, really curious what this kingdom looks like. I want to see the activities, the arts and crafts, music being played, the people, and most of all, see them do sorcery. I remember Althalos and Ryia conjuring their sorcery to get the boat into and sail across Lake Michigan, and Forthwind using his sorcery to bring my weapons to life. Just thinking about them and mostly about Ryia makes my heart sink and I don't know if I'll meet another great woman like her again. Plus, the memory of the fight we had when they were protecting me got them killed, and just thinking about that one evil wolf that shot Ryia with an arrow makes me grab and tighten my fist around the thick, insulation tarps that are draped around inside this tent.

I hear the curtain being pulled and I turn around to see it's Tristen. He and I exchange our usual greetings and medical checkup talks. Obviously, it requires me to lay back down onto the bed so that he can examine me. During the examination and the time I've spent here, I've grown to really like Tristen and I'm pretty sure he's grown to like me. During the past month, he was curious about what my life was like before I got here. I did tell him straight out that my life is right on his tablet, but he wanted to hear from me, so I told him everything. Now, on this day, Tristen pulls out some object wrapped in a towel from one of his pockets, which takes me by surprise once he unfolds it.

"Here," as he holds out my iPod with a smile, "I kept on forgetting to give this back to you. You have a very unique taste in music."

Calmly grabbing it, I ask, "How'd you get it?"

"Well, it was part of the procedure to remove any sort of items from your clothes when we were getting you ready for the I.C.U."

Looking down at my iPod, I can't believe I forgot about it. It's just that the music that I listen to is the most important thing in my life which influenced me through different types of social classes and kept me going through life with some ease. I say "Thank you" to Tristen and look back at the insolated tarp wall of my room wondering what Sparta looks like. I mean, I'm healthy enough to go outside and experience the interesting high-tech, medieval, humanoid wolf culture. I want to ask Tristen if it's absolutely okay with him that I go outside; plus, I do remember that he's going to be my mentor and show me around the kingdom of Sparta.

He answers, "Certainly, you can go outside and I will show you Sparta, and we'll do it after you had your breakfast." He pulls in a cart with my food on it.

After I'm done eating, I hear voices coming alive outside the tent along with music that sounds Celtic.

Anyway, the sounds outside make me even more excited. Tristen places his hands on my shoulders, looks at me right in the eyes, and says to me, "Alright, Will, as your doctor, you can tell me if you're getting exhausted, about to pass out, or that the environment overwhelms you. Moreover, it is a bit chilly out there with the sun shining bright and there's snow on the ground."

"Doc, you're talking to a country boy who had some hell in his life. I think I can handle what I'm about to see."

He sighs a laugh and brings over clothes that are winter-designed, which also seem to fit my size. Surprisingly, he brings me a brand-new robe that has the same colors. Getting dressed is a bit of a hassle, especially with the jeans, though they are bigger so that they can go around and fit along with the cast. After throwing my new robe on, putting on my camo hat, shades, and grabbing my crutches, Tristen and I head out toward the entrance of the medical tent.

"You ready for this, Will?" he asks while he grabs the flap of the tent with a bit of excitement on his face. I nod with enthusiasm and he continues, "Welcome to Sparta."

Stepping outside, I'm greeted by the chilly air as it touches my face and by the blinding light of the morning sunrise. Putting on the shades, my eyes adjust to the light and what I see completely blows me away. Where I am standing, the entire medical tent, is surrounded by more tents that are set up as houses and shops which have the same kingdom colors, except for the medical tent because its fabric walls and roofs are an off-white color with darkish red medical crosses. Anyway, the paths between the structures are beginning to be crowded with people emerging from their tents. It's not just the humanoid wolves, but there are also humans mixed in with the crowd and start exchanging small talks with the wolf race like it's not scary or weird. Well, I do remember that Ulric told me the two reasons why these two kingdoms are established: one, they are like refugee camps to keep humans safe and two, they are to capture their enemy and transport them back to their planet, which I think is the idea.

Tristen pushes me gently saying, "Come, there's much to see." And surely, there is.

Making our way into the crowd, there are several beautiful stone fountains that are absolutely carved with precise crafting and look very smooth. There are torches burning in different shades of colors of red, blue, purple, and green. There are shops selling very authentic jewelry that have real crystals with different colors in them and they are embedded in interesting metal frames for necklaces, earrings, wristbands, and rings. Even some of the necklaces take shape of wolf symbols and other interesting symbols that are created from silver, copper, bronze, and gold. The other shops are selling toys in all shapes and sizes that even young adults like me could enjoy, and the most intriguing thing is that on one of the wall's display shelves are high-tech electronics that have all-glass pane tablets in different shapes. Seeing these toys makes me wander in and take a closer look. Just looking at them puts me in an awe moment; naturally, the owner sees me and he and I start talking about them. After a brief moment into our conversation, Tristen starts slowly pulling me away with a smile and tells me again there's more to see. Continuing moving through the market, the most interesting tent really catches my attention.

This tent is set up like glass, metal welding, and furniture workshop. The heat and the sound make it so exquisite it makes me just want to step inside and start crafting my own like whatever they are crafting. However, a familiar head, then a face, shows through the crowd. Later on, other familiar faces started to form next to the first one. After a while of scrutinizing, a lightning bolt goes off in my head and in my stomach. The first familiar face looks at me and breaks out a huge smile.

The person runs toward me, shouting my name, "Nos!"

Instantly, familiar people look in my direction and also come running toward me giving huge hugs. Now for introductions, the first person I know is Chris October. He's about my height, slightly built, brown eyes and hair, and a little crazy because he grew up in the Jemez Mountains in a small town called La Cueva. If you're asking what makes him crazy is that he can perform well-executed stunts on his dirt bike, get his only A.T.V. to do wheelies, and drive it on two wheels on the left or right side. Plus, he has thrown some awesome parties in the neck of the woods and does some crazy shooting tricks using different guns from his family's gun safe. All in all, it's great to see him and my other friends.

"Nos, it's so good to see you man, but what the fuck happened to ya?" Chris asks.

"Yeah man, what happened to you?" Another friend of mine called Alice Cole, a few inches shorter than the rest of us, really cares. She loves to wear Mossy Oak camo all the time and she still is. Alice loves to hunt elk during the season, and I wasn't able to go along with her and her family when we were in high school. However, the rest of my friends have eagerness and concern in their eyes, wondering how I got this way.

"Well," I go into the details of how my life was going when I was in the truck driving business, to the part where I was filling up in Ottawa, Kansas and read the article about Tristen's race, which I introduced him, to where I met up with the scout group of Ulric, Ryia, Forthwind, and Althalos. At that point in my story, I went into complete detail about how our journey was going when we were coming here. When I got to the point of the story about the battle that got all four of them murdered, my friends gasp in horror. Then they shed a few tears when I told them that I buried them and went on. They got even more shocked in horror and amazement about the last fight I endured when I took on that one evil wolf one on one.

I gesture my hand to my leg and told them about the painful night after the fight and finally tell them the end of how I collapsed just a few yards away from the West Gate.

"No wonder we heard that horn being sounded a month ago. We didn't have a clue what was happening and still when the doctors rushed by us," says Austin Black. He's a tall guy, about six feet, lean, fit, and built. Plus, he joined the Marines after he graduated a year before our class. I thought he was going to be based up in Oregon.

Must've been transferred to another one to be this close and be ushered here.

"So, how long have you guys been here?"

"Well, over a month and a half, Nos," says Hugh Smith. He's another friend, an older adult actually. He's the auto shop teacher who gave me the name Nos and let me hang out at the shop every lunch period when I was a freshman at Los Alamos High. The only time when any freshman was allowed in the shop is when he or she had him as their Driver's Ed teacher. If they didn't have them, they weren't allowed in. It's just how he rolls. Anyway, he's another person that likes country music and likes classic rock music. He wears cowboy boots, sometimes a cowboy hat, but mostly wears a greasy, dirty, camouflage Bass Pro Shop hat. Plus, he has a daughter called Emily Smith and it's also great to see her, too. Once, she and I are about to engage in a conversation when Tristen taps my shoulder. Looking up at him, he gestures his head that I should wrap it up because a superior wolf dressed in a robe with finer detail that represents the king is walking toward us. The superior wolf's fur is pure black, he has brown eyes and has some weight around his stomach, but I can't make out his age.

I ask Tristen, "Who is that?"

He sighs, "That's Marcus Lowsbroth. We better get going, Will, before he gets impatient."

By that moment, this Marcus guy is three feet from us and he replies, "Yes, I do get impatient. Especially that the time I heard that you, Doctor Maverick, were given is now up and the royal family wants to meet Will. Plus, it's nice to see you, young man, up and about."

Something about this wolf, guy, or whatever you readers want to characterize him, feels off like this man is not feeling so great seeing me out of the medical tent. I don't know what else to think of it; I simply nod to him in acknowledgment. When he mentioned the words "royal family," my friends made noises that something interesting is happening to me and as I look at their faces, they all want to know how I got into this situation. But Marcus clears his throat in impatience, so I tell my friends that I'll see them later and Tristen places his hand on my right shoulder, like a guardian, and we both follow Marcus to a cliff that has all sorts of vegetation growing and hanging from it. Still, strolling the market area, I still want to see the interesting shops and talk to the other wolves, but that'll have to wait.

CHAPTER FIFTEEN
Meeting the King and His Kingship

AS MARCUS, TRISTEN, AND I get closer and closer to this black cliff face of the Appalachian Mountains, the marketplace gets thinner and thinner. Looking at the cliff blows me away because the entire cliff face looks to be carved out with well-sophisticated craftsmanship that probably took years to do. On the flip side, this "alien" race has technology that is far more advanced than ours. So, it might've taken the builders just days to do it. The craftsmanship of the carvings takes the form of a medieval castle with two large towers that seem to run up to two hundred feet with coned roofs and faded redwood shingles; on each tower, there are two small balconies that seem to have several floors spacing between them. There are marvelous, detailed carvings of statues that seem to be popping out from the stone walls and each figure seems to be holding a different weapon about annihilating an enemy of some kind while portraying some really interesting battle scenes.

In between the two towers is the main structure that is also carved out, forming the rock into smooth stones. At the base of the main structure are two large wooden doors with four wolf guards holding staffs. The interesting thing is that their cloaks seem to be woven out of finer and luxurious material. On their right sleeves is a woven gold outline of the wolf symbol that represents Sparta and has two gold stripes below the icon. Looking above the guards are huge, thick flags that represent Sparta slowly flapping in the wind due to their weight, suspended a hundred feet in the air, and attached to iron rod polls that stretch out fifty feet from the structure. In between the two flags is a large, circular stained-glass window that also has the icon of the kingdom placed in the middle and it's made out of beautiful different colors. Behind the window seems to be torches or some other light source illuminating it from the other side. Back at ground level, there are three torches on each side of the wooden doors, burning a dark, rich purple. Putting my eyes back up at the stained-glass window, I keep on looking up and there are only two balconies. The first one is large, but small compared to the one above it because the second balcony seems to be four times larger. Both of them have rod iron or wood French doors that are closed and behind them are curtains pulled shut.

Getting closer to the doors, we are brought to a halt by the four guards. Marcus talks to them in a different language, the same one that I heard when I woke up in the hospital, and points at me probably saying that their king is expecting me and Tristen. Looking at the guards closer, all of them have green eyes, light golden fur, hair on top of their heads that seem to be cut in a military-style, and are medium built. Two out of the four guards come toward Tristen and me, especially me. One of them puts a smile on his face and pats me on the back in a friendly gesture which gets me a bit confused.

"Should I know you or have we met before?" I ask.

The wolf laughs and answers in an Irish accent, "Of course, I met you, mate. It's so good that you pulled through. I thought you were a goner."

This blows me out of the water and I can't hold myself back to what I'm about to say.

"Holy shit, you're the guy that told one of your guys to relax and gave me some water. Thank you so much."

He laughs, "It's not a problem, lad, I'm glad to help. So, Doctor Maverick, how's his recovery?"

Tristen replies, "Slow, but speeding up. Within a two-week time or less, his leg would be fully healed and that includes all of the other scratches on him," while patting my back with a smile.

The other guard inspects me to make sure I'm not carrying any dangerous objects or weapons. Tristen assures him that I'm not a threat and I'm a simple, innocent human that's just recovering. Now, the innocent thing is kind of off because I may look innocent on the outside, but on the inside, I'm a rebel. Please, I'm not going to repeat myself of the subject that I told you guys back in chapter one.

However, I will tell you this: after spending the second year of high school and hanging out at the auto shop, I was taught how to stand up by fighting for myself. As the days progressed, one of my Special Ed teachers crossed the line by acting as a guidance counselor instead of a speech therapist. Why, you ask? She thought she had the right to pry herself into my personal life, asking me what has been happening, about the new friends I am meeting, and what stuff they like. This is what happened on that day.

Location: Room 215A, Los Alamos High School
Time: 10:30 AM
Date: Sept. 9, 2010

"Now, tell me, Will Young. What things do your new friends like to do?" Chase Tiger asks me while still prying her way into my privacy.

I sit on the couch in her little classroom that I and a lot of her students that I also know call "the prison" in silence, with my arms crossed and completely reclined on the couch, sticking true to my first and fourth Amendment Rights. Tiger, the so-called best Special Ed teacher, leans forward and pushes her odd, gold-rimmed rectangular glasses back up her nose. This is the fourth time of this fucking, stupid ass session that she's asked me about the friends I have met in the shop. It's none of her goddamn, fucking business; her job is to make kids speak better, *not* teaching or prying about their private lives. That's the guidance counselor's job. Still, Tiger lets out a quiet yet furious sigh through her nose and looks back at me with intimidation.

"Will," she begins, trying to hold back her frustration while folding her hands in her lap. "I am asking very kindly about what your friends like to do and also, do you have play dates with them at their houses?"

It's none of your fucking concern. I'd rather be helping Samantha on her white Chevy Camaro right now.

I look at her sternly. "I don't want to talk about them," I answer calmly, holding back my frustration.

"Well then." She leans back in her chair and looks down at her clipboard. "I guess you'll have to miss Auto Shop 1 entirely unless you tell me what's happening in your life."

I throw my hands up, slap them on my legs, and remove myself from the couch. I slip between her and the old 1950s heater in "the prison" and begin reaching for the doorknob. Suddenly, Tiger grabs my left arm. I snap my head in her direction and see an evil glare or perhaps evil, happy, sinister expression, something like the Joker will show from the recent Batman movies.

"If you leave this classroom, I'll send out a hitman to murder your family back in Wisconsin that you hold dearly to your heart."

What the fuck?

Hearing this threat makes my blood boil, officially. How dare she threaten my family? My heart races with speed and my adrenaline starts kicking in. I released her grip from my arm by thrusting her away from me with my right arm and she collides into a bookshelf. Then, I grab her hair with my left hand, bringing her head onto the table where she made me and other students do stupid first-grade work; next, I tighten my right hand into a fist and wind up the tension in my shoulder for a few seconds. During these few seconds,

I look right into her eyes, and all I see is fear. Soon, releasing all the force from the shoulder into my arm, my fist punches her right into the nose, sending her flying into the couch. Her nose is completely broken and a lot of blood is pouring out. She examines the small pool of blood in her hands and looks up at me. I slowly walk over, then deliver a hard smack across her face.

I grab her head again, holding it real tight in my hands, and I whisper this message into her ear, "Threaten me that way again, consider yourself six feet under. Report this to any other official, you'll still end up six feet under. You have made a monster, not a friend. We're done here, Ms. Tiger. Now, fuck off."

After sending that message, I push her back onto the couch; I see fear, all-out fear across her face. As I am about to reach for the door, I flip her off with both hands. I open the door real fast and slam it real hard behind me that makes the window above the door frame crack across the entire pane. Right after that, I march straight back to the Auto Shop, fuming, but with pride in my chest that I showed that teacher she crossed the line with the *wrong* student.

Now, bringing you guys back to the present, I am injured and it is best that I should behave and follow orders. These guards have staffs as weapons and can do serious damage and kill any living creature within a second. Anyway, Tristen and I are clear to enter. One of the other guards taps a piece of stone on the frame of the doors on the left side. The stone reacts and turns one hundred and eighty degrees revealing a communicator of some kind and he speaks into it in the same language that he and the other guards used when talking to Marcus. The stone immediately turns back to its original nature and the two big, wooden doors open up.

The doors open with ease, but there's a quiet noise of gears and chains clashing with one another as the doors open. Once they stopped, the four guards surround Tristen and me leaving Marcus in front, and we enter. This makes me nervous like we, or just myself, did some crime. Tristen brings his right arm over my shoulders, assuring me that everything is going to be okay and it's just a protocol. By the time we clear the doors, they start closing; the quiet sound of gears and chains come to life again; looking around at the smooth stone walls and ceiling, up in the highest corners, I can see them moving, just barely. Looking behind us and seeing the stained-glass window, it is indeed illuminated by torches that are slightly angled outward and circle the entire circumference of the window. What's interesting is that the colors of the fire blazing are the normal ones you see in our reality.

"We should keep moving," says Marcus in a slightly annoyed tone.

Hey, go easy on me. It's my first time to see "all" of this.

Moving on, the ceiling of this entrance area descends fast to meet another ceiling that's about ten feet high, with Gothic or Celtic architecture cones in its long hallway illuminated by normal burning torches. The only sounds that I hear are quiet steps of bare paws stepping on the floor, quiet breathing, the crackling of the burning torches, and my crouches tapping the stone floor, which, in a couple of feet, is replaced by thick, dark purple carpet that has amazing gold lines forming the same pattern over and over again. Walking onward, we pass another set of faded redwood doors on our left with signs above written in their language I can't read.

"What's behind those doors, Tristen?" I asked in curiosity.

"Behind those doors is our sanctuary. It's closed today, but tomorrow, it will be open for worship."

Wow, these people do believe in a god or the God that we humans worship to on our planet. Tomorrow is going to be so interesting.

After walking a few more yards, the same type of doors appears in front of us. Marcus straightens out his robe, pulls out some kind of a hat, but as he's about to knock on the doors, he looks at me in a very serious way right into my eyes.

"Now, Will Young, through these doors is our king, King Borin. You must address him by that or by your majesty. Look right at him when he asks you questions. If you look away from him, he will give the order to execute you right on the spot. You do not pay attention to any other kingship that serves him. You do not look around the throne room when our king is talking to you. And most of all, you do not speak freely unless you are given permission to speak. Do you or do you not understand these terms?"

At the same moment, Tristen lets out a heavy sigh and rubs his thumb and index finger at his closed eyes.

Looking right back at Marcus and feeling frightened, I reply, "Yes, sir. I do understand the terms you have set upon me."

"Good. Now, stand up straight."

Again, Tristen lets out another heavy sigh.

I do my best to stand up straight. Marcus rolls his eyes like my posture isn't good enough for his satisfaction.

Hey, I'm on crutches, you asshole. Give me a break.

Then Marcus knocks at the doors loudly three times and they open inward to the great, well-designed, well-furnished throne room of the castle of Sparta.

Here's my best description of this room: the carpet goes on, the walls are white marble with gold lines, about half an inch thick, running down from the ceiling to the floor. The main floor we are on is very wide although on each side it's raised by five steps that stretch the entire length of the throne room from the doorway we walked through and all the way to the far wall where they create a stage where two thrones reside. On top of the raised floors, both left and right, are columns that are carved out of dark blue marble stones and stand very high, about fifty feet, toward the ceiling where at the very top of each one is capitals painted in or carved out of gold. It's hard to tell. The marble columns become support beams as they angle themselves at fifty degrees and continue higher until they connect to a similar marble beam that touches the wall where we came through. This beam stretches all the way to the fall wall and is outlined with gold stripes. The gold stripes are also found on the beams that angle toward the center beam and on the support columns.

There are five huge, circular, polished steel chandeliers well over twenty-five feet in diameter with two levels of smooth, bright blue lights that cover the entire circumference at both top and bottom. Along the walls are also the same exact lighting except they are singular and spaced apart by four doorways on both sides with curtains drawn back revealing passageways to areas I don't even know. The five light sources seem to be made out of some kind of electrical liquid between the doorways on both sides and they seem to be about a foot long vertically.

Finally, at the far wall are two thrones that are both exquisitely carved from the same blue marble with very fine and great detail. Both of them have thick cushions on the bottom and back sides with the colors of the kingdom, including the symbol. Above the two thrones, the marble rock climbs up the wall and forms itself into a giant wolf head with golden pupils in its eyes. Above the giant wolf head is the biggest flag of the kingdom of Sparta that I've ever seen being held by two heavy-duty hooks on the wall. Back down at the thrones, one is bigger than the other and it comes to me that the bigger one is for their king who occupies it.

So, the throne on his left is for his daughter. Where is she anyway?

Still, the entire throne room is occupied with the highest authorities abroad because all of them are wearing delicate cloaks, gowns, and superb jewelry. Looking at all of them, their fur colors range from ginger, gray, white, to black. All of them are deep within conversations with one another while holding chalices, and all of them look young, like from the twenties to the thirties, which is odd.

Looking back at the king, his cloak is much fancier than the others being outlined with fake fur around the hood, down the zipper, and around the openings of the sleeves and pant leggings. His cloak is halfway opened revealing an undershirt that is also made out of the finest material. He is wearing a crown made out of gold with diamonds inserted, three necklaces (one of them is a cross), numerous gold and silver wrist bands, and a few diamond rings. What's interesting is that he too is deep within a conversation with one of his associates and doesn't seem to notice us until the doors we came through shut behind us.

Once the doors shut, everybody ceases their conversations, including the king, and looks right at us, especially at me. Within a second, the terms that Marcus told me kicks in so I keep my mouth shut and place my eyes right on the king.

Marcus kneels down on his right knee and speaks, "Your majesty King Borin, I bring you, Will Young," while he sways his right arm toward me with his head down but eyes looking at me, sending the message I should bow. I feel the presence of Tristen and see that he too bows, so I try to do the same, but it seems that I can't do it. On the flip side, I really try.

Then, King Borin speaks up loud and clear in a friendly tone, "There's no need for you to bow, young one. Please come closer."

Marcus snaps his head back up to the king and tries to protest, but the king waves his right palm to silence him and gestures Tristen and me to come forward. Looking slightly down at Marcus while walking past him, I flip him off with my left hand. The closer we get to the king, he stands up and descends down from his throne to meet us. Then the king gives Tristen a sign to stop with a nod of his head. I can feel Tristen slightly pushing me to keep going because I am absolutely terrified.

The closer I get to the king, he throws his arms open, wraps them around me, and says in gratitude, "Welcome to Sparta, Will Young. Also known as Nos."

I still remain silent because I don't want to be executed.

He pulls himself away and looks right at me in the eyes, "Marcus, did you scare this young man with your terms before you entered?"

"Yes, your majesty. You are the king and must be highly respected." He slowly gets up from the floor. "This is a human that must understand—"

"Silence!" The king put up one of his free hands since the other one is wrapped around my shoulders as he looks at him with annoyance in his eyes. "Can you clearly see that this poor creature has suffered enough? How dare you force him to kneel down since his left leg is still in a cast?"

Marcus tries to come up with a good excuse.

"No excuses. You've done your task, now leave us." Again, Marcus tries to protest. "Marcus Lowsbroth, I order you to leave this room and return to your chambers. If you don't, I will order the guards to escort you out."

I give out a sly smile to him and Marcus growls in annoyance and leaves the throne room by going through one of the five doors on our left.

While the king lets out a small sigh, he turns his attention to us and resumes in his friendly, normal tone, "Now, how 'bout we have some brunch. This includes you, Doctor Maverick. And thank you Sean and your watch for escorting these two men in here. You may return to your post and there's some food waiting for you."

"Thank you, sir," says Sean in an Irish accent as he and his men snap their legs together, bow their heads, and exit the room.

Soon, King Borin pulls me with him as we go up the steps on our left, through the doorway that's close to the thrones. The hallway we enter also has white marble walls with the same carpet and on the corners where the walls and low ceiling meet is the same light source that runs continuously down the corridor until it's stopped by another wall with another door. Looking behind is Tristen and the guests are behind him while we walk down the hallway and into a large lounge room that has low tables and silver platters with multiple kinds of food on them. Next to them are couches, well, more like lounge couches, kind of like the ones professional psychiatrists use in their offices. Spread out on them are polyester fur rugs and they are also spread out on the floor along with thick pillows.

The room itself is circular that looks like a fourth of the size of the throne room in diameter. The ceiling is flat but stands nine feet high above us. The walls are covered with fancy wood paneling and are stained caramel to give it a warm welcoming atmosphere. Speaking of this room being warm, it does feel warm enough that not just me but everybody else remove their cloaks. There's one fireplace that has been lit and is burning great; the same light fixtures take place, but in the ceiling, like recessed lighting, except they're just small tubes forming circles four inches in diameter, giving a soft brown glow. I haven't seen a coat rack or hooks around this room, yet it looks like the other people remove their cloaks and throw them wherever they want.

"Have a seat, Will. Or would you like to be called Nos?" says King Borin.

"Either one, I'm not really picky," I say as I gradually sit down on one of the lounge couches. Obviously, Tristen sits right next to me to monitor my condition and the king sits across from us.

"So, introductions. You know who I am, Tristen, and Marcus. Forgive me for his actions. He has more respect than he shows though he's been disobeying my orders during the past weeks," The king says while he grabs for an apple.

"Why has he been disobeying your orders?"

"To put it simply, my daughter, whom you shall meet or should I say, have met," with a little chuckle in his throat, "had rejected his in-hand marriage and has been bugging her for two years. In my opinion, I don't find him as a perfect suitor for her, but you, my dear boy, she already has fallen in love with you."

The rest of the wolves giggle.

But my question is this, "Who are these people with us?"

His eyes widen and he swallows the bite of the apple. "Ah, yes. The man who I was talking to and standing at the fireplace is Admiral Zachariah Blitz. He's the man who organizes my military."

"What about me, my lord?" asks a female who's helping herself to the snack trays on one of the low tables.

The king just smiles, "And this is his wife Lupa Blitz. She's the person that organizes and sends out search parties to find your kind that's caught in the crossfire. Without a doubt, she is well in touch with another person that does the same thing at the Kingdom of Troy."

When King Borin says the words "search parties," my heart begins to sink and I feel sad that I lost my search party when they were just doing their job. Again, thinking about them brings up the memory of Ryia which makes my heart sink down even further. I glance up to see Lupa Blitz approaching me, kneeling down, and putting her hand on my shoulder.

While looking at me right in the eyes, she says, "Yes, it is indeed sad; especially for me when I saw the memory of you, Forthwind, Althalos, and Ulric fighting our enemy. It really broke my heart when you buried them and sent a prayer to the same deity that we believe in."

Wait, what about Ryia? She was part of the search party. Why wasn't she mentioned? I have to find out.

"There was a woman named Ryia and she was part of that search party. Why didn't you mention her?"

Lupa looks back at her husband and at King Borin. Then both men hang their heads and breathe heavy sighs, which brings up more questions for me to ask but mainly one, "What the hell is going on here?"

Then another man clears his throat. Turning my attention toward him, he's also standing at the fire but on the opposite end of the mantle, and he looks a bit older than the rest of them.

"The reason why Mrs. Blitz," he speaks in a low, gravel, Irish tone, "did not mention Ryia is because Ryia was not an existing wolf. She was animatronic. To put it in simpler terms, we have manikins that we simply make out of tin, then we conjure a spell that uses numerous amounts of chemicals that are combined in a cauldron and the main ingredient is our DNA. It could be a single strand of hair, saliva, or one drop of blood. Once that's combined into the caldron, we pour it out onto a manikin that's laid onto a table. Before long, the manikin will take the form of the original person, yet we can change the fur color and the color of the eyes. Not the height, of course. Oh, and I'm Rollo Greenwood. I believe you've met my son Sean a couple of times and I'm the head of the guardsmen that protect this kingdom."

Feeling shocked or surprised, I immediately stand up, "So, Ryia was a made-up wolf person? I was falling in love with a fake humanoid wolf?"

All of them nod in agreement and Rollo continues on the subject, "Yes, but when the subject adds his or her DNA, they can control their animatronic from a great amount of distance, well, the distance is unlimited. The consequences are that their senses of smell, touch, and hunger are cut in half. Their animatronics can rest but a few minutes before the controller goes to sleep. Their hearing is twenty-twenty, so they can hear their surroundings."

"Then who created Ryia?" I ask.

Then King Borin speaks up, "That's something you'll find out in the coming days. Anyway, let's get this private ceremony underway."

Then, he stands up and his officials gather around Tristen and me, but Tristen stands up and joins the circle putting me in the center. The king reaches into his robes, pulling out a small wooden box with excellent carvings that go around the walls of the box and show Celtic design amidst the smooth twist and turns of the lines. For a moment, I think that I'm going to see the symbol of the kingdom on the lid, though as the box is fully revealed, there isn't one. Yet once King Borin opens it, I am blown away from the object that lays inside and on top of the small, dark blue pillow.

The object is an award medal of some kind and this is how it looks like: the shape of it forms a rhombus, made out of silver, and very neatly polished. In the center are three gold stripes traveling horizontally that are also neatly polished. Layering on top of that are two forms of wolves helping each other out. One of them is pulling the other back up on its feet while both are holding staffs. So, it looks like the wolf that's being pulled up seems to be injured. These two figures are painted navy blue and there are fine gold lines outlining the mouth, ears, arms, etcetera. Finally, at both ends of the rhombus metal are three gold stars beside each wolf figure in a row.

Man, these people really like navy blue, silver, gold, and purple.

Looking up at King Borin with astonishment all across my face, he replies back with a smile and says, "This is the highest medal of Bravery and Respect when you, Will Young, stood up to our enemies multiple times and brought back the identification tags of Ulric, Forthwind, and Althalos representing that this kingdom has lost its comrades in action."

Then he gives the box to me and I have no idea what to say.

"Also, have this as another token of gratitude for respecting our fallen brothers," says Zachariah as he pulls out a smaller box and reveals a crystal, triangle base, pyramid necklace.

Once he pulls out the necklace and places it around my neck, a small burst of light ignites inside the pyramid and then combusts into a light purple and blue explosion, and within half a minute, it forms itself into a miniature galaxy with all sorts of stars shining bright. Holding the metal in one hand and looking at the necklace, I feel so much gratitude that I can't come up with the words. Just looking at all of them, it's just that I can't believe I'm being honored this much. My mind feels like it's going to explode until a warm liquid falls out of my nose. Then a few more drops follow.

"Are you okay, Will?" asks Tristen with some concern in his voice.

Shaking my head to relieve the trance I'm in, I finally speak, "Oh," while touching my nose and looking at the blood on my fingers, "I'm . . . sorry. It's just that, um, I've never received an award like this in my life. I am very grateful and thank you so much."

"Come on, let's get you back to the hospital."

"That sounds like a good idea, Doctor Maverick. It was nice finally meeting you, Will," says King Borin.

"Likewise," I say with a grin on my face but feeling a little embarrassed. Mrs. Blitz hands me a handkerchief and Tristen and I leave the relaxing lounge room, making our way back to the front door.

CHAPTER SIXTEEN
Sanctuary and Weaponry
Location: Hospital
Date: November 23, 2014
Time: 7:30 AM

IT'S BEEN A LONG time since I attended a church sermon, let alone being inside a sanctuary. But, I still wake up. When we got back to the medical tent, Tristen checked me over trying to figure what caused it. I simply told him that I was just overwhelmed by the gratitude and respect that I received and that I have never received any award of that kind. Plus, when we got back to my room, it was made a bit homier. I mean, the hospital bed is still here and the E.K.G. along with the other equipment, but now, there's a nightstand with this awesome, hologram alarm clock with a small calendar being displayed and a cool-looking, book-reading lamp. There's also a dresser filled with jeans and shirts, both t's and long sleeves that are decorated out with American brands. Finally, there's a tall speaker stand where I can plug in and play my iPod.

Getting back to the main point, I get up and limp toward the dresser to find any nice-looking shirts since I might be going to the sermon today. Sure enough, there's a black and white, plaid, button-down shirt. My question is, how do these guys know my social life and what I like to wear? Getting dressed before my injuries usually took me two minutes. After getting fully dressed, I power up a small, glass pane panel on my new crutches that I also received yesterday when Tristen and I got back. Swiping my right index finger across the main E.K.G. screen, the display automatically pops up on the small screen on the crutches. With that done, I can leave my room and walk around the tent, but as I reach for the thick curtain, it's immediately pulled back revealing my new friend and doctor with a small trolley that has my breakfast on it.

"Good morning, doctor, how's it going?" I say with a smile.

"Good morning, Will, it's going good. I should ask though, how are you feeling today?"

Hobbling back to my bed and taking a seat, "Well, I'm doing okay. Slept very good and looking forward to this day."

Tristen sits next to me and pulls out a clipboard from the holder in front of the bed while he checks the statuses and compares them to the info on the small screen. Without a doubt, he swipes it back to the main screen so that he can get a better view. After a while of checking, he scribbles a few notes and does the usual check-up on my vitals.

Then he asks, "Has your nose begun to bleed?" while he tilts my head upward and points a small flashlight up into the nostrils.

"No, sir, it hasn't. Like I told you yesterday, my mind was on overload drive due to the awards I received and I couldn't come up with the words."

"Alright, just making sure. It's just that I've never seen a human body act like that." Then he continues scribbling down more notes.

When he looks up at me and looks at the clothes that I'm wearing, he asks, "Do you want to attend the sermon today or wait till next Sunday?"

Looking at him very seriously but in a happy tone, I say, "Tristen, I feel fine. Plus, it's been a while since I attended a sermon because, well, you read it in my profile, I was an asphalt cowboy and drove very long hours, especially on the Lord's day."

"When you say asphalt cowboy, it means being a truck driver, correct?"

I nod my head.

"Wow, you humans, especially you, Will, surprise me with the littlest things every day that I spend here on this planet." He chuckles a little bit.

He pats my good leg, gets up, but before he leaves, he says, "Alright, eat up, and meet me at the front entrance."

"You got it, doc."

Without wasting another minute, I dive right into my breakfast enjoying every bite of it. Ten minutes roll by fast and I hop over to the restroom area, which isn't far from the patient rooms. It's like up the center aisle, completing the end piece of the corridor. I shave, brush, floss, and grab my winter robe, throwing it over my shoulders, zipping it up, and throwing up the hood like I'm some sort of a model. Just thinking about it makes me snicker a little bit. Oh yeah, I did get a new robe and instead of being the kingdom's colors, it's white with the sleeves and hood outlined in the color of silver. It has a half-inch, thick woods camouflage stripe that starts at the beltline, travels up and over my left shoulder, and stops at the same location. Plus, it's also outlined in barbwire print on both sides. So, like I asked, how do these guys know the things I like to wear? Still, I re-swipe the E.K.G. back to the small screen onto my crutches and meet Tristen at the front entrance.

Arriving there, he smiles and says, "I have to say, you look really good in that robe, but you're missing one more thing."

I smile back, "Now, what am I missing?"

Tristen still smiles, "This." He reveals a white baseball hat that also has thick woods camo forming a pair of racing stripes, stretching out from the brim toward the Velcro strap with a barbed wire print that starts at the left corner of the bill and stretches all the way to the right side of the back of the hat. "I promise you that this is the final gift that you'll receive in a while."

"Ah, c'mon doc. You're putting too much enthusiasm into your patient, which I think is bad or something, but thank you anyway." I take the hat from his hands and put it on.

"Now," Tristen says, "you complete the outfit, let's go to church."

We set outside and there's already a line of people, both humanoid wolf and human, walking toward the castle. The weather today shows a calm, clear blue sky without a little hint of wind. However, I can still feel the bitter cold air on my skin.

While we both join the parade, there's a sudden sound of heavy bells chiming off in the calm air. Looking at the top of the mountainside, there are no other structures housing the bells. So, the bells might be held and housed inside the mountain, which would be awesome to see once we get inside the cathedral and I am very, very curious what the cathedral is going to look like.

Now, as the parade progresses, more and more people join the crowd; soon, there's a hand tapping my shoulder and as I look around, there's Alice Cole along with her boyfriend Alex Rodriguez who's also a friend that I've met at the auto shop. We exchange greetings, and in the middle of our small talk, he takes notice of my crutches.

I ask him, "Do you want the long version or the short version?"

Alex simply shrugs and says, "Nah, I don't want to hear either. Alice told me everything that she could remember. All in all, it's great to see you, Nos."

Before long, there's a beautiful wolf howl that sounds so harmonic it makes me slowly turn my head and urge me to keep pressing forward. Again, that sound is so beautiful that it makes my curiosity burst forward and I want to see who is howling. Tristen laughs and tells us to keep moving since the sermon is about to start.

Entering through the main gate, the line of people comes to a crawl since the passageway that leads to the throne room isn't very wide and the doors that are the entrance to the church are also not that big, which makes perfect sense. After shuffling our feet for about ten minutes, we finally enter the cathedral, which absolutely takes my breath and blows my mind away at the same time. This is how the cathedral looks like: the doorway that we just enter is greeted by an eight-step stairway with neatly polished railings that are placed in the middle and inserted on the left and right walls. The stairway seems to stretch a hundred feet in width from one wall to the other where the crowd disperses and filters down five separate aisles that consist of hundreds of rows of beautifully hand-carved wood pews that all have slots where hymnals and Bibles are placed. And they are in the wolf's language and in our language. The doorway that's placed in the wall wastes no time as it springs up another several hundred feet where domes for the ceiling are curved out to represent the medieval, Celtic style of their culture. The arches are neatly illuminated by some light source that might've been conjured by their magic. Each arch has four columns that intersect one another like an "x," come down at a curved angle for twenty yards and touch the bottom of the other columns that form the eight separate, huge, bottom openings for the domes.

At the very center of each dome are long, thick chains that hold huge chandeliers that are suspended well over a hundred feet over the pews and the audience. Instead of bright blue lights that line the top and bottom edges of the chandeliers, there are torches burning strong and bright in normal fire colors. Alongside the walls are more torches that are burning very good, illuminating this gigantic area.

Some people gently push past us and that makes me keep moving forward down the steps and filtering up through the center aisle. As my friends and I move on, there are huge stained-glass windows that depict some of the ancient stories in the Bible, and some of them I recognize. But the weirdest thing is, instead of human beings, they are all humanoid wolf beings portraying the stories. One of them is on the right wall, near the front of the cathedral, where Jesus is being baptized by John the Baptist and receives a blessing from God. Each of these stained-glass windows towers over us close to a hundred feet and are also being illuminated by another light source developed by magic or by more torches since there are no windows letting the sunlight dwell in.

Getting closer to the front, the floor is raised back up to its original level by the eight steps and stretch over ten feet toward the walls that curve into one another to complete the area. On the floor is a podium that's constructed out of wood and is stained in a caramel color. On top is a microphone to allow the plethora of humans and humanoid wolf beings coming in to hear the sermon. There are loads upon loads of humans and wolves coming in to hear the sermon. Behind it is a chair which I presume is for the priest. To its left is a two-row bleacher set that I'm guessing the choir uses. To its right are two thrones created out of the same navy-blue marble, completed with cushions, and are both occupied. Behind and above these three objects is a suspended wooden cross with a metal statue on it that seems to be beaten, cut, and jabbed with some sort of sharp objects, has a crown of thorns on his head, and has his feet and hands nailed into the cross.

"Oh. My. God. Is that?" Alice and Alex gasps in awe and horror, or either one. I don't know.

"Yeah," I say with a sigh of my own amazement, "That's Jesus. The son of God. Instead of being a human, he's a humanoid wolf."

"So, these, um, people worship the same God that we worship?" Alex asks.

"Yep," I say looking at Tristen with a confident smile on my face. In return, he gives back a sheepish smile, like he's embarrassed by his own race.

Again, the same beautiful howl sounds off; this time, it's louder, clearer, and even more beautiful. We all turn our heads in the direction where it came and back at the two thrones are indeed King Borin and his daughter, I would assume, who's standing tall and holding her hands together as she howls. King Borin on the other hand is seated. Both are well-dressed in clothing and jewelry that seem totally church-appropriate than me wearing a white hat and cloak that has a thick forest camo sewed in silver barbed wire thread, which reminds me to remove my hat since I'm in the house of God. We take our seats, which is three rows in front of the stage. I can't help myself looking at the king's daughter. I do my best trying to make my expression as normal as possible instead of gawking at her.

"That's Tara Borin. You've met her at the hospital on the first day we started your recovery," Tristen says.

The memory sparks bright in my head and hits me like a brick wall. She was the one who brought me food and got annoyed with Tristen since he didn't like her being there.

"You serious?" I ask looking right back at him. He nods while trying to hold back a smile.

I turn my attention back toward Tara. She has her attention pointing right at me and our eyes meet each other. Soon, they lock on. She keeps her gaze on me as she sits next to her father, crosses one of her legs, and licks her lips in a very friendly, pleasurable gesture. Looking right into her eyes lasts for a good minute and my heart begins racing. I break the gaze by looking down at my feet in embarrassment and a little bit of fear. Of course, my ears pick up a hint of laughter that echoes from her mouth.

Alex nudges my arm with his elbow, "Like we said at the auto shop, 'Nos is really good with ladies when he drinks Dos Equis.'" He begins to snicker at the end of his sentence.

I just roll my eyes, "Shut up, Alex." I know he was messing around, but I still feel embarrassed that I met Tara's eyes with mine. On the other hand, Tristen looks a bit confused, but I explain to him about a beer commercial and that my friends and I have made a satire out of it. Then, he gets the gist of it.

When all the humans and humanoid wolves take their seats, there's a soft chatter of multiple conversations until they come to a sudden cease as another set of two, faded red doors open up on the right of the stage where the deacon enters with his hands placed together, palms flat. His outfit is pure white, from the robe to the hat he's wearing. The robe is decorated with two large, sewed, silver thread crosses that cover both sides of his chest. His hat has the same cross on it except it's outlined with a golden thread that represents the light of God shining bright behind it. He also has a large, golden cross hanging around his neck and the cross is decorated with the finest gems. Then the deacon bows his head and sings a hymn in their language that the choir follows, repeating the same lyrics over and over again. The robes that the choir wears are also white but with a pair of purple stripes that flow from the front, over the shoulders, and down the backside of their robes. I count about twenty singers. Still, the wolf choir sings the same language in their native tongue as they take their positions on the bleachers. It's not just me, but the rest of our race is getting confused about what the choir is singing so a small burst of quiet conversations breaks out. Looking back at the deacon, he smiles at the crowd as if this sort of commotion is interesting. He gestures with his left hand to cease the singing from the choir and looks at King Borin and Tara with a grin and they grin back.

He taps the microphone. The thumping noise echoes through the area, although I see no speakers, and he says smoothly, "Oh come, oh come, Emmanuel. And ransom captive Israel. That mourns in lonely exile here. Until the Son of God appear. Rejoice! Rejoice! Emmanuel shall come to thee, o Israel."

Every human, including my friends and me, quietly let out the word, "Oh," with the nodding of our heads that we finally understand the lyrics that they were saying.

The choir sings the remaining stanzas of the song. During the song, I quietly ask Tristen, "Isn't it a bit early to start celebrating Christmas?"

He laughs and answers my question that in their society, November 23 is the first day they start celebrating Christmas and goes to December 26. During our little talk, Alex and Alice are also interested in this little information as they too are getting a bit more interested in the humanoid wolves. Soon after, we turn our attention back to the choir as they finish the song and take their seats, then the deacon starts to speak.

"Welcome, brothers and sisters, both humans and Wolfinoids. Today is the first day that we celebrate Christmas and the birth of Jesus."

Afterward, he repeats the same sentence in the Wolfinoids' language.

"Today is also the day where our ancestors have discovered their sorcery and used their powers against the werewolves, our enemies, which nearly wiped out our planet and made it as their home. But our ancestors would not allow that. The remaining six hundred from the Kingdoms of Troy and Sparta joined hand in hand, rose up, and used their newfound powers to eliminate and capture our enemy. When the battle ceased, they set across our planet replenishing the forests that were burned during the battles."

Again, the deacon repeats the story in their language and there's a simple English word that comes out from their mouths.

"Amen."

What's interesting is that a few of our race, including me, quietly say the same word along with them.

"But now," the deacon continues with a heavy sigh, "our enemies are slowly trying to take over this beautiful planet and harm these humans by slaughtering or turning them so that their numbers could increase," as he gestures with an open hand and waves it from left to right. Small conversations of the agreement broke out between us and the Wolfinoids.

But this sort of information is completely new to me and I can't hold my mouth shut. "Holy, fucking, shit," I say under my breath.

Tristen pats my shoulder in comfort, but it doesn't seem to help because I thought of my family up in Wisconsin being slaughtered and I was too late to reach them. Thinking about it makes me ball up my hands real tight and lower my head so that nobody can see my pissed-off expression.

Immediately, somebody clears their throat, which catches my attention. Looking back up at the stage is Tara holding her right hand, in fist form, in front of her mouth, and gestures with her eyes to the deacon to grab his attention that the information he just said made me upset. He looks down at me and what I see on his face is sympathy. He turns his attention back to the congregation.

"Nevertheless, there are scout groups of our kingdom and from Troy that are sent out each week to find our new friends and bring them to safety. Let us pray." From here on out, the deacon prays for the safety of the scout groups and for the safety of our race, and that God punishes the enemy with a mighty smite.

Again, but this time, both humans and Wolfinoids say, "Amen!" in a louder tone that echoes off the walls and ceilings. The deacon continues with the sermon that's laid out before him. I have to say, there are a lot of similarities between their version of worship and our version of worship. To break it down, in some churches, like the one I used to attend back in White Rock, New Mexico, the pastor gave out announcements of what's coming up, and one of the similarities is that the deacon gives out an announcement—that Tara has found a mate. Let me step away from reality, have you guys ever heard a noise that has been used like in T.V. shows and movies where a record makes a breaking noise when someone or something says or happens spontaneously? Well, that sound went in my head and I look at the deacon with the message in my eyes begging him not to say my name. I shake my head left and right in short shakes really begging him not to announce me. If you guys are asking why, well I don't do very well in crowds, and the embarrassment it gives me has started to rise to the back of my neck, then turn red. I'm not ready to be announced and again, I hardly have met her and I know nothing about her. I don't want to stand and show up in a crowd of well, over, um, three hundred people that I'm the king's daughter's mate.

Overall, there's Tara watching me with curiosity in her eyes. She decides to get up and talk to the deacon privately, away from the mic. Their little conversation doesn't take long and both of them return to their spots. At the time Tara returns to her seat, she winks at me and then gestures with her hand for the deacon to continue on. He does say he will not announce the person due to some issues and continues. During the sermon, more similarities come together when we read along some Bible passages. After the passages, we sing hymns, which is interesting to hear as it is in the combination of our language mixed with the Wolfinoids' language. Halfway through the sermon choir sings a beautiful hymn in the Wolfinoid language in the most beautiful way. After the choir has sung, the deacon announces a prayer time session where all of us announce our prayers out loud or in silence. For me, I choose to pray in silence for simple reasons. Wait? What? You guys want to know what I'm praying for? *Sigh.* Fine. I'm praying for the safety of my family, that they are escorted here or to Troy, and have sought safety.

The deacon ends the session by saying amen and reads another story from the Bible and this passage is about standing up to your enemies and shouting out back at them that you're not alone because God is always with you. Then, he relates the passage to today's events and that we should never give up hope. We should always stand tall and we will find a way to defeat our enemy. Every person and Wolfinoid stands up, applauding the deacon with that awesome lecture; the deacon takes one step away from the podium with a serious and pleased expression on his face.

"May the Lord Almighty always be with you!" the deacon shouts at the top of his lungs as he raises his right hand giving us the blessing.

He returns his hands together in the same position from before and exits off the stage with the choir following him through the same set of doors where they entered and they close it behind them. Then everybody starts exiting the church. Once my friends and I get up and walk back to the aisle, I look back at Tara to see that she and her father are exchanging a few words. Tara is mostly looking at me and when King Borin turns around, he turns back asking his daughter a question.

Looking at her mouth, I can make out the words that she says, "Yes father. He is truly the one for me." Both look at me with causal expressions and I just nod to both of them before I exit.

When my friends and I get outside, the sun is shining so bright that I have to pull down the brill of my hat to reduce the sun rays reflecting off the snow and shining bright in my eyes.

"Hey, Nos?" says Alex interrupting my thoughts.

"Yeah."

"Do you want to join me and Alice at the blacksmith tent?"

Hearing about the blacksmith tent activates my interest in creation and tools because I love working with tools and love building things with my own hands, but I look at my crutches, and then I look at Tristen.

"Doc?"

Tristen smiles and slips his hands into the pockets of his cloak, "Yes, you have my permission to go. I have some other tasks that need to be done back at the hospital tent. I hope your friends will look after you."

"Of course, Doctor Maverick," answers Alice, with a big grin on her face as she gives me a side hug.

We go separate ways and my auto shop friends take me to the blacksmith tent. During our walk, I ask Alice and Alex what they've been up to before all of this happened. Both of them tell me that they were accepted down at New Mexico State University in Las Cruces and tried their very best to have classes together. However, both of them were studying in two different areas of fieldwork. Alice is studying to be a marine biologist and Alex is studying to be a top-of-the-line welder for one of the custom auto shops in the nation. Later on, they told me they ran out of town when the werewolves started to move in, but they still stuck together. During their flee, they rode numerous commercial buses filled with other people, transporting them to one of the military bases in Tennessee, probably one in Nashville. Alex did confirm to Alice that it was in Nashville and after the first night they stayed there, the city was taken over.

I stop and ask the date of that event, and they both tell me, "September 15."

The information takes my breath away in some horror, then replaces it with a smile, "What a coincidence. I was there on that date dropping off a parking garage of brand-new Priuses."

"No way," they say to me, much surprised that all three of us were in the same city at the same time. I nod my head for Alex to keep on explaining their adventure here. As he continues, on that same day, they are both founded by a scout group of two Wolfinoids and were swiftly escorted here to Sparta with no problems at all.

Continuing across the grounds of Sparta, a small cheer rises from the people spontaneously which makes us wonder why. Turns out, we're crossing the path where the north entrance of the kingdom is and as we turn our attention to it, the sight of what we see makes our hearts sink a little bit. Nothing terrible happened, it's just . . . shit. A scout group of four female Wolfinoids has returned unscathed with five kids: three girls and two boys; all are well under the age of ten. The kids, well, they seem a bit terrified, so the four female scouts calm them down and coax them in. The kids cling tight to each of the Wolfinoid's cloaks as they slowly walk in. Nonetheless, all I see are happy and pleased faces around me probably because all of them survived. Naturally, two questions come to mind, where did they travel from? Are they siblings or come from different families? The scout group turns in our direction and we all step aside so that they have a clear path probably toward the hospital. When the group passes us, one of the boys looks up at me with big, terrified, but curious eyes and I simply shrug at him saying that, "Yes I am on crutches and yes, this place is definitely different." The two questions still linger in my mind.

"Excuse me," I say to the last female scout.

She stops and looks at me with a curious face, "Yes?"

"Where did you guys travel from?"

She looks at her group, turns her head at the gate, and then back at me, "We traveled from a state that you humans call Vermont."

That far up north? Damn, it must be very cold up there by now, "Are those kids siblings, or are they from different families?"

She lets out a sigh, "They're siblings, but we found them three miles away on the far east side of that region where their parents . . ." Small tears begin to form in her eyes. "Their parents were slaughtered. Thank the Lord and his mercy to let those children live and give our search party time to find them. Now excuse me, I would like to make sure that these children are absolutely healthy." She turns away from me and jogs up the path to catch up with her group.

"Fuck me." I turn and keep heading down the path to the blacksmith tent. Five kids, all under ten, were found three miles away from their slaughtered parents. Now, I can fully understand and picture what I looked like to the crowd's faces as a small group of Wolfinoid guards is running through the crowd while carrying a stretcher with a young adult male that completely looked like he was barely hanging onto life.

Damn those werewolves!

Soon, Alice and Alex catch up and the three of us walk in silence toward our destination.

Winding our way through shop tents that soon became housing tents, we finally make it to the blacksmith tent. The location of the tent is on the edge of the kingdom, still within its borders, a few yards away from the housing tents. On the other hand, the layout of the structure seems to be in stages. In time when my friends and I get closer, the stages of these tents stand out quite differently from one another; in detail, the first tent is organized to be a drafting tent where there are drafting tables with high chairs and at each table, there are numerous amounts of paper, loads of different ruler sizes, pencils, color pencils in all colors, and stencils for all shapes. The next tent is where all of the metal material for creating something extraordinary is and has twenty stations where melting the material takes place. Then, the boiling hot liquid is poured out into narrow casteners that vary in length with different types of design on them. However, the detail of the designs is so fine and small that the overall look of all the casteners looks the same. The third one, oh, it gets very interesting in that tent. The final tent is where the sorcery takes place. In that tent, there are tables that have cauldrons with mixing tools and different types of potions that can be and are already made. There are also ingredients like different types of vegetation that could be added to a potion that's being made or has been created.

While the three of us approach this awesome-looking area, an old Wolfinoid male comes around the furnaces from the second stage tent. When I mean old, his muzzle is completely gray and so his hands and feet. He's wearing thick, bright copper-rimmed glasses, has a long white beard, and a long mustache. His fur color is gray but darker than Tristen's. His cloak used to be green, but it's covered in soot, grime, grease, and has additional burn marks on the sleeves, leggings, and torso. Finally, his weight is being held up by a tall, wood pole that's almost his height. Once he approaches us, his eyes are two separate colors; one is normal green while the other is normal blue. Finally, he smiles at us in greeting.

"Well, welcome back, Alice and Alex," says the old man. Next, he turns his attention to me.

"Ah, welcome, Will Young. My name is Atticus Whitehall. Welcome to my weaponry staff tent."

How did this man know my name and that I was coming here?

Atticus chuckles, "Lad, if you're wondering how I knew you were coming is that I was blessed with a gift many years ago."

"And what is your gift?" I ask.

Again, he chuckles, "To put it simply, many years ago, my eyes used to be liquid gold, but during one of my projects when I was assembling a spell for my own private weapons, there was an explosion which blew me off my feet and backward toward a wall. The liquid from the spell burned my eyes, changing them into these colors. The green eye can look briskly into the future. That's how I knew you and your friends were coming. The blue eye can look into your soul and give me a brief description of your likings in life. With that, I can give you better ideas and help you create your own weapon staff whatever you want it to be."

"But how did you know my name, sir?"

Atticus gestures his head at Alice and Alex, "I've heard these two, possibly more of your friends, throwing your name around."

That basically explains everything.

"Catch you later, Nos," says Alex as he takes off and heads into the melting tent. Alice departs and heads toward the drawing tent. Then, another wave of reality hits me. As far back I can remember, when I arrived here, well, a few yards away from the West Gate, I arrived with Ulric's staff in one of my hands. My question was, what happened to that staff? Just pondering over this question, I don't see Atticus showing up at my side, gently pushing me forward to his weaponry shop.

"Is there something bothering you?" he asks, interrupting my thought.

Looking back at him a little startled, then relaxed, I say, "Yeah, a little. It's just that when I arrived here, I had one of the scout's staff because none of them didn't make it. I'm just wondering what happened to it when I passed out and was taken to the hospital."

He closes his eyes, breathes in deeply, and looks back at me, "I believe that staff was returned to its original owner. I do remember receiving that staff on that very night. I remember examining it, finding Ulric's name on it, and then sensing his magic on it faintly because there was a stronger presence on it. The magic that was still reminiscing from it smelled dark, desperate, angry, and sad. Looking at you, I sense that bit of that magic reminiscing very faintly off of you."

I look at the man, feeling scared and embarrassed that I used dark magic so that I can survive long enough to get here. He pats my right shoulder with a grin.

"Not to worry. You were in desperate need of survival and you had to do what you had to do. Overall, you're here and you can create and conjure your own weapon staff." At the end of his statement, he ushers me into the drawing tent, pulls out a chair, and sits me down in front of a large piece of paper with no ideas running around in my head.

It's been a long time since I drew something good, in my point of view, because the way I draw now, I tend to draw two-dimensional without using a lot of shadow details to make it stand out.

Behind me, Atticus snaps his fingers, like he knows how I feel. Wait, that was a dumb statement to make. He's a Wolfinoid. These people are descendants of the canine breed; they pretty much still have the sixth sense. Looking at him, he has one of his hands rummaging around one of the pockets of his cloak, then he pulls a syringe that has clear liquid inside and the needle is capped.

He removes the cap and says, "Hold still, lad, this should help you with your creativity." He pushes up the left sleeve on my cloak, revealing my arm, and with one swing, he sticks the needle into my arm and injects the liquid in.

I don't feel the needle entering or exiting my skin, but within a few minutes, my creativity starts to take off. I immediately grab a couple of different shapes of blue, a pencil, an eraser, and a ruler while mentally playing a song called "Covered by Darkness" by Parking Lincoln. Within ten minutes tops, I have my weapon staff drawn out and I reveal it to Atticus. He nods and gestures with his hand to follow and he brings me to several measuring sticks, all of them seem to travel up to eight feet.

"What are these for?"

"I like to have the staffs to be at the right height for my customers. Stand up straight for me please."

And so, I do. He brings down a piece of wood that's attached to a rail that runs vertical with the measuring sticks down to my head. As my head and the wood make contact, Atticus writes down the height, and both of us press forward to the furnace tent.

The heat, the smell, and the sound of the furnaces echoing get me really excited. Walking around the tent and getting a closer look at the casteners, the detail of different styles stands out finer than from the distance I was standing at. Each castener design is organized by shelves with the name of the style in both the Wolfinoid and English languages separating different designs. Each castener has the size of the height of the customer, literally starting at two feet and ascending up to eight feet. So, my height is five feet and ten inches and Atticus points out the styles that are in that height zone. I look at a few and soon, two of them stand out; the first one has lightning that goes around the top and bottom of the rod for about three inches and the second one has flames that completely travel up and down the rod and break out into smaller flames that still lick the staff. The creativity shot that Atticus gave me keeps firing off and proposes with an image of the final outcome of my staff.

I smile up at the man, "This one. This is what I want."

"Okay, young man. Now, what metal material do you want to use?" he asks while he sways his right hand toward another shelf system that has all of the metal material known to our race, yet there are others that are more extraordinary and possibly possess magical abilities that I think these guys invented on their home planet.

I walk over to the shelving unit, scrutinizing the material and finally picking stainless steel.

"And so, it begins," Atticus says.

Next, Atticus breathes in deeply a couple of times, then a faint glow starts appearing around his body and it becomes brighter and brighter. He turns his attention to the frame castener, magically pulling it from the shelf and placing it in front of one of the furnaces where a spigot lies for the hot, liquid metal to pour into. Then, he waves his hand over thereby commanding the castener to close, seal, and be pushed up against the spigot. The furnace itself has already been lit and has been operating for quite sometime before my friends and I showed up here. So, melting the stainless sheet wouldn't take very long.

Then Atticus looks at me with calmness in his eyes and says, "Now, Will, before you grab hold of that metal, put some safety gloves, goggles, and an apron on."

I nod without hesitation and obey his orders. I grab the sheet while asking him where I insert it into the furnace. He points his right index finger at the opposite end where a gravity roller conveyor lays in front of a chain that opens and closes a metal hatch. I place the stainless-steel sheet onto the conveyor and use all of my might to open the hatch. It lets out loud, squeaky noises and the heat of the inferno slowly slips out through the opening. The heat is so intense that it slowly stings my eyes. I slip the goggles on, asking Atticus what's the temperature inside the furnaces, and he replies that they burn at one thousand degrees Fahrenheit. Without wasting another minute, I push the ten-pound sheet of metal across the conveyor and gravity takes control of the material, letting it glide into the inferno. The sheet of metal disappears into the flames. I close the hatch and lock it up.

"Now, what do we do next?" Looking at him, placing my hands on my hips.

"Now," he replies, "we let the metal melt, but to save some time, let's move onto the potion and sorcery tent."

The potion and sorcery tent totally reminds me of science lab classrooms back in high school, except that there are mini cauldrons set on tables steaming with liquids that stay as one solid color and there are others that change colors rapidly. On another table lays herbs of different plants that can change and possibly make the potion or sorcery come to life. Some of the herbs that I see before me are totally not from this planet. For example, there are some flowers that look like roses and conduct a soft glow of light that lets out little flares of magic swirling around the petals. To me, these look very astonishing and each one represents the different kinds of elements; one has fire softly swirling around the petals and another conducts little lightning bolts.

Atticus shows me my own workstation where a cauldron sits empty with a small fire pit unlit. On both sides of it are tools that can be used to cut, stir, and reshape the plants (don't know how that works). Also, there's a box of matches and without pause, I grab it, pick a match out, and ignite the dry wood underneath the cauldron. Again, the creativity shot still kicks in; grabbing my cauldron, I take it over to a fountain that's gushing fresh, clean water and let it fill about halfway. Then limping back to my station, I grab a small knife, making a small cut on my left index finger and letting a few drops of my blood fall into the water. Then, I grab a few of the flaming flowers that burn in the normal color scheme of fire and a few of the electrical discharging flowers, plucking a dozen petals from them. I combine water, my blood, and the still burning, electricity-discharging petals for a couple of minutes; during that time, the liquid in the cauldron begins boiling. After stirring the flame, colors turn into blood red with lightning surrounding them, but overall, I don't want this color. I want the color admiral blue. On the other hand, I don't know how to make it.

"On the other end of this tent, there are cauldrons that I've set up and have different colors in them," Atticus points out.

Following his gaze, there they are and I happily limp toward it. Reaching the table, I again scrutinize the colors. Luckily, there're labels announcing which color is which. Getting to the blue section, I find the admiral blue, pick up one of the small eye droppers, and fill it up completely. Returning to my station, Atticus hands me a few extra ingredients that are simply powder in small, thin tubes. I try to ask, but he winks at me. I pour the powders, squeezing the admiral blue liquid in, and I began stirring everything together. Within minutes, the blood-red flames turn into admiral blue with a hint of tiny, golden flakes. The little lightning bolts dissipate, never to be seen again. The aroma of this potion that I've created, with a little help from Atticus, feels a little bit energized like it wants to do something active. I feel the power of justice rising from it, but only a small hint and that hint is still very powerful. Something in the back of my mind tells me to pick it up and view it closer. However, when I place my hands to raise it closer to my face, a source of light comes to life making the flames burn bigger and brighter. The energy intensifies in both good and bad ways, and finally, the power of justice expands to greater lengths.

"What have I created?"

Atticus places his hand on my shoulder, "Come, Will, let's pour it into the castener to combine with the stainless steel."

We both move our way back to the furnace tent. Simultaneously, Alex and Alice have already inserted their own chosen metal material into their furnaces and their eyes widen with the glow and flames that are arising from the cauldron.

"What have you created, Nos?" Alex asked.

"I don't know, but we'll find out," I replied.

Atticus moves toward the hatch of where the spigot lies, opens it up, and lets the intensely hot stainless steel pour into the castener. As the last drop goes in, I examine the castener for an opening to pour my potion into. I find it at the top, in the center of the cover. Alice places a funnel into the hole and I pour the potion with caution.

The last drop of it goes seeping through the funnel, silence comes upon us, and Atticus says, "You all might want to put your goggles on and probably, really step back."

The tone in his voice is not joking. He sounds pretty serious and we all follow his instructions.

Suddenly and simultaneously, there's a loud ping noise, like a coin is thrown into an open, empty space, and clatters the first time onto the floor; the same blue light source seeps through the crack of the top and bottom parts of the castener and it grows brighter and brighter. The sound from the light source sounds like a large, electrical machine consuming so much electricity up to the point where it starts shaking the ground that we're standing on.

"Everybody, get down. *Now!*" Shouts Atticus and we all hit the deck.

Kapow!

The light source sends out a shockwave throughout the entire tent and extinguishes the flames that lit the lanterns of all rooms, the fires in the furnaces, and fires underneath the cauldrons in the potion and sorcery tent.

"Jesus Christ, Nos. What the fuck did you create?" Alex asks.

"Pop it open, Atticus. Let's see what I've created," I say, nodding my head at him.

He also agrees and we all stand up and gather around the castener. Atticus undoes the locks and waves his right hand in the opposite direction to open it. Our breaths, especially mine, are taken away. Looking down at it, our eyes are wide open. Apparently, the type of staff I've created is a pretty powerful one. The stainless steel shines beautifully. The flame print that runs up and down the staff glows faintly blue yet begins to dissipate, and around the staff are little golden lightning bolts that discharge for a few seconds, giving off that electric discharging noise. At the top lies the glass orb; instead of being an oval orb, it is flames that stick out and stretch a good five inches with the faint, dissipating admiral blue light inside.

As I'm about to reach for it, I ask, "Is it going to be hot?"

Atticus shakes his head and I press forward to grab it. Once my right hand wraps around it, the same ping noise sounds off and the light begins to grow in brightness. I immediately stand it on its butt and say to it very softly to be still. By that time, the inside light fully dissipates.

Looking at Atticus, his face is full of shock and awe. This includes my friend's expressions as well.

"Atticus, what have I created?"

"My boy, you have created one of the most powerful and lethal weapon staff I have ever seen in my entire life."

"A very powerful one indeed, lad." That voice makes me turn around and discover Sean all by himself, holding his weapon staff in one hand and a piece of paper on the other that looks like it's made out of gold.

"Sean," I say feeling surprised, happy, and embarrassed to see him, "What uh, brings you here?"

"Well, mate." He approaches me with some caution in his footsteps. "I'm here to give you this invitation. This also includes your friends because you'll need them for what is planned for you."

He hands me the invite, turns away, and says to me, "You have one week from today to be prepared."

Be prepared? For what?

I unfold the invite and it tells me straight forward, *"Dear Mister Will Young. Also known as Nos. You are invited to attend Tara Borin's birthday on November 30. She has also requested that you play one of your dearest country songs to truly win her heart and that is her only request present from you. Your friends are also invited and can help you orchestrate the song. The equipment is already in your hospital room. You have one week from today to be prepared. Have a lovely day."*

Oh man, one week. What song should I play? And what do they mean by equipment? Oh well, I guess I have to find out myself. Man, this kingdom just keeps getting better and better.

CHAPTER SEVENTEEN
Preparation and Party Time
Time: 6:00 PM

I ARRIVE BACK AT the hospital completely stunned by the invite and the event that took place back at Atticus's blacksmith workshop. Still, I hold my very own weapon staff with pride inside as I push through the thick door flaps. The temperature has indeed decreased at a fast pace and snow began to fall from the sky. Before I returned here, I asked my friends where they stay and they told me that the kingdom arranges housing tents within a snap once they get checked over at the hospital. I'm curious and a little worried if I have to pay a very large bill due to the usage of machines, medical supplies, etc. Plus, due to the number of weeks I have stayed here, I'm pretty sure that I've racked up one hell of a bill. Passing the registration and nurse's counters, right on cue, there's Doctor Maverick emerging from one of the hallways looking at a glass tablet, reviewing other patients' profiles. Then, he looks up with an expression that shows concern.

"Will," he says, rushing over, "I've heard the news that an explosion took place at Atticus' compound. Are you injured?"

Looking right at him, I shake my head to get my stunned reaction out of me before I can answer.

"Yeah, yeah. I'm okay. I wasn't seriously injured, nor my friends and Atticus. It's just that we're still a bit shaken up. All in all, I'm quite pleased with myself of the weapon I created."

Simultaneously, I bring up my staff, holding it in both of my hands toward Tristen. His ears perk forward. The exposed hair starts standing up and he takes a couple of steps back as the weapon staff discharges a couple of lightning bolts. This action also makes the other doctors and nurses stop and look upon it in awe and shock.

Tristen tries his best to remain calm. "You do realize that we still have a sixth sense and my senses are telling me that your weapon seems pretty dangerous."

But my senses are telling me that there's some excitement in your voice.

"Yeah, apparently, I've created a nuclear reactor that's combined with my emotions which probably makes it so strong and dangerous." I place the butt of it back down to the ground, yet again, the ping noise goes off and the staff starts glowing. Finally, the remaining medical staff starts slowly backing away from it.

I let out a heavy sigh, "Will you just relax!" Giving that command, the staff goes completely dark, making a heavy machine noise that has just been turned off.

"Thank you," I say, rolling my eyes at it. Turning my attention back to the room, I gesture with my free hand that everything is okay. The other doctors and nurses return to their duties though still remain on edge of the uncertainty of my weapon. Again, I turn my eyes back to my good doctor and friend.

"So, Tristen. I have a question to ask."

"And what is that?" he replies, stepping forward with curiosity in his eyes but with a little uncertainty.

"I know I've stayed many weeks here and your service, including everybody else, has been great and I thank you all for getting me this healthy this far. My question is—"

Tristen folds his arms, letting out a laugh, and says, "You're wondering if you have to make payment for the medical services that we have provided for you?"

That threw me off. "Yes, sir. How much do I owe?"

He looks around with his eyes, then sway his body, building the intensity inside me that I probably have to pay close to or well over one-hundred thousand dollars. I don't how much that costs in Wolfinoid cash or if they even accept American currency. He still ponders, making the pondering noises as if he is, or is, really deep in thought. For me, the intensity keeps on building up, my heart is picking pace, and some sweat starts building on my forehead and on the back of my neck. A couple more minutes go by.

Goddammit man, just tell me the freaking price already!

Then Tristen looks down at me. "Nothing."

"What!"

"You owe nothing. We don't charge. Our medical system is free and always has been," he says, putting a smile on his face.

I'm completely shocked. "Are you shitting me?"

"No, I'm not."

"Truly?"

"Yes, I'm totally telling you the truth."

Oh man, what huge ass relief this is. I am so glad that I don't have to pay a penny for the services. This amount of relief makes my legs buckle, letting my crutches fall to the ground, and I grab my staff with both of my hands. Luckily, the staff remains deactivated. Tristen moves forward, grabs me by the armpits, and moves me to my room. Behind us, one of the nurses grabs my crutches and follows us. We enter my room and there's a large white box sitting on my bed with another golden piece of paper with a golden bow placed on the lid.

"Ah, yes," says Tristen as he places me on the bed. "That arrived for you a few hours ago. I'm pretty sure you've received an invite?"

I reach into my cloak, retrieving the invite and showing it to him. He nods at it and at the nurse who places the crutches against one of the tarp walls and swipes her finger across the E.K.G. screen that flies onto the bigger one powering up immediately as it receives the data. Other than that, Tristen again examines me as if something is seriously wrong. I assure him, waving my hand and telling him that I'm okay, I'm just relieved that I don't have to pay a huge medical bill. He asks if I'm hungry, so I look over at my hologram clock, showing it's 6:17 PM, and I reply that I'm not. Maybe later on. Again, Tristen nods and tells me that I can page him if I'm hungry and he'll have food delivered.

Before he exits, I immediately blurt out a question, "Hey, Tristen, how are those kids doing? The ones that were brought here around eleven and twelve o'clock."

He looks back really calm and confident, "Well, they're not on my patient list, but from what I've heard and talked with my colleagues, those kids are good, but they're still frightened. Overall, they're doing fine."

Hearing this kind of news makes me relax, "Okay, thanks for telling me."

Then Tristen leaves, pulling the curtain close to give me some privacy.

I get up, place my staff alongside my crutches, and return to my bed. I look at the large box and retrieve the golden piece of paper on the lid.

Opening it, it reads, *"Good evening, Will Young. As stated in the invite, Princess Tara Borin requests that her present from you is that you play one of your country songs to win her heart and that your friends can help you play and they're invited as well. Below this message are instructions to use this device that we invented two years ago. This device will make you and your friends play and sound like the singers and instruments in the song of your choice. The instructions and* the use of the equipment are quite easy, plus, the more time you spend practicing the notes and lyrics, the device will implant the rhythms of the song in your mind(s) thereby relying on the devices the first time around. Enjoy."

I place the note to one side and with eagerness, I put the box on my lap and remove the lid. The contents that lay inside the box before me are interesting, clean, very high-tech, and modern-looking. Also, there are two pieces of golden paper that are folded. I take one of them out and unfold it.

It states, "Please write on the dotted line how many of your friends will be orchestrating the song of your choice thereby receiving more of this equipment. Reply soon."

Looking back at the contents, there are a pair of solid gloss black wristbands that are constructed out of some sort of metal and are completely smooth and slick. Each one has a gray dot of the sort that might be a power light indicator and while I examine one of the bands, trying to figure out how to open it, my index finger slides around the outside of the hollow circle and a set of a sky-blue lights pulses around one time. Then, the wristband opens. I slip it on and the wrist band closes smoothly. Again, I slide the same finger around the outside of the hollow circle until the same light pulses around and reopens it. The next band is of the same color, design, and texture as the wristbands' but it is larger. I glance down at my ankles and decide to try it on my right ankle. I do the same test and it opens. I close it around my ankle and it fits perfectly. Repeating the same test, the ankle band reopens with ease. Up next is a pair of wireless earbuds that are also constructed out of the same material and have little gray spots to indicate power; overall, nothing feels special about them. The final item is most definitely made to be used on the neck with the same color scheme as the ankle bands', the pair wrist bands', and the earbuds'. The difference is that there's a small square that's an inch on every side and in the middle, there's the same gray circle that might be the power indicator light. The square is solid and is constructed as the previous items, but there are two pieces of stretchable fabric that extend off the small square. At both ends of the fabric is a clip that clicks together and can be unclipped. I put this device around my neck and click it into place. Instead of the same light source setting off one pulse, it says in a quiet, computer tone voice, "Voice changer, activated."

"Hello, testing, testing, 1, 2, 3." My voice doesn't sound different so I take the device off and it says in the same tone, "Voice changer, deactivated."

Okay, if these devices are made to help me and my friends or anybody else sound and play like a real singer or band, then I should follow the directions. But what song should my friends and I play for Tara?

I reach for my iPod.

What is the best way to win a girl's heart? I browse the entire library for a moment. *Bingo, country music.*

Looking through my country music section, I still have to pick a song, but which song should it be? I look at artists after artists for a few minutes until I find him. Tapping on his name, I browse through the album files, then one song stands out the most. I put in my earbuds and listen to it very closely. I put the song on "Repeat," listening to the instruments and the lyrics. Nearly ten minutes go by and I count off on my hand the number of instruments. The result is four. To make my decision easier, I grab the second piece of paper and glance through it. From what I read from it, I decide to make it four, and I write it down on the previous piece of paper. I hop my way over to the registration counter. Once I get there, I hand the note to one of the nurses and I tell her it's urgent. Right away, she gets the message in my face and tells me that she'll send it right out. I return to my room still not feeling hungry, but I am filled with eagerness, nervousness, and the feeling that I don't have a lot of time to mess around. I need to start practicing. I need to put on a great show.

Date: November 27, 2014
Time: 2:30 PM
Three Days Before Tara Borin's Party

In just four days, my leg was completely healed. Tristen took off the cast, asked me to wave my foot in all sorts of directions and wiggle my toes, then he signs off on his tablet that I am totally healthy and discharges me. Soon after, a group of six Wolfinoids came into my hospital room and started packing up my things. I asked Tristen what was going on and he told me just two days before he discharged me, a housing tent was being set up for me and at the very moment he signed the computer screen, it sent out a signal to the movers' group to come here and move my stuff to my new home. Within thirty minutes, my personal belongings were out and all that was left in the room is the bed and the E.K.G. It dawned on me that Tristen was no longer my doctor and it was the last day I'll see him. The emotion of saying goodbye or "see you later" was strong in me that tears started to form in my eyes. I tried my best to hold them back because Tristen became my first Wolfinoid friend who showed me what the kingdom looks like and brought me back to my full human health. We looked at one another and he was about to shed some tears, too, but we shook hands and told one another we'll see each other around. Then, I departed the hospital tent, following the movers to my new home and carrying my staff.

Now, here I am in my new home. My housing tent is very large, measuring out thirty feet by thirty feet. Another plus about it is that it has removable curtains and that I can turn the entire tent into one large room or with multiple rooms. When I arrived here, there was already a bed, a fire pit, and a surprising number of electrical outlets. Anyway, the tarps of my new home are thick, but still, cold air leaks through the littlest cracks, so I stride forward toward the fire pit and grab the same box of magic matches. Upon observing my house, there is no ventilation shaft or hole of the sort to let the smoke file out. Thinking really hard, I push my memory to the point of my journey where I found the matchbox and used it on the first night. The flames that engulfed the wood created heat, yet no source of smoke accumulated from the blaze. So, I guess I won't have to worry about smoke billowing up in here and making me suffocate. Eventually, something catches me off guard. One moment as I was approaching the fire pit and retrieving the matches, there was no wood, but the next thing I see is there's already firewood in the pit, stacked together as a perfect cone with a rotisserie over it.

"Hello?" I asked, looking around with nobody in here but me.

How in the hell did this firewood get here? I mean, there's only one entrance and that's also the exit, plus the wind is sort of blowing and I would've felt the cold wind coming in. Oh well, it's one of those sorcery spells that might be common here at the Kingdom of Sparta. A fire pit senses that you need heat and magically pulls firewood out of thin air with a rotisserie at the ready for food to cook. Anyway, I strike a match and throw it into the pit. With one second passing, bright orange flames erupt, and within another few seconds, my tent becomes very warm that I don't need to wear my cloak. I also forgot to mention that once I entered here for the first time, there was already a medium-sized fridge plugged into one of the outlets and inside the fridge is filled with different kinds of meat, fruit, vegetables, nuts, and liquids like water, milk, orange juice, and apple juice, which I find completely weird. However, I feel like it's really nice for a kingdom like this to know how to make their people really comfortable. Yet, I'm in a bit of a snacky mood and decide to head toward my refrigerator. Immediately, as I'm about to reach the handle, the door flap opens and closes behind a Wolfinoid that I don't really want to see. And now, just seeing him in here sparks my hatred against him.

"Marcus Lowsbroth," I speak with a displeasing tone in my voice.

"Hello, Will. Do you like your new home?" he says with a little evil smile and simultaneously crosses his arms.

"What the hell do you want?" I ask, leaning against my refrigerator and also crossing my arms. "Are you still pissed that your king told you to shut up and piss off?"

"Ha! A little bit, but that's not why I'm here."

I lower my head and slowly ball up my hands because I know that a fight between me and this idiot is about to breakout.

"Then, why are you here?" I ask, sounding a bit more defensive.

Marcus just smiles as if he's enjoying my anger and says, "I'm here to tell you, no, I'm here to order you to stay away from Tara. She's mine," taking one step forward and gesturing his right thumb to himself.

I burst out laughing, throwing my head back a little.

"What's so funny?" he asks, getting a little sizzled from my laughter.

I turn my attention at him, "Man, you're some kind of stupid. You see, once King Borin ordered you to get the hell out, I had a meeting with him and his highest associates in this awesome, relaxing lounge room where he told me that he and his daughter don't like you, especially Tara."

His eyes widen and go narrow. Then slowly, he puts back his ears. "That's not true. Tara loves me and I do the same. If you cross our path or mine, I'll tear you apart!" At this moment, his cloak starts slowly tearing and his sharp teeth are sticking out.

For me, I face my torso toward him, lowering my hat, popping the bones in my neck, and popping my fingers because the first rule when you're about to engage in a fight, you don't rush to your opponent. You let the opponent rush to you. In that case, I let the anger I have for him boil a bit more, letting my heart to pick up more pace and my adrenaline to activate and surge through my veins. Another rule of engaging in a fight is that you should study your opponent and from what I see, Marcus has fat around his stomach, arms, and legs. So, he's a bit slower, but that doesn't mean he's weaker than me. For my physical appearance, I am slim. I've been eating the right foods and have been exercising. So, I am faster and agile.

"Well?" he asks with a hint of impatience in his voice, as always.

After sizing him up, I put on a sly smile. "Bring it on. You fat bastard."

Marcus charges at a full speed at what his fat, stubby legs would allow as he growls and snarls at me. I still hold my ground and wait for the right moment. Once he reaches me by arm's length, I dodge to avoid his mouth, grab hold of his cloak, and throw him into my bed at full strength. His back crashes into one of the sharp corners of one of the posts and whelps out a bit of pain. I take four long strides, thereby jumping into the air as high as I can and slamming my human, military boots that I still have into his stomach. Then, I ball up my right hand very tightly and slam it into Marcus' right side of his face, hopefully blocking out his vision for a few moments. Again, he cries in pain as he covers his left eye with his left hand and holds his stomach with his right. He lays down sideways on his left toward the ground; right before his head makes contact, I deliver one swift, hard kick with my right boot into his face which makes him sit back up.

"Owww, my nose!" he bellows in pain.

"Oh, I'm 'sorry.' Let me help you with that." I grab his muzzle with both of my hands and using all of my might, I bend the nose in the opposite direction which makes a loud cracking sound.

"Owww!" he says screaming much louder, closing his eyes, holding his ultimately broken nose in his hands, and leaning forward.

"Get your lazy, fat ass ego up," I say, grasping the collar of his cloak and trying to throw him out of my tent with little success.

I turn my attention briefly away from him. I grab my staff that still remains deactivated for some odd reason and head outside. Exiting my tent, Marcus tries his best by standing up. His eyes are filled with hatred as if he wants to kill. By that time, a small crowd forms around us, talking in soft voices and pointing at us.

Marcus removes his hands, revealing his dislocated bloody nose, "I am going to fucking *kill you!*"

I tighten my grip on my staff, look at him with a stern face without a hint of fear, and slam my staff into the ground, thereby creating a louder pinging sound that rings out from it. The light source inside the staff ignites, letting admiral blue flames erupt from the staff and forming around a glass, flame orb. Golden lightning bolts discharge themselves at a powerful rate from the staff, but I don't feel the heat or burn from the flames nor the electricity coming off it in my hand and on my arm. The crowd, both human and Wolfinoid, back away from us slowly. I look at Marcus dead on with the intent of murdering him first. Although his eyes widen and show fear, he still charges at me, pulling out a sharp dagger.

My defense instinct kicks in. I swing my staff a good one-eighty-degree arc at him, letting the admiral blue flames scorch him with the sound of my best war cry in the wind. The flames knock him over and yet again, he screams louder in pain. I slowly walk over to him, then I push his face real deep into the earth with the same boot. Through his right eye, I see a plead of mercy, but to me, it is already too late.

"Perhaps I should put you out of your misery right here. Right now." I raise my staff in the air, flipping the flame-shaped orb to ram right into his face, and the flames around it converge into a sharp arrow, resembling the movement of the flames. "Time to die, Marcus Lowsbroth." Right at that moment, when I'm about to release the tension in my right shoulder and let the staff run straight down into that pleading eye, a voice bellows out.

"That's enough!" I look up, only to see King Borin and Sean Greenwood with his group of guards. "That's enough, Nos." He gestures with his hands that I should calm down and back away.

I do it without resisting. I breathe in a couple of times to let the fire inside and outside of me subdue to a calmer tone. Feeling a bit more in control of my anger, I say to King Borin, "Sir, with all of my apologies and respect, this is the man who started the fight," pointing the flame-shaped orb at Marcus with no flames erupting around it. The admiral blue light glows on the inside.

"I know, Nos, I know," the king says, still gesturing with his hands that I should calm myself down even further. "I don't blame you and I understand you are innocent. I did take notice of Marcus leaving the castle in a weird fashion that rose my suspicions. For now, you've done your part of defending your ground. Now, let Sean and his men do the rest." He gestures with his hand and four out of the eight come toward us, carrying a stretcher. They lift Marcus up and start carrying him away.

Despite gasping for breath, Marcus says to me, "You're gonna regret this day."

"Shut up, you bloody idiot," one of the men says.

As they reach King Borin, he says to them, "Take him to the hospital inside the castle to get him stable and once he is, throw him to one of the cells deep within this planet we're visiting. Then, arrange for a portal to our planet for immediate transport to await further justice."

"Yes, my lord," another Wolfinoid answers him and they take off jogging.

At this time, it's just Borin, Sean, and the other four guards. Behind them is a large, white box with edges chromed out. Underneath it, you wouldn't believe this, is nothing. There are no wheels of any size nor style supporting and transporting the weight of the box and whatever contents that lie inside. The entire box is just floating in the air, a couple of inches off the ground, with a faded color of purple glowing underneath. There are no handles or any other device I see that can be used to control the floating box. King Borin takes notice of the way I stare at the box, looks at it for a brief second, and returns his eyes at me.

"What's in the box, sir?" I ask.

"Let's bring it inside your tent." We all move toward my home, except the four guards that stationed themselves around my home. Sean, King Borin, and I go in with Sean pushing the box. He taps a few touchscreen keys and the box settles itself slowly onto the thick, plush, artificial pelt floor. Then, he taps a few more keys and the box opens itself, revealing five different instruments, two amplifiers, and four speakers, and two microphones with two floor stands for them. The odd thing is, I wrote down four as the number of friends I'll need help from. So, why are there five?

"Why are there five instruments? I wrote down a count of four a couple of days ago," I ask directly at King Borin.

With a calm face and smooth movements of his arms, he reaches into one of the inside pockets of his lavishly designed cloak and hands me the same piece of paper. "Tara has an interest in this song. I believe you already picked a different one in advance, but she and her friends want you and your friends to play this song."

I look down at the note and I do recognize the song and the country singer.

"Is that going to be a problem?" he asks with some uneasiness in his voice.

Looking back up at him and Sean, I put on a confident smile, "Naw, it's not going to be a problem. As long as nobody purchases a shot or two of Patron. If they do, my friends and I may have to stay and do our best to shut that party down." Then I wink to them. Both the king and Sean look at one another with confused looks, trying to calculate if my reply is a compliment or that I'm going to have an issue in performing the song that's written before me.

I assure them, "Don't worry. It was a joke. Tara and her friends will indeed love the performance. However, am I really trying to win her heart so that she truly falls in love with me?"

"What?" Sean says. I repeat the previous note I received about four days ago.

Both of them are surprised and King Borin says, "No. No, no, no, no. You're just performing that song as one of her presents. Again, my daughter already has her sights on you. For some reason, your character made her fall in love. Of course, first sight love in our race, especially for women, happens quite often."

Well now, that makes me really nice and warm on the inside. All of my blood rush into my head turning my skin red. Plus, it makes me turn my attention away from them so that they don't see my huge embarrassment. However, my eyes continue to observe eight small spheres that are encased in the black foam in the upper hatch that encases the five instruments.

"What do those do?"

King Borin looks at them and back at me, and replies, "Ah. Those spheres are designed to create a sound barrier. So, when you and your friends are practicing, the noise that you create will not exit your house and disturb the neighbors."

"How'd they work?" I ask, leaning onto my staff with curiosity.

"Simple," answers Sean. "You just activate any one of them and they'll fly out into the eight corners of your home. Then, they'll shoot out eight separate beams of light that connect all eight spheres and create the sound barrier that will cover all four walls."

"What does that mean?"

"It means that you and your friends can walk through it when you enter or exit the tent."

"Okay, that sounds pretty interesting." I walk forward, grabbing one of the spheres and analyzing it in my hand.

Then, King Borin pats my shoulder, "Enjoy, Nos. Just show up at the party between the hours of six and ten. The party doesn't start until five o'clock and goes to one in the morning."

Right after that, he and Sean begin exiting my tent, then King Borin turns around, "Oh, you do realize you have three days left?"

"I do indeed know that, sir," I reply with a confident smile.

"Practice hard and enjoy the party," the king says with a smile as he and his men leave and head back to the castle.

I'm pretty sure you guys are still wondering what types of instruments lay in the case. Are you? Good. Okay, so, in front of me is a completed drum set, one bass guitar, one electric guitar, one electronic keyboard, one steel guitar, two wireless microphones with stands, and a pair of earbuds for everyone to listen to the music. I did forget that every house tent comes with a glass tablet that's programmed as an address book, so I immediately put down my staff and pick up the tablet to start searching where my friends live. Once I write down their addresses, I pick up the instructions of the device that may help me and my friends sound like the country singer's band, and I started to study them for the remaining time of the day.

Date: November 28, 2014
Time: High Noon
Two Days Before Tara's Birthday

"Alright, Nos, can you tell us again how this device works?" Austin Black asks as he cracks open a Mountain Dew still looking confused, and so do Hugh Smith, Chris October, and Alex Rodriguez. Along with the group are Alice Cole, Whitney Silver (dating Chris), and Emily Smith (Hugh's daughter). The girls themselves, well, they're just tagging along to see how this karaoke device works. All in all, they're mixed in with their own conversations. The crazy thing is, I'm not the only one who's getting in a love relationship with a Wolfinoid. Chris and Whitney have been dating and Whitney is a Wolfinoid. Anyway, I sigh and pick up the directions to read them out loud.

"Okay," I say, rubbing the brow of my nose with my thumb and index finger. "It says: Step 1, turn on your musical device. Step 2, turn on the wireless transmitter and connect the wire to the musical device. Step 3, once the wireless signal is connected to the musical device, a small tab will pop up on the screen. Once there, tap on it and the tab will show the number of voice changers, wrist bands, ankle bands, and wireless earbuds. Then, select the instruments that are being used."

I follow those instructions and everything that was explained happens and comes together perfectly. Before I put on the voice changer, wrist bands, and earbud headphones, I continue reading.

"Step 4, select the song(s) that are going to be played. You can create the pause time to last longer in case you want to change song(s) or you want to pause the music. Step 5, have fun."

"That's it?" Hugh asks.

"Yeah," says Whitney, "our race invented that so it can be really easy to use for our fun or for your fun," gesturing her right hand toward us.

"So," Alex says, sounding like he gets the idea of how the device works, "what type of song are we going to play?"

I look at my friends, cross my arms, and start leaning against my refrigerator again. "Well, we were going to do 'Asphalt Man' by Mike Path since my previous job was being an asphalt cowboy. But, when King Borin stopped by to drop off the equipment, he hands me a note of Tara's request."

"And what song does she want to hear?" Chris asks.

I look at him and then to the rest, feeling really good, and say, "She wants us to do 'Oh Man' by Josh Black. And I think that'll be a great party song."

Every one of them nods in agreement and also compliments that the song does have a nice party tune to it.

Then, Austin asks, "So, which instrument do you want to assign us since you're the leader?"

I clap my hands together, "Alright. I'll be the lead singer a.k.a. Josh Black and be playing the electric guitar. Austin, you'll be playing the drums. Chris, bass. Alex, steel guitar. And Hugh, keyboard."

They all nod their heads and start grabbing the instruments. All of them grab the wrist bands, headphones, ankle bands, and voice changers. We all activate the devices and each light on the wireless transmitter glows blue. Then I pick "Oh Man" by Josh Black on my iPod and put the beginning pause time at fifteen seconds to give us some time to get situated at our positions and ten at the end. Next, we all take our positions, ready for whatever happens; I watch the countdown on my iPod very closely. I feel really nervous for what if these things really work and they control our bodies when a song actually starts to play? I look around, the rest of my friends have the same feeling—nervous and unsure, possibly even a bit scared.

Then I look back at the screen, "5, 4, 3, 2, 1."

Simultaneously, as the song starts playing in our ears, my right hand starts strumming the strings on the main part of the guitar while my left hand follows moving up and down the neck. Soon, Austin's hands start bagging the drums with the sticks and pressing the pedal for the bass drum, and at the same time, Chris' hands are doing the same thing on the bass guitar. Suddenly, my voice starts sounding like Josh Black as the lyrics begin. Seconds later, Alex joins in with the steel guitar and so does Hugh on the keyboard. I am pretty sure everybody feels that they still have control of their conscience; we look at one another with amazement in our eyes. When the chorus comes up again, Chris joins me, sounding like the backup singer from Black's band and he does it a second and a third time. As the song comes to an end, everybody, except me, stops as I strum the final chords to end the song. Then, the countdown for the pause section activates and I immediately rush over to officially hit the pause button. Once I did, we're all in complete shock, awe, and amazement. And so are the girls, except Whitney, who is laughing her head off by the expressions on our faces.

She gasps for air and says, "Oh man, you humans are so amazing to us. Not just to me, but to all of *us.*"

"Holy shit," Chris says, "did we just do *all* of *that*?" while he points to the transmitter. We all look down at the device still in awe and amazement.

Then I look at them, "Yeah. Yeah, I guess we all just played the song 'Oh Man' without actual practice."

"We gotta do it again," says Alex.

"Oh, hell yeah," says Hugh. "If we are performing at the princess' party, we gotta look like we actually mean and enjoy it." Then he winks at me.

I just laugh, shake my head, and look around the circle. All of them look at me and looking into their eyes, I can tell they want to go at it again. I shrug, smile, and set the beginning pause time at ten. We play the song all over again. Then, I put the start time down to five seconds.

We practice the song over and over again until we all start to feel and know the chords, rhythm, and lyrics of the song by heart. After practicing several times, I look at my clock and it says six. We decide to take a break and have some dinner, then meet back here after thirty minutes.

Coming back, we practiced some more, but this time, I messed around with the equalizer on the iPod so that my voice kind of overtakes Josh's and now it's the real me singing. Finally, we take another break and we're all exhausted; Chris's fingers and mine start to bleed a little bit, and yet I look at the clock, it's already eight-thirty.

"Alright, guys, let's call it quits for the night and meet back here around the same time. Agree?"

"Agreed," says Austin, Chris, Alex, and Hugh simultaneously.

They all exit until Whitney pulls me aside, "I know you guys are going to be great at Tara's party. She is going to love it."

"You sound like you know her."

"Because I'm one of her closest friends." Then she and I bump our fists and she turns in the direction of the castle.

"Have a great night, Nos," she yells over her shoulder.

I close the tent flap and zip it up. Then, I turn toward one of the counters to grab the first aid kit and start wrapping up my fingertips. Without wasting more time, I turn off the wireless transmitter and iPod, extinguish the light in the lantern that hangs bright in the center of my tent, throw some magic powder into the existing fire to lower the light but still to keep me warm, and finally crawl into bed falling right to sleep.

Date: November 30, 2014
Time: 7:30 PM
Approaching the Gates of the Castle

Why in the hell should I be nervous? Why am I nervous? My friends and I have practiced multiple times that we practically know every chord and rhythm. Ah shit, who am I kidding? We, especially me, are going to fuck it up! Ah man, I don't know if I can do this. No, yes you can! Think positive stuff, Nos. Nothing but—"

"Are you feeling okay, Nos?" Hugh asks, interrupting the argument in my head.

I snap my head to the left to look at him, "Do I look like I'm nervous?"

"Yeah, you kinda do."

Sigh. "Yeah. Yeah, I am nervous."

I turn my attention back toward the path as Hugh, Austin, Chris, Alex, and I hike through the thick, snow-packed roads of the closed market. The weather today has an overcast of dark gray clouds with very thick snowflakes falling continuously. It has been this way since we all got up and met at my house around noon. When we all met outside, another group of movers wearing cloaks that represent being king's guards came in, packed all of the instruments and equipment, and took them away. I was about to ask where they were going, but one of the movers told me that they're moving the stuff to the party. Then, he asked what our names were and where we lived. When I told him our names and our addresses, he hands me five gold-colored cards with large words that say, "*V.I.P.*" with our names included, tells me to keep them with me, and carries on. For the remaining hours, my friends and I hung out and caught up with each other's lives, including the stories of how they were escorted here.

As of now, we're approaching the main doors that lead into the castle, and it's already 7:30 PM. We all begin to feel the temperature dropping. Same as my last visit, there are four guards in total standing by the doors. I signal with my hand for my friends to stop and we stand twenty-yards away from the gate. I turn around saying in a serious but friendly tone:

"Alright." I reach into my cloak. "One of the movers gave me these cards. These are V.I.P cards. Each one has your names on it. Take one and show it to the guards before we go in. I'm pretty sure we'll meet more on the way, so keep these with you."

They all nod and tell me that they understand what is bound to happen. Without hesitation, they take their assigned cards and I gesture with the same hand to keep moving. Approaching the large doors, the Wolfinoid guards seem to be a little in-depth with their topics, probably speaking in their own native tongue. As their ears perk forward, their conversations stop. One of them gestures with his hand open toward us to stop and we do.

"Have your cards out at the ready," I tell my friends.

The guards approach us. They do the same routine by patting us down, asking if we're carrying anything that can be used as a potential weapon and our V.I.P. cards. Upon request, we show them to the guards. Immediately, the guards agree with one another, then one of them punches in a code on the same stone that turns around and reveals the same keypad. Instead of the large doors opening, a smaller regular-sized door appears out of the air from one of the main doors and opens for us. Before we could all step inside, the same guard that told us to stop also tells us to follow the signs of where the party is located. Then, we all head inside.

While entering the great foyer, the same door closes and disappears. My friends give off noises of amazement, but for me now, it's just another part of the Wolfinoid's culture.

"C'mon guys. I don't want to be late. I mean, we shouldn't be late."

"It's okay, Nos," says Alex.

Without spending more time, we press forward down the long corridor toward the throne room. Within five minutes, yeah, the corridor is that long, we reach the doors that lead into the throne room. Before I knock, there's a sign nailed onto one of the doors in the same writing.

"If you're proceeding to Tara's party, there is no need to knock, just come in. Follow the signs. Don't stray onto a different path."

I turn around to look at my friends, "When we enter through these doors, you guys will be absolutely amazed by the architecture and design in the throne room."

"Is it really that awesome-looking?" Chris asks.

"Yep."

I open the doors and all of their jaws drop to the floor. They gasp in awe as we go down the aisle that leads up to the thrones on the far, opposite side of the room. For me, it is pretty, damn awesome to be in here because from what I stated before, the architecture of this place is just purely awesome and I still am curious how they crafted it, along with the kind of tools they used. However, I have to focus back on the existing task; so, turning my head at every angle, I look for any other signs that will show us the direction we should follow.

Turning my head to the left wall, I see the sign that's located on the third doorway away from the entrance where we came in. But before I can press on, my friends are still in total awe and are turning around to get every inch of the room etched in their minds. Their actions just make me roll my eyes and laugh a little. I grab Austin and Alex saying to the rest of the group that we should keep moving. All of them realize the task at hand and keep on following.

Going through the corridor, the same carpet continues onward and instead of torches, there is the same electric light source that continues to the corners where the wall and ceiling meet. The difference is the color of the light—it is in a soft golden glow that seems to get dimmer as we go down the hall. Then, we reach a staircase that spirals down and we begin to head down. During our descent, we start to hear music. I expect the sound to have a Celtic tone, but it sounds like a dance club. With a mixture of old club music, that might be from the 1990s to our now-modern club music.

"Seems like these guys aren't old-fashioned after all," Hugh observes.

"Yeah, you have a point," says Alex.

"Agreed," I add in.

Nearing the bottom, the stairway goes completely dark and makes us slow our pace on the steps. After several steps, we reach the bottom where the music is much louder and the light fixtures are replaced with little LED lights that softly pulse into numerous different colors located in the ceiling and from what we can see in the blackness, there seem to be several strobe lights reflecting off the walls. There are also several laser lights. This sort of commotion brings up our courage and we quicken our pace down the hall and around a corner.

Once rounding the corner, we stop because right in front of us is literally a nightclub. The carpet abruptly changes into a metal mesh because it becomes the catwalk that circles around where all of the action is taking place. The size of the club is very large and judging through the strobing lights, flashing normal lights, spinning lasers, and rising fake fog, the place looks like an octagon. Both on our left and right are switchback stairs that lead right into the action below us, and from the height we're at, I guess we have to be thirty feet high. We walk over to the railing and looking at the walls, they're all covered in metal diamond plates with rivets and poles running parallel with the walls alongside all of the strobe and laser lights attached to them. In front of us, there are several metal beams held by the thick cable that connects to the ceiling which holds more of the same lights and speakers. Then, something taps on my left shoulder.

I turn to see the source and off to our left, there are three guards but not wearing the cloaks. They're wearing black shirts with neon colors that glow brightly in the black light. They're also wearing jeans but no footwear of any kind. Turning my gaze to their faces, they're also painted in neon colors that still glow brightly. Plus, two of the three are wearing different colors of glow sticks around their necks and wrists.

"Hey!" the leader asks loudly but still in a gentle tone. "Are you guys the band that plays that one song for Tara?"

I become hesitant for a bit, but I still reply back, "Yeah, we're Tara's present request."

"May we see your special invites?"

"Yeah. No problem." Feeling a bit more enthusiastic, we all hand our cards to them. The guards look at them over and nod to one another.

"Alright, you guys, have a great time."

"We will," I reply, shake their hands, and so do my friends.

We descend down the right stairwell, then a familiar tune comes out. I listen closely, then it hits me. It's "Dustbowl" from L.E.D. (Electronic Exotic Dude) and that just makes me bound down the stairs a lot faster. We reach the party level and from what we can see, it's not just Wolfinoids jumping and dancing around having a great time but there are also humans in the mixture. Plus, everybody has their bodies painted in neon colors and have glow sticks. The heat in the area is enough for us to remove our cloaks and we find the closet to store them. Right next to the closet is a long table that's full of glow sticks and I grab a handful of them, crack 'em, shake 'em, and wear 'em. Then, we decide to split off and go have some fun. For me, this experience is just purely awesome. Across the room where I'm standing, I see the bar and walk toward it. The bar itself has a stainless-steel backsplash with a black countertop and below are more LED lights that smoothly change colors. On the wall is just a large mirror lined with glass shelves displaying various choices of soda. Letting my eyes scan toward the right end of the shelves, the soda choices become alcohol choices. I mean, there's a choice of any kind of beer, wine, whiskey, vodka, and you won't believe this, there are different flavors of Moonshine. Also, this bar I decide to sit in is very long and is operated by four Wolfinoid bartenders.

"Holy shit," I say with a big grin on my face.

One of the bartenders notices me and walks over with a smile, "Hey, man, welcome to Tara's party. What's your choice of poison?"

I look back at the alcohol choices and ask, "Is there an age limit?"

"How old are you?" she asks.

"I'm twenty-one years old."

"Well, in our culture, we let our people start drinking at fifteen. So, what can I get you?"

Wow, fifteen? But let's play it safe for tonight, so I reply, "I want a cold, regular Mountain Dew on the rocks."

She shrugs with a smile and pulls out a glass, fills it with ice, and at the same time, starts pouring the Mountain Dew. She says, "Are you the kid named Nos or Will Young?"

I simply nod.

"It's 'bout time you showed up. Tara was beginning to worry," she says while she gestures with her head for me to look to the left. Turning to face the left end of the bar, there she is—Tara Borin— completely different from what she was wearing from church last Sunday. Her hair is dyed in different colors to reflect the black light. She's wearing a white sleeveless shirt with the same camo pattern like in my hat and jeans, and to my surprise, a belt buckle. She's also wearing glow sticks on her wrists, along with leather bracelets that have metal studs sticking out, a choker that is also leather with a waterdrop hanging from it, and earrings that match her choker.

"Damn" is the only word. Tara looks so beautiful that it makes my heart start thumping. She doesn't notice me because she seems to be in a deep conversation with her friends.

"Here you go, man, enjoy," says the bartender as she hands me my drink.

I take a swig of it and calmly look back at Tara. I do notice Whitney in the mix and she takes notice of me, taps Tara's shoulder, and points in my direction with a smile.

Before all of this happened, I've trained myself to read lips and I can tell that Whitney said, "Look who finally showed up, girl. Your man is finally here."

Tara looks at me and does the same action in church last Sunday, licking her lips in a friendly, pleasurable gesture, and I can see it in her eyes that she really wants me. This increases the speed of my heart and triggers the butterflies in my stomach. I snap my head back at my drink and take a long swig of it.

"Right, where are my friends?" As I get up and search for them, I look over my left shoulder and I see Tara, Whitney, and their other friends giggling at me. Still, my heart increases speed and I begin to lose focus on the task that I have to do.

"Nos!" I turn around and there's Hugh with a Coors Light in his hand.

"I saw what happened. Is that the girl that wants you because, damn, it looks like she's really into you." At the same time, he elbows me in my side and I try to put a confident smile on.

"Yeah. That's the girl. That girl is also the king's daughter in this kingdom."

"Really!" He looks at her and then back at me. "Holy shit! Nos, you're going to be one hell of a fucking man after tonight. And you told us back in the shop that there's no woman in the universe that doesn't want you."

Well, he does have a point and I have been proven wrong. Even though I don't know Tara, she does look like she has a strong interest in me. But my question is, how does she really know me?

Then a voice booms out from the speakers above us, "Alright, alright, party people! How are you doing tonight!" A loud cheer rings out and we turn our heads to the D.J. on the stage in front of us. In the faint blue lights, I can see our equipment already set up and ready to be used.

"How's the party girl feeling tonight!" Tara lets out a loud, beautiful howl in the almost-silent room.

"Alright! Okay, tonight, the party girl had requested that her new mate she met over a month ago play one of his songs for her and for us tonight!" Another cheer rings out from the crowd.

I chug the rest of my Dew to steady my nerves.

"Okay, her man and mate is Nos, and man, if you're out there in the crowd, you got ten minutes to get up here and ready to jam *out*!" Then the D.J. cranks the music back up and a timer in orange LED lights appears above our equipment, counting down from ten minutes.

I've just had one Mountain Dew. I need to get more.

I rush back to the bar and have several shots of my favorite soda.

After having my last one, I crack my neck and say to Hugh, "Alright! Let's do this because I'm *ready*!" Then I move my way to the stage with Hugh following me.

When we get there, Austin, Alex, and Chris are already gearing up.

Alex looks at me, "Are you ready to do this?"

I reply back with more enthusiasm, "Are *you* guys ready?"

"Hell yeah!" they say together.

We settle into our instruments and stations, and I tell my friends that we should just listen to the song as a review before we start playing it and they agreed.

We listen to the song a couple of times and when it ended, we look at one another and we can tell that all of us can do this. On the stage, Austin sits behind me on a two-step raised platform. I am standing in the center front. Chris stands on my right side with Hugh on his right, and Alex stands on my left. I walk to the D.J. and tell him that we're almost ready. He nods and lets out the announcement while I set up the pause time before the song to five seconds and the after-pause to fifteen. Walking back to my mic, all of our instruments, speakers, and headphones are activated and live. The D.J. taps a few buttons on his very large glass tablet turntable which sinks into the floor and another floor moves over it, covering the machine completely.

Then, he yells clearly in my ear, "I've listened to your song. Tara, her friends, and everybody else are going to love it! I've also calibrated the lights to change colors and shapes as the song plays!" I nod and he exits the stage. I look at my iPod and the countdown from five begins.

"Here we go," I quietly say to myself. Then, the songs start to play and so do we.

During the entire song, I looked out at the crowd feeling completely calm and having fun with my friends. At certain points of the song, I looked right at Tara's eyes and she really enjoyed it. When the song ended, everybody cheers so loud that my friends and I make several bows to them. I rush over to my iPod immediately pausing it before the song starts playing all over again. We make more bows to the crowd and surprisingly, they start throwing roses at our feet.

"Thank you," I say in my normal voice. "Thank you all for letting my friends and I play that song for you tonight."

I return my gaze back at Tara and she makes the gesture of blowing a kiss for me. The butterflies return to my stomach, but I don't break the gaze between us. Somehow, I am beginning to feel a bit more comfortable just by looking at her. My friends exit the stage and join the crowd back on the floor. The lights on the stage go black, but I still see their faces. Then something moves on the catwalk like some sort of movement of an arm. Out of nowhere, the curtains start closing from the left and the right, making the stage completely dark.

"What the fu—" Suddenly, I get punched right into the face and fall backward onto the stage.

Movement of feet, I don't know how many rush toward me, and I get blinded by a second punch. This time, in the jaw. Before I blackout, I feel a bag being thrown around my head, my hands and feet being tied up, and all of me being dragged away. By that time, I blackout completely.

CHAPTER EIGHTEEN
A Fight to the Death
Location: Unknown
Date: Unknown
Time: Unknown

MY CONSCIOUSNESS BEGINS TO reboot after a heavy sound of a couple of doors with steel and lumber materials being opened and closed. I feel my body, although my legs aren't doing the movement, flying through the air. Paying close attention to my stomach, I feel like it's bending over some object. I feel the object moving, swinging back and forth. I focus more on the object for a while longer. Then, it comes to me.

Shit. I'm on somebody's shoulder.

Then, the memories of the curtains being closed, the stage going completely dark and being punched in the face twice.

I'm beginning to panic. *Where the hell are they taking me to?*

The shoulder stops as the final door opens, moves again, then the door closes in front of me. Suddenly, I'm thrown to the ground. The feeling of the floor is cold and hard like slabs of stone. As my consciousness keeps on rebooting, I try my best to roll over on my back. However, my body feels like it doesn't have the strength.

"Look at him," a voice sounds out. "Completely pathetic and absolutely skinny. How in the hell was this kid able to throw you out?"

"I don't know and I don't care. Just shackle him up and give him five good licks. Then, throw him into the arena."

That voice. That voice sounds so damn familiar.

"You got it, boss," the first voice replies and I see hands cutting the binds, pulling the bag off, grabbing me by the armpits, thrusting me up, and then suspending my body weight in the air now by my wrists. My sense of touch keeps on improving and I can feel my nose and right side of my jaw aching. My nose hurts so much that I think it's broken and I feel my blood, slowly pouring down my face. Or maybe it's dry. I can't tell.

"Ah," says a female voice, "it brings me great joy that this autistic man is finally going to be punished for what he did to me three years ago."

"Anything for you, Ms. Tiger, soon to be Mrs. Lowsbroth," says the second voice.

"What!" I shout out loud while thrusting my eyes open.

I see that I am in a circular room constructed out of heavy boulders and lit up by torches burning in a bright red color. Looking around and seeing the equipment, it all hits me that this room is made for one thing, torture.

"Ah, look who's finally awake," says the female.

A heavy-set Wolfinoid male, dressed in black with his face covered with a black hood, brings down a pair of cold, metal shackles, and cuffs my wrists in them. Quickly, he moves down to my ankles and does the same thing to them. Following him with my eyes, he moves toward a wooden, gear wheel sticking halfway out of the floor and begins to turn it. Simultaneously, the shackles around my wrists and ankles are being pulled in opposite directions that I think they're going to be brought out of their sockets. The man dressed in black stops, comes back to me with a knife, and cuts off my shirt.

"My God, you look disgusting. I can see your entire rib cage. Oh well, at least your family doesn't have to deal with you anymore," says Ms. Tiger.

I can see her clearly, leaning against one of the torture machines, which for some reason, I don't want to know how it works. Her arms are crossed and she puts a grin across her face. I can see pure evil in her eyes. Just seeing her makes my blood boil in a second and I let out my best menacing growl.

Ms. Tiger just throws her head back, laughing, "Ha! You think you have the willpower to come over here and smack me?" She approaches me and says, "You don't have the power. Plus, you don't have the right to be with Tara anymore. Aside from that, I tried my best to make you miserable as possible so that you won't be able to have the confidence to get another job. You'll just be stuck at home, with your mommy taking care of you, and still be washing golf carts," as she strokes my face.

I try to lunge at her, snapping my jaw, but the chains restrict me; in essence, I was trying to take some skin off her hand. I look at her straight dead in the eyes and swear, "When I survive this, I will find you and when do, I will fucking kill *you!*"

She slowly withdraws her hand and puts on the same sinister smile, "You see, Will, that's where you're wrong; you'll be dead and Tara. Well, she's also going to die, too. And there's nothing you can do to stop it. Tah!"

She spins on her right heel and walks to a door that's indeed made out of heavy lumber and riveted with large, steel plates. Ms. Tiger walks through it, tells the Wolfinoid tormentor to give me several good licks in the back, and closes the door. Just hearing the news that Tara is going to be murdered makes the blood in my veins run faster. I know, it's crazy because I've only seen her twice, but to feel this kind of emotion makes me want to break loose and tell her, even her father, about this. Again, I can't escape and the fear of being whipped sinks in.

I shake the chains, screaming at the top of my lungs, *"Fuck!"*

The tormentor just stands there with a whip in his hand, laughing, "Scream all you want, puny human. No one can hear you scream. And no one," walking behind me and taking his position, he continues, "will save *you*."

Then, he strikes the whip against my back and I scream in pain. The man just laughs and strikes my back several times, over again. Suddenly, he throws the whip to my right side. Turning my head, he picks up a medium-sized bucket filled with whatever liquid.

He sloshes the liquid around, intimidating me, and says, "Here, this will help heal the wounds." He throws the liquid onto my whipped back.

The liquid inside was sea water.

"Oow! Fuck You! Fuck You! Fuck You! *Fuck You!*"

"Enjoy the fight, Nos." Simultaneously, he pulls back a wooden lever on my left, opening all four shackles and a trap door right below me that I didn't see before.

Gravity pulls my body down into a dark tunnel. I travel straight down for how long I don't know until the tunnel curves at ninety-degrees. Two things rush into my head: first, the tunnel is not made out of rough stones but of smooth metal. Second, my whipped back touching the metal surface hurts like the pain of a thousand flames igniting as if they came from hell itself, especially with the speed I'm going. Then, the slide angles slightly down, increasing the speed. Suddenly, a bright light illuminates in front of me and I go sliding right into it.

I am suddenly blinded by bright lights as I crash-land into a soft surface. The soft surface moves, splashes around me, feels dry on my exposed skin, and stings my back.

Oh, good. It's just sand.

Letting my eyes adjust to the lights, a deafening sound of a hundred voices sounds off at once with trumpets blowing some sort of a battle tune. Lifting my head and slowly looking around, my breath is taken away by the sight that surrounds me. I am both in awe and fear of the area, perceiving it as a fighting arena. It seems to be mainly for very brutal fights because sticking out and laying on the sand floor are shovels, chains, ropes, spears, daggers, axes, bats, and swords. Slowly getting to my feet, I see no other weapons for self-defense like a shield or the likes. The deafening roar keeps on, making me look up, and above me are three levels of seating that have bleacher seats carved into the rock apparently for every spectator to look over each other's heads and have a good view. The first level is a good twenty feet above the ground and in front of me is a door. Looking behind, the hole where I came through is a metal plate that must've rolled in from one of the sides when I exited the tunnel. Above it has a sign that states, "The asshole."

"Oh, good, I'm the asshole," I say in a distasteful tone. Turning my head back to the door in front of me, I see that it is also constructed out of metal, looking like it opens inward, and above it, it states, "The victor."

I keep on examining this arena, standing fully on my two feet, but my back still stings in pain. At my right is an observer box with one throne made out of wood and behind it is just one simple doorway with a curtain covering the other side. Below the box makes me shiver; there is a flag of Sparta probably torn in some areas in purpose. The wolf head is turned upside down and there are bloodstains. I don't know if the blood is fresh or not; I rather leave it at that. The bright lights come from multiple recess lights in the ceiling that still has stalactites hanging. To sum this all up, the arena I'm in totally resembles an arena in a video game that I have recently played in my semi. Overall, there's no other way to escape. It looks like I may have to fight to the death just by seeing the weapons strewn across the sand floor.

Then the trumpets burst out again, with hidden cannons blasting lime-green and black powders, then back up at the observer box, an overweight, male Wolfinoid comes around the curtain and stands in front of his throne.

"Marcus Lowsbroth," I growl at the same time, balling up my hands; the sight of seeing him really makes my blood boil.

He's not wearing any cloaks that resemble the colors of this kingdom but of the colors lime-green and black. He smiles, waves at the crowd, and the crowd cheers back. He shouts his full name in such a high positivity. Yet, looking back at the crowd, it stuns me that there are a few humans, my kind, shouting his name like they really want our nation to fall right into the wrong hands. They must be very high liberals or fuckers who joined Nomads. Either way, in my eyes, they *all* must *die*, including the Wolfinoids who support this asshole. Turning my attention back at him, he begins waving his arms to settle them down. They all get the message and begin to quiet down and take their seats.

Marcus looks around at his audience, then down at me with an evil smile, and back to his supporters, "My friends, thank you so much for coming together on this fine night. We are here to see this man die since all of you agree with me that he is not the right suitor for Princess Tara Borin." The crowd begins to boo at me and throws trays and cups that they got from some sort of a concession stand, directly at me.

Yeah, keep on throwing your crap at me. If I make it out here alive, I'm going to hurt you all really bad.

I turn my attention back up to him, "And who the fuck am I going to battle against, Lowsbroth?"

He smiles and says, "He is an enemy of yours. You might remember him from your youth." Then he spreads out his right palm to the door ahead of me.

"Gentlemen, I give you Gurtruit McFuze!"

I know, right? What kind of dumbass name is that? I mean, listen to me closely—Will Young a.k.a. Nos; Gurtruit McFuze. Which name sounds better? I'll let you guys decide. Anyway, the door opens and there he is, a chubby bastard with his squinty eyes still covered with his long, thin hair. He's also shirtless, showing his fat hanging over his pants and arms that wiggle when he waves at the crowd with a bright smile. Compared to me, I'm basically skin and bone. I do have some muscle buildup on my arms and legs, but when

I suck in my stomach, my ribcage sticks out and people can clearly see it. Plus, you can feel every bone around my collar and shoulders.

Some parts of the crowd cheer, while others mumble among themselves in confused tones. Nonetheless, Marcus crosses his arms and has a pleasing smile across his face. In my case, I let my adrenaline and anger against this guy buildup. If y'all are asking why, here's a brief history lesson—Gurtruit was one of the many kids in elementary school who never had let me join them as I was from Green Bay and I support the Packers. Plus, he and his friends really made my life a living hell in middle school. However, during high school, I didn't see him or any of his friends, which made my last four years in public school enjoyable. Yet, seeing him now brings back those memories and I am totally ready to get my revenge on this motherfucker.

As Gurtruit approaches me, he stops, looks right at me, and says, "Ah, Will. How are you doing? Are you still feeling bad that your beloved Packers suck and still suck today?"

"Why, you little . . ." I reply grinding my teeth, simultaneously reaching for the nearest shovel with my left hand.

"*Not yet!*" Shouts Marcus and turns back to the crowd. I do retract my hand, but looking around, there are no guards. As Gurtruit and I look up at Marcus, I glance with my left eye and position my hand into hovering a mere inch away from the wooden shaft.

"The rules are simple," Marcus states. "Place your bet always on the victor and never on the asshole. If you do the latter, you will be removed and beheaded. If the asshole wins, he would be still be put to death. So, Will," he threatens, looking down at me with death in his eyes, "You better die."

Unlikely. I look back at him with revenge in my own eyes. I wonder how in the fucking hell he escaped from his captivity.

"Let the fight begin!" Marcus shouts, the crowd cheers, and the cannons blast the same color of powders all at once.

Immediately, I grab the shovel, bringing it to my right hand and whacking it hard across Gurtruit's face. His reaction is priceless;

he didn't see it coming. He goes flying to his right and lands on the floor. The crowd continues to boo at me, but I flip them off. I raise the shovel, preparing to whack the back of it on the back of his head, but out of nowhere, he throws sand in my eyes. I mumble a moan of pain, dropping the shovel, and rubbing the sand out. Once I get them clear, Gurtruit pops me hard right in the jaw, making me fly to the ground. The punch was so hard, it makes the inside of my mouth open and bleed. I can feel his presence as he hovers over me and kneels down.

"You, your family, your team, all fucking suck! I'm going to marry Tara; she and I will have so much fun. In case you didn't notice, back in school, women have always been attracted to me. You? You're a lousy piece of—" During his little speech, I let enough blood pool in my mouth and spit it right into his eyes.

He screams and stumbles back while I deliver a much harder right hook into his face that makes him fly backward. I crouch, leap on top of him, delivering more of my right fist punches into his face. Some automated bell sounds off. I don't care. I keep on punching. My adrenaline is running high with my anger and there is no way to turn it off until a chain wraps around my neck and pulls me away hard onto my back. Once I'm brought down to the ground, a large foot comes down and stomps on my bony chest, twice. And then another shovel comes out of nowhere and whacks me right in the face.

My vision is blurry, but it begins to clear up. Once my vision is clear, my anger turns into fear as I recognize Gurtruit's two other friends from school. Both of them are male and slightly built, but one is taller than the other. The short one holding the shovel with my blood on it is Max Kill and the taller one is Andy Xavier who's holding the chain around my neck.

Looking up at them makes my eyes widen and I say just one word, "Shit."

"Are you alright?" asks Max still looking at me with the intent to kill.

"Yeah, thanks for the rescue," Gurtruit replies as he slowly gets up to his feet.

"What should we do with him?" asks Andy with the same look wanting to kill.

Gurtruit rubs the blood off his face and looks at me, "Kill him. Kill him good."

"Will do, boss," they say together.

My anger completely shifts into fear—the fear of being dead; the fear that I'll never see my friends again; the fear that I'm never really going to meet Tara and have a conversation with her; the fear that she is going to marry such assholes or be killed. My heart races again in anger. I want to protect her since I am beginning to like her. As Max raises the shovel to deliver another hard swing to my face, my feelings for Tara get stronger and a song by Quintin Gill called "Fight It Out" begins to play in my head.

Max brings down the shovel and I deflect it with both of my feet. That counteraction makes the shovel fly right out of his hands. Then I pull the chain away from my neck, spin my body around crisscrossing Andy's hands, and pull the chain away from his hands. Both get really surprised, but I don't stop as I keep on listening and replaying that song in my head. Everything starts to go in slow motion as I spin around, thrashing the chain across Max's face and doing the same with Andy's. Next step, I kick right into Andy's ball sack to immobilize him. Returning my attention back to Max, he thrashes a spear that barely cuts my chest, missing the major parts. Stepping away from that attack, I throw the chain around the pole of the spear, pulling it from his hands. I grab the spear and throw it right into his left foot. He screams as he bends down to hold the wound. This where I make my move to walk behind him and as I do, I grab another shovel and smack it hard against the backside of his scalp. His cries of pain falter, his body goes limp, and he crashes into the sand headfirst.

Turning back to Andy, he thrashes a dagger at me that makes me lose grip of the shovel and the blade cuts my left eyebrow with his left hand while he holds his balls with the other. Once his arm has reached its full extension, I grab the wrist with my left hand, tugging him forward and delivering again another fast, hard punch with my right fist into his face. He begins stumbling backward. I rip the dagger from his hand, and he retracts it to his face.

"Big mistake."

I toss the dagger to my left hand and throw my right hand up and tight around his neck, bringing him down below my eye level. Gasping for air and wiggling around, I tighten my grip even more. I spin the dagger one-eighty degrees in my left hand where the blade is facing him. Andy removes his left hand, revealing all-out fear in his eyes.

"Please, Will . . . I . . . I mean Nos. Have mercy. I am so sorry."

Still thinking of the same song, I look right at him, and all of the memories of being bullied play over smoothly in my head, "You treated me like shit. You and everybody else hated my ass just over a football team. You didn't let me show you what I can be. After those years, it's a little too fucking late to apologize."

"No!"

Thrusting the dagger right into his head, his plead for mercy cease and I push his dead corpse onto the floor. The cheering of the crowd ceases and spinning around, all of them are in shock and horror. Marcus is also in shock. The expression on his face shows that he can't believe I was able to do all that. He's just sitting there, in his throne, looking dumbfounded.

"My friends. My closest friends," says Gurtruit, which makes me look back at him. "You killed them."

"Well, they were about to kill me. Survival of the fittest, asshole."

"I'll kill ya!"

"Bring it on, fat ass!" He grabs the nearest spear and I grab the same shovel lying next to Max's corpse. The blood from my eyebrow flows down into my eye, but I wipe it and pick up some sand to cover it. Once I was done, Gurtruit didn't come after me. He was still just standing there several yards away from me, tightening his grip on the spear. I do the same with the shovel, intending to take him down once and for all.

He and I stare down, waiting for one of us to charge. Seconds tick by, then a minute or two, until he decides to charge at me at full force letting out his best battle cry. I too begin charging at him, letting out my best battle cry. As we get closer and closer, a force looking like a mist and ice blue knocks us away from each other and onto our backs.

"Stop!" says a voice simultaneously.

I lift my head back up to see who created such power. The gentle force that knocks us back happens to be a silhouette that leaps from the second balcony and lands between us. The silhouette is fully revealed in the bright lights. My anger slips away realizing that the silhouette is Tara's and she's the one who created that force.

She hangs her head while performing a superhero landing. To my amazement, she's still wearing the clothes and jewelry from her party. Around her is an ice blue light glowing bright, then Slowly dissipating to a softer tone. She gets up to her feet and looks around at the crowd with seriousness burning in her ice-blue eyes. The crowd begins to mumble. Some of them begin to look afraid and decide that they should leave.

"All of you," shouts Tara and points at them, "should leave before both the royal and normal guards arrive here!"

They all shuffle and suddenly freak out when whistles blown in tunnels that lead into the stands begin echoing off the walls and lights of some source reflect off from them. Instantly, the entire crowd begins running toward the other tunnels that don't have both of the guardsmen coming down on them.

"Tara," shouts Marcus, standing up in disbelief. "How dare you end my fight! That man, Gurtruit McFuze, is the perfect man for you!"

"Ha," shouts Gurtruit, pointing at me, "she picks me! She picks me! Ha, ha! Loser!"

"*Shut up!*" Tara shouts at him in anger, then ice shoots out from her, glowing and sticking into the ceiling.

This also made him shut up in fear because from what I am seeing, Tara is a very powerful woman. She's the princess, so it would be wise that he and I should just keep our mouths shut. Plus, seeing her throwing ice into the ceiling makes me a little afraid of her.

She continues, "None of you are good enough for me. I don't like how you act and smell both physically and spiritually!"

Marcus walks closer to the wall of his box and continues to shout, "This is absurd. I'll tell your father of how reckless you are acting and that you still reject me and my love for you!"

Tara slowly turns her head at him, growling and baring her teeth at him. This is going to sound odd, but damn does her teeth look nicely clean and very white! Anyway, the ice-blue glow intensifies in her eyes and around her body as she slowly extends and raises her right hand like she's reaching for something. The expression on Marcus' face turns from frustration to confusion to alarm. He slowly raises his hands in surrender, but looking back at Tara's eyes, she has the intention to kill him. She quickly snaps her cupped hand sideways, destroying Marcus' neck with a loud snap and killing him instantly. His body slumps over the edge. Pretty soon, gravity takes over and brings his corpse down to the ground where we are.

By that time, both guardsmen have entered and begun looking for the crowd who witnessed the fight I was just in. Looking back at Tara, I am now afraid of her having witnessed her power, making me feel stuck in the position that I'm in. She turns her attention toward me. The anger in her eyes settles and is replaced by gentleness. The glow in her eyes and around her begins to subside, too.

Once she examines me, her eyes begin to fill with concern and sadness, then she slowly walks toward me, speaking in a soft tone, "Oh, Nos. What have they done to you? What have they done?"

She starts crawling on her knees as she gets closer, which makes me back away slowly from her on arms and legs.

"Please," she says, stretching out one hand. "Please, don't be afraid of me. Let me help you. Let me take you to my bed chamber and heal you. Again, don't be afraid." As she gets closer, I'm right up against one of the walls, trembling with fear and nervousness.

"Don't be afraid. Everything is going to be alright," Tara speaks to me in a lower, softer tone.

At this point, I am starting to feel the strong heat from her fingers as they slowly inch closer toward my face. Looking in her eyes, there's no anger but sadness, concern, and gentleness. Something in the back of my mind makes me look at my left and once I do, Gurtruit isn't there. He suddenly appears right behind Tara with a shovel in his hands, raised to swing, and looking very pissed off.

"Your highness, look!" I screamed but it's too late.

Wham!

When Gurtruit brings down the shovel, the gentleness, concern, and sadness are replaced by astonishment. Tara reaches behind her head, touches it, and brings it back; what she sees on her fingers is her own blood. The astonishment turns back to pure anger and she slowly turns around to him. Surprisingly, the back of her head where she was struck is bleeding but a light appears from the wound and closes the opening. The bleeding ceases instantly from the wound. Gurtruit looks like he is pleased by his action, but he automatically turns afraid as Tara arises, growling and baring her teeth. His legs begin to tremble, then his entire body, and he decides to make a run for it, dropping the shovel and crying out for help at the top of his lungs.

Tara lets him get some distance and suddenly bolts after him with great speed and immediately tackles him to the ground. Gurtruit still cries out for help and tries to push her off, but it's no use. Tara and her race are Wolfinoids. They are taller, faster, and stronger than us. Within a blink of an eye, she tears right into him. His cries for help turn into blood-curdling screams as Tara rips him apart. It's such a gruesome scene I am witnessing—every human organ being ripped out and bones being broken and torn with loads of blood spewing out. Within seconds, Gurtruit immediately dies and Tara turns around to look at me.

Her mouth and clothes are just covered in blood; some of Gurtruit's organs hang from her mouth. The sight makes me so terrified that my broken ribs throb in pain, making me hurl out blood so hard that I begin to lose consciousness.

"Somebody, get down here and take Nos to my bedroom. Stabilize him, don't heal him! That's an order!" shouts Tara and then I fully pass out on the sand.

CHAPTER NINETEEN
A Lovely Surprise and the Truth
Location: A bedroom
Date: Unknown
Time: Unknown

I DREAM ABOUT THE fight. I dream about the large number of spectators cheering with the pleasure of me being murdered. I dream that I almost die, but suddenly, Tara arrives and ends the battle with her soft ice shock wave that pushes me and Gurtruit away from one another. I see her turn around, looking at me with sadness, concern, and gentleness. She begins to walk toward me. Each step creates a beeping sound. The sound just gets louder and louder every time she gets closer. The noise is so loud that the dream and my subconscious dissipate. I can feel my mind and body slowly waking up. My sense of touch returns and as I move, I feel the surface extremely soft and comfortable. My sense of smell slightly returns and I can barely breathe in the fragrance that smells like wilderness like a pine forest that has been just softly soaked by the rain. I can also smell the fragrance of rain-showered flowers. Actually, reactivating my nerves, the rest of my body feels damp. Am I lying outside, in the forest? On the flip side, those two fragrances are so good. I take a deeper breath through my nose, but an enormous amount of pain rolls through my face and chest.

I let out quiet moans of pain through my mouth. I want to return to my deeper slumber and replay the memory of Tara approaching me with caution and gentleness. Nonetheless, the beeping sound keeps on, so I guess I'm back in the hospital, hooked back to another E.K.G. However, I don't remember the hospital bed feeling this soft and the room smelling like a lightly soaked pine forest with flowers blooming and feeling damp. Then, another texture of some substance comes down to my body. The substance feels really warm, like being wrapped up in a blanket and sitting next to a fireplace on a cold winter night. Focusing more on the substance, it feels soft like skin with fingers spread out. My mind fully kicks in and tells me it's a hand, then this hand lightly strokes my forehead.

The hand, the smells, and the fabric are so inviting that I decide to open my eyes. Once I do, the E.K.G. picks up my racing heart; a familiar tune from a particular video game soundtrack starts playing in my head because the hand belongs to a beautiful woman and that woman is Tara Borin.

She smiles at me the same way when I awoke on my first day in the hospital here in Sparta. Her eyes are filled with comfort and gladness. She continues rubbing my forehead and glancing down, I am still bare-chested with a large bandage.

"Hello, Nos," Tara says to me very softly.

I move my eyes back at her for a moment and then away from her calm eyes, curious if she's wearing the same hospital cloak that she wore on that same day, but she isn't. Instead, she's wearing a white, plush lingerie around her waist, like a thong, and a plush bra on her chest that just wraps around to the back, hiding no lines of her beautiful shoulders that connect to her neck. Her legs, feet, arms, and body are completely exposed. Plus, she's wearing white feather earrings that have the shade of ice blue on the ends. Looking at her replaces my fear with love. The warm fuzzy feeling reawakens in my heart and soon, spreads out through the rest of my body like a wildfire.

Tara keeps on smiling and looks up at the glass tablet, "You're starting to fall in love with me. That's good, that's really good. I guess we don't need this silly machine anymore." She turns it off and removes the wireless adapter from my right hand's middle finger; at that moment, she places her right hand softly around my face. Looking back at her beautiful body, she is also built. She has a four-pack, strong slim legs, and strong slim arms. All in all, Tara definitely looks like an angel.

"You like what you see?" she says, gesturing with her free hands up and down her almost-nude body.

I just slowly nod, feeling completely astounded and speechless.

"Good." She brings her head down to mine, lightly licking my forehead, and continues, "I want to replace the scene that you witnessed two days ago. I want you to feel like you're in heaven and feel completely safe. I am sorry that you had to see my reaction back there, but I promise you that I won't let anybody take you and harm you again. Anyway, how do you feel?" She goes back to rubbing my forehead.

Hold on! I've been out for two damn days? What's the date? What's the time? Aw shit, my friends are probably freaking out and still are at this moment!"

At the same exact moment, she moves her hand from my forehead and places two of her fingers on my lips. "Shhh. It's okay. Don't worry about the date nor the time. If you're questioning how your friends are reacting to this situation, I've told my father and Sean to tell them that you are safe with me. For now, it's my turn to heal you in my own fashion. Again, how do you feel?"

I slowly lift my head to examine the damage. Looking down at my chest, it's covered in deep blue and black bruises. Laying on top of them is the same bandage covering the cut from the spear Max thrashed at me. Looking further down, I'm relieved that I'm wearing white sweat pants and that I'm not lying completely naked next to Tara because I don't think I'm ready to have intercourse with her. Examining my knuckles, the right is completely bruised, bleeding a little, and swollen, while it's almost completely opposite in the left. I try to breathe through my nose again, but it hurts so much that I lean forward while holding it with both of my hands. I decide to breathe through my mouth, but once my jaw opens, it also hurts beyond the one-to-ten scale.

"Okay, okay. I think I should start healing you right now. Just lay back down and take it easy," Tara says, gently pushing me back onto the soft fabric that has soft, plush pillows stacked up.

Next, Tara sits up, cross-legged, and reaches behind her. Again, her body is slim, rugged, and beautiful that I decide to move my eyes away because I respect a woman's private parts and I believe I should not stare at them for a very long time.

Tara laughs, "You don't need to feel embarrassed. You can look at me all you want since you're mine forever. I trust that my father told you that in our race, we women pick whichever man we want, fall in love, and have sex with them to seal the relationship after four days."

I nod my head in response, keeping my mouth shut to reduce the pain, but I am completely thrown off when she says that they have sex four days after they meet. So, if I was out for two days, oh man, I have two days left being a virgin.

Tara cocks her head sideways while she reveals two granite bowls with cylinder mixers and interesting-looking ingredients and says, "Have you ever had sex, Nos?"

This time, I shake my head left and right saying, "No."

Tara shrugs and starts preparing whatever she's going to create, and keeps on talking, "It doesn't have to happen in two days, well, in a day now. We can take this relationship slowly and learn about one another."

Thank you, that sounds a lot better.

"But I would like to do it soon since I've been waiting for a hundred years."

Really? Say what?

She just laughs at my reaction and continues on with her business, "Heh, you look so funny when some outrageous stuff are told to you. I really like that."

The way she says that makes me very curious about her. The tone in her voice sounds like she knows and has known me for a very long time. How could that be even possible?

Anyway, I am just watching her, adding the ingredients into the bowls and grinding them into smaller bits. She reaches over me to grab something and as I follow her arms, she grabs some glass jars on a shelving unit above me filled with clear liquids inside. Surprisingly, as her hands touch them, they begin to glow certain colors like purple, ice blue (no doubt), pink, boysenberry purple, and ocean blue. When she begins to descend back to her seating position, she looks at me and I look at her and again, she just smiles with giggles slipping through her lips. It brings me happiness and I try my best to smile back. As time progresses, water keeps on falling on us, and looking up, I see indeed a large pine tree with roots that grow around the rock shelves. It's fully healthy, green, and has waterdrops falling off the branches and pine needles.

Slowly lifting my head a little bit more, I am indeed laying on a bed that has a fake or real fur covering it, shaped like a large oval, and has a three-step stairway all the way around it. Looking beyond are more pine trees with the inclusion of cedar, sycamore, and a couple of weeping willows all fully blossoming with leaves and looking very green. All of these trees are in a cavern, so how could they be surviving in this environment? My curiosity grows and I do my best to sit up, but Tara places her warm hands on my shoulders.

"Are we a little adventurous today? I'll show my chamber after I fully heal you," she says and gently pushes me back down, again.

On that occasion, Tara begins humming a tune that slowly sounds a bit Celtic as she continues grinding, mixing, and pouring away. Later, she pours the liquid that she finally created in one of the granite bowls, pours it into the next, and repeats the action a couple of times until the liquid in the first bowl begins to glow. Tara sets the other tools on the shelf, grabs the bowl in her hands, and begins singing the Celtic song to it, then the liquid glows brighter and brighter. Soon after, the song becomes a chant and her ice blue, calm eyes begin to glow; the same mist channels down her arms, and around her hands, it begins to glow.

Soon, Tara stops chanting and looks at me, "Are you ready to be healed?"

I nod with some excitement.

"It's going to feel cold, like the device your kind uses to numb the swelling. Nonetheless, there will be no pain."

At that point, she drinks from the bowl but does not swallow, climbs on top of me, brings down her muzzle, having both of her hands cupped around her mouth, and finally starts licking my face very slowly. Her breath, tongue, and hands do feel cold, but the swelling and the pain around my face begin to fade away. Tara starts at the right side of my jaw, then slowly moves her head and hands up to my cheek. Next, she moves over to my nose, rubbing it gently, then to my left cheek, up to my eyebrow, and finally down the jaw. Miraculously, I can fully breathe through my nose without a problem although when my chest moves, it still aches. The outside of my entire jaw doesn't hurt anymore. Soon, Tara puts two of her fingers through my lips and gently opens my mouth. As her mouth molds around mine, she sticks her tongue in and starts licking my gums. When her tongue passes by some of my teeth that have fillings in them, the coldness stings the nerves but subsides the pain. What surprises me is that I feel her tongue hitting some gaps between my teeth.

Did I have some of my teeth knocked out during the fight?

Apparently yes, yet as the tongues move on, I can feel new teeth coming through the gums. Man, does it feel extremely weird and awesome. Tara continues licking around my mouth, perhaps making my teeth clean, white, and all-natural again. Looking into her eyes, they're halfway open, yet they are filled with pure love and care. To me, I do feel love pumping through my heart and out of my body. I feel no stress; I feel completely serene. I've never felt this way in my entire life up to this point. Not having my adrenaline galloping through my veins twenty-four-seven feels really nice.

After healing my mouth, Tara moves away, sending a smile that I send back with pleasure and no pain. Next, she scoots down, slowly pulls away the bandage on my chest, bends over, and repeats the same process. She then rubs her hands around in circles that make the dark purple and black bruises disappear. I again breathe deeply and there's no pain on the front side of my body. Yet, as my back arches, the wounds I received from the whip sting like hell again. Still taking her time, she grabs my right hand and licks the knuckles and the rest of the hand slowly, savoring the moment. She does the same thing with the left, except in a quicker fashion since there were little nicks on it. After that, Tara moves back to my right side. She signals with her index finger that I should roll onto my stomach and takes another sip from the bowl probably to reignite the power of the potion in her mouth. I follow her command and rollover. Tara slowly and cautiously peels away the bandages; as fresh, moist air touches the wounds, it sends off the pain muscle on high alert in my head and I decide to muffle my moans of pain into the pillows. With no hesitation, I feel Tara bending down and repeating the process. From what I'm feeling, it seems she has one index finger in front of the mouth, pushing up, her tongue following, and another index finger in tow. While feeling the movement of the tongue and fingers, I count eight lines. I was whipped eight times before being dropped down into that arena and had to fight to the death.

Tara rolls me back to the previous position, and she's still smiling with eyes filled with joy and pleasure. The potion still lingers in her mouth. I ask, "Are you finished?"

"Not yet," she mumbles as she places her hands around my face, comes back in, interlocks my mouth with hers, and blows the remaining of the potion in and down my mouth and throat at such a gentle force.

The force spreads around my heart, which a lot of people believe is where the soul is located, and throughout my body. This action lasts a good minute and she pulls away with the mist of the potion dissipating from her mouth as I, too, see it disappearing from me. In the end, I feel like a completely new man.

"What was—?" I begin to ask.

"That," she states with a smile, "was for healing your soul. From a distance, I smelled great pain coming from you, especially from your soul. Now, you are a healed person one hundred percent. Through and through."

She stands up immediately, stretches her right hand toward me, and I take it with mine. Getting up, out of nowhere, a chilly breeze blows through, making me shiver. Tara walks around me, analyzing me with her eyes and letting her finger travel up and down my body.

In one simple step, she's behind me, pressing her warm body up against mine, rubbing my shoulders, and then she breathes into my ear, "You are so skinny. Why?"

"I'm a very, hyperactive person."

"Is that why they call you Nos? Because of your adrenaline rush?"

"Yeah," I sigh out.

Tara moves her hands down to my chest, pressing firmly on my skin and taking deep breaths of my scent, and says, "It's so nice to smell you. When the stage curtains closed for no reason, I began to worry. As some time ticked by, your friends began to wonder. My concern was also rising and I decide to look for you on the stage. When I got up there with the stage normally lit, you weren't there, but there a few drops of your own blood on the floor. Your scent was very faint from the blood. Nonetheless, my senses still told me where you were taken to."

Another cool breeze comes through out of the blue and I tremble again. Tara bends down, picks up a thick, plush quilt, and throws it around us. Next, she leads us out of the large, sunken bed toward some couches that are surrounded by a fire pit with a fire blazing strongly. Again, the fire is one of those special-colored ones, the color of ice blue. Next to some of these couches are tables and only one has food and drinks on it. As we begin to sit down, Tara lays down, props her back up against the armrest, and pulls me down to lay on top of her. The vibe throughout her and her bed chamber are completely calm and steady. I look up at Tara and she brings down her head and licks me affectionately on my face.

Then, she grabs a banana from the table and hands it to me, "Eat. I'll tell you more."

I take it and bite it. Tara continues, "Once I was following your scent, it led me down strange tunnels that were built in secret. I had Sean and his men following me during my search. In moments, we hear cheers echoing off the walls. At that exact point, the faint trail of your blood stopped and we decide to follow the sound of the cheers. When the cheers got louder, we entered a small area where the tunnel had several other ones going in different directions. I told Sean to split up his men and as I gave more directions, our ears perked forward when we heard Marcus' voice. We immediately split, I took the tunnel ahead of me and sprinted down. Soon, I hear you yell, then another person yells back at you. I quicken my pace and when I exited the tunnel, I see you and that fat bastard running toward each other. Shouting. Seeing you injured made me angry, thereby I summoned my sorcery, sending out that shockwave to end the fight and leaping from the stands. In the end, I saved your life. I took care of those two idiots. Loads of people were arrested and given trials. Aside from that, thank you so much for playing that song for my birthday."

"You're very welcome," I softly answer with gratitude for performing that song and for saving my life. Without wasting more time, Tara hands me more food and later, hands me a glass jar that may have milk in it. I analyze it with some suspicion. Before I can take a drink, she moves us both upright.

"It's okay. It's just milk."

I sip it; the taste seems off but really good. It's probably better than cow milk. Or is it cow milk? I should ask Tara, but another question forms in my mind.

"Something on your mind, Nos?"

"Ah, yeah. I've been curious for a while. From what I'm about to say is that I'm not trying to sound offensive."

"Well now, I'm really curious about it. You can ask me anything."

I take a deep breath, putting the question together and breathing out, "The way you have been looking at me, treating me, and sounding like you've known me for a very long time have me confused. I've only seen you twice and talked to you up to this moment. How do you know me so well?"

Tara just lowers her head and huffs a laugh, "Let's stand up and I'll show you."

We do and Tara lets the quilt fall to the floor. Next, she stands behind me again, places her hands on my hips, and slightly jerks them up as if I've been thrown into the air. Next, she comes around me, brushing the tips of her fingers across my face with a wink in a flirty way. The only memory I have of that same motion is when Ryia threw me up on that boat and did the same action. Now, I start to replay both actions in my head and compare them.

Within minutes, it all hits me. I look at Tara, completely astounded.

"Ryia?"

Tara just throws her back laughing, "Ha, ha, ha, ha! Yeah, it's me, Nos. Ryia."

I fall back onto the couch. "How can that be possible?"

"I'll tell you everything." She sits next to me placing her left arm over my shoulders.

"Have you been told that we use animatronics to simulate ourselves?"

I nod in agreement.

"Well, you can tell that I'm the princess. Actually, make that the future queen of Sparta, but I'll tell you about that later. Anyway, I can't leave the premise of this kingdom. When my father, mother, and I received the news that our enemy has escaped and was ravaging your planet, we immediately opened up portals to transport all of this here. Once my father and I arrived, we were flabbergasted by the scenery of this place, but more shocked by how thin your forests were. Other than that, as this kingdom camp was being set up, multiple search parties were being sent out. I wanted to go and explore this whole new world, but my father said no. So, I went to our sorcery tent, extracted a small bit of my D.N.A., and created my own animatronic."

"After changing the color of the fur and eyes, I came back here to control it. Then, I joined Ulric, Althalos, and Forthwind. Those three guys did not know about my true identity and they let me tag along. After leaving and exploring the northern states for about a couple of days, we got news about you from another search party and that they gave you the box of magic matches and that portal device. I don't know why Ulric told you that they were the ones who gave that stuff to you. Anyway, that search party watched you from a distance. What's interesting is that one of them can predict the future in two days' time and that they told us that you were going to that city called Green Bay trying to rescue your family. With that info, we sprinted to the fullest to Green Bay to meet you there, Nos."

"When we arrived, of course, you remember there was a blizzard. We waited for you. After nearly an hour passed, the portal opened and you came through. Seeing you with your cowboy hat on made me fall in love with you. As we approached you, my heart really sunk when your hat flew off in the wind and you looked so disappointed at it. All I wanted to do was to comfort you. So, after coaxing you to talk to us, I was really starting to fall in love with you."

"Then, when our mission to bring you here went to shit and when all the three of them died, it really had me worried. When my animatronic died, seeing you shed tears brought me to tears. I cried and prayed really hard to God that you make it here alive every day. On the day I decide to overlook the kingdom from my balcony, I heard the medical horn being blown and that brought my gaze down to the West Gate. When I saw you severely injured but alive, I cried out in joy and started to make a plan to meet you, greet you, and heal you in my own fashion. In the end, you are with me and that's what counts."

Holy shit. I am absolutely blown away by her story. Now, I truly understand her feelings toward me. Also, my feelings for Ryia, well Tara, now have gotten stronger and I don't want to ever leave this beautiful woman's side. Ever.

"Are you okay, Will?" Tara asks. I lean forward with no hesitation and I kiss her back passionately. While I'm retreating back to my end of the couch, Tara grabs my chin and returns the kiss. Then, a glint of light comes through a window.

I get up and move toward that light and turns out, it's being blocked by thick, dark purple curtains. Slightly looking through them is a pair of French doors that lead out to the balcony where Tara stood and saw me being brought in. Pulling back one of the curtains, I get immediately blinded by the sunlight and I stumble back, shielding my eyes. Within a moment, I yawn and Tara wraps her arms around me, gently swaying me left to right. The exhaustion rolls in very heavily and I let out another yawn.

"Let's go back to bed, baby," she says while she strokes my head and I nod in agreement. Returning back to the large, oval bed, Tara waves her left arm at the fire pit and it goes out. Some other light sources also begin to go dim and finally go black once we reach the bed.

Tara grabs hold of my body and lowers me gently back onto the soft fabric while humming a Celtic lullaby that also increases my exhaustion. Soon, she slowly lays and wraps around me like an infant and pulls another thick, plush quilt to keep us warm because the temperature in her bed chamber begins to drop quickly to a point I can see my own breath rising from my nose and mouth. On the other hand, feeling the warmth from Tara's body makes me warm within a minute.

As I'm about to go to sleep, Tara whispers this message in the dark, "Welcome to Sparta, Will Young. Sleep well tonight." After that, I drift off to sleep.

CHAPTER TWENTY
From Blue Color to Royalty
Location: Tara Borin's Bedroom
Date: December 3, 2014
Time: 8:00 AM

IT IS A BEAUTIFUL morning. Last night or yesterday . . . just wow. I thought the events that took place were a dream. Waking up this morning, I'm really warm and comfortable. It's a bit unusual, yet the memory of the events that happened makes me turn my head around, only to find a beautiful creature that's still asleep and still has her body wrapped around mine. My simple movements awaken her and she opens her eyes and also throws a smile.

I smile and retract my head back. "I guess what happened yesterday wasn't a dream."

Tara moves her head above mine, licks my face, and replies, "Not at all. You were great last night."

"I didn't do anything. You're the one who did all the healing which was the most interesting sensation I ever went through, especially when you stuck your tongue in my mouth and licked my gums to bring back my teeth."

"Ha, ha. That's true."

Then I turn onto my back to look right at her, lacing my hands together behind my head. She moves her right hand across my chest looking sorrowful as her hand traces the curvature of my ribcage, and rubs the pit where my stomach sinks inward when I'm lying down. Tara turns her attention to the tree above us and blows air out of her mouth, then a sorcery of lights come to life and light up the bed. She looks back at me and still continues to let her hands press down and feel my body.

"I can feel every bone. Don't you ever eat?"

"You stated the same thing last time."

"I know, I know. But I think it's time that you should be on my diet and workout schedule. Speaking of food, let's get something to eat."

After she said that, we both get up with energy and she leads me to her large wardrobe that's constructed out of cherry oakwood. The designs totally represent her Celtic and Medieval culture and people. She opens the doors of the wardrobe and the inside looks like a large walk-in closet; on the right side is her clothes and jewelry; on the left side, surprisingly, are my clothes with a couple of robes that have very different designs and colors. Tara walks in, turns to the left, and starts picking through the items. From where I'm at, I just lean against one of the doors, smiling at her. Tara opens up a drawer and pulls out a camouflage leather belt with a buckle that says "Air Force" and a pair of dark blue jeans; within a flash, she tosses them at me. When I'm about to catch them, she then throws the same cloak that Tristen gave me on the day I attended their church, plus the hat. After that, a white shirt lands on my head.

"Get dressed," Tara says in a happy tone.

I obey, start to get ready, and within minutes, I am ready to take on the day. But, oh man, as I turn around, my eyes just widen because Tara is just standing in the door frame straight-up naked.

"Aw, man!" Immediately turning back around, shaking my head in disbelief, I say, "Tara. You're being such a femme fatale."

"Oh?" As she comes over where I stand and wraps her warm arms around my shoulders, she says, "So, you're saying that I bring destruction onto you when you look at my beauty."

"Yeah."

Again, she laughs, "Oh, Nos, you have to get used to it. I mean it's nice that you respect a woman's privacy and I'm glad you do, but I have desires to really settle and be intertwined with you." She steps away. I can hear the movement of clothes flying through the air and she comes in front of me fully clothed and wearing a marvelous tiara.

Next, she takes my hand and we both exit her bed chamber. Going through the doors, we enter a brightly lit hallway. The same carpet, as before, still comes through here, and what makes this hallway bright is that it's painted white, walls and ceiling, and has the same light fixtures that illuminate the throne room. The ceiling is much higher than the other ceilings in the other passageways I've walked down and running down the center is the same navy blue, marble beam. To our right is a stairway that probably spirals upward to King Borin's and her friend's bed chambers. Tara tugs at my hand and leads me down the passageway; we walk in silence, passing very large portraits of Wolfinoids that served in the military and the kings and queens. Other portraits are much bigger than the others because they show the kings and queens that ruled this kingdom.

Yet, a question begins to formulate in my head. If Tara is one hundred years old but still looks like to be in her twenties, how old are the other officials? On the other hand, my thoughts are interrupted when we both come to a flight of stairs that also slowly curve downward. While we descend, I take notice of Christmas decorations that are green tinsel with glowing lights wrapped around the banister and solid glass balls of light blue, white, green, and red hanging from the ceiling; soon, Christmas reeves from small to large sizes hang at the walls of the curving stairwell. As we set foot on a different lower level, my jaw drops and my eyes get wide.

"Whoa."

The stairway leads into a very large royal dining hall with the walls and ceiling continuing the white color but has the same navy-blue marble columns with gold pieces on the top just like the ones down in the throne room. Surprisingly, the purple carpet turns into ocean blue and has silver lines running along the edges. The light source is still the same as the exact type of chandeliers that hang in the throne room except on a smaller scale. All around the hall are all sorts of decorations that celebrate the most wonderful time of the year. Hanging around it are navy-blue marble beams holding up the ceiling down to the very large mahogany table with matching chairs that also have cushions on the armrests, backs, and bottoms in the same color as the carpet. On the table lays numerous and various amounts of food from pancakes to different types of breakfast foods.

At the other end of the hall and table stands King Borin and his associates, some I recognize. When Tara and I step further into the hall, King Borin ceases conversation as he takes notice of us. His expression from calm turns into sadness when our eyes meet.

"Oh, Will Young. I am so sorry." At the same time, he begins a fast pace toward me with his arms open. Tara steps aside to let her father softly crash into me and gives me a huge hug.

Then he steps away. "I am so sorry that you were taken, forcibly beaten, and were forced to fight."

"I truly accept your apology, but I don't blame anyone of you. Nobody could've predicted it. It was spontaneous, although the fight," I shrug both my shoulders, "was truly personal. That guy Tara tore up was an old elementary school bully and so were his friends. Yet, I had the situation under control; I've been waiting for years to get even with that guy and I was ready to end his life," looking at Tara, I continue, "I am grateful that you ended the fight and I'm very glad that you ripped that bastard apart." Tara gives out a sly smile and looking confused if that was a compliment or a complaint. For King Borin, he just pats one of my shoulders and lets out a sigh.

"Well, it does look like you were well taken care of," he says with a confident smile, looking at his daughter.

I look at both with a smile, "Indeed."

"What are we standing around for? Let's have breakfast," says Tara.

"Indeed," says King Borin, "and discuss how your life is going to change, Will."

Say what? My life is going to be changed? This is going to be an interesting morning.

We all gather at the opposite end of the table. Joining the three of us are Admiral Zachariah and Lupa Blitz, Rollo Greenwood; the entire group of Tara's friends that include Whitney Silver, Crystal Tundra, Dawn Sunset, and Faith Solar. Then, Maddox Nightrunner, Trent Wild, Gothraigh Borin, and Cora Stone. I'm very curious about what services Maddox, Trent, Gothraigh, and Cora provide to the kingdom. I know those things would be explained to me once we've all have our breakfast. As time goes on, we all don't waste another minute as we dig into the food and during the meal, it occurs to me that it's strange and cool to be the only human to sit at a large table, be surrounded by new creatures, and learn and see a new culture that has kept the medieval times alive to this day. It also amazes me that they share a balance of sorcery and very advanced technology while they maintain the government of a monarchy. Yet, how do they transfer the source of power and authority to another Wolfinoid if the royal family or anybody else has the power of immortality? Plus, how do the people of Sparta and Troy not fall into the annoyance of the authority who's been in power for all eternity and try to restrain themselves from revolting? On the flip side, the real question should be, what's going to happen to me? Specifically.

Being wrapped up in my questions, I feel a warm hand touching mine which makes me jolt a little bit.

"Are you okay, Will?" Tara asks. When I turn my head to look at her, I see concern in her face and eyes.

"I don't know. I'm a little stressed about some things and I'm very curious about how your government works."

Tara leans closer to me. "I do sense some anxiety from you with the mixture of curiosity, but what are you mainly stressing over?"

Before I can answer, King Borin claps his hands twice and some servants come through a couple of passageways and start clearing out the plates, platters, and excreta from the table. Once the cleaning was done, King Borin leans forward and laces his fingers together, looking a bit serious.

He sighs through his nose, looks at me, and says, "Right, let's get down to business. Due to your current situation, Will, which is good, you are now part of this royal family, and being part of this family is that you need to know how this government works. Thus, knowing how to be a king, although Tara is the next person to rule and you'll be second-in-command if she's ill or doing some tasks."

"So, from what I'm hearing, I'll be the vice president and Tara will be the president of Sparta?" I ask.

"Yes," says Borin. "Our government sort of works like your government system. Also, this is the perfect time to know what Cora, Trent, Gothraigh, and Maddox do." Then he nods to them as their cue to speak.

"I guess I'll go first," says Cora, in a confident tone. The woman sits across from me at the table. Her clothing resembles the medieval era and royalty. Her fur is brown but in a lighter shade than Tara's. Her eyes are also ice blue. Her hair is pulled into a long ponytail that lapses over the hood of her dark purple cloak that has silver stripes on the edges of the sleeves and a stripe running up and down the center where the zipper is. On the left side of her chest is the symbol of Sparta also sewn in silver thread. The jewelry that she's wearing is simple yet elegant. Her earrings are created out of glass that swirl around her ears and in some areas form into little waves colored in bright red and orange, probably to represent fire or lava. On her head is a tiara that has a small, gold chain, and hanging between and just above her eyes is a piece of glass forming into a drop with the same color on her earrings.

"I'm Cora Stone and it's very nice to meet you, Will. Or would you like to be called Nos?"

"Either one and likewise. What do you do, Cora?"

"Well, I'm the queen's head assistant and I teach Tara," she says, gesturing with her right hand and a smile to Tara, "of how to be a queen. Which brings me to this question, is it alright with you that I take a picture of you and send it to Tara's mother? Ever since I sent the word back to her, she's been dying to know what you look like."

Whoa. Whoa. A picture of me being sent to Tara's mother. Man, this feels a bit awkward. Oh no, please not now.

At this moment, my heart races again. The feeling of embarrassment rises up in my head, making the skin on my arms, neck, and face turn red.

"Nos, are you okay?" asks Tara with a hint of concern in her voice.

I swallow. "I'm sorry. It's just that . . . when something like this happens, I get nervous and feel embarrassed. That's why my skin is turning red." And yet, my skin gets redder and burns hotter.

I look at Tara, then at Cora, and I try to take a couple of breaths to calm down. Cora on the other hand looks a bit ashamed, decides that she'll hold off on the picture, and wait until I tell her I'm ready.

I look around the table and ask if there's anybody else who wants to introduce themselves and tell me their positions.

"I'll go next," says Trent Wild. This man has black fur with some brown appearing around his muzzle and hands. His eyes are green and his hair is cut in a military format. His cloak is black with purple stripes forming three separate arrows underneath a crescent that forms a box, yet at the bottom, forms into an arrow to complete the shape. Inside the box is a solid-filled symbol of the kingdom in the same color thread and on the front are a few metals of award for doing combat in the field or having executed well-thought-out plans for battle.

"It is a pleasure to meet you, Will. As you can see from my appearance, I am the Tactical Officer of the Army for Sparta. Rollo and I will be introducing and teaching you how to place and give out orders to your army."

"Um, wow. But don't you mean Tara's army since she's the next ruler of Sparta?"

Everybody at the table burst out laughing. For me, I'm just sitting here feeling like an idiot, yet I come to the point of also laughing.

Trent gasps for air and looks back at me. "Yes, yes, that is true. But still, you need to know your own military."

"Okay," I answer, also gasping for air. "That sounds reasonable. Anybody else?"

"I'll go," says Gothraigh Borin. Now, with this man sitting on the right side of the table, near the head, he's wearing the same outfit as his brother's, yet the jewelry is less fancy than King Borin's and his hair is combed back to look professional. Plus, he looks a bit younger. But if he, Tara, and the rest of the royal family are immortal, how in the hell do their facial features show signs of age?

"Is there something on your mind?" Gothraigh asks.

"Sort of, but please, tell me what you do?"

"Well, I'm the new right-hand man for my brother and I very do enjoy this position. I am very sorry that you had faced Marcus. I've never really trusted that man. Plus, I agree with my brother. He wasn't a very fine suitor for my niece."

"Aw, c'mon uncle, don't embarrass me," Tara replies, throwing out a smile and trying to hide her face in her hand.

Gothraigh smiles back then leans forward. Elbows on the table, hands laced together, and looking very curious at me, he says, "But tell me this, how were you able to throw that fat bastard out of your tent?"

I look back at him, leaning onto the table but placing my right arm on it and looking serious at him. "The reason I got the name Nos is because of my adrenaline rush, which activated because of the hatred I had for him and that is why I was able to throw him out to the best of my strength."

"And did you have the intention to end him?" He tries to hold back a smile.

"Yes, sir," I reply, still looking and sounding serious at him.

Gothraigh lets his smile out and leans back into the chair, "I like him, Cedric. I really do. I think he's a very fine suitor for my niece."

"My thoughts exactly," says King Borin or should I address him as Cedric. I don't know, but when he replies, he looks at his young brother with a smile.

"Who else hasn't introduce themselves to me?" I ask.

"That'll be me. I'm Maddox Nightrunner, I'm the head of all sorcery of the kingdom, and I'm the teacher for Tara, Whitney, Crystal, Dawn, and Faith."

The sound of his voice also sounds Irish but in a heavier tone than Sean's. His robe is created out of the normal blue fabric and is decorated to represent space that includes galaxies, stars, and planets near and far in such rich colors. The color of his eyes is also green, but a bit brighter; half of his head is made into spikes with tips dyed blue to match his robe while the other half is also gelled and covers his left eye. On the right side of his face is an awesome tribal tattoo that circles around his eye and travels to the backside of his neck. His choices in jewelry are a small, silver chain necklace that has a crescent moon and a simple silver ring earring in his left ear. I think I'm going to really enjoy hanging out with this guy if and when I have the chance.

"That's really cool," I told him, "What type of sorcery do you teach?"

He smiles, "All kinds, mate. One of them is teaching students of how to use their staffs to the fullest advantage if the creator has a very strong, spiritual connection with his staff. Which," he ducks under the table, reaching for something, "brings my attention to yours."

He sets down my staff onto the table. Everybody here leans forward to take a better look. I'm surprised because I completely forgot about my staff. The memories of practicing and playing at

Tara's party, being taken and forced to fight, and finally waking up in Tara's bed chamber and being healed by her rush through my head all at once.

"Wow," says Trent, "that is indeed one interesting-looking staff. The style, especially the glass orb, I've never seen that kind of design ever in my life."

"Indeed," says Cora who sits on the left side of Maddox.

"Well, let's not waste any time. Let's see what it can do," says Crystal.

"Agreed. Well, come on, Will, stop sitting there and come over here," says Maddox with enthusiasm.

I immediately get up, walk around, and as I approach him, he gets up and hands my staff over with care. Looking at him, his face simply states both enthusiasm and curiosity. The same goes for everybody else around the table. I examine my own staff in my hands taking in the beauty and craftsmanship and just simply being amazed at how it turned out when Atticus unlatched the top half of the molding case.

"Atticus told me that the source of power that comes off it smells and feels like justice and authority. Do you want to seek justice and have authority in your presence, Will?" Maddox asks.

I stare at the staff a little more and then look up to him, "Yeah. I guess I do, especially to eradicate your enemies from my homeland, the homeland of the United States of America."

Simultaneously setting the butt of the staff down onto the floor, the exact ping noise sounds off, admiral blue shows, and in the flame, the glass orb starts to glow. While the glow begins to brighten, the same sound of a heavy magnetic machine rings out and gets louder, encouraging me to tighten the grip of my right hand around the shaft. Looking around, the expressions vary: the looks on Tara's friends' faces show a bit of fear but mostly amazement; Tara herself is in complete amazement and I think she's more in love with me as she places her elbows on the table and puts her head on top of her hands; looking past her, Sean eases further into his seat showing that he's uncomfortable for being in the same room where my staff is; his father, Rollo, also shows the same signs but tries to show some interest; looking at both Admiral Zachariah and Blitz, they both have their ears perking forward and looking interested; turning my attention to Cora, she's in complete astonishment as she places one of her hands over her breast, trying to remain calm; looking down on her side, Trent is trying to remain calm, but some fear shows in his eyes while being completely amazed by the sight before him; looking down at the head of the table, both Gothraigh and Cedric get up and begin to walk to where both Maddox and I stand with caution in their strides; and finally, looking at Maddox, he is both amazed and terrified from what he sees, slowly backs away from it, and returns to his seat.

Looking back up, Cedric and Gothraigh still approach with caution, yet looking at their faces, both of them are really curious what my staff can do. Looking back onto the table, I think it should be time to ease down the power. So, I slowly loosen my grip and take heavy breathes to calm down; my staff acknowledges as it, too, begins to slowly power down. This gives me an idea. If I told a verbal command, will it obey it? Let's give it a shot.

Looking right at it, I speak to it, "Power down." Miraculously, it obeys and shuts off with no hesitation. Some of the guys let out sighs of relief and both Cedric and Gothraigh stop a few feet away from me still expressing caution with a few hints of curiosity.

"May we observe your staff, Will?" Cedric slowly lays out his hands. With caution and order, I swiftly hand my staff over to him and both brothers examine the beauty of my weapon. They stare at it for a solid five minutes, which makes me feel uneasy. The silence just grows stronger and stronger that some drops of sweat start forming on the back of my neck.

Cedric takes in my emotions and breaks the silence, "Maddox?" still looking at the staff.

"Yes, sir?"

"Are you capable of taking in another student?"

Maddox looks at me with curiosity, then turns his attention to Tara and her friends where all of them start nodding their heads, looks back at me with a smile, and says, "Of course, sir. I'll be glad to take in another student since Tara, Crystal, Whitney, Dawn, and Faith have advanced to an area to help me out in teaching this young human."

"Very good," he replies, looking over his shoulder and handing back the staff.

On the flip side, something in both Cedric's and Gothraigh's eyes throws me off like they both forgot to tell me something. To further increase my curiosity, Cedric looks at Tara with bad news in his eyes. Tara immediately gets it and shoots back with a pleading look while slightly shaking her head left and right. Cedric tightens his stare, trying to force his daughter to say something bad. Yet, Tara continues her pleading expression and lets out small whimpers. From what I'm seeing, I feel like something is totally bad and it might involve me; the dews of sweat build up more.

"Tara . . ." says Cedric in a stern voice.

"No father," Tara replies in horror and plead.

"Is there something wrong?" I cautiously ask, slowly backing away, yet placing my left hand on an open chair preparing to bolt for it.

Both brothers let out a heavy sigh and Gothraigh answers, "Not really, but since you're now part of the royal family," looking at me that whatever he's about to say is so painful, "there is one thing. There's a catch, as you humans say."

Tara stands up abruptly to cease the talk from her uncle and father, "No uncle! I just healed him last night! He's still new to all of this!"

"He still has to know, daughter," Cedric replies with a growl

"What's the, um, catch, sirs?" I ask, taking another step back.

Cedric looks at me seriously yet sad. "Tara has to turn you, my boy."

"Turn me? Into one of you?" All of them nod their heads. Tara falls back into her chair, hides her face, and lets out some tears.

"Yes, my love," Tara replies, slightly choking on air, "turn you into one of us, which means I have to literally bite you so that you can become immortal and rule with me until we have grown and raised children, then they find their mates."

"Holy shit," I say while almost falling backward onto the floor. I immediately grab the chair to stop and pull myself back up to my feet. Fuck. I got to be turned into one of them? How much time do I have now being a human? Shit, I should've known this was going to happen. Aw, hell, who am I kidding? We humans can't predict our own futures; there wouldn't be any way I could've seen this coming.

I look back, frantic. "So, that's how your kingdom works? A king and queen vice versa rule for an entirety, have kids, and still rule until their firstborn finds a partner?"

"Yes," replies Cedric sounding calm. "That's how our kingdom works. It's the same thing in Troy. But for you, in your current position, Tara chooses you. It's good, but bad because you're a mortal and you're not a Wolfinoid."

I close my eyes, putting my hand against my face, trying to contain my anger and fear. "Yes, I understand that. My question is: how much time do I have of being a human?"

"Three months," replies Tara, still holding her head in her hand.

"And what happens then?"

"A wedding and the ceremony where Tara takes the crown with all the responsibilities. Of course, you'll be there to share some of those," replies Gothraigh.

"From this point to the wedding will be my final months as a ruler and it would be the time where we teach you how to be a king, Will Young. This includes knowing the military, strengthening your karma connection between you and your staff, and knowing the history of our culture."

Aw man, what have I gotten myself into?

The room suddenly became quiet and remains this way for some time until we hear the sound of heavy breathing. It gets louder and louder. I turn around to see where the sound is coming from. Soon, another Wolfinoid emerges from another stairwell directly opposite from one where Tara and I descended from. He does not stop. He keeps on jogging toward us. With one quick step to my right, he passes over me and stops in front of Cedric and Gothraigh. The man tries to bow down to his king, but Cedric waves his hand which means there's no need for it.

"What is it?" asks Cedric.

"My lord and lady, there's been trouble stirring up in the kingdom."

"What kind of trouble?" he asks, perking his ears forward.

"I think it would be best for you to hear it from the civilians."

"Tara, Crystal, Dawn, Solar, Whitney, Sean, Gothraigh, and Will," Cedric says in a commanding voice, "let's head down to the throne room and hear about this conflict."

After he says the command, he leads the way down the other curved stairway and we follow him down. With Cedric and Gothraigh ahead, Crystal and Dawn walking in front of us, Tara walking beside me, Solar and Whitney behind, and Sean covering the rear, we climb down in silence. As for me, I'm a bit stressed and frightened. Wait, that's incorrect, I've always been stressed out; that's how I got the name Nos. I am mostly frightened from what I just learned and from what lies ahead. Then, Tara takes my right hand and holds it tight. I look up at her and in her eyes are sympathy, calm, and a hint of happiness.

"I know you're scared, Nos, but let me tell you something. From this day on, you and I are granted the authority to give out any order. Plus," she pulls us both to the side, coming to a stop, Sean looks at us a bit confused, but Tara tells him to move on. Looking at her, she looks completely sad and sympathetic and continues, "I don't want to turn you. I really like what you are," while brushing her free hand across my face.

I want to reply, but she presses her index finger against my lips to keep them shut. "Don't speak. I'll still have to turn you, though I'll figure out a way to put you unconscious so that you don't have to endure the pain. Do you understand?"

I do and slowly nod. Understanding and hearing her voice completely shows me that she's sad, she doesn't want to hurt me, and that she truly loves me for the person that I am.

"Good." She bends down and kisses me. "I love you. Now, let's hear about this trouble."

I nod again in agreement and we both continued down the stairs, but I'm still on edge.

CHAPTER TWENTY-ONE
One More Parasite to Deal With
Location: Throne Room
Time: 10:00 AM

OKAY, REPOSITION YOURSELVES AT the doors that lead into the throne room while looking straight down the two thrones where Tara and King Borin sit. Remember, there are four passageways on each side leading to different rooms or caverns, if you want to call them that. Do you remember? Yes? Good for you. If not, you should've paid attention or read this book straight from the beginning to get the whole idea. Anyway, we enter through the last passageway on the far left where we are greeted by a few families, all of them Wolfinoids. Some of them vary from couples to single fathers and mothers. All of them are wearing basic robes with different colors. Some have interesting patterns like stripes that decorate them, plus all of them still have the colors of the kingdom printed somewhere visible. The color of fur ranges from black, orange, to white and so does the eye color from blue, green, to a golden brown. What really grabs my attention and I'm pretty sure everybody else's, is that these families have brought their kids; some of them seem to be under ten, or I might be wrong. Also, it makes my heart sink because some of these kids or pups, if they're characterized like that, look sad. Some are quietly crying. But over what?

We resume walking across the stage to the thrones. Tara and King Borin take their seats. Gothraigh stands on his brother's right side; Whitney, Crystal, Dawn, and Solar stand on Tara's left side looking attentive; Sean takes his position by the passageway and crosses his arms; for me, I don't know where I should stand. Looking around, trying not to look confused, I find my spot and decide to lean against one of the marble support columns, also crossing my arms.

King Borin sighs and I look at him. "Forgive me, Will, that I haven't given out an order for a throne to be created for you."

I give him a sly smile, "It's alright. Sean, Whitney, Dawn, Solar, Crystal, and Gothraigh don't have thrones either."

He sighs again in a tone that means he also understands, rubs his eyes with his index finger and thumb, and looks forward to the civilians, "Now, what kind of trouble has stirred up in my kingdom?"

Looking onward to the people, they stare back at me, some with irritated looks. The impression they're giving off makes me feel uncomfortable. The irritated looks get tenser and I feel like I've done something wrong. What have I done? I haven't done anything wrong.

I look at Tara and Cedric, waving my hand sideways, gesturing that I'm completely confused. Both of them get my message and Cedric clears his throat loudly to get their attention, which works, and he descends down the steps to show authority.

"Has Will Young done something bad or horrible that you are giving him dirty looks?"

"No, my king," states one of the males, "but the reason for our visitation does involve his kind."

"Can you elaborate?"

"It deals with a human female," says one of the female Wolfinoids. When she said human female, her child, a boy, clings tighter to his mother's robe, shedding more tears.

A woman? My kind?

I examine the crowd. Some of the other kids do the same thing, cling tighter to their parents' robes, and shed tears. I lower my hat and look down at my feet to think this over.

What kind of woman would make Wolfinoid children cry, especially for a crowd of kids that look under ten or over? I dilly-dally the thought over in my head.

Tara gets up and moves down to the crowd. She kneels down to one of the girls and talks smoothly to her, "Hi, what's your name?"

The little girl slightly looks up and answers quietly, "Stardust."

"Stardust," she replied, sounding interested in the name, "Stardust, why are crying?"

Stardust looks at me, then back at Tara, "This human hurts my feelings."

"Hurts your feelings, how?"

"By calling her names," sounds off the mother in an irritated voice, then looks at me baring her fangs.

"Hey!" says Cedric, bringing her attention back to him. "Leave him out of this. Can you tell what names this human female calls your daughter?"

The woman sighs to calm down. "She calls my child stupid, weird, and an odd word that I find offensive. I can't pronounce it correctly, but Stardust wrote it out for me once and I remember it started with au."

A woman that makes kids cry and calls them names? Time for me to investigate.

"Is the word 'autistic,' ma'am?" I asked, still looking at the floor.

"Yes," says a different man, "and my two sons have told me that she does more than call our kids horrible names."

Before Cedric or Tara could ask, I beat them to the question, "And what does she do?" I begin to pace the raised balcony at the left while at the same time I remove my robe, still holding the staff in my hands.

Then another man speaks, "By making our children do such meaningless work and telling them it's worth it. On the contrary, our children are a bit more intelligent than your race. No offense."

"None taken, continue."

Then, the same woman replies, "She does these mind games to lower their personalities and try to get into their lives. Before all of this, she's told us she's a speech therapist, but from what we've heard from our kids, she seems like an evil counselor."

"That's right," says the previous man. "My sons have told me that she's tried to get in their lives and I've taught them that if anybody tries to get into your personal lives, growl at them and snap your jaws. My youngest son did that just this morning and he told me that she smacked him and said, 'If you do that again, I will tape your mouth shut.'"

The other parents agree and I keep on pacing the balcony.

Kids crying very easily. Having their personal lives being pried into. Doing meaningless work when they have a better I.Q. Receiving threats when they were trying to hold their ground. Then I come to a sudden stop, raising my head up. *It can't be.* Before I can ask, Tara beats me to the question.

"What does this woman look like?" I ask, sounding discouraged from the information I'm receiving.

Another woman answers, "About five and a half feet tall, reddish-blonde hair, golden circular glasses, dresses like a human school teacher for all sectors, and looks like to be in her fifties."

It is. My heart rate goes up, so do my anger and adrenaline.

"What's her name?" I ask with some growling in the back of my throat.

The same woman replies, "Her last name sounds related to a feline category."

"Tiger?" I ask, frustrated.

"Yes!" all the parents reply with enthusiasm.

I turn around to look at them, "Chase Tiger?"

"Yes!" they all say even louder.

Now, I am really, really pissed off. That bitch never quits. I'm pretty sure she still thinks that this is Los Alamos County School District when it ain't! The memories of me being mentally tortured by that dumbass, autistic skank flows back through my head. The memories of doing those stupid first-grade classwork when in reality, I was a sophomore in high school and that final memory of her, smiling so evil that I deserved to be whipped eight times, receiving the news that she was probably part of the team to assassinate Tara, my ever first girlfriend, and hoping that I died in that arena. Oh, now it's full-on payback time. It's time to show that woman what kind of monster she created in her little room back at Los Alamos High.

Suddenly, a clap of thunder echoes so loudly close by, making me snap my head to the right to figure out where the source of the sound came from. Then I see my staff fully activated. The admiral blue glows bright and moves around like lava inside the staff; the flame, glass orb shines the same light inside with full flames licking and dancing around it. From top to bottom of the shaft, small storm clouds move and circle around in small separate groups with lighting exploding inside and around the clouds, also sounding off an electronic discharging noise. As my eyes continue down the staff, they stop, only to see that my right hand is extremely tight around it with the skin over my knuckles already white. Looking back to the parents, kids, and the royal family, all of them are frightened with their ears slightly laid back and eyes showing all-out fear.

"You know," Tara tries to swallow her anger, "this woman?"

Her question brings me back to the torture chamber where I heard the news that she was going to be assassinated. I have to tell her and everybody right now.

Before I could answer, I have to take a couple of deep breaths to calm down before I truly become a loose cannon. Then I look right at her and say, "Yes, Tara, I know her. She's probably one of the reasons why I was taken before you could congratulate me and my friends on our performance of that song and," looking at her family to deliver the final news, "she's also the one who wanted you to be assassinated."

"*What?*" King Borin barks loudly and abruptly turns around, looking at me with fear and anger. He quickly strides over and places both of his hands on my shoulders. "Are you sure about *this*?"

I immediately answer, "Yes, sir. It was going to be her and Marcus to do that job. She didn't mention any followers. Thankfully, again, Tara stopped the fight to save my life and also used her sorcery to break that man's neck."

"I knew that man was bad news!"

"I agree with you, Gothraigh," says Sean.

King Borin takes a heavy deep breath and looks at his civilians, "Thank you for coming in and telling us about this information. We will take care of the problem."

They bow and leave the room; once the doors close, Cedric wraps his arm around me and walks me back to the thrones. He gently pushes me in front of his throne in a gesture that I should handle this, takes a few steps back, and crosses his arms. Tara walks up the steps also looking angry, yet she takes my free hand in a calm fashion, trying to calm herself down. Next, Gothraigh and Sean walk up and stand behind Cedric looking serious. Looking back at Tara, she breathes in and out of her nose and looks at me in the eyes.

"So," she asks, "how do you want to handle this situation?"

"Sean," I say, still looking at her in a serious way.

"Yes, sir?"

Then I look at him, "Do you have a tablet on you?"

"Yes, I do." He pulls it out and activates it. "What do you want me to look for?"

"Does your tablet contain the addresses where both human and Wolfinoids live?"

"Yes, it does." He taps and swipes his fingers on the screen, then shows me a web page like Google Map of the addresses that appear on the roofs. "What do you want me to look for?"

"Search for the address of Chase Tiger. C-H-A-S-E T-I-G-E-R."

"Searching." We all stand in silence until his tablet chimes off. "Got it, it's 44458 C."

"So, what's the plan, Will?" Tara asks.

I look at all of them and finally answer, "Sean, get some of your men and meet Tara and I in the main entrance. After that, I'll give you and your men more directions."

"On it, sir." He snaps his legs together, bows at me, which is new, and walks down the center aisle. Before he reaches the doors, he turns to our left and walks through the last passageway entrance.

Tara and I stand in the cold main entrance wearing our thick and warm cloaks waiting for Sean to bring out some of his men. Actually, my cloak is a bit thicker than hers and I'm wearing gloves that match the color and design of my cloak and insulated military boots that are just black. So, pretty much, I look badass. For Tara, her cloak is simple and refined. It reflects the layout of the colors of the flag with a base color of dark purple and the head of the tribal wolf, blue and outlined in silver. Her cloak is off-white. The edges of the hood and cuffs are outlined in purple and then followed by silver. Plus, she's not wearing footwear of any kind and no gloves.

Both of us are just standing, waiting, exhaling our body heat through our noses and letting it evaporate in the cold air, and hearing the faint sounds of the fire thriving on the torches. Tara and I are armed with our staffs and I forgot to mention her staff. It is as tall as her, six feet. The rod of the staff is constructed out of white granite, perfectly smooth from the top to bottom. Surrounding the rod are shards of glass to represent crystals and at the top the glass orb is a wave-like shape frozen in motion, crescenting over. Focusing on Tara, she's completely irritated and wanting revenge. I, too, want revenge, but this is my problem. This problem was created years ago and I alone should handle this, but throwing in the information about the planned assassination, the entire royal family wants to know the answers. Yet, looking back at the large doors, my anger builds up and the memories flow back of how that woman treated not just me but other people who aren't that completely disabled as I am. *Sigh.*

"Could this be the woman that had you tortured?" Tara asks, arms crossed, looking intensely down the hall.

Her question throws me off. "Oh, um, possibly. I don't know, but I want her to also confirm about it, too."

"Good," she replies, looking at me, "because I was on the verge of tears when I saw you in that arena, damaged, broken, and bleeding." She sighs, looks back at the hall, then speaks in a quieter tone, "Curse you, Maverick, you should've let me take him in."

By that time, Sean and five of his men are dressed for the weather because today, the sky is clear, but the temperature is ten degrees. They are also armed with their staffs. When they get closer, Sean is carrying a small bag and I'm curious about what contents lie inside.

When they arrived, they all look ready to take on orders, but what's throwing me off is that Sean and his men, including Tara, are looking at me. This position is starting to make me feel uncomfortable for three reasons: first, I'm still a human. Second, Tara is specifically the next ruler of this kingdom, so she should be the one giving out the orders. Finally, being told that I have some authority immediately is a little awkward. I don't know why, but c'mon, being told now that I am officially the "king" is too fast and I'm still adjusting to what's happening right in front of me, especially being told that Tara has to bite me to turn me into a Wolfinoid to officially make me a king. However, Tara is against it and that brings me some relief because she did heal me completely last night, and looking at her, she still wants me to remain human. Now, don't get this mixed up with that strange book series about a whiney girl who believes she has nothing in her life and then throws herself upon a supernatural being, pleading to turn her! Tara, from what you've just read, is *way* much better than that supernatural being and I'm *not* that whiney girl. Our personalities are completely different and better than those lunatics. Anyway, due to the current situation, I guess I do have the authority to carry out this small mission and bring that woman to justice, which brings me back to what's in the bag in Sean's hands.

"What's in the bag, Sean?"

"Ah, yes." Sean opens it and reveals what looks like a pair of sunglasses except for the frame for the lens is solid from left to right and likewise for the lens. It does have a pair of folding arms, yet on the left arm, there's a microphone near the front and on the right arm is an earbud hanging on a wire connected to the arm. I want to ask him, but he beats me to the question.

"These are our communicators. Not only do they provide shade for our eyes; they are also computers that give live data of the geography, location to and from, heat signatures of any individual inside a structure, night vision, and where the other users are."

Blinking a couple of times with pure amazement in the device in front of me, I slowly reach for it and Sean hands it over. I probe the interesting-looking device over in my hands, and what puzzles me is that the lenses are clear and not shaded.

"You said that these are sunglasses?"

"Yes, I did, sir. They automatically taint when they interact with the sunlight." By that time, he's handing each one out to his men and to Tara.

We all put them on, insert the earpiece in our ears, and adjust the mic. Instantly, the heavy-wooden doors open slightly to give us enough room to walk through and close immediately as the last royal guard walks outside. The moment we step out onto the snowy ground, we're greeted by the ice-cold air and the bright sun; the lenses automatically shade our eyes. Sean did say that these are computers. So, how do we activate them? At an instant, my question is answered when all of them, one by one, give the command to turn on. I do say the same command and amazingly, half of the back of the lens turns on revealing a screen that's blank, yet I can still through the tinted lens with my right eye. Tara places her hand on my shoulder smiling.

"Do you like these?" With enthusiasm.

I smile back, "Yes I do, but how do I turn on the GPS?"

She shrugs, "Just tell it."

And so, I do. Soon, the screen gives me a bird's eye view of the kingdom; lime green digital lines pop up and zip around the screen; little numbers and words pop up in the same color giving me coordinates and information; next, several dots show up revealing the names and locations. Also, in the upper left-hand corner of the lens, a smaller screen appears and displays a compass.

"This. Is. Simply. Awesome," I say, feeling flabbergasted by their awesome technology. I'm curious of how I can zoom in and out; luckily, the map automatically does it. I think about it again and the computer responds immediately.

"So, Will?" Sean asks, "what's the game plan?"

"Can you upload the address to these?"

"Sure can." He pulls out his tablet, taps, swipes, and soon, the address shows up on the map.

I study it. Tiger's tent is located northeast, about a mile and a half away from us; surrounding it are more homes and a couple of shops. I input the thought command of having the image activate thermal imaging and the computer responds to that. Studying the map more, the majority of people, both human and Wolfinoid, are inside their homes, a few shops are open, and a few are walking around doing some errands. Since there are eight of us together, my plan all comes together with ease.

"Alright, we all hike together to her tent, but once we're twenty yards away, we disperse into pairs and try to look normal. I'll bring Tara with me as we get closer, and Tara," I turn my attention to her, "you cover the front door while I head inside." She nods in agreement and I turn my attention to the rest. "For the rest of the pairs, I want you guys to form a huge circle just in case this woman is going to bolt and there's no doubt about that. Once we capture her, we'll bring her back here and take her down to the arena if it's still there. Is it?"

"Yes, sir, it is," says one of Sean's men in a confident tone.

"Alright, let's move out!" We start jogging through the snow to our primary target—my primary target.

We reach the location where Chase Tiger's tent lies within ten minutes. We're about fifty yards out when we slow down to a walk. To them, a mile and half jog is easy. For me, man, I am out of shape. I mean, yes, I am skinny, but I haven't jogged or run that much and far in a few years so I'm basically huffing, puffing, and wheezing my head off. On a positive note, I still keep on walking. Surprisingly, Tara wraps her left arm around me and pulls me in, then whispers.

"I'll get you on my diet and exercise and you'll be as fit and athletic as me."

I want to tell her ha, ha or lay off, but all I can get out is a smile and long, wheezy breaths of air. She just laughs and so do the other guys. During the time we're approaching the tent, our sunglasses chime off and we look at the mini map; we're indeed twenty yards away. I wave my arm for us to disperse into pairs and surround the tent. Looking back at the map, I see Sean and his men moving around, still maintaining twenty yards, creating the circle.

I raise my right hand to the earpiece. "Is everybody in position?" All of them reply yes, so Tara and I move forward. Then Sean's voice breaks out in slight panic.

"Hold up you two, find some cover, we've got some company."

We look at our maps and sure enough, it's true, there are three occupants approaching from the west. One of the three body signatures is warmer than the others, similar to the body signatures of Tara's kind. All in all, we both hide behind the nearest tent.

"Does anybody have a visual?"

"We do, sir," says another of Sean's men. "We have eyes on Chase Tiger. She's, um, almost pulling one human, a male, probably over ten, and one of our kind. Also, a male almost in his teens." I can hear some irritation in his voice when he mentions the Wolfinoid kid.

"Stand down. Let them enter the tent and Tara and I will move in."

We hide our bodies behind the tent, only to keep our heads in view. Minutes tick by. I can hear her voice trying to sound calm but getting angry with the kids. One of the kids shouts that he doesn't want to do the work and Chase quietly yells at him to be quiet. Next, they appear in our vision. The human boy tries to escape, but Chase grabs him by the collar of his coat and drags him back to her. At this moment, we can hear them speak.

Chase kneels down, holding each one's cloak and coat in her hands and scowling at them, "The next time you run away from me again, I'll make you relearn the 'A B C's' a hundred times, the shapes, and read first-grade books."

The boy protests, "I already know my 'A B C's,' shapes, and I'm in the sixth grade, you woman."

She smacks him in the face. I let out a furious growl. Tiger continues, "I don't care if you're in the sixth grade. The way you are acting is very childish and I don't tolerate that!"

"Will you leave my friend alone?" says the Wolfinoid boy. He too gets slapped in the face.

"And you, you rebel against me one more time, I'll muzzle your mouth shut like we humans do to bad dogs. And you are also acting very childish."

"I'm thirt—" Tiger immediately grabs his mouth and holds it shut with her hand. She then breathes in and out, then returns her gaze back to them with the same evil smile.

"Get inside. Now," she commands, pushing them slightly violent into her tent. I, again, let out my most evil growl, yet it's overtaken by Tara's.

I look up at her, giving her the face that she was overachieving. She looks down and replies, "Oh, don't worry hon. I love your growl, but it needs some work."

I simply shrug and make a gesture with my hand to move forward. We approach the tent as quietly as we could. Before I go in, I look up at Tara to make sure that she understands the plan. She understands it in my eyes and nods in agreement. I enter the tent as slowly and quietly as possible. Once in, I'm greeted by the sight of the Wolfinoid boy's mouth with a muzzle on. Both of them are sitting in kindergarten chairs with fear in their eyes. The human wants to speak up, but I put my finger to my lips that he should remain quiet. I mentally give out the order for the GPS to turn off. The tint on the lens dissipates, giving me a clear sight of how Tiger has set up her tent. There are about eight feet between the tent's flap and a curtain that creates the room we're in to be a waiting room. There are another five chairs made for kindergarteners and I shake my head in disbelief. Perhaps, on the other side is her "classroom," which I don't want to give much thought about. I immediately kneel down, remove the muzzle from the boy's mouth, and I quietly tell them to leave and go back home as fast as they can. They both nod in gratitude and quietly slip back outside. Once they leave, I stand up, holster my staff in the back pocket of my cloak, and cross my arms.

Then I hear Tiger rummaging around on the other side. She starts pulling back the curtain with enthusiasm while speaking, "Okay! Who's ready to do first-grade math!" When she sees me and not her students, her happiness turns into pure horror and shock, not just on her face but also in her eyes.

"S'up, *Tiger*?" I begin cracking knuckles and giving out my evil smile.

Again, she gasps in horror for a few seconds and bolts for it, screaming and tossing her school supplies in my way to slow me down. She breaks through the back wall, still running and screaming. I start chasing after her, jumping over the debris and yelling into my mic.

"She's running! She's running!" At that moment, I yell at my glasses to reactivate the GPS and it gets a lock onto her. I can see on the map that Sean and his men also get a lock on her and move in; Tara bolts around the tent and catches up with me.

"Did she just bolt for it?" she asks, sounding excited.

"Yep, she saw me and ran," I reply, also sounding excited.

We follow her down the alley, heading east. Some of Sean's men close the escape ways, which makes Tiger keep on sprinting forward. My adrenaline is at a full-time high. It rushes throughout my veins, courses in and out from my heart, circulates down to my kidneys, and orders them to push out more of the juice. The juice travels down to my legs and orders them to work even faster. They send help signals to my brain and it responds by flashing the memories of how I was treated, repeating the process all over again. Suddenly, Tiger makes a hard left run and I react immediately by sliding in the snow like a car drifting around a sharp corner with the E-brake on and tapping the gas pedal. Once I straighten out, the E-brake is disengaged and the gas pedal is back down to the floor. Looking at the compass, it shows that I'm head southeast.

"I'll cut her off, babe!" shouts Tara still filled with excitement.

I just smile and press on even harder. I glance at the map and see another dot coming down another alley of the tents that's adjacent to me, just a few rows up. The dot pops a little name tag: "Sean Greenwood."

"I see you, Will!" he says with determination in his voice.

After a minute passed, he rounds the corner and he's in front of me by sixty yards. He and I close in on her. Tiger lets out a small shriek but keeps on running toward Sean. I get closer and closer, start stretching out my hand to grab her by the collar, and pull her down. Within a second, she bolts left and Sean and I smack into one another at full speed and ricochet backward from the ram.

Sean and I groan in pain; for Sean, he holds his chest in his hands. For me, I place both of my hands around my head, especially around my jaw. It feels like I just ran into a soft, concrete wall.

"Are you okay, Will?"

I roll around in the snow for a while, rubbing away the pain, "Yeah . . . I think so. Ah crap, where's Tiger?"

Then we both hear a loud thump noise in our earpieces and a response, "I got her guys! I got her. Where did think you were going?"

Sean and I look at the map and follow the coordinates where Tara has captured Chase. Of course, during the walk, we both groan, but I groan the loudest. At the moment we reach Tara, Sean's men have already surrounded them, pointing their staffs at the primary target and Tara, oh boy, has Chase pinned face down in the snow with one of her arms about to be dislocated from the shoulder and the other stretched out with fingers spread across the snow. The rest of Tara's body weight is pressing down onto her back and every time Chase wiggled, Tara just tightens her hands on both of her wrists. With every step we take, we can see that there's fresh blood on Chase's face, and as her eyes meet mine, she screams and tries to break free from Tara's mighty grip.

I can't hold back a smile, but I try not to laugh, "What did . . . um . . . ha, ha, you do Tara?"

She looks up at me with a smile. "When I saw how she diverted you two, I looped around and waited. Once she rounded the corner where I was hiding, I punched her right on the face and immediately pinned her down where we are."

I bend down and kiss her on the head. "Thank you." Then I kneel down in front of Tiger's face. The look in her eyes, the sudden realization that she's been caught, and that she has to finally face the crimes that she's committed all explode in her eyes and on her face. On the flip side, she tries to retain the fear and convert it into anger.

"You! And your . . . friend are in so much trouble! Do you hear me, Will Young?"

I smile back, acting calm and sarcastic. "Yeah, I'm in so much trouble. What should I do? Let me think, nothing." Then I return to my feet and say, "Let's get her to the arena where the real prosecution can happen."

"*Arena!*" Tiger shrieks.

Tara rolls her eyes and does a karate chop on her neck to knock her out. Next, one of Sean's men puts a bag over the head while the others tie her up like a hog in a rodeo. Soon, two of the guards pick her up and we all return to the castle. For me, this is the greatest victory in my life.

CHAPTER TWENTY-TWO
Prosecution
Location: Back in the Castle
Time: 2:05 PM

THE FIRST OFFICIAL INTERACTION I had with Marcus Lowsbroth is when he exited through one of the four passageways on the right side of the throne room. When we re-entered, Tara went ahead of the pack and gestures with a wave of her hand to follow her. This also includes Cedric, Gothraigh, Dawn, Faith, Whitney, and Crystal. Tara leads us through the third passageway designed the same way as the one that leads into the lounge room except we descend a flight of stairs. The bottom of the hallway stretches another twenty feet until we're facing a T-intersection. Our right leads to other areas that I'm not aware of and the left probably leads to what used to be Marcus' chamber.

Tara sighs in slight irritation. However, her sigh includes satisfaction from what she did to him; then she turns left and says, "This way."

We still stay on her six, walking in a calm fashion. She looks over her shoulder, directly at me. Her eyes are calm with both sorrow and pleasure in them.

"Come up here, Nos." I follow her request and join her side. Next, she takes my hand in hers and grips it gently. We keep on walking for a while until she comes to a stop.

"We're here," she says then looks down at me. "This is how Sean, his men, and I found you."

I'm a little confused because when we turn our heads to look at the right-side wall, I see nothing but stone bricks. I search every brick if there's a keyhole, a lever, or anything else, yet each one is clear. I search again if there's supposed to be a painting or something, yet the color of the bricks is the same. There's no hint of different color or shade, so there's really nothing here.

"Just look forward, slightly above your eye level." When she says that, she removes her hand and places it on top of my head in comfort and encouragement.

I look forward and slightly up, setting my eyes at the one brick that's nearly in front of me. I study it real hard for a moment and I finally see the answer. At the bottom, left corner of the stone brick is a little engraved circle with the initials that say "M.L."

"No way," I say in astonishment.

Suddenly, Tara balls up her left hand and smacks the brick with the butt of her fist. Hard. The brick reacts by sliding back a bit, activating a lot of pistons, springs, and gears on the other side. The opera of the noises continues for a minute until the entire section of the wall, ten feet wide and nine feet tall, jerks backward releasing a gust of pressurized air, stalls for a moment, and slides back about five inches. Next, the wall slowly slides right showing a secret passageway where dim torches ignite and light the tunnel system.

Tara looks back, sets her eyes on Tiger who's still unconscious, lets out a small but furious growl, and jerks head toward the passageway. Right after that, we all start moving down the corridor. The sound of our footsteps echoes off the walls and ceiling. Further down the tunnel system, the secret passageway closes up making all of us, except Tara, stop and look back.

"It's okay," she says in a calm tone, "we'll be able to reopen it from this side. Let's keep moving forward."

We continue onward. Dim light torches ignite themselves while lighting the way; we pass a large wooden door that has cast iron hinges and plates to hold it together. Above it is a sign written in their own language that makes me stop and look. Tara notices and places both her hands on my shoulders.

"What does the sign say?"

She leans forward, placing her head on mine and breathing a heavy sigh. "That leads to the torture chamber. I wanted to follow your scent through that door, yet the roar of the crowd grabbed my attention."

I look at her, slightly terrified by the information she just told me. Tara understands and senses my fear; she strokes my face to comfort me. Feeling the warmth of her hand immediately makes the fear melt away and it pleases her very much. Again, she grabs my hand and leads us toward the arena.

The journey through this tunnel continues until we reach an intersection that has several different ways. Tara, again, doesn't stop. She leads us right through the center opposite of the tunnel we came through. Soon, the tunnel starts curving to the left and keeps on curving until it straightens out. Directly ahead of us is an opening. As we all enter simultaneously, stadium-like lights come alive and show what surrounds us.

We enter the arena where I almost fought to the death. From where we're standing, we're on the second balcony of seats. Being up here shows that each balcony has carved and leveled rocks for seating, with three rows of benches. Below us is the arena, still littered with weapons. What strikes me is that there is still blood on the sand— the blood of my three enemies; two I took down with my own hands and the third brutally torn apart by my lovely future wife. Looking down at the large empty space, I wonder, how do we get down to the floor? I do remember Tara leaping from one of these balconies and landing perfectly on the floor, but from where we're standing, we got to be at least forty feet above.

"Follow me," says Tara, still in a confident tone. Again, we follow her.

She leads us to the far-left side of the balcony. Next, she picks up a plank of wood covering a hole, and she calmly steps through it and disappears.

"It's alright. It's just a slide. It leads to the victors' room."

I look up at the other guys. They look a little uncertain, as do I.

Then, there's a groan and movement. I look at one of Sean's men and it looks like Tiger is regaining consciousness. I immediately drop through the hole. Just like Tara said, it's a slide, and so I whoosh down into a room that has an all-out metal-plated door to the left and empty to my right in a matter of seconds. Still, dim torches magically ignite to light up the room. Tara greets me with open arms and pulls me off and away from the slide to let the others come down. One by one they come. Tara briskly moves toward the door, pulls back on a lever, and the door opens onto the battlefield. We all pour out and the man that's carrying Tiger wastes no time and dumps her onto the ground. She groans some more. The same man pulls out a small dagger, cuts the ropes, and pulls off the bag from her head.

Looking around, this place looks like a great opportunity to act out like an insane villain from another video I have played. I kneel down and get into character mode. I let Tiger roll around the sand some more and soon, she begins opening her eyes.

"Did I ever mention the definition of insanity?" I speak with an evil grin.

"Hm . . . what?" she replies.

Then I stand up and speak, gesturing my hands, "The definition of insanity is doing the exact same fucking shit over and over again, expecting for shit to change."

Tiger's eyes burst wide open with horror and realization that she's been caught and she can't escape. Tiger just lies there, on the sand, completely stunned.

"Where . . . where am I?" Her voice trembles.

I continue quoting the main villain, "The first time I heard that, it was from a guy. I thought he was crazy, so I shot him and you know what . . . he was right."

"What are you talking about, Will?"

"You see, my definition of insanity is when a certain group of people, like you, mistreat a person or people, like me, and make them think that they, well, should've fucked it in their incubators. So, when their minds are really soft, they absorb what they hear and told to do; thereby, it lowers their self-esteem, unless they meet a great group of people that makes them realize their true potential and they learn how to stand up and hold their ground. But the damage is done. The voices that made them feel like assholes drive them, I don't know, *insane*! And they want to beat up their bullies as payback."

After shouting "insane" at her, Tiger slightly curls up in a ball, trying to remain calm. "How are you even alive?"

"Oh? I was supposed to die here. Well, I'll let Tara and her family give that answer to you." I step away and all of them, Tara, Cedric, Gothraigh, etcetera, gather around her. Some of them are angry; others are growling and slightly baring their fangs. Tiger begins to tremble.

"Is it true that you had a part of the assassination plan for my daughter?" bursts Cedric.

"What?" Tiger shrieks.

"Why did you have Will tortured and forced to fight?" Tara snaps.

"Where's Marcus?" She scours the arena for her fake boyfriend hoping that he'll come to the rescue.

"Marcus is dead and gone, you peasant woman," Gothraigh scowls at her.

"What? How?"

"I snapped his neck and that killed him instantly!" Tara snaps again.

"You what?" Standing up abruptly, Tara pushes her back down.

"Stay down, you bitch."

Tiger gasps in horror like she's never heard of the word "bitch" before. And I really mean that. Her reaction to that word is so authentic. Yet, her horrified expression transforms to anger and she starts grinding her teeth.

"How dare you call me that? You autistic skank!"

Oh! That's really a bad choice of words, especially to a Wolfinoid female who's now the queen of Sparta. Looking at Tara and especially Cedric, both of them are now baring their fangs. The hairs on their arms are standing up and both of them are unleashing their most furious growls. For me, I start laughing for no reason. I try to muffle it but it bursts out. Through my squinting eyes, I see Tiger looking at me all-out confused with anger and disbelief.

"What do you find so funny, Will?" Her question slips with fear through her mouth like sand in an hourglass.

I just keep on laughing so evilly that I drop to the ground rolling in the sand. I do my best to catch my breath and after a couple of minutes, I reply, "Tiger, Tiger, Tiger. You are most definitely some kind of a stupid."

"What do you mean? All of this is not real."

I get back up, still shaking with laughter, "Oh, it's all real. All of this," spreading my arms out. "All of this is real and you're trying to deny the fact that you were part of the plan to have me tortured and forced me to fight to the death and also have Tara, my lovely girlfriend, to be murdered."

Tiger shakes her head in disbelief. I let my arms drop and I walk over to Tara. There's still the vibe of hostility coming off her, so it would be wise not to touch her. Then, I get serious and cross my arms.

"Answer their questions, Tiger, or you'll most definitely be torn apart."

In her eyes is yet again fear but trying to be smothered by anger and resentment.

"You are in so much trouble, young man. Just wait until—"

"Until *what*?" I bark at her. "Report me to Principal Jacks?"

Her eyes dart back and forth from the ground to me, "Yes."

I roll my eyes, "You think that this is still Los Alamos County and that your teaching career has authority wherever you go?"

"Yes. Yes, it does," she replies as she slowly gets up and tries to stare me down.

I roll my eyes again and gesture with my hand toward Sean to bring out his tablet and hands it to me; as he does, it's already on. Surprisingly, he has changed the language on the screen from theirs to ours, making it really easy for me to navigate the machine. The tablet is indeed like our iPods and I'm able to find an Earth icon that brings up a satellite image of our planet. It also amazes me that the satellites are still working. I twirl the sphere and stop it to see the United States of America. Then I zoom in on our location. That's when I find out that we're in Pennsylvania, in the Susquehannock State National Forest located in Potter County. I glance up only to see Tiger trying to beam at me with her demon eyes. *Sigh.* I twirl the tablet in my hands so that the screen faces her and at the same moment, I grab her hair and smack her face into the screen.

"Does it look like we're in Los Alamos County?" I ask while smearing her face over the screen so that she can understand the picture.

"No," she muffles.

"What?"

"No," she says a bit louder.

"I can't hear you!" I say, sounding a bit like a Marine drill sergeant.

"No!"

"No!" I push her back onto the ground. "You have absolutely no authority of any sort here in Sparta. Again, answer their questions."

Again, Tara and King Borin growl at her and so do everybody else. Tiger finally comes to her senses and realizes the huge trouble that she's gotten herself into. She takes a couple of deep breaths and keeps her eyes on the ground. To me, I think that's a wise choice because after telling the truth and nothing but the truth, I think both Tara and her father, or just Tara, will immediately start tearing her apart.

Tiger breathes a heavy sigh once more and speaks, "Yes. I was in partnership with Marcus to have Will kidnapped, tortured, and thrown into this arena in hopes that he'll die for the way he treated me three years ago."

Tara growls much louder. Her source of power, the light of ice blue, starts glowing around her and in her eyes with the indication of tearing this woman into confetti. King Borin calmly places one of his hands onto his daughter to calm her down so that they'll continue to hear the truth.

"What happened three years ago?" he asks, trying to hold back his anger.

"That man punched me and yelled at me when I tried to restrain him from leaving my classroom," she replies, still looking down but points her right, index finger at me.

Both of them look at me with some shock and disbelief. The rest are showing disbelief on their faces, too. For me, I'm blown away by the fact that this was the reason that I go through all of that shit. I have to defend my side. "Because you were prying yourself into my private life and the way you were talking to me was making me angry. That's why I got up, to remove myself from the situation before I let my exhaust pipes blow fire out of them. But you restrained and threatened me that if I left, my family back in Wisconsin was going to be murdered."

"I was trying to be funny," she looks up at me with pleading on her face.

"For shit like that I don't find funny!" I look around at the royals. "She made it sound so real that I had to take a stand and show that I don't take that kind of crap."

"I stand by Will," says Gothraigh. "Threatening another man's family just to hold him back when he was removing himself from a situation that you created; I don't find that acceptable."

Everybody around us agrees with him.

"Now," speaks Cedric, "Were you in partnership with Marcus Lowsbroth in the attempt to murder my daughter?"

Tiger looks at him, ready to be turned into confetti, "No, sir. I wasn't."

Cedric, Gothraigh, Sean, and everybody else breathe heavy sighs of relief, but Cedric remains serious. "Due to your actions, Chase Tiger, and your partnership with Marcus Lowsbroth to have my future son-in-law tortured and forced to fight in this arena, I'll let Will deliver his verdict." He pats me on the back.

I look at my bully—the monster that created me into a monster. I want to remove my staff from its holster, channel my energy into it, make the flames that surround the glass orb into an arrowhead, and thrust it into her head. Or let Tara tear her into tiny pieces. However, I feel a hint of mercy tugging at my gut. I decide to follow it.

"Since you think that you're so tough, Chase, I'm giving you just one hour to pack up whatever shit is necessary from your tent and we'll escort you to the West Gate of this kingdom. Once your hour is up, I hereby banish you from Sparta. We'll send out some intel about you to Troy and make sure that they don't ever let you in if by any chance you make it to the Rocky Mountain Range." I check the tablet for the time and it states 2:59 PM. Then it reads 3:00. "Your one hour starts now. If you dare of escaping us or not meeting us by the West Gate with your things, you shall be beheaded and your corpse soaked in gasoline and lit on fire."

"You heard the man!" Sean shouts, "Move it!"

And we all usher Tiger out of the arena.

Sean, Tara, and I escort her all the way to her tent. Very interestingly, word about Chase Tiger being evicted by my verdict got out quickly. At every alleyway of the housing and business tents, both humans and Wolfinoids start gathering around. While we walk through, some of the people start yelling things like, "This is what you get for threatening my son! This is what happens when you have no business in their lives! Who's the autistic person now?"

More people join in, yelling and shaking their fists at her. Tiger hangs her head really low and tries to be invisible, but it doesn't work. Pieces of food start flying and hitting her. We all just let it go for the people to have their revenge. I, walking the closest to her, can hear her whimpering and trying to hold back tears. Yet again, I roll my eyes.

"I thought bullies were supposed to be tough and show no other emotion except for when they feel pride and anger toward their victims for no damn, good reason after destroying them, whether it be physical or physiological."

That last sentence makes her burst out crying.

My God, this woman is such a poser.

"I wanted to make friends in my own way so that we can be the same," she says while she gasps through the tears for air.

I just shake my head in disappointment. No less than five minutes later, the foods increase in mass, becoming larger and softer, so when they impact, they "explode" on Tiger, thus making an absolute mess.

We just let this happen; after a couple of minutes, to tell you the truth, I feel like I've brought enough shame on her. Looking back on my comrades, their eyes agree with what they're witnessing. I bring out my staff and slam the butt onto the ground, sending out a shockwave of flame that's not so hot but gets their attention.

"The next person who throws any kind of food will spend three days in jail!" They all stop immediately and then I look at Sean, "You do have a jail system, correct?"

He nods in agreement.

We continue the march toward her tent, which feels like an eternity. Approaching it, Tiger grabs the flap but refuses to open it.

"Thank you for stopping them," she mumbles, head still hanging.

"Yeah. Well, don't get comfortable. I'm still banishing you," I reply while looking the opposite direction.

She breathes a heavy sigh and proceeds. We all follow and stand in her "waiting room" in silence, watching her browse through her stuff, probably trying to find a large bag that she can carry with ease. I look down at Sean's tablet to check the time.

"You got thirty-five minutes left."

She spins around, scared all-out, "That's not enough time. I . . . I mean . . . it's—"

Sean rolls his eyes, reaches in his cloak, and tosses her one of their enchantment bags, "Use it."

Chase looks down, confused, not knowing what to do with it.

"C'mon! Chop, chop!" Tara says, still looking frustrated.

Chase scrambles for her fridge and starts pulling out food and water. Then, she stumbles around to the other side and throws in clothes, toiletries, and cookware. She looks down at the bag and realizes its pure power. Then, she rushes toward her school equipment in hopes that she'll be able to take them. I immediately stop her by sliding between her and her school supplies.

"No. Only survival stuff only." She gets the message and proceeds for her bed.

Once there, she throws in pillows, warm blankets, and other personal items. She looks around the tent, calculating if she's forgotten something. Her eyes bounce back to her school supplies, but I glare at her and release an impatient growl.

"Got everything?" I ask, trying to hold back my frustration. Chase nods quickly in response. "Then, let's move." Now, we escort her to the West Gate.

Approaching the gate, I look back at the tablet. Tiger has ten minutes left, but I, including Tara and her people, do not want to see another minute of her. We stop about ten feet from the threshold and my bully turns around, trying to get the last few sights of safety and security from the werewolves. Gathering around is almost the entire population of Sparta watching the parasite, my problem, the bully, to be officially banished. She tries to open her mouth to form the words, "I'm sorry." But Tara, Sean, the normal guard, and I point our staffs right in her face to say that she should immediately leave. Until now, Chase hesitates and her hesitation really wears out our patience, especially mine.

"Get outta here," I say quietly and violently.

Chase steps back, throws the bag over her shoulders, turns, and walks away. As the parasite proceeds away from us, we lower our staffs. Some parts of the crowd dissipate; the rest watch in bravery. The further away it gets, I decide to turn my attention to the guards and give out my next orders. Yet, something else makes me turn back and I watch it disappear into the woods. I do my best to ignore it, but the feeling gets bigger and bigger. I stomp my foot in frustration and look back. In hopes of seeing an empty trail, the parasite has stopped and is looking back at us from about twenty-five yards away. It makes one step forward to us and that makes the flames erupt from my exhaust pipes, hopefully for the last time.

"Get outta here!"

The parasite is immediately shaken by my screaming command and bolts off into the woods never to be seen again.

Finally, I turn my attention back to the guards and give out my final orders, "Alright. I want you guys to work in shifts. One group is awake while the other is asleep and vice versa. I also want you to tighten the security around the entire perimeter to make sure *it* doesn't get back. Y'all understand?"

"Yes, sir," they say in unison.

I clap my hands together, "Okay, let's have a celebration."

Everybody who hears that last sentence agrees and celebrates.

CHAPTER TWENTY-THREE
Getting to Know My Powers
Location: Maddox's Sorcery Arena
Date: December 13, 2014
Time: 1:00 PM

CLANK! CLANK! CLANKADY CLANK!

My staff sounds off while colliding back down onto the floor as I attempt the tenth time to bring it to life by using my inner power where I use my DNA that's coursing, dying, and reproducing throughout my body as a wireless transmitter. To bring you guys up to speed, this is literally the first day of my sorcery training with Maddox and for my friends Alex, Chris, and Alice. If you're curious about how they got accepted, well, they also created their own staffs and with me being booted up to being the future king, I can bend the rules. Of course, Maddox was also glad and flexible to let them in, so from the day I banished Chase Tiger from Sparta, I and all of my friends were able to meet up and discuss what happened the night I disappeared. They didn't have much to tell me except they were all worried, so I told them my side of the story. After that, nothing in particular happened until now. Anyway, assisting them are Whitney (who has completely fallen in love with Chris and likewise with him. Plus, Chris has told me that they already hit it off. *Sigh. I'm such an asshole to Tara.*), Crystal, Faith, and Dawn. Assisting me, well y'all can guess, it's Tara. She practically knows everything so Maddox is just supervising but will hand out some methods and hints to us humans.

To describe Maddox's arena, it's basically carved and formed like a dome. Its purpose is to be an observatory and to give well-enough space throughout the area if any mishaps take place. A certain number of safety mats have been laid out for us, if, yet again, things get out of hand. There are a few scaffolds with different levels to stand on. Plus, there are some ladders for us humans to climb. Back here on ground level, there are only two passageways directly opposite from one another. The first one leads out of the arena and back to the throne room. The second leads into Maddox's chambers. There are also a bar and grill stocked with kinds of food and drinks to indulge ourselves. Interestingly, the bar has the exact design and color as the one used during Tara's party.

Back onto the matter, my staff falls back onto the floor and I'm sweating a lot, likewise for my friends because we've been at this for two and a half hours.

"C'mon, mate. You almost had it," Maddox encourages me while he leans against one of the scaffolds.

I heave a heavy sigh and place my hands on my knees to steady myself. "Can't you see I'm sweating buckets over here?"

"C'mon, Nos! You can do it," shouts Chris also in encouragement while he, Alex, Alice, and the rest sit at the bar having a drink break.

I remove my hat so that I can cool off a lot faster. Tara comes over in a calm fashion and brings me to the bar. "He's right, Maddox. Look at him. He needs a break."

She reaches over the counter bringing out a large cup and dumping in a few scoops of ice.

"I can see that, Tara." He laughs a little and walks over. "But did you witness how he almost had the staff levitating?"

"Yes, we all saw that," Alex answers and proceeds, "but we agree that Nos needs a break, just like we do."

Maddox just rolls his eyes at him.

Tara sighs, still ignoring Maddox. "What do you want to drink?"

I look at her and reply, "Ice Blue Gatorade."

She nods, brings out a hose from underneath, and presses a button that releases the refreshment into my cup. I take it and chug a bit from it, still breathing in and out through my nose. Having the cold drink splash down through my throat and into my stomach feels so refreshing. Alice brings up a towel and pushes it across the bar. I grab it and wipe the sweat off my face.

Maddox takes a seat at the other unoccupied stools and faces the mirror wall. He places his head in his hands and lets out a heavy sigh. We all sit in silence, enjoying our drinks. The silence, as time goes by, grows more intense and so does the awkwardness. We can all feel it, growing stronger and stronger. Somebody needs to break the silence, like right now. Looking down at my right, do both of Tara's friends and mine have anything to say to break the silence? Nope. I look at my left to see if Tara or Maddox has anything to say, but that's also a no. *Sigh.* I guess it's gonna be me.

"So, Tara?"

"Yes, Nos?" she answers with enthusiasm that the silence is broken.

I look at her and asked, "What are your interests?"

"What? You've got me a bit confused."

I laugh a little, looking down at my half-empty cup for a moment, then I look back at her and say, "On the night you healed me, you and I agreed that we should know one another before we officially hit it off, just like Chris and Whitney," gesturing my thumb toward them but looking at her with a crooked hillbilly smile. When I said it, both of them snicker in agreement.

Tara perks her ears forward. Confusion is gone from her eyes and she smiles, "Oh yeah, now I remember. I would like to hear what you like first." Then she folds her arms on the bar and places her head sideways, looking very interested.

I take another gulp of my drink and put my hat back on.

"Okay, from what my friends and I performed for your birthday that night, you should know that I like country music. Of course, when you had that animatronic, you were browsing and listening to my iPod on the first day we set off from Green Bay. So, you also know that I like rock, some rap, some dance, and metal."

Tara sticks out her tongue, like a dog on this planet, as a smile and waves her tail back and forth. Then she replies, "Yeah, that's true. You do have an interesting taste of music and I would love that you perform all of them, but I would like to know what you do in your spare time." Alex leans over, elbowing his elbow into my right side, making noises that they know I'm really into her. Again, I smile and shake my head at him.

"That's simple." Soon, Maddox and Tara's friends were interested. "Before high school, I used to draw a lot, mostly cars in 2-D, and I used to build things out of a toy product called Legos."

Her eyes light up. "What kind of things?"

"Buses, skyscrapers as tall as me, but mostly planes. During high school, I mostly rode my bicycle around town at night."

"Do you like cars, Nos?" Maddox asks.

I look at him and reply, "Yeah. From stock to tuners. From muscle cars to lifted trucks."

He smiles, "That just proves my hypothesis."

We all look at him confused. He just laughs at our confused expressions. "Before you and I met, I studied your staff for a moment and also talked to Atticus about it. He and I agreed that your source of power is based upon your interest in music and your liking for cars."

Then he gets up and walks to the opposite side of his arena. When he reaches his destination, he taps the smooth, curved wall. What blows our human minds is that every time he taps the wall, circular shockwaves of dark purple erupt from his fingertips. Once he taps the wall one last time, he steps back because the same color of light sets off sparks like a welding machine when the intense heat from the hot wire touches a metal surface; two lines appear opposite from one another by fifteen feet and travel upward to eight feet. Next, both lines turn toward each other and come as one. Once they do, the trail of light behind them disappears and the section of the wall slides down toward the floor. In front of Maddox is just a blank, dark space, then the stadium lights sound off, revealing the objects that lie in the shadows.

I drop my cup onto the floor and Maddox turns back to face us and gives out a smile.

"Do these vehicles please you, mate?" he asks as he crosses his arms.

I get up and walk toward him to get a better look at the large, hidden garage. Inside lies two 2010 Dodge Challengers, several 2012 Ford F-350s that are crew cabs with duals, along with several 2012 Ram 3500 crew cabs with duals, two Aventadors, and three Jaguar F-Types. What blows me away is the 1969 Dodge Charger. I look around at all of these cars and so do my friends. Our mouths and eyes are wide open. Each of these vehicles absolutely looks brand new; there's no hint of it being abused or driven. They all look like they just came from the factories. Turning back to look at Maddox, he's just standing three feet away from me with his arms still crossed and with a fine satisfied look on his face.

"Maddox. How'd did you come across these cars?" I'm still completely surprised.

"Does it please you, sir?"

I just nod. Tara walks up behind him, holding my staff with excitement in her eyes and face. Seeing her brings me back before all of this happened. Again, I'm curious, what should I learn from her?

"What do you like to do, Tara?" She just shrugs and hands forward my staff. I take it, still waiting for an answer.

"We'll get to that, but let's get back to business," she says with a smile.

I smirk and shrug, returning my gaze to the cars. I twist my staff in my hands, trying to comprehend how to bring these mechanical devices to life. Yes, it's true that I do have a liking for cars like these laid out before me. Yes, it does appear that I have a thirst for justice to bring down the people who've brought me down. And yes, I do have a liking for intense music. All of these interests and likings have combined themselves into my DNA and have prospered throughout my blood and veins. The question lingers in my head—how can I bring these vehicles to life? I look at Maddox in hopes for an answer.

"Do you . . . by any chance . . . have a stereo system of some kind?"

His eyes light up. "As a matter of fact, I do." Then he strides forward to his chamber, opens the door, and closes it.

We all look at each other and back at the door. I look at Tara to see if she has any answers. She nods and winks at me while raising up her index finger, signaling that I give Maddox a moment. Again, I turn my gaze back at the door. As time passes, I cross my arms. Minutes pass and I look back at Tara in question. Again, she just raises her finger to give him more time and winks. More minutes pass and Maddox reopens his door, pushing out a dolly that has three panes of glass, each one framed in stainless steel. Two of the three panes of glass are about five feet tall, slightly curving backward, and are skinny. The last one is large as the size of a thirty-inch screen T.V. Surrounding these objects are the same white spheres that produced a sound barrier in my tent when my friends and I were practicing "Oh Man." Instead of eight small ones, these are larger, like the side of a basketball, and there are twenty of them. I raise my eyebrows amused at the sight before us.

"What are those for?"

Maddox stops, engages the brakes, and touches each large sphere that activates and flies out to the opposite ends of the arena, "Let's see if this system boosts up your energy." Then he looks at Tara, "Do you have his iPod?"

"Of course." She takes it out from one of her pockets with a smile.

She hands it over to him. Maddox eyes my iPod in fascination then pockets it. He turns his attention to the three panes of glass, breathes in deeply probably to summon his sorcery, claps his hands three times, and stretches out his arms to them. Immediately, a faint light starts forming around the edges of his body. He brings his arms up and all panes of glass levitate off from the dolly and he then settles them down to the floor. Next, he takes out my iPod and touches the upper right corner of the rectangle glass pane that activates the power icon. It glows for a few seconds, then shoots out lasers across it and to the tall skinny ones. Amazingly, the lasers form the knobs, volume meter, buttons, levers, speakers, and absolutely everything to operate an all-out, extremely awesome stereo system. Next, a little slot pops out in the center of the main stereo and Maddox inserts the iPod into it. Suddenly, the arena gets dark, like the lights dimming in a movie theatre when the trailers of the future begin to play. All of us humans look around only to see that the basketball spheres are the cause of the shade. On the flip side, Maddox clears his throat.

"Shall we continue, Nos?" He spreads his arm toward the garage with an encouraging smile. Without hesitation, I walk up to the stereo and scan the library on my iPod to find my intense music mix. Within a moment, I find it, but before I press the first track, I look at Maddox and the rest of the group with a smile.

"Yeah, let's." I press the first track and the song "New Canyon" by Parking Lincoln starts playing loudly on the system and the spheres throw different light sources, making the arena into a large dance club floor. I grab my staff in both of my hands, inhaling the air, and tuning into the song. At the same time as the beat, I slam the bottom of my staff onto the floor. At that moment, it truly comes alive and so does the lead singer's voice as he sings the opening lines.

I look up at the garage of cars and say, "Awake." Every car and truck comes to life and I gesture with my hand, saying, "Come to me."

And they all start pulling out one by one like a convoy. My friends back away, but my sixth sense is telling me that both Maddox and Tara are very pleased and excited by what's happening right now; soon, the vehicles surround me, waiting for their next command. All of a sudden, I hear a battle cry and look up to see Maddox coming back down onto the ground, pointing his staff right at me with the intent to harm me on his face. I immediately swing up my staff to deflect his attack. Once our staffs collide, a huge mass of sparks come flying out between them. His weight is so strong that it makes me bend down to the floor while still standing on my two feet. I glance at my friends. They look concerned but with a hint of encouragement underneath.

"Am I too strong for you, your majesty?" he asks.

I look back at him; he's really enjoying this moment. I look back at the army I summoned; they haven't moved an inch. I clench my jaw tightly, tighten my grip, and let out my battle growl. I recoil my arms a bit, building the intensity to launch them forward. Then, I smile at him. He cocks his head slightly sideways and I thrust my arms forward, making him fly off of me.

"No," I say, getting up, "Not really." I run toward the nearest Ram and jump onto the bed, slamming the bottom of the staff into it. It makes the truck move forward and start circulating the arena.

Holy crap, this is amazing.

I set my right foot on the side of the bed, leaning my weight into it. The truck still continues to circulate, but I give the command to increase its speed. It responds and I can tell that it's traveling at thirty miles per hour. Maddox is beyond surprised, perhaps scared. His gaze follows us as we still continue to circle.

"What's wrong, Maddox?" I shout over the sound system as the song "I Hate You" by Grace on Three Days begins to play. "Are you afraid? Or are you going to keep on standing there and try to attack me again?" He smiles and charges at us. I smile and point my staff at one of the Dodge Challengers and quietly say an order to it.

"Take him out, but gently."

It lunges forward. Maddox doesn't see it coming; as he's about to jump into the air, he gets impacted from behind and flies up in the air. While in the air, he totally looks confused. As gravity takes him back down, he moves like a ninja to stabilize and lands back on one of the high scaffolds looking frustrated yet pleased, trying to figure out his next attack. I laugh and command the Challenger to follow us. When it gets behind the Ram, I am suddenly thrown forward from the bed to the cold stone floor. On impact, I lose grip on my staff. Dazed and confused, I look back to figure out what happened. Looking upon the crash site, I see Tara's staff activated, standing tall and strong like a steel street lamp post. Molding around it is the crumbled and destroyed front-end of the Ram with the grill destroyed beyond recognition. The hood is crumpled up like a piece of paper, likewise for the front fenders. Headlamps, too, are destroyed. The windshield is cracked into a million pieces along with both front airbags deployed. Turning my attention to the Challenger, it has the same results. Both vehicles have smoke billowing from their crumpled hoods.

"Sorry, baby," says Tara with a mocking smile. "I couldn't let you have all the fun."

She walks toward her staff to retrieve it. I look onward at her, struck with shock. I didn't see her place her staff in front of me. I look back at my friends. All of them just shrug. Tara's friends are smiling at my failure and trying to hold back their giggles. I shake my head and slowly get back up at my feet, swiveling my head to find my staff. Within minutes, I find it. Once I proceed to retrieve it, Maddox leaps from where he landed and gets in my way, grinning. Tara leaps and lands on his right side. Dawn, Whitney, Faith, and Crystal join them and surround me. All of them have their staffs in their hands at the ready.

"Aw, c'mon!" Alex shouts from the bar. "That's not fair!"

"He's the future king. He needs to learn how to get out from one of these situations," replies Dawn, still looking down at me.

"Bullshit!" shouts Chris as he slams his staff into the ground creating huge cracks. He and Alex get up and proceed forward.

Faith notices and says, "Stand down. Please."

"*No!*" they reply in unison and point their staffs at them.

Apparently, both of their staffs are created out of solid bronze. None of their staffs have any slots revealing the source of power like mine. Both do have glass orbs shaped like buck's heads with ten antlers and both are glowing emerald green with some bright yellow shining brightly in the heads. Alice gathers the courage to join them and points her staff. The difference in her staff is its winter forest camouflage prints all over with a hot pink outline. The glass orb is formed as a doe's head and the light inside glows pink. Dawn, Whitney, Faith, and Crystal turn their attention to my friends.

"Are you sure you want to do this?" asks Crystal.

"You're cornering our friend. We don't let any of our friends be cornered," Alex firmly states, glowering at them.

I glance at Tara and Maddox. Both of them are looking at my friends surprised and curious by their actions. I look around Maddox and I see my staff still activated and shining brightly. Within that moment, I form a plot, double-check it, and breathe in and out a couple of times. I immediately drop down and swing my legs to knock out Maddox's. Again and surprisingly, all of them, Maddox, Tara, Crystal, Whitney, Dawn, and Faith, didn't see my attack coming. I leap to my feet and push a few of them aside while I bolt for my staff. I stretch out my arm, signaling it to fly off the floor and into my hand. It responds. I suddenly wrap my fingers around it and I swing around to find Tara was in pursuit, but she comes to an abrupt halt when the glass orb points right at her and my entire staff erupts in flames. The heat does not singe my hands because I sent out a mental message to keep the flames an inch away. I glower and smile at her.

"Fuck off, baby."

She lets out a sly smile, puts up both of her hands, and slowly backs away from me.

"That . . . was a very well-executed attack," she replies.

"I ain't finished yet."

Her smile disappears and is replaced by confusion. I cock my head to one side, changing the fire into lightning bolts. Then, I send a mental message to have the bolts fly out and command the remaining vehicles. In seconds, they respond. The remaining trucks are ahead of the convoy. They swing open their doors; the seat belts stretch out to retrieve my friends and bring them back inside their cabins. One of the Aventadors does the same, grabbing Crystal and locking her inside. Two of the Jags and the remaining Challenger have the same command and they grab Dawn, Whitney, and Faith. All of them yelp for help but are silenced once the doors close. I leap onto the back of one of the Ford 350s while it is in motion and look at Tara and Maddox. The vehicles still circulate them. During that time, Chris, Alex, and Alice climb through the back windows and stand in the beds.

"Nos," Chris shouts out with enthusiasm, "that was totally amazing!"

I just smile at them. Looking at Tara and Maddox, both of them couldn't believe what just happened. I turn my attention to her friends; they bang and scream from the cars, but it's no use. These cars are under my command!

I look at my Ford and the three Rams and commands, "Slow down and form a circle around Tara and Maddox." In a funny way, they reply with a honk and obey. All four trucks creep in a circle at ten m.p.h.

"Halt," I say to them and they come to an easy stop.

At this moment, I forgot my iPod is still playing and now, it is on the chorus of "Journal of Sam" by Heart Breaking. In the end, all four of us point our staffs at them and let the chorus play out.

Tara and Maddox look nervously at one another, debating what their next move should be. Tara looks around and through the gaps of our trucks, she sees her friends entrapped in the other cars, also circling Maddox's arena. She again looks back at us, sets down her staff, and puts her hands up in surrender. Maddox understands the situation and follows Tara. Then he snaps his fingers to turn off the stereo and have the spheres return and deactivate upon landing on the dolly. I, too, snap my fingers to stop the cars and release my captives. My friends and I raise up our staffs and let our power drain from them, smiling in victory.

"How? How . . . were you?" Whitney stutters in confusion as she and the rest approach us in caution. All of them are completely shaken and unarmed.

I walk to the other side of the bed and say, "Like my friend Alex said, 'We don't let our friends be cornered,' especially me. I've been cornered far enough and it was time to show that I had enough of it." I examine my staff in both of my hands, then return my gaze to the arena, shocked and amazed.

I can't believe I just did all that.

The truck moves as Tara comes up, places her arms around, and lays her head on one of my shoulders and we just stand here in a moment of silence.

"So," I begin breaking it, "am I going to learn a few things about you or should I talk more about myself?"

She sighs and gazes at the sight. "No, you've proven yourself to learn a few things about me. But, are you and your friends hungry?"

"No." Then my stomach growls. Big time. And so do Alex's, Chris's, and Alice's.

Maddox walks over to the main stereo system and swipes the screen which transfigures into a clock. Our eyes widen because the last time we knew, the time was 1:00; now, it's 5:15.

"Perhaps, we should have some dinner," Maddox says with a smile.

We all nod in agreement and exit the arena. Tara and I are the last ones to leave, but before we go up the stairway, I look back at the site. It's such a mess. I give three light taps of the bottom of my staff to the floor and order the vehicles to put themselves away. Again, they obey, drive themselves back to their spots, and turn off. Tara tugs at my hand and I let her lead the way back to the banquet hall.

CHAPTER TWENTY-FOUR
Christmas Celebration,
Party, and Confession
Location: Lounge Room
Date: December 24, 2014
Time: 8:00 AM

I WAIT IN THE lounge room for the rest of my adjoining family. The entire room is fully decorated in the Christmas spirit. I mean there's a pine tree decked out with lights and candles, ornaments, and tinsel. Plus, the tinsel and L.E.D. lights lay on the tables and the mantel of the fireplace with a fire burning warm and bright in its normal colors.

I'm just sitting here on one of the couches, waiting. My wardrobe has been completely changed from wearing a simple t-shirt with some designs or a robe that has camo barb wire in a single stripe with a matching hat to now a full royalty. In detail, the robe I am wearing now is created out of a more extravagant fabric, making it heavier and thicker on me. It is indeed dyed in the colors of the kingdom, decorated in silver and gold fabric that have studs attached to form the crosses of the Celtic and the Christianity cultures, which also repeat themselves on the back as the fabric drapes over my shoulders.

I am also wearing highly decorative, royalty jewelry of necklaces and bracelets. One of the necklaces is just a silver chain; the other one is a chain that has a purple diamond encased by silver. The bracelets are made out of brown leather with some small, loose hanging chains. Each one covers the entire length of my wrists, which is insane yet cool. Plus, I'm wearing my Medal of Honor and Bravery that I received when King Borin and I exchanged a few words for the first time, making me feel like a medieval pimp. The only thing that's missing is a well-carved piece of wood formed into a walking stick that has medieval markings on it. And to top it off is a big, real, purple diamond, like the size of my fists, to match the necklace.

Please, let not be one of those. I feel and kind of look ridiculous. What's taking them so long?

Within minutes, my question is answered as Cedric, Tara, Gothraigh, and Cora enter the room. What grabs my attention is that Cedric is holding another well-carved box just like the one before, except this one is bigger not just in size, but in height. I stand up as they get closer. My curiosity rises. All of them look serious. The energy in the room makes me feel nervous but not on a huge scale like before. You see, from the past weeks of sleeping with Tara, not the other way around, my stress levels have reduced over time and Tara has told me one evening that she sees and senses it, which makes her happy. I do remember reading an article on Facebook a few years back that once a person finds somebody they like and fall in love, their stress levels go down and so do other things. I gotta say it's really nice not to be on edge twenty-four seven and worry about almost everything. I'm getting curious about what's in the box.

"What's in the box, sir?"

Cedric sets it down on the table and looks at me with pride in his eyes, "In this box is to show our race and your race that you are now royalty. It is also to complete your outfit since it's Christmas Eve."

I look at Cora, Tara, and Gothraigh; all of them are trying to conceal their smiles. Cedric opens the box and inside lies the most astonishing, awesome-looking crown. The sheer beauty of it makes my jaw drop and plop back into the couch. The crown is created out of silver, neatly polished, and has a few purple and admiral blue diamonds embedded. The crown also has a nice, thick purple cushion on the bottom to fit comfortably on my head. Still, I feel like I have no right to wear this and I have not, one hundred percent, gotten used to their culture.

"Go on," Tara encourages. "Put it on. You'll look fantastic with it on you."

I rub the back of my neck still feeling uneasy about it. I know that this is reality and these guys and their culture are very real, but playing dungeons and dragons in our culture is a child's play, and when we grow up, some of us find it childish.

Ah hell, I couldn't predict this coming. Might as well try it on.

I carefully grab the crown and study it. I walk over to a tall skinny mirror, observing myself in the reflection. Seeing myself in the clothes that I have on kind of, I don't know, works with me. I look back down at the crown in my hands.

Here goes nothing.

I slowly lift the crown up over my head and then set it down on top. Looking at my total transformation, I'm still appalled by what I see. I feel like I should immediately take it all off and just attend the sermon in a normal human suit. Cedric then walks over and places his hands on my shoulders to comfort me.

"Will, you do look great. You are part of this royal family and tradition. Now, let's not, as you your kind says 'dilly dally' some more and head toward the church."

"Yeah, let's go," I reply with a nod, trying to sound confident, though I'm still not satisfied with the things I am wearing.

We proceed out of the room with Cedric and Gothraigh leading the way side by side. Tara and I follow and Cora covers the rear. While walking down the hallway to the throne room, Tara bends down and whispers to me.

"Don't worry, once I receive all the power, I'm gonna make a few changes. I'll give you the details at the party tonight."

I look up at her and she winks. We continue down the hall into the throne room and the entry hallway to the chapel doorway. We proceed down that hallway and very interestingly, the passageway is empty. Not one human person nor Wolfinoid is waiting in line to enter, yet the time has passed since eight o'clock and the sermon starts eight or possibly at nine. This type of atmosphere makes my nerves rise. We arrive at the double doors. I try to swallow my fear. Of course, Tara squeezes my hand and Cedric and Gothraigh push open the doors. Bits of sweat slide down the back of my neck because the entire sanctuary is completely filled with our race and theirs.

This is one of my fears, being on a stage and in front of a *very* large crowd. More sweat slides down as all faces look at us while we proceed down the stairway and up to the center aisle. The entire area is quiet and heads turn to follow us making our way up to the stage where the deacon and the choir wait for us to sit. Looking at the stage, instead of two chairs, there are now five. The sanctuary is also decked out with Christmas decorations in a much more extravagant way than the lounge room. Anyway, we ascend upon the stage and we take our seats: Cedric sits in the middle, Gothraigh, Tara, and I are on his right, and Cora sits on Cedric's left.

I look uncomfortably out to the crowd, trying to remain calm as possible, but it's not going to work because every Wolfinoid can sense my fear and I am pretty sure some or the majority of the humans can see the fear slowly revealing itself across my face.

While glancing around, my eyes stop at a certain row. In the middle of the sanctuary, sitting on the far-left side, are my friends, all of them. They look at me surprised, shocked, and can't believe it's the real me. I give out a weak yet comforting smile with a slight wave of my hand to confirm it's me. They reply with sly smiles and almost the same wave back. Then, our attention is broken by the deacon's voice.

"Friends. Humans and Wolfinoids. Welcome to this glorious day that our savior Jesus Christ is born on this coming cold, winter day."

A lot of people shake their heads and murmur in agreement. The deacon raises his hand to end the conversations and continue.

"Today is the first time that we celebrate this great day with the human race and I have to say, when we arrived here and learned that both of our religions share the same aspects, I thought we would get along very well with one another. And now, looks like my prediction came true."

Everybody laughs in agreement, including us. I do agree with him. Looking from the stage, it does look like our races have gotten along with one another quite well. There might be some rough patches, but every society can't be absolutely perfect.

"For further announcements, the reason we are celebrating this early is that," he lets out a sigh with some aggression, "Princess Tara is having a party after the sermon and she has told me about this celebration in advance. So," he tries to retain his frustration, "every person is welcome to join. Moreover, as my fellow Wolfinoid brothers and sisters can see," while he spreads his right hand toward our direction, sort of putting me on the spot, "Tara has found her future ruler and husband, Will Young."

Correction, exactly putting me on the spot. Every Wolfinoid turns their attention at me. Tara waves to her future kingdom calmly. However, I try to contain my fear and not let the skin around my head turn red, while still waving to the crowd.

The deacon smiles with satisfaction at Tara and me, and continues, "Now, let us celebrate this glorious day. All rise."

We all follow and sing the first hymn and again, it's the same one, "O come, o come, Emmanuel," but we sing it together and the choir joins in. After singing that song, the deacon proceeds the usual way of how things go in our churches. We confess our sins and our wrongdoings, we pray in silence, and we hear a few bible passages. I find it very interesting that our cultures have so much in common.

We sing another hymn, then hear the story about Jesus Christ, and sing another hymn.

Finally, the deacon raises his hand and speaks, "May the Lord our God be with you."

And we all reply, "Amen."

Everybody gets up and disperses.

Tara sighs and looks at me with satisfaction, "Well, that took hours."

I look at her, feeling a bit offended, but relieved that I can change back into my normal clothes. I reply, "It did take hours. About three at the most."

"Yep." She stretches her arms up and flexes her shoulders. "I'll send the rest of my friends to get your friends and you to meet at the club in a few or so hours." Then, she gets up.

"Wait . . . what?"

She turns around smiling, probably finding my confusion funny. "I'm the party host and you're the main D.J. Like I told you a few nights ago. I love to hear you play more of your songs. Anyway, let's change and meet Maddox there."

I erase my confusion and follow her out.

Following Tara back to her bed chamber, just looking at her makes my heart beat faster. The rushing warmth of love spreads throughout my body. Having the feeling of butterflies fluttering around my stomach makes me slow down and just admire her. I mean, I can't believe I am truly falling for her. Plus, being with her for the past weeks makes my legs quiver a little in a positive way. Yet, I still have little knowledge about her. In her case, she knows me one-hundred percent. And again, being with Tara calms down my cylinders and keeps the revolutions around fifteen-hundred. All this time following her and describing how I feel about her to you guys, I don't realize we're already walking through the dining hall and about to ascend up the stairway to the royal chambers. Still, admiring Tara from the same position, I feel like I should tell her or perhaps when the party's over. During that time, I'll pick the right words and develop them to be very authentic or I can pick a few songs for the show to really butter her up for the right moment.

Yeah, let's go with that plan.

"I sense you're admiring me very much, Nos," she says in a flirty way. "Is there something you want to tell me?" She turns around and looks right at me with eyes filled with love and pleasure. I stop in shock, stumbling through my mind to find the right words.

"Um . . . ah . . . yeah," is my only response.

Tara comes down to my step and traces her index finger up and down my neck, continuing her flirtation, "Is there something on your mind you wish to tell me?"

The warmth of her finger on my neck, the love, and pleasure in her eyes with the flirtation in her voice make me want to fall apart and tell her how I truly feel about her.

No, no. Don't fall apart. Keep it together, Nos.

You know what? Since she likes to play hard to get, perhaps it's my turn to turn the table around. I lock my eyes with hers and slip out a smile. She cocks her head sideways, curious what's going on in my head. Man, thank the Lord she's not that gay, sparkling vampire.

"Possibly. I might tell you when the party nears closing time. If there is one."

She shakes her head in disbelief and closes her eyes, "So close."

Then, she withdraws her hand and keeps climbing the stairs. I let her get a few steps ahead of me before moving on.

When we both arrive at her room, she opens the door and I let her enter first like a true gentleman. Once I enter, I stop for a moment to get a really good view of her room. She does have several types of trees and the same ones I stated weeks ago. Yet, interestingly, there are large pieces of fabric in different shades of blue stretching from one wall to the next and overlapping one another. When I mean "large" pieces, the fabrics reach up to possibly ten feet wide or more to cover the stalactites hanging from the ceiling of the cavern. Surrounding the chamber are the same torches that come to life once we entered; now, they burn in a canary color. Off to my left is Tara's large oval, sunken bed. Beyond it is her wardrobe. Opposite them is the same fire pit with the same pieces of furniture that surround. Surprisingly, there is a set of outdoor cookware. I look at Tara with raised eyebrows.

She gets my amusement. "I like cooking in here. Perhaps you and I should have a private meal together. How does that sound?"

I walk toward her. "Yeah, sounds like a really good idea."

She throws a smile.

Anyway, beyond the pit is the French door that leads to her balcony. I continue toward the wardrobe, slowly taking off the crown since I respect the craftsmanship. Then, I remove the thick leather bracelets and place them on one of the benches inside the large wardrobe. Next, I remove the chains at the back of my neck, rejoicing that the weight is finally removed. Soon, I unbutton and unzip the heavy and highly decorative robe, struggling to remove it from my shoulders. Tara notices, removes it with ease, and places it on a heavy-duty hanger. I thank her and she gives me a quick lick on the cheek. After that, I hear a rustling sound—metal rings being pulled along a pole. I look behind me and see a curtain has been drawn.

"I'm still respecting your wish, but I would like to hear what's going on inside your head. Just to let you know, Will, my patience is starting to go down."

Aw shit, the pressure's on. I gotta, no, I have to confess my feelings to her tonight before I upset her big time. I don't want to end up like Gurtruit McFuze.

Hearing that, I throw off the silk shirt, socks, and shoes, and I run toward one of the drawers where my jeans are kept. I grab the best blue ones, throw them on and my camo belt, then dash toward another drawer for a shirt. I throw it open and look at each t-shirt, scrutinizing the designs and figuring out which would be the best for the party.

"You okay over there?" Tara asks with the teasing sensation in her voice.

"Yeah, yeah, I'm fine," I reply, trying to sound confident.

"Really? Cuz you don't smell like it," Tara continues to tease.

I try to take deep breaths, which kind of works but by like eighty-five percent. Looking back at the drawer, I settle on a black, Harley Davidson shirt that has an eagle's head on the front and on the back. Its wings are spread wide open, talons are extended, and the print of the company is enlarged on the backside of the shirt. Next, I grab two simple brown, leather wrist bands and put them on, a simple leather necklace with a metal tiger tooth on it, and a black and camo hat with a barbed wire stitch design. I pocket my iPod and finally put on a pair of Nike shoes.

While I exit, I wait by the fire pit for Tara. She comes around from the door, all dressed up like on the night of her birthday, except some of her jewelry have tiny Christmas ornaments. She closes the doors like nothing has happened and approaches me with caution. She gets three feet from me, places her hands on my shoulders, and on her face is sorrow, not in a cheap way.

"I'm sorry to frighten you, but that's how I feel. I really want my urges to be settled once and for all."

I nod in agreement and answer with caution, "I understand through and through. I will tell you everything after . . . say three songs?"

She bites her lower lip, "How 'bout making it four and those songs better be some fucking awesome ones."

I smile, shift my weight from one foot to the next, then look right back at her. "It's a deal. Now, let's head down to the club to discuss further arrangements with Maddox."

"Yes, let's."

And we both somewhat hustle out, almost like a race down to the club.

Turns out our little walk turned into a race. Once we both reach the metal catwalk that circulates the dance floor, we're both heaving air in and out. We both look at each other, laughing and nudging each other. My eyes widen with surprise when I return my gaze back to the dance floor. It retains the shape of an octagon except it's four times bigger. The stage is wider and deeper. The bar has increased in length and spreads onto two walls of the octagon with more stools. Finally, were greeted by Maddox's voice.

"S'up? It's about time you two showed up. We could use your help getting the new lights and shit set up."

He's not kidding. Strewn all around him and still in neat piles are equipment boxes that house the speakers, more lights, fog machines, and more cables. Plus, some of that equipment lays around Maddox. The other people helping him are the D.J., Whitney, and Crystal. We head down to join the renovation crew. Reaching the dance floor, I am totally confused about where to start. I haven't dealt with this type of equipment for lights and sound, even for the little things like hooking up a T.V., a game console, and a few simple light fixtures. With this, it's a whole new ball game. Interestingly, looking at Crystal, Whitney, the D.J., Maddox, and Tara, all of their outfits seem to be modern and high-tech.

"So, is this the type of change you're going to bring once you're a queen?"

Before she could answer, Crystal beats her, "Yeah, Nos. I mean it's nice and all that we've stuck to our ancestral ways, but we all think that it's time to shake things up a bit. I mean we can keep the castle and tents, but it's time to change up the style of the robes and jewelry or get rid of them."

I look around with my hands in my pockets, "Sounds reasonable," while nodding my head. Still, I'm confused about where to start.

"You alright, bro?" the D.J. asks.

I don't know how to respond. He and the rest seem to understand what they're doing. So, I guess I should stay out of their ways, and I just shrug both shoulders.

"Yeah, you're confused." He scratches the back of his head. "I can see and smell that. LED is the name." We bump fists. "C'mon, I'll teach you." Immediately, we set off to work.

Within five hours, we get the entire space set up for the Christmas party. Nearing the end of those five hours, I browsed through my iPod, slowly picking each song that could easily flow from the end of one song to the next. Once I picked those songs, my friends were brought in.

"Damn," says Hugh, "this place is a hell a lot bigger than the last time."

"Yeah, no shit," says Alex.

"Gentlemen," I set down my iPod and descend down from the stage. "How y'all doin'?"

"Nos," Austin says with relief in his face, "You look much better. Well, more like yourself than when you were in that church."

The rest of the three also have the same expressions.

"Yeah, I do agree with you all. Prior to the service, Tara assured me that once she receives power, she's bringing this new reality to the kingdom."

They all look around, taking in the equipment that we just assembled and nod in agreement. I look at one of the digital, hologram clocks on one of the walls. It's five minutes past five, so we have less than an hour and a half to practice maybe twice. Of course, Tara announces the reality of the time, too.

"Well, Nos, are you and your friends going to set up and practice the songs?" she asks while she helps the same bartenders assemble the final drinks and food at the bar.

I nod and wave my hand for my friends to follow me to the stage. As we get on the stage, I lightly sweep one of my hands over the small, sound barrier spheres, and they take flight, activating the shield.

"So, Nos, what songs are going to do?" Alex asks.

I look at the iPod and announce the playlist, "We're going to play 'Rockin' in the Woods' by Quintin Gill, 'Trust Is Back' by Diamond Back, 'Screw the Law' by the Duramaxes, and," I glance over my shoulder to look at Tara, then I show the final track to my friends, "this song by Luke Shell." They get a good look.

Hugh's eyes widen and he lets out a smile, "*Oh* Nos, getting really good with the ladies."

"Nos, I think she's gonna love that song more than 'Oh Man,'" says Austin.

"Yeah, when we were changing, she told me that her patience . . . you know." They all lean forward, curious. "To go all the way are running low."

"*Oh!*" they burst out in surprise jumping up and down running around while laughing hysterically on the stage.

Man, this is embarrassing. It's a good thing that none of the other guys can hear this.

"Nos! You dirty, dirty dog! Or should I say wolf," Chris bursts out, still laughing.

"Yeah, yeah," I reply, trying to hold back my laughter but also trying to be serious. "Let's pull ourselves and start practicing these songs." They still laugh. "*Guys!*" They tone down but still laugh while they assemble into their positions. As the minutes pass, they calm down, and I start the playlist.

After practicing for an hour, we were able to practice the songs twice. So, with about a half-hour to spare before all guests start pouring down the stairwells, we head to the bar while avoiding the alcohol and get ourselves jacked up on our favorite caffeinated drinks. During that time, I talk to LED and he's agreed to carry out the rest of the party if Tara and I decide to split. To tell y'all the truth, I'm really both nervous and excited about it. I haven't been able to be this close to a woman in my entire twenty-one years of existence. Without a doubt, I'm pretty sure she will mostly be in charge. On the other hand, I need to focus on putting on a great show for the party tonight. Not a moment too soon, people start pouring down the stairwells and the main lights are slowly toned down letting the black lights, lasers, and strobe lights come to life.

Whitney, Crystal, Dawn, Faith, Tara, and Maddox start handing out glow sticks and have neon face paint kits at the ready. LED sets up his system and starts playing some songs. We all finish our drinks and proceed to the stage. We assemble into our positions and check our equipment to make sure everything is good. We kill some more time and just let the crowd start building up. More minutes pass; the place is starting to build up and we all agree that it's time to jam out.

LED shouts out the announcement with excitement, "Alright, party people! How we doing on this awesome night!" A huge ass roar erupts from them. "Okay, tonight I'm gonna let my man, Nos, and his crew perform a few songs from his playlist tonight. Y'all cool with that?"

The crowd cheers again, I activate my iPod, the lights on the stage come to life, and my crew and I start playing "Rockin' in the Woods."

The crowd roars again. Apparently, that song made them rush to the bar and order every kind of alcohol. Onto the next ones!

"Alright, this next one is called 'Trust Is Back' by Diamond Back." After ten seconds, we start playing that one.

Then I step up to the mic and speak in my normal voice, "Alright, um, we're going to play two more songs because," I look at Tara; she gets the idea and nods in encouragement, "Tara and I . . . we're gonna split and enjoy the rest of this night by ourselves."

Everybody gets what I'm saying, even though it's a bit embarrassing, but I'm really getting tired of sweating the small stuff. When I look back at my crew and ask if they're cool with that, they all just pat my shoulders, give out words of encouragement, and thumbs up.

I smile and return to the mic, "Okay, this next one is called 'Screw the Law' by the Duramaxes, and the last one, Tara, I specifically picked this one just for you. Hope y'all enjoy." When I told her that, she walks right up to the stage looking thrilled, and we start to play "Screw the Law."

When the song comes to a close, we play "Angels Gave You" by Luke Shell to wind everything up. For this one, I deactivate the guitar and sing the song. Well, I had the guitar off before 'Screw the Law' started and Chris and Hugh were the other singers.

As the song finishes, I look right into Tara's eyes looking completely aroused and I guess I totally melted her heart. She grabs the collar of my shirt and pulls me right off the stage. While I'm brought down, she pushes me against the wall and deeply kisses me.

Then she whispers in my ear, "Is that how you really feel about me?"

"Yeah, I do. I think I'm ready to go all the way," I whisper back. She kisses me one more time and holds my face in front of hers.

"Wait here for an hour or so and come up to my room." I nod in understanding and then she leaves in a hurry with excitement bouncing from her feet.

Everybody congratulates me and my crew on such a great show, especially the Wolfinoids. They all tell me that my taste in music is interesting and I thank them for their compliments. I nod my head at LED and he retakes the stage and starts jamming out Dubstep. For me, I just wander over to the bar feeling really great about myself. The rest of my friends come over and we celebrate.

The one hour goes by fast and slow in my universe. The anxious side of me acts up again and I feel excited and somewhat worried. However, I'm twenty-one and I can have any type of alcohol so I order just one shot of patron. It does loosen me up a little and I bid my friends a good evening. While climbing the stairs to the catwalk, I'm still on edge like I've always been since high school.

CHAPTER TWENTY-FIVE
Home Run
Location: Approaching Tara's Bedroom
Time: 9:30 PM

I WALK UP IN silence to the long, curving stairway leading to a massive, high-rise hallway that connects to the doors of Tara's bedroom. The noise of the dance club was immediately smothered by the stone walls when I got to the top of the spiral stairwell and exited the hallway that connects to the throne room. This entire hike has been so quiet that I can hear my heart racing and pulsing through my ears. And it's weird that I can feel my blood rushing around the edges of my stomach. At this moment, I am a bit shaky and lightheaded as I climb the center part of the stairway.

Soon, my vision starts going sideways and I trip on one of the steps. Before collapsing, I put my hands out to stop me from falling.

Why I am struggling? Why am I having this panic attack? C'mon Nos, pull yourself together. You can do this. Straighten up and climb this stairway like a man.

I grab the banister and hoist myself to my feet. I shake my head a couple of times to straighten out my vision and proceed upward.

I reach the top and walk toward the doors. Still, bits of sweat slips down the back of my neck and my heart proceeds to increase its speed. Getting to the doors, I stop, taking huge breaths of air to really try to accomplish remaining calm. The only question is, why do I have the song called "Can't Breathe" by Flying Spark playing in my head? It's weird, but it seems quite relevant to the situation I'm going through.

Sigh. Here's goes nothing.

I open one door and step in. Surprisingly, in front of me are thick curtains that are extended, cutting off a section from the room. I step forward with one hand stretching outward to pull back one of the curtains until Tara speaks from the other side.

"Don't pull it back," she says in a soft, pleasurable tone. "Just remove your shoes, stand where you are, and close your eyes."

I raise my eyebrows. "Um . . . okay." I follow her directions still nervous about what is going to happen.

"Are your eyes closed?"

"Yeah, they are."

"Okay, I'm coming through."

The curtains move. I can feel her presence nearby. Soon, I can feel her body heat radiating off from her. Then, I feel her stepping behind me; the warmth of her hands come in contact with my skin as they slip under my shirt and she slides them upward. While they slide upward, my body reacts by shivering slightly and having goosebumps.

"You're on edge. There's nothing to be worried about. You've been with me for months so there's nothing to fear."

Her warm breath strokes the side of my face while most of it enters my ear. Her hands stop on my shoulders and rub them gently. I let out a heavy sigh to try to calm my nerves.

"It's going to be okay, Will, I'm going to guide you to my private pool room. Once there, you can open your eyes."

I nod in agreement. She gently starts escorting me forward; entering the room, I can feel the cool air wrap itself around my exposed skin. I expect to be walking on the cold, stone floor, but I guess Tara put down thick, warm rugs. We continue to move forward, taking our time. I feel the warmth of fire blazing in the pit in front of me as we get closer, but Tara gently turns me to the right and continues forward.

I can feel that we're getting close to a wall, but we still press on. Tara bends down to my ear, "Okay, there are a few steps ahead of you. Just take them one at a time."

Within two slow strides, my right foot touches the first step and I slowly ascend upon it. Soon, my left touches the second one and I repeat this process eight times. Then we reach the level ground and Tara tells me to stop. Suddenly, there's a sound of stones grinding against one another. As it slides away, a wave of hot yet comforting humid air travels from the other side to greet us. The stone stops. Tara pushes me onward for about six more strides and tells me to stop. After that, the previous sound of stone happens again and seals off the cold air from her room. The atmosphere feels humid, tropical to put it, and I can feel the steam, moist air touching my skin.

"Now, you can open your eyes."

I open them and what lays before me is a large, rectangular room that has a floor, ceiling, walls, and pillars constructed out of limestone tiles. Off to my left is indeed a very large pool already filled with water with steam rising from it. Farther to its left are three fountains, equally spaced from one another and formed into wolf heads that have water spewing from their puckering lips. They are also created out of limestone. Behind them is an open shower area that has six polished square stainless-steel showerheads attached to the ceiling, but no knobs are attached to the wall. Surrounding the entire pool room are tropical plants. Some of them have full-grown fruits on them ready to be plucked and eaten. On the opposite wall from us, spanning from the floor to the ceiling, from the left corner of the wall to the right corner, is an all-out mural. Painted in extravagant colors, the mural shows a lovely, friendly, and inviting beach view with the ocean cresting over in different areas and a beautiful sun shining bright in the sky. It is completed with palm trees and some smooth boulders. In front of us are a few comfy pool chairs and right next to them is a simple shelving unit made out of bamboo with thick, white towels and different types of lotions. Illuminating this tropical pool room are recess lights. After taking this all in, I look back at the pool and wonder how big it is.

Tara laughs, "The pool is thirty feet long, fifteen feet wide, and has a depth of eight feet. Are you a good swimmer?"

"Ah, yeah. I swim okay."

"Good." She comes around and walks in front of me.

She's wearing a simple, white robe and has her attention on the tie she is undoing. Then she spreads the robe, spreading her arms out. As they are fully extended, she lets go of the robe and it falls to the floor, revealing her pure, true form. She then turns around slowly. I do not let my eyes fly down to the floor; I keep them on the beautiful Wolfinoid angel. With her facing me, I can see everything: *all* of her beautifully sculpted body. All the fear that I was experiencing immediately melts away, yet my knees shake, wanting to move forward to get a closer view and feel though I still want to maintain this distance.

She giggles while biting her lower lip, "Come closer, you silly human," while she gestures with her right index finger with the same command.

I walk closer, still admiring the sight. Getting closer, my heart is still racing, pumping blood, mostly sending it down between my legs, and letting my stick come alive.

Tara stops me and inhales my scent with pleasure, more deeply than ever. "Hmm, lovely than ever, but there's still a problem."

What problem? I don't a see problem. I'm just letting my eyes gaze upon your beautiful body.

She grabs a small dagger that is hidden in one of the towels, then she grabs the bottom of my shirt and pulls the dagger upward, letting the pristine, sharp blade cut through the fabric like paper. As it reaches the top, she squats down, undoes the belt buckle, and pulls the rest of the belt off. Next, she cuts through my jeans from the bottom to top on both leggings. Looking at her eyes, she seems to really enjoy this moment of cutting my clothes off and taking in what is becoming my naked body. She then removes the jeans and shirt and tosses them both behind me like they're trash. Tara places the dagger on the lower shelf, then picks my right leg, removing the sock and likewise for the other. Next, she stands up and removes my hat, necklace, and simple leather bracelets.

We look into each other's eyes filled with pleasure and yearning to be closer with one another. To break the silence, Tara breathes a sigh filled with relief and says, "I think it's time to reveal the package. Don't you think?"

In my breathy tone, I reply, "Yeah."

We keep our eyes locked onto one another as she slowly squats back down while pulling down my boxers. Once my boxers touch the warm limestone floor, Tara breaks the gaze and looks down at her prize. She gasps in awe, lets her free right hand stretch out, and slowly grasps my penis. The warmth of her hand, aw man, makes me lean forward onto her shoulder and close my eyes while I enjoy the feel of her fingers rubbing and almost stroking it.

"It's a good size and so soft like the rest of your body."

Uh-huh.

She retrieves the hand from her prize, then I hear the movement of her saliva and that same hand returns wet. That feeling of her saliva continuing to rub my penis makes my eyes burst open and I immediately wrap my arms around her shoulders to steady myself.

"Do you like that?" she teases.

I try to talk, but I can't form the words.

Then I feel her head tilting up. As I look down, her eyes are filled with sexual intentions. "How about this?"

Next thing, she places both hands on my hips, looks back down, and begins stretching out her tongue.

"Oh, God," are the only two words that come out of my mouth. She wraps her tongue around, pulls her mouth around it, and begins slowly sucking it with her eyes softly closed.

Oh my God. I'm getting a blowjob from a Wolfinoid! Fuck. Shit. This feels fucking amazing. Fucking hell. Her tongue feels great!

While in reality, I'm beginning to pant with my eyes closed while I enjoy the feel of her tongue moving up and down my cock.

Right after that, she removes her mouth and after my penis has been soaked with her spit, the air in this room feels cold instead of warm. Next, she adjusts her head and begins slowly sucking my balls while lightly massaging them. Just minutes of feeling her soft tongue on my only exterior organs, my knees buckle, the gravity bringing me down. At that moment, Tara removes her head from "harm's way" and catches me from my armpits. Through my half-open eyes, I can see Tara's face filled with lust, love, and happiness.

"And now, it's your turn," she says as she lowers me down onto the floor gently and reclines onto one of the pool chairs, stretching her arms up behind her; her fingertips are nearly touching the wall.

I roll onto my stomach, slowly shaking my head to retrieve my entire eyesight. Tara just giggles as she watches her human boyfriend struggle to get back up. And I do with all my might. As a few minutes go by, I finally steady myself on my feet and as I look onto Tara, she lowers her right arm while stretching her legs and begins to open them wide while letting her hand brush against her breasts and then slowly inserts two fingers from her left hand into her paradise hole. She moves them slightly in, out, and around a little. After that, she pulls them out and holds them toward me ordering me to come closer.

"Taste it," she says.

I come forward, slowly getting down on both of my knees at her right side. I slowly raise my hand to grab her wrist, yet she forces the fingers through my lips and swirls them around my mouth, letting my taste buds make contact with whatever juices dwelling on them. I don't know how to describe the taste, but my sex endorphins made me enjoy it. I do. Suddenly, Tara immediately pulls out her fingers and fully grabs the top of my head. Her eyes now show a glint of seriousness.

"Now that you have tasted it, it's time to feast upon it." She then begins lowering my head toward it and I don't resist. As I'm just an inch away from her vagina, I look up.

"You better feast on it real, good human," Tara says in the same tone to match the mood in her eyes. Immediately, my lips collide with it and I begin to suck and lick while rubbing her stomach. The more I moved my tongue around, the firmer she pushes her hand onto my head as she moans with pleasure.

"Yes. Oh, yes, Nos. Right there. Right there. Oh, fucking God yes!"

Since she has blown her breath down my throat during the times when we have deeply kissed, I inhale air through my nose and blow right into her. Hard.

"Oh, my fucking God yes! That's it! Ah, shit, Nos! You're such a dirty human!"

Her gasps for air become heavy while she slams her other hand onto my head increasing the force to bury my face into her pussy. The taste and aroma are so damn strange. It smells really weird, but the same neurons fire off to convert those things into something satisfying.

Later, her hands slip down to my jaw and she brings up my head. I was able to squeeze one more lick before it happened; Tara, filled with adrenaline, pulls me forward and kisses me deeply once again so fast, throws my back on the chair, and gets on top of me. She sits on my legs and rubs my chest firmly. I begin to reach up and gently grasp her breasts. The feeling is just amazing. Tara also places her hands on mine to continue the rubbing while she bites her lower lip and looks up at the ceiling feeling quite pleased about what is happening. In seconds, she rips off my hands (not literally) from her breasts, places one hand on my shoulder, and uses the other to continue stroking my cock; she and I lock eyes; both of us are gasping for air; I quickly glance down to my cock and then back up at her. In her eyes, she wants to move up. I slowly nod to give her consent. She nods back, removes that same hand, then slowly and smoothly moves over my stomach and up the chest, clasps her right hand over the left side of my face, and bends down licking my lips.

"You sure?" Her warm breath rolls over my face.

"Yeah," exhaling the word.

I completely settle onto my back fully relaxed while Tara grabs one of the lotion bottles and massages the liquid all over my penis and balls. Next, she raises herself only inches, sliding upward a bit while placing her hands on my shoulders for support and positioning herself over my crotch. She licks her lips, smiling for the ride she is about to have. In an instant, she comes down; the feeling inside her is so warm and liquefying that I place my hands on her hips as I look up at the ceiling and just enjoy the sensation. She exhales in happiness and begins to ride it.

The ride gets faster and faster. Both of our hearts and our gasps for air increase in speed. The adrenaline, the pleasure, the need to be very close with one another intensifies. We hold onto one another as if a huge storm with a tornado is passing at a slow speed, shaking the structure with its high velocity. We look at each other through our half-open eyes. I can tell that the pressure is beginning to build.

It's building. I feel it. I need to take it out.

I try to pull away and adjust my body in a position to remove it from the warm, liquid tube, but Tara notices it and destroys my plan by holding me tighter against her body, almost smothering me into her breasts.

She gasps through her breaths, "Don't . . . don't take it out. Almost . . . there." She still increases her humping; on my end, the pressure is much intensifying I do my best to hold it back, but I can't. This is feeling way too damn, fucking good.

As Tara comes down, I push upward, releasing my white liquid within her while letting out a high groan of pleasure. Tara lets out a small howl of pleasure too while slowing down her humps every time I pulse into her. Her rides keep up the pulsing for a good moment and once there is no more, she lays us back onto the chair. Both of us are breathing in relief from the huge rush we both shared, and she whispers into my ear:

"That was fun. We should do it more often, but how 'bout we retire to bed and sleep in each other's arms closer than before?"

"Yeah . . . that sounds good."

We get up, holding each other close, and Tara grabs one of the towels from the shelf and drapes it over us. On the contrary, I shiver from shock at what happened a few seconds ago. Tara licks my forehead and takes us back into her room. As the stone door opens, the cold air rushes in, making both of us shiver. We descend the steps. Tara moves one of her hands outside the towel and waves it around in slow motion, making the fire in the pit grow bigger and warmer and likewise for the torches on the walls. Interestingly, the light grows dim and the atmosphere starts to feel warm.

Getting closer to the bed, she lets the towel fall down to the floor. We enter the large oval bed in slow motion and again, Tara lowers me down first and she follows by lying on top, wrapping herself around me. Then she brings on top of us a thick blanket to keep us warm. Well, mostly for me. Still, the same shiver from what I experienced lingers in my body; my whacked-out brain from being told in the past what is allowed and not tries to calculate whether I should be happy or scared. The voices from the majority of the Special Ed staff sound off, yet the warmth radiating off my girlfriend's body combats those voices and replays the moment. For some odd reason, this makes me shiver; it also grabs Tara's attention.

"What's wrong, Nos?" she asks with concern and strokes my forehead. "Why are still shivering? Did I do something wrong?"

I shake my head and try to form the words, then I speak, "No . . . you didn't. It's just that," I look right at her, letting tears form and then bury my head into her chest, "don't leave me. You're *the closest* I've ever got to in my entire existence. I've been shattered enough by people like Chase Tiger and by myself."

Tara rubs my back in comfort, "Oh, Nos, my poor baby, I will never leave you. You did really great back there. Especially how you blew that air into my pussy, it was . . . exhilarating. Plus, I think we'll spend the next few days or weeks just in here. The two of us, learning more about each other's past. Does that sound good?"

I nod in agreement with my head still buried into her breasts. Tara kisses my head and soon, we both start drifting off to sleep, closer with each other in this warm chamber on a Christmas Eve night.

CHAPTER TWENTY-SIX
Tara and I Finally Get to Know One Another
Date: December 25, 2014
Time: 6:45 PM

I WAKE UP TO the smell of food being cooked followed by their sizzling sounds. The aromas of the food touch my nose and my brain tells me that they're sausages, bacon, eggs, and hash browns. I move around realizing that Tara is not lying next to me. I slowly open my eyes and they are greeted by the rising winter sun that shines brightly through the open curtains. I wake up feeling totally relaxed and refreshed. I've never felt this way since, I don't know, elementary school, possibly back in the first or second grade. I raise my eyebrows at that and flex my shoulders and neck to shake off the slumber. Thinking about last night, the adrenaline rush comes back to me and makes me realize I truly slept like a baby. My brain, replaying that night, finally accepts and chooses that it was a happy moment, and I should not regret nor feel guilty about it. All in all, just thinking about last night makes me smile.

"Good morning, Nos."

I look behind me and there's Tara, sitting on a couch, cooking breakfast over her fire pit, and wearing a silk ruby-red robe tied to her waist but still revealing her chest. I smile more, shaking my head at the sight. I stand up to my feet, stretching and realizing that the atmosphere here is still warm like a summer morning in late May. I look around to put something on and as my eyes look at the stone-shelves above the bed, in one of the cubbies lays a pair of white sweat pants. Perhaps, those are the same ones I woke up in for the first time in this chamber. Other than that, I put them on and join Tara.

"Tsk. I really enjoy seeing your true form. I don't like seeing clothes on you."

I smile, sit down next to her, and kiss her forehead, "And good morning to you, too."

She shakes her head and continues cooking.

I place my right arm around her shoulders and watch her cook. I have to say, it really feels great to be next and be this close to a woman, especially when she's the one who falls in love first, then both of us make the full home run. Plus, this is really relaxing that I don't realize I lay my head onto her shoulder. Tara removes one hand that was holding the skillet and massages my back with effort. I can definitely feel her warm, comfortable hand against my skin, bones, spine, and the backside of my rib cage.

"Are you going to tell me why you're shaking last night?" she asks concerned.

That question makes me raise my head from her shoulder, yet I let it hang in front of my chest, feeling a little stupid about that reaction almost right after we had sex.

"What's wrong, Will?"

Looking at the corner of my right eye, I can see her turning to me. She brings up her other hand and lifts my head up to her while flattening her other hand on my back. Looking into her eyes, they are filled with concern, curiosity, and desire to cheer me up. I glance at the food wondering if she's done. She gets the message and moves the large skillet to a sturdy wood table, her eyes pleading why I was shaking last night.

"Are you going to go into full detail about your life after I tell you mine?" I ask, hoping that Tara is still keeping her promise that she made last night.

"Yes, yes. I will."

"Okay." I get up and walk toward the French doors.

Looking out, I can see the snowy peaks of the Appalachian Mountains. I let my eyes glance down and through the gaps of the stone railing of Tara's balcony, I receive a decent bird's eye view of Sparta. I return my gaze to the mountains and let the thoughts of being bullied by my "classmates" and faculty flow combined with what happened in my parent's house in Los Alamos. They're mostly negative. I just let the history of the insane mental roller coaster ride I've been on, throwing me side to side on the deep embankments and trying to throw me out of the train car. At this moment, I can feel Tara's eyes mining themselves into my back and get loaded with more concern. I let out a heavy sigh, briefly going through my history as far back I can, making sure I can tell my future wife the hell I've been through. Then I turn around, looking at her seriously and folding my hands behind my back. Next, I proceed to walk.

"Okay, Tara. Here's my history."

I start telling her where I was born in Wisconsin and which town I lived in. After that, I tell her the town I lived in was so small it didn't have a school district and I went into full detail about it. After that, I tell her about the town I traveled to by bus to go to school and I do my best to describe what I did during school hours. Then, I move onto the subject of me and my family moving from Wisconsin to New Mexico and proceeded onto my academic life in Los Alamos County School District. In that part, I go all-out walking around everywhere, waving my arms while explaining my social life, my minor learning disabilities, my relationship with some of the special education teachers, what happened in those classrooms, what happened to me when I brought some crap from home to school because some of us were struggling to adapt to our new home and how I was treated by my "classmates," and how most of them hated my ass. The details of my social life in school just get darker once I hit middle school. Yet, I do throw in that I met some nice people, but on the flip side, that's when the majority of the special education staff started not giving a damn about people like me. They started treating our I.E.P.s like they were the same and just mainly pointed out the negative shit.

However, once I talk about high school, the mood becomes positive. I tell Tara everything about the new people I met, receiving respect, and all that. However, the history goes back to being dark of how my dad was starting to be in and out of jobs and how during high school, teachers like Chase Tiger tried to put the final brand on my mind that I'm an autistic bastard, and that life was going to be so much "simple and easy" once people like me graduated from that campus. I do my best to explain to Tara how I was torn between two different kinds of people: the ones who can defend themselves and live on their own and the others who physically and mentally can't. I tell her how I was treated at my parents' house; all of these created barriers in my head, especially making me feel that I wasn't good enough for any woman and that I was not going to have an actual dating relationship.

"That's why I was shaking last night. I was trying to tell my whacked-out mind that our . . . actions were really special and that I should not regret it. I should feel happy, but my messed up, programmed mind was trying to slip through those memories of hell I've been through and made me think that I crossed the line. Of course, it was probably a mixture of shock since that was my first time doing it with you."

Tara has her hands over her mouth. Her tears start forming and falling from her eyes. Looking at her, I feel relieved explaining all of my past while observing her expression of sadness and sorrow. I feel slightly terrible by destroying a very good morning. I look away scratching the back of my scalp, feeling terrible that I just broke her heart after she heard my mostly dark history. Then suddenly, she turns me around and her hand tilts my head up so our eyes meet and lock onto one another. Her eyes still have tears falling, though they show hope.

"Have I . . ." She sniffles a little. "Have I brought down all of those barriers in your head?"

I smile, "Every day that I spend with you, you constantly tear them down in large chunks and make sure that they stay down. Some areas of my mind where the barriers once stood have now been destroyed and you walk over the rubble, place your warm welcoming arms around me, and hold me close. Very close."

After saying that, her eyes completely light up with joy. She bends down, kisses me, and lightly tows me back to the couch. As we both sit down, she sets up another table, brings around the still-hot skillet, and sets plates out. After that, she dashes toward the pool room while carrying a silver platter. Tara shouts over her shoulder saying it's alright for me to start eating. I just shrug and dive in. Minutes later, she comes back with the platter filled with fruit and joins me.

We eat in silence. Expect in my head I always have songs playing ranging from rock, metal, country, hip hop, to R&B. It's like a never-ending boom box in here. After creating it during elementary school, I've gotten used to it. I am curious what's going on in Tara's head. What is she thinking about my history, of what type of human that I am now? Probably thinking how I could be treated such an asshole for eight years. Oh well, it's simple science, survival of the fittest, and I wasn't one of the fittest. *Sigh.*

"Do you want to learn about me?" Tara asks, looking under her eyebrows.

I swallow. "Yeah, I would like to know a few things about you."

Tara stirs the food around her plate for a while, probably gathering her thoughts, then she fully looks up at me. "Well, for starters, from what you've seen, I can conjure nature and ice by will. I am a very smart woman and can destroy any type of opponent. Just like the time where I told my staff to fly and stand still in front of that rolling mini semi."

She throws out a smile.

The memory of me being thrown forward from the bed of the Ram when it collided with her staff makes my ribs ache a bit.

"Obviously, you can see that I am the future queen of Sparta." She raises her hand to display her room. "But before we came here, my life was a bit troubled. Kind of like yours, except the bully incidents."

I lean back and cross my arms, still remaining calm and interested. *Oh, this is going to be good.*

Surprisingly, she gets up and paces the room like I did. "For a long time, I've been reserving myself for someone special. Another Wolfinoid on our home planet. No offense."

"None taken. Continue."

"But none and I mean absolutely none seemed to interest me. Some have come up to me and try to win me over. Others have tried to use force; at those moments, I have used some of my skills to tell them how you humans say "fuck off." The majority of them received the message, but a small piece of the pie thought I was joking and that led to their deaths."

Wow and I thought I was too serious.

"And then," Tara continues, bringing her hands to the sides of her head, running her fingers through her hair, and letting out a heavy yet aggravated sigh, "there was Marcus Lowsbroth. That man, that bastard, never understood I wanted him to fuck off and stay the hell away from me. I have told my father about his actions and he took my words seriously. Soon, that man got some prison time and was let out on good behavior. He did leave me alone for a while but returned to his old ways. I had to use my close combat skills to fend him off. To sum it up, he ended up with his left shoulder dislocated, right kneecap shattered, and a few ribs broken and cracked."

Okay, I think it would be wise for me not to leave her, cheat on her, or anything like that to get her really pissed off.

"Other than that, I like music. I'm into the Celtic music that our race has been playing for years. However, I'm more interested in dance club songs. Although," Tara continues as she walks behind the couch and tilts my head back, "I'm really getting into your type of music and I have to say it's really interesting."

"Thank you. Anything else?"

She ponders a moment. "What other things do you like?"

I lean back and think for a moment. "I like log cabins."

Tara cocks her head sideways. "What are those?"

I explain to her what cabins are, what they're constructed of, and their variations from small to large mansions. After that, I tell her that I've always imagined living in one that's located in a low altitude valley or in one that's concealed by trees in the mountains, yet in between the massive trunks of the trees, I can still have a good view of the snowcapped mountains. Next, I move onto the likings of classic muscle cars and lifted trucks. Again, Tara is curious about them. I tell her a very fine example of one classic car lying in Maddox's garage. She gets the idea and walks over to her bed to grab a tablet. Her eyes widen with wonder as she searches for the famous '69 Charger, the lifted trucks, and the log cabins. While she looks at the images of the log cabins, she turns the tablet toward me to make sure they're the right thing. I acknowledge and turn the tablet back at her. She then pops something like a note tab and starts writing notes about the places in her native language. This makes me wonder.

"Why are you jotting down notes?"

"Hm? Oh, for the heck of it." Then Tara powers down the tablet, puts it away, and joins me back on the couch. To sum it all up, we both fall into deep conversations. Most of the time, I try my best to describe the history of this nation, although I do fetch her tablet and search for all the answers.

Tara throws question after question at me. Since I'm very good at American history, I answer the questions, but most of the time, I have to use the tablet to fill in the gaps. During one of my searches, a small piece of my mind wanders off and recalls the architecture of the poolroom. My typing in the search bar slows as I think about it. The way it's built and designed resembles a tropical beach and resort.

Comparing to how this place is constructed and laid out, it's the complete opposite.

Well, duh! It's cold here in the Appalachian Mountains and that goes for everywhere else that's going through this winter!

Still, I think the poolroom totally resembles their home, so is the original kingdom of Sparta in a tropical location and constructed next to a beach?

"Why did you stop typing?" Tara asks.

"Oh, um, I'm just thinking. Since I'm answering your questions about this nation, how 'bout answer a few of mine about your world?"

Tara nibbles her lower lip and answers, "You do have a point. What do you want to know?"

"Is the original kingdom of Sparta located on a beach? Because, from what I've seen from your poolroom, it's built and designed like a beach resort."

She nods and smiles, "Yeah, that's true. The original kingdom is located at a beach."

After that, she spirals into detail about her people's race and shows me the geography of her homeworld. My amazement shoots high as she portrays her planet on the tablet and then shows the animal life both in land and sea, the vegetation—everything. She even uses a time-lapse control system to show how they migrated over the million years and how Sparta and Troy set up their proper boundaries of which area they cover and control. I do turn the table around and throw question after question at her and that just makes her smile.

Throughout the morning and into the afternoon, we teach each other's history and hammer each other with questions.

CHAPTER TWENTY-SEVEN

Spontaneous Hand-to-Hand Combat Training
Date: December 29, 2014
Time: 9:12 AM

ANOTHER CALM, WINTER SUNRISE passes by the windows of the French doors as Tara and I eat another fine and fulfilling breakfast in her room. This time, she has her own iPod playing some music that's a mix of tropical tranquility lounge and Celtic music. Also, she's made the atmosphere to be more tropical. When we both got up and dressed, she used her sorcery to have tropical plants grow right out of the stone floor and produce their fruit. After that, she casually walked over, picked the fruit, and combined them with the other ingredients.

Other than that, we eat in this relaxing environment wearing summer clothes. The funny thing is both of our clothes do have camo prints on our sleeveless shirts, her shorts, and my blue jeans. She questioned why I'm wearing jeans and I told her that my body adapted to the heat of the high New Mexico desert and it's my preferred style.

Once we finish eating and I help Tara with the dishes, she comments that I'm such a gentleman and I just tell her it's like the country music that I listen to. When the minutes pass and the dishes are put away, Tara glances at me in a serious way. It catches my attention when I glance back. In a weird way, Tara walks away from the fountain where we're washing dishes. Her posture and movement show that she's a little stern and makes me concerned, wondering if I've upset her in any way. If I had, I might end up like my rival back in the arena. I slowly stand up and proceed with loads of caution on how to act and what to ask.

"Tara," I ask in a concerning voice while remaining calm, "have I said anything to upset you this morning?"

Tara walks to the French doors, pulls back one of the curtains, and looks out, possibly ignoring my question. This makes my heart pick up some pace, sensing I might have pissed her off. I don't how, but it sure does look like it. I slowly back away and move to the doors to exit her room. During this retreat, my fear begins to slowly rise, yet I try to keep it as low as possible; on the flip side, it just creates sweat to form and slide down the backside of my neck. Again.

"No," Tara answers in a calm voice with some sternness. Her answer makes me freeze when I'm about twenty feet from the door. She continues, "Do you find me, my race, terrifying?"

Okay, this question throws me off. I need to find the right words, "Um . . . yes."

I answer in caution but still remain where I stand. "From what I've seen . . . especially when you rescued me in the arena . . . I do find you terrifying. Why do you ask?"

Taking another step back, Tara turns around, glowering at me. I don't know if she's being serious or funny. I stop. Looking into her eyes, they do seem pretty damn serious and they make my blood turn to ice. My nerves break and my fear rises.

"Good." She slips an evil smile, crouches down, and growls at me. She continues, "Do you remember that I told you I know close combat skills and that some of the victims ended up dead?"

Ah, shit. Don't tell me where this is going.

My voice trembles, "Yeah."

Tara growls again, tenses her legs even more, then suddenly springs and charges at me while yelling with enthusiasm, *"Let's see how good you are!"*

As she gets closer, she leaps up into the air having her teeth and claws exposed.

"Fuck!"

My adrenaline rush immediately kicks in and I bolt for the fountain. Tara snarls and chases me swiftly. Nearing the fountain, I literally dive into it, grabbing the cast iron skillet and within a moment's notice, turning around, I see Tara snarling with continuous enthusiasm. I slam the skillet across the right side of her face in quickly and seriously that sends her flying a few feet away from me.

She lands on the floor on her chest letting out an "Oof" sound and remains there.

What the fucking shit and hell did I just do? I can't believe I just smacked a cast-iron skillet across my girlfriend's face.

I slowly stand up; my legs are trembling in fear and mighty concern. The thought of knocking Tara out and putting her in an unconscious faze frightens me to the extreme. To check on her, I slowly step toward her on-guard just in case she springs up and pins me down. She is breathing normally, which makes me stop in fear, yet I'm grateful that she's still alive. After five steps, she groans while shaking her head and pushes herself off the floor. Next, she kneels on her right knee, touching her lower jaw with her right hand. Withdrawing it, there's blood on her few fingers. Turning around, the damage reveals itself. The cast-iron skillet not only broke the skin on her lower lip but also the skin around her right eye. Within seconds, a faint light appears, sealing the skin and making the blood stop dripping. The expression in Tara's eyes is filled with surprise, satisfaction, and revenge. She closes them, calmly wipes away the blood that once ran near her eye and lower lip, and fully stands up. My fear reaches its highest. I slowly back away from her, gripping the skillet tighter in my hand. Then Tara opens her eyes and they are filled with revenge and desire to push me off the edge seemingly to release the beast inside of me. The one that was created over the years from bullies and putting myself down to please others—the one I've kept locked up tight in an iron cage.

"Heh," Tara laughs. "One more attack to push you over and let your dark side come out." At the same time, she takes one strong step forward to make me flinch.

"Tara," I caution her, raising the skillet yet holding out my left hand open at her so that she doesn't proceed forward, "Tara, please don't do this. I really don't know my own strength. I really don't want to hurt you or perhaps kill you."

She smiles and takes another step forward while brushing her hair behind one of her ears. "You don't want to really hurt me? Ha, sweetie, that's the point of this day. I really want you to release your beast inside and take me on. I'll show you new moves while showing the chinks in your attacks."

Again, she bends down and growls at me. This time, without running, I too crouch my legs, embracing her attack and converting the fear into strength while playing battle music in my head.

Seconds tick by so fast as she springs forward. Her movements are so swift, I don't have the time to react. She immediately tackles me down; as my back hits the ground, I lose grip of the skillet. Tara gets full grip around both my wrists, spreads my arms wide, and lays her entire body weight upon me totally immobilizing me. Struggling in hopes to break free, Tara tightens her grip and seeps out a mocking laugh. Immediately, she opens her mouth and inches it closer to my face perhaps to maul it off. Surprisingly, an idea went into my head and it seems to be the only plan so I tighten my neck and wait for her mouth to get closer. Nearing less than an inch away from my face, I snap my neck forward, dropping my jaw wide open, and latch firmly around her nose. I bite tight, hoping to break her skin. Tara's nerves recognize the pain. Her eyes burst wide and she pulls upward, releasing her grip on my hands and having me in tow. Within an instant, I open my mouth to let her back away and place her hands around her nose.

I sit up, bringing up my right leg yet letting the left lying flat on the floor. I place my right elbow on top of the right knee, glower, and growl at Tara. She sits cross-legged still holding her nose in her hands, but surprisingly, she begins to laugh with amusement combined with some revenge. I tense up, prepping for the next attack. I'm pretty sure that this situation is heating up real good because she just keeps on laughing.

Oh, man. This is starting to get awkward and scary.

"Ha, ha, ha, ha! Oh, Nos." She removes her hands from her nose and stares down at me. "Now we're getting somewhere because this is going to be so much fun." Then she bolts at me.

I roll immediately out of the way. Again, she follows and attacks me by bringing me down. I counteract by balling up my right hand and smacking it against Tara's right eye. She hollows in pain; I jump up and kick her back down, pushing her back toward the floor. Immediately, I scramble my legs around her head, interlocking them tightly. Next, I wrap my arms around her legs and lock them, too. When Tara struggles, I just tighten more and more. Of course, I forget that Tara and her race have claws in their hands. She bares and scratches them into my legs a little deep. The pain is unbearable, making me release my captive immediately. Tara sees the open window and springs upward. Like a kangaroo, I kick both of my feet into her face. We stand up quickly and circle one another; putting my body weight onto my legs ignites the pain even more. After that, I feel something warm and wet seeping down my legs. Still, Tara and I watch each other with our defenses highly up.

Every time I step, the pain in both legs intensifies and the mass of the warm liquid increases. The pain becomes too much to bear that I decide to look down to figure out why I'm in so much pain.

Once my eyes go down, they widen. "What the fuck?"

Then I look at Tara, shocked and in disbelief. Her amusement suddenly turns into shock. Turns out, Tara dug her claws a little *too* deep into my legs and I'm bleeding kind of bad.

"Nos," Tara speaks apologetically, "I am so, so sorry." Then she examines her claws and her eyes widen. She looks back at me while I stare at my bleeding legs.

"Nos, baby, I didn't mean . . . to be . . . this rough. Please, baby, I'm so sorry."

I'm listening to her but now on a small scale. Turns out, her last attack has finally unleashed my beast, my monster. Everything in my head goes silent. My shock turns into anger. I look at Tara and zero in. She puts up her hands in surrender.

"Will, please, listen to me. I am so sorry. Calm down, please."

I stretch out my right arm with an open hand. I close my eyes, concentrating on my staff. It flies right into my hand and my hand automatically closes around it tightly. Suddenly, it comes to life, sounding off the original chime. At the same time, the admiral blue flame erupts around the flame, glass orb, and I reopen my eyes.

"You want the monster? Well, you got the monster."

Tara tries to speak, but I try to charge right at her. She darts away. I swing my staff sending an arc of fire. Tara frantically picks up speed. She ascends in one of the trees also commencing her staff to come to life and fly into her hands. I continue zeroing in and keeping on charging, but the pain becomes too much. Yet, I use it to fuel my adrenaline rush that unleashes my insanity.

In the middle of my attack, I don't notice where her staff is until it collides into the back of my head. The force is so strong that it knocks me right off my feet. I face the stone floor, scraping my face and releasing my staff from my tight grip. After that, Tara jumps down, but I am filled with so much anger that I try to get up and throw a right hook. Tara counteracts by swinging her staff, knocking out my legs, grabbing my fist, bringing it behind me, and dislocating my shoulder with her foot. I shout in pain and again try to stand up. She tries to knock me down, but I back away as fast as I can on my bleeding legs. Looking at her, Tara's face is filled with pleading and sorrow, shedding tears while shouting stop. However, my anger and my adrenaline are operating at full speed that I ignore her plea and throw my best left hook; Tara counters it by blocking it with her left and finally throwing out her right hook which crashes into the left side of my skull, knocking me out completely.

While my hearing fades, Tara speaks through her gasps for air, "I'm so sorry, Will. I am so fucking sorry."

As my brain and body slowly return to normal operations, one of the songs by the Duramaxes begins to play loudly in my head. I slowly begin moving my arms and legs, yet something comes down soft and firm and restrains them. Since I can't move any of my four limbs, I slowly open my eyes. The brightness of the lights is dim and soft, so my eyes quickly adjust to them. Once the colors and shapes start taking form, the details follow. When everything in my head becomes fully operational, I raise my head wondering where I am. The same force that restrained my arms and legs comes upon my forehead and gently pushes it down.

"Don't," says a familiar voice. I look up to see Tara sitting next to me like before, except wearing her summer clothes. Looking onto her face, there are relief, exhaustion, and sorrow.

"Nos . . . Will. Please forgive me." She places her hands around my head and tears form in her eyes. "I am sorry. So fucking sorry. I should've restrained myself and I shouldn't have pushed you over like that." She sniffles. "How you acted did terrify me. I guess I let out my animal side and should've watched the rising levels of our actions."

I want to speak, but as I open my mouth, Tara seals it with her index finger.

"I am truly sorry that I clawed at your legs and made them bleed. I am truly sorry that I dislocated your right shoulder and knocked you out. I just had to do those last two things to make you stop because you weren't listening and you were fully enraged. On the other hand, making you that angry was my mistake. Today should've been a calm yet exciting day for the both of us to learn and teach each other new moves. Oh my God, the damage that I—"

I remove her hand from my mouth and abruptly sit up. "Tara!" She stops and looks embarrassed. *Sigh.* "You're beginning to sound like me. Hammering yourself down with a sledgehammer over the mistakes you've made when it was an accident." I sigh again. "I, for years, have hammered myself down very hard a thousand times over on the little mistakes that I've made in hopes that destroying my self-esteem would please other people. But when I became an asphalt cowboy, I stopped doing that because I got out of that town. Away from those people. Away from those thoughts. So, please, baby, don't be like me because it hurts me seeing you act this way."

Big tears form and fall from her eyes. She hugs me tight and lets the tears fall. I wrap my arms around her and comfort her. That makes her cry even more but in a way of relief that I'm no longer angry at her and that I accept her apology. The curious thing is we had breakfast around 9:05 in the morning and cleaned everything up around 9:14. So, how long was I out when Tara healed me? I mean Tara dislocated my shoulder, practically broke my jaw, made some deep cuts in my legs, and had my face scraped on the floor. So, the healing time would take about a couple of hours or so, including the time I was unconscious when she fully healed me.

"You were out for four hours."

I guess she sensed that question by how my body was acting like I was thinking about it. Other than that, her kindness still amazes me. After a moment of hugging, she gently pushes me away so that we can talk face to face.

We stare at each other's eyes for a brief moment, so I decide to break the silence, "Perhaps we could start over again. Take this training slow, steady, and easy."

She agrees with me and we both stand up and move ourselves to an open space in the room. Just as we both agreed, we start off nice and slow. So, just like we did before, we circle one another but calmly this time. We stare at one another waiting for one or the other to make a sudden move, or close to it.

CHAPTER TWENTY-EIGHT

Hospital Visit and Wedding Plans
Location: Castle Front Gate
Date: January 20, 2015
Time: 1:00 PM

AFTER BEING WITH THE royal family of Sparta for the past three months, I have learned a lot. In detail, I have learned how a king should act, how the law system works, and how the military operates. Most of all, I learned more about the history of this kingdom and Troy. During my teachings, I did point out a few of the stuff I learned from Tara and that made the lessons go a lot faster. The way I learned is not by our dumbass teaching system where we sit at desks, stare at a thick textbook, and let the teacher lecture on and on. The way I learned was through their advanced technology. I not only used their tablets but also their table that produces very authentic holograms just like our Google Earth, though more advanced. With that type of hands-on equipment, I was able to witness time-lapsed videos of how their geography was formed over the millennia and how both Sparta and Troy agreed about sharing land and becoming allies. For the lessons being a king, those were taught by going through the process of mostly just walking around in different patterns for certain matters and what to wear during certain events. On the contrary, since Tara is going to be the person in power, most of the clothing and other things are to be tossed away and replaced with her new ideas. The most interesting thing is that the system around the rules and regulations is just like our government's. The best part of going through these different subjects is that I am not tested or quizzed every two weeks. Being hands-on with the equipment also made me retain and remember the lessons a lot easier and more fun.

After nearly three months of those lessons, Tara decides that we both should check on how the rest of the kingdom is doing. This includes the housing, businesses, relationships between both our races, and finally the hospital. The hospital visit is at the top of Tara's priority list and it's been a while since I've seen Doctor Tristen Maverick. Another reason she wants to visit that place first is that she studied medicine back on her home planet and wants to lend a hand if there's a shortage of staff on call. If it's true, then the situation outside our safe haven has gotten worse. Why you ask? I'm sorry to report this; there haven't been many returning search parties. There have been some, although most of the time, their outcomes have been like mine. These get all of us on edge. We try to figure out why they're not returning given the other factors such as the weather, the difference in age, health, and distance. Perhaps it's because most of our search parties are so far west that they are founded by the search parties from Troy. Plus, put in the possibility that most of the eastside of this continent is clear and there are no other people to rescue, or that the U.S. military are full-on guarding and protecting the towns and cities that they couldn't send out their search parties to round up survivors. Still, some communications, from what I learned, are fragile.

Sigh. Perhaps our own satellites are beginning to lose power.

Anyway, Tara and I put on our winter wardrobe, the same ones that we used when we "arrested" Chase Tiger and head toward the hospital tent. Stepping outside, the air is too cold. I think Tara and

I have spent too much time in her place enjoying a tropical, relaxing atmosphere. Today, the sky is completely covered with gray clouds, blocking out the sun. Thick snowflakes heavily fall down. The wind is blowing at ten or so miles per hour. Yet interestingly, there's a good mass of Wolfinoid and humans meandering around the business sector. However, the cold makes me shiver, making Tara laugh, then she nods forward with our mini quest. I did forget to mention this—another similarity between our races is that they also celebrate New Year's Eve and man did we have one hell of a party.

Arriving at the tent and entering, Tara's prediction came true. Turns out, there aren't even enough doctors and nurses on the clock. On the reception desk are huge stacks of files. Doctors and nurses are almost running through the tent trying to attend to their patients and most of them look like they haven't gotten enough sleep. Farther in, we do our best to stay out of their way, yet the sight of the rooms being filled with both of our kind is concerning. The patients' health ranges from completely healthy, to minor injuries, to severe. I can even see an I.C.U. or two down one of the corridors. In those rooms, I recall the thoughts when I was severely injured, barely making it here alive. They evoke the memories of my traveling here and the battle where Ulric, Forthwind, and Althalos perished and I had to bury them. Those memories moist my eyes. Before tears could fall down, I immediately wipe my eyes.

Oh, for God's sake, Nos! It was not your fault. Those werewolves completely outnumbered the search party you were in. Don't blame yourself and don't go back on your words when you told Tara that she shouldn't hammer herself for the actions she had no control over.

"You okay?" Tara asks.

I wipe my eyes once more to answer her. She cocks her head to the side in question, but it's interrupted when Tristen runs into us. His momentum is so strong that it knocks us down and the files he was carrying go flying everywhere.

"Ah man, look at this mess." He scrambles on the floor, gathering and organizing them. When he looks up and realizes who he ran into, Tristen's face turns from frantic and on-edge to relief.

"Tara, Will, I'm sorry and thankful that you're here. Especially you, Tara."

"Well," Tara answers as she too gathers the papers, "you could definitely use the help. I mean, my plan was to heal Will and be done with it sooner. But, that's in the past and I'm here to help." At the end of that sentence, Tara hands over the rest of the paper files.

Tristen gives a confident smile and says, "Yes, both of those are true."

His smile fades away when he turns back to the chaos that's happening. Suddenly, a computer voice comes alive over the P.A. in their own language and blue, LED lights begin to strobe. Doctors and nurses that don't have their arms full immediately rush to a specific room where the action is taking place. It doesn't take me long to figure out what's going on because rushing past us is a hovering cart that has a crashed box used to bring people back to life.

Doctor Maverick sighs and mutters, "Another one today."

Tara hands half of the files to Maverick and reassures him. She suddenly bolts off to work. Maverick also leaves by going back to his business, and I realize I'm a dead weight and I have no professional medical knowledge. What am I supposed to do?

Before Tristen can get far, I shout out to him, "Hey Doc, what am I supposed to do? I have no knowledge in this field!" He stops, returns quickly, and sets down the remaining half of his files.

"Oh, I'm sorry. It's a good thing we've invented this type of shot." He reaches into his cloak and reveals another syringe. Next, he pulls off the cap, rolls up my right sleeve, and tells me to hold still. In an instant, the needle goes through my skin, into one of my veins, and the liquid surges through my bloodstream. I look up at him curiously.

"Within moments, you'll know everything about the medical field. Good luck."

He turns on one of his heels and proceeds back to his practice. Interestingly, he's right; once the liquid enters and combines with the neurons in my head, within moments, I know everything—from minor cuts, severe injuries, to the big and small tools used during the practices. As the shot takes full effect, I immediately set off to work.

Time: 7:10 PM

Tara and I have spent so many hours in the hospital to aid the doctors and nurses on their workloads. During that time, a search party of two Wolfinoids returned with a group of fifteen humans. Their ages range from teens to thirties and most of them have suffered serious injuries. One of the Wolfinoids was on her last leg and she needed to be administered to the I.C.U. The other one was still going and I was taking care of the lacerations on his arms and face. I asked him about the status outside. He told me most of the towns and small cities are well-protected and supplied with food by my own military race, but their enemy has put a huge gap between us and Troy, covering the Great Plains starting in the northern part of Illinois to the Northern part of Mississippi; thus, spreading to the west to the far eastern edges of Wyoming, Colorado, and New Mexico. He included that a few of our search parties were trapped in those regions. Nonetheless, the search parties from Troy have found them and taken them back to their kingdom.

He pulled out his tablet and showed me the geography. In purple: Sparta covers all of Pennsylvania, New Jersey, Delaware, Maryland, West Virginia, Virginia, Connecticut, and Rhode Island. Half of Ohio is covered from the eastern state line to mid-central and that goes for Kentucky. Half of North Carolina is covered starting from the northern state line to mid-central. Finally, the entire Southern end of New York is covered.

The entire Great Plains and Northern parts of the Southern states are covered in black and that's where the enemy has inhabited.

In marigold, the kingdom of Troy covers all of Montana, Idaho, and Utah. Their range also covers almost over half of Wyoming and just beyond the northern state line of Colorado.

Finally, in red, white, and blue, the Unites States military covers all of Washington state, Oregon, California, Upper Michigan, the Northern part of New York, Vermont, New Hampshire, and all of Main, South Carolina, the Southern half of Alabama and Georgia, majority of Florida, and the other remaining halves that I stated before are covered by them.

Now, the reason I did not mention other states is that those territories are in gray which means they are vacant or a neutral zone. There are similar spots around the nation; most of them form lines between our militaries, Troy's, and the US's.

Before we left the hospital, I showed Tara the tablet and she shook her head in disbelief from the hell that's raining down across my homeland. During her observation, the image gets pixelated, jerky, and goes blank after she looked at it for a few minutes. On the screen, it said in both languages, "Signal lost." We both sigh and I do my best to hold back my anger from seeing the results. It is a good thing most of the US military covers almost the exact same range as the werewolves have taken over the Great Plains and parts of the South. Plus, with the ranges covered by Sparta and Troy, we equally match the size of the US military. For now, Tara and I change clothes and head out to the camp to check on the other facilities.

Walking around the dark is not so eerie since lots of high-tech lamps and different colors of torches light up the walkways. Another interesting thing is that there are loads of people moving about during this Tuesday night. Tara and I get hungry and we stop by one of the local food vendors and eat. After that, we proceed with our little mission and when two hours have passed, we both agree that everything is okay and turn back to the castle. During our walk, I stop and look at a group of the normal guard that's protecting our borders. Seeing the group reminds me of the day when I banished Chase Tiger and told them to make sure she doesn't re-enter.

I walk toward them calmly and steadily. Approaching their earshot, I announce myself,

"Prince Will." Some say in surprise, making them all stand in attention.

I wave and smile. "At ease, men. Any sightings of Tiger?"

"No, sir. We haven't seen that woman since you banished her."

They're right. It's been well over two months and I didn't have a clue what the coverages of the regions were back then, so I think I'll give these guys a break. "You know what, ease up fellas. Spread the word to the other groups and just worry about our main enemy."

"Yes, sir," they reply in unison.

After that, I return to Tara and we head back to the castle.

Time: 9:20 PM

I walk out of the pool room after taking a shower and as I enter the bedroom, I notice that Tara is on her tablet. She's talking out loud in her native tongue and is in deep conversation. Listening more, the other voice from the tablet sounds female and my curiosity rises.

Will, stop. You have no authority nor right to know whom Tara is talking to. Plus, you don't know what she's talking about.

I shake my head to rid of my curiosity and move toward the wardrobe to get ready for bed. On the other hand, she sees and calls me over in joy.

"Ah, Will, just in time. Can you come over here? I would like you to meet someone."

I nod in agreement, grabbing a shirt to be decently presentable. Walking over to her, she's grinning ear to ear and holding the screen part in the front of her chest. When I get closer, she tells me to stop and then looks back down at her tablet grinning even more. Soon, she nods to whoever is on the screen and takes a deep breath to calm her excitement.

"Will." Her eyes are sparkling like stars. "Meet my mother. Athena Borin." Within a moment's notice, she turns the screen toward me and everything inside me freezes.

Seeing Tara's mom, she most definitely looks like her daughter with the same eyes and fur except a little older. The one thing that throws me off is that I was expecting her to be wearing the garments and jewelry like her husband. Her hair is almost styled like Tara's, yet the ends are dyed emerald green. The jewelry is pretty much the same as Tara's, modern and simple. Plus, since the original kingdom of Sparta is located on a tropical beach, the clothes her mother is wearing are fitted and designed to the climate. Interestingly, it's daytime on her end and I can perfectly see some palm trees swaying in the wind and behind them is the ocean. Still, I remain frozen where I stand.

"Well, Tara," Athena speaks, breaking the awkward silence, "I must say you picked one lovely and cute human."

Ah, cute? I've never thought of myself that way.

Tara looks down, acknowledging her mom, "Thanks. He is so sweet and nice but furious when I rough him up in the right way." She winks at me.

My head snaps up at her, "Seriously?"

"Oh, he does talk. I was beginning to worry," says Athena while she giggles.

I turn my attention back to her, "Um . . . yeah. Of course, I can talk. It's just . . . um . . . I wasn't prepared to meet you, your highness. Anyway, it's great to finally meet you."

Both Tara and Athena start laughing. I slowly begin joining them, still feeling nervous while scratching my head, feeling awkward and embarrassed. This event has my heart rate increased and I try to contain my embarrassment, yet the same thing occur as in the past.

"Anyway, should we get down to the business, you two?"

Tara agrees, takes my hand, and sits us down on the couch near the campfire pit. She sets down her tablet on a stand that's already on a nearby table. Two questions pop into my head: one, how is

Tara getting this kind of signal when the satellites belonging to the US government are dead or slowly failing? And two, what type of business are they talking about? I guess I'll find out soon.

"So, what is the theme of the wedding going to be, Tara?"

Come again?

"Well, I'm pretty sure father still wants to keep it traditional, yet I want to include the modern way and perhaps," Tara slowly turns her head at me with a smile and continues, "some country into it."

Athena raises her eyebrows. "'Country? Never heard of that before. What does this country mean?"

"Well," I do my best to explain, "It's another type of social life where people live in small towns, work in factories like steel mills or on farms and ranches all day, every day. They like outdoor activities that include fishing, hunting, and riding ATVs. This social life is where people listen to country music and hang out at bars that are called honkey tonks."

To further my explanation, I let Tara assist me in sending one of my country songs to her mother. The song I sent is "Lots of Country Out Here" by Tom Joshington. She gets it and listens to it with earbuds on and with her eyes closed.

After four minutes, Athena looks at us. Her stare is calm and relaxed, but it makes me nervous a little bit. Eventually, she shows a warm smile.

"That was an interesting song. Tara's right, you do have an interesting taste in music. I think I get the idea what your country lifestyle is. So, onward with wedding plans?"

Tara and I look at each other that we should proceed.

After several hours, all three of us agree with our ideas about the theme, food, and the whole nine yards. So, here are the details: the wedding will be traditional, yet we will incorporate a country/western style. My friends and I will be wearing authentic, cowboy suits and hats while Tara and her friends will wear simple elegant dresses and gowns with hush hush designs. Well, I made the cowboy suits also a hush hush. At the reception party, the theme would transition from country to dance club. The food courses have been decided yet are bound to changes. The drinks shall remain the same. We decide the seating is kind of ridiculous when we put our guests in specific order and finally, all three of us have agreed to have one formal wedding dance song, although when it ends, we'll let LED turn up the music. On that note, when we were picking songs from my rock playlist, Tara came upon "Alive and True" by Cold Water. I play the song out loud and Tara tells me that we should totally perform that song. For further preparations, Athena would take care of the details on her end and send the rest of the things through the portals. After that, we lose communication but are grateful to get the wheels turning.

Lastly, the crowning ceremony where Tara is announced as queen and I king of Sparta will happen after my transformation, which brings Tara to sadness. She looks at me, doing her best to hold back tears.

"Will, when my mother and I started talking in the beginning, I asked her if there's any way to numb you so that you wouldn't be in pain."

"And?"

She looks at the empty firepit with sad eyes and closes them. "There isn't. Once I bite you, you're going to be in some pain, but as the hours go on and the transformation takes effect, the pain will increase by the hour and you'll be in excruciating pain. I'm sorry."

I look away, heaving a sigh and trying not to imagine the pain I am to be put through. To put my tensions at ease, I need to know when the wedding is happening.

"So, when is our wedding going to happen?"

I can feel Tara turned her eyes to me and replies, "The fourteenth of April."

I nod my head in acknowledgment. "Okay. Okay then." I look at her putting on a brave smile. "I'll let my friends know and make arrangements with them." Then I glance at Tara's tablet and the time makes my eyes widen.

"Well look at that; it's past three in the morning." Tara looks and her eyes widen the same. After a split second, the thought of sleep settles in our minds and we go to bed feeling excited, anxious, and sad that I just have over two months left of being human. After that, I'm a Wolfinoid, a new king, and there's no way of reversing it.

Holy shit, I'm so fucking scared right now.

CHAPTER TWENTY-NINE
Wedding Day
Location: The Outskirts of
Sparta, on the East Side
Date: April 14, 2015
Time: 8:00 AM

BREATH IN, BREATH OUT. Breath in, breath out. Breath in, breath out.

Okay, Nos. You can do this. You can definitely do this. You thought you couldn't have a girlfriend and man, you were proven wrong, though you didn't know that relationship was going to escalate to an actual marriage in roughly five months.

I stand in a tent that was pitched for my friends and me to cowboy, suit up, and prepare for the actual event. I stand here trying to remain calm, yet my fear gets the best of me when things like this happen suddenly. On the flip side, we did have two months to get this wedding prepared and have everything set in the right place since there were two teams of people assembling it together in two different worlds. We did use the teleportation devices as planned to bring some of the necessary supplies such as the fabrics of Tara's and her friends' dresses. Tara, Faith, Dawn, Crystal, and Whitney used their sorcery to make this end of Sparta comfortably warm for the perfect outdoor wedding. During the past two months, I went to tell my friends about the wedding, they congratulated me, then I told them about the plans for the event. I asked all of them to be my best men and they agreed with enthusiasm. Yes, I know only one person could be the best man, but it's our wedding, and whatever we say can and will happen.

Bringing you guys up to speed, my friends and I stand here making sure we're ready. Well, for Austin, Hugh, Alice, Chris, Emily, and Alex, they're ready for the big event. For me, I'm not because the relationship I got into escalated so quickly that I tried my very best to slow it down, although time was short and relevant to the situation happening outside these borders, and finally, as Tara said, it's their way of life. *Sigh.* I know I can do this though I feel like I'm going to finally have a nervous breakdown.

"You okay, Nos?" asks Hugh as he pats my shoulder.

It takes me a while to answer, "Yeah. I think I'm okay. Possibly. Possibly not."

"Why'd you say that?"

I look at him, trying to be confident, "Because . . . I've felt like I had no chance with any girl all thanks to the majority of the Special Ed staff back in L.A.C that always pointed my problems during my dumbass I.E.P.s and made me hammer myself down almost every day. I was truly proven wrong when I got here. It surprises me still that the relationship between Tara and I escalated this quickly, especially after we did a homerun."

"Hold up," says Austin. "What do you mean homerun?"

I look at all of them seriously. "We had sex when we both left the party during Christmas Eve."

All their jaws drop in amazement. I smile and shrug saying it's the truth. Now, all we hear is the light spring breeze and the music that's happening outside near our tent. Soon, footsteps come close and open the main fabric tarp. We all turn to see who it is. Our eyes adjust to the sunlight and we see that it's Gothraigh.

"We're ready. Are you?" he asks in a confident tone.

We all check ourselves over and we are. We all grab our cowboy hats and follow Gothraigh out of the tent. For us men, our hats are black to match our black suit jackets, slacks, cowboy boots, brown vests, ties, and white shirts. For the ladies, they're wearing white dresses perfect for the weather conditions, white cowgirl boots and hats, and the finest, most elegant, and simplest silver jewelry that Sparta can provide. Anyway, we move down an alley that connects with one another right across from us. Nearing the second one, rounding the corner, comes Whitney, Faith, Dawn, and Crystal. As we team up, I follow Gothraigh from behind while Chris and Whitney join behind me, Alex and Alice, Austin and Faith, Hugh and Dawn, and finally Emily and Crystal.

We follow the path that leads to the center aisle of the outdoor chapel. The usual procession you hear at weddings begins as we head toward the altar. There are rows upon rows filled with people already standing as we file in. Standing at the altar is the deacon with a Bible in their language, waiting. Getting to the front, Gothraigh stands next to Trent and the others in the very front row. I take my position on the deacon's left side and my friends stand next to me in this order: Hugh, Austin, Chris, Alex, Emily, and Alice. On the right side, Whitney takes her position and the rest falls into this order: Faith, Dawn, and Crystal. We all stand for a moment, giving me the perfect opportunity to describe the scenery. All the trees are lusciously green, the leaves are fully bloomed with small flowers in the mix, the grass is perfectly green, the chairs the guests are sitting in are perfectly white like fresh snow shining in the sun, the sky is clear giving the sun a room to warm up this lovely spring morning, and the altar is built out of white-painted wood with red and white roses. The dresses that Whitney, Faith, Dawn, and Faith wear are created out of white silk and designed to resemble this early season. To our right is a small orchestra playing the introduction tune with a Celtic theme mixed into it. Finally, the orchestra changes the tune and plays the symphony where Cedric leads his beautiful daughter Tara down the aisle. All of my attention is drawn to her.

The gown she wears is stunning, modern, yet holds some traditional style. The bottom of the gown is white, but almost midway up, there's a transition into ice blue and the blue shades turn into a dark blue, like the ocean. When the ocean blue shade is about to reach the shoulders, it becomes a mulberry purple, covering shoulder to shoulder. Tara is wearing a white veil with her lovely face underneath all polished with makeup. Her hair is pulled back fully revealing her left eye; what also grabs my attention is that the tips of her hair on the side are dyed to match the purple on her wedding gown. Her ears are pierced with silver earrings that curve around, and in between the gaps are purple diamonds. She's also wearing a silver chain necklace and the gem that's connected is formed into a purple, heart diamond that looks centuries old.

Hugh nudges my arm and quietly says, "Damn, Nos, you've made one hell of a catch. One hell of a catch indeed."

It takes me a moment to hear his statement because I am completely in awe of my future wife, "Ah . . . um . . . I guess . . . I did."

Immediately, my gaze is brought upon Cedric. He looks down at me with regards, gratitude, and most of all, satisfaction—the satisfaction that his daughter has found the right man knowing that he will treat her with respect, love, and care for all eternity. I look up at him with gratitude and respect.

With his free hand, he grabs hold of my right shoulder. "Continue giving Tara an excellent life with your human ways."

Next, he releases Tara, kissing her on the forehead, and I let Tara hook her right arm in my left arm. We look into each other's eyes. At this moment, I thought this was going to be so nerve-racking, but it turns into an exciting moment. My heart race and adrenaline want me to burst into a dance. I do my best to gain control of both when all my heart wants is to leap into my throat. My imaginary *Nos* tanks want to break free from their brackets, letting the hoses burst out of my skin while spewing the liquid. My adrenaline is all over the place completely out of control. I'm pretty sure Tara is feeling the same way, yet her presence feels calm and relaxed since we're finally doing it.

The deacon clears his throat and that grabs our attention.

"Would everyone please take their seat?"

The onlookers do what they're told and he continues, "We are gathered today to celebrate the joining of two unique creations. Our kind, Tara Borin, is marrying a human, Will Young. At this moment, I feel the presence of the Lord has brought us even closer than before. Our worlds are no longer separate. Today, on this fabulous spring morning, our worlds are one. At this moment, listen to the words of the Lord from Ecclesiastes 4: 9-12, 1 Corinthians 13: 4-12, and Genesis 2: 18-24." He opens up his Bible and reads the scriptures. Once he concludes on Genesis, he looks at both of us.

"Tara Borin, do you take Will Young as your husband and future king?"

Tara looks down at me with love in her eyes and says, "I do."

"Will Young, do you take Tara Borin as your wife and future queen?"

When he asked that question, I was looking at Tara with the same emotion in my eyes and replied, "I do."

Next, the deacon pulls out two small boxes from his robe and opens them. Both of them are rings that bear the designs of marriage and power. Then he holds each one in each of his hands.

"With these two rings, they combine two completely different creatures as one in holy matrimony and as future rulers of Sparta." He then hands each one to us. We take them and slide each one on our marriage fingers.

"By the power invested by me from the kingdom of Sparta, I pronounce you husband and wife and as king and queen. You may now kiss."

Within an instant, Tara throws back the veil and grabs me by the shirt, picks me up, and presses her lips firmly against mine. I, on the other hand, wrap my arms around her neck, enjoying the passion of her kiss. Once she sets me back down, we look at our guests and they are out of their chairs, applauding enthusiastically. Looking at my friends, some of them are really happy. For Emily and Alice, they're shedding tears of joy, so I walk over to give them a big hug, which makes them cry even more. Looking at Faith, Whitney, Dawn, and Crystal, they're also shedding tears of joy. Tara walks over and gets them into a group hug.

Then the deacon shouts, "Wolfinoids and humans, I give Tara and Will Borin, your new queen and king of Sparta!"

Tara and I grab each other's hands and we jog down the center aisle with rice pouring onto our heads and great happiness inside.

The wedding moves swiftly toward the reception. We take the time for all of us to change into better clothes because the temperature outside is steadily rising past the seventies and could stop at the mid-eighties. Plus, this is where the formal dress code becomes more the . . . how do I put it? The dance club dress code. On the other side of the same clearing where the ceremony took place, a stage has been assembled that has all of the equipment brought up from the original dance club arena. A long bar has been designed to look like the ones from the saloons during the old times of the West. Long benches and tables were assembled and designed to seat our over one hundred guests. Interestingly, both pieces of furniture have a small touch of modern look, like the glow-changing LED lights. On the opposite side of the bar and benches lies a massive buffet table with various kinds of food from humans' and Wolfinoids' culture. A large piece of wood flooring that has been smoothly polished laying in front and below the stage has been prepped for the celebration. Finally, to the right side of the stage are bench and table made for us.

Within minutes, our guests take their seats; we do the same. Once everybody has settled in, the time comes for the speeches. Hugh is the first one to stand from his chair and he grabs the mic.

"Afternoon y'all. I'm Hugh Smith. I am the man who gave Will the nickname Nos. The reason I decided to give him that name is because of his adrenaline rush. I tell him to get something from the tool room and he'll get it within a minute. The first time I met Will is when he was a freshman at Los Alamos High. I started talking to him during the passing periods about cars because he always stopped, looked at this '95 Ram 1500, and imagined putting it back together. When I talked to him, I can he tell he was a different kind of freshman."

Before long, he goes into this history about me and how our friendship turned out to be, and mainly talks about how great of a kid I was. He also tells the guests that there shouldn't have been a way for me to be part of the Special Education System back in L.A.C. After Hugh sits, Whitney gets her turn.

"Thank you for that interesting story about Will, Hugh. Before all of this, I didn't know much about Will, but I could tell, just by smelling him, that he was a good man and a good partner to Tara. There are two main things that blew me away about Will: first, he has an interesting taste in music and shows a passion for those songs. Second, he is one interesting fighter with his staff and the way he captured me, Faith, Crystal, and Dawn by having the . . . the . . ."

"Seat belts," I say.

She continues, "The seat belts flying out of the doors from those mighty machines really terrified us. That proves that Will, a.k.a. Nos, is not the type of human to mess around with. Anyway, I'm pretty sure you humans want to know how all four of us know Tara." Right off the bat, Whitney tells us a brief history of Tara and how their service turned into a friendship. Plus, a few other things.

After hearing both speeches about us from our best man and woman, LED appears on stage and makes an announcement.

"Alright, ladies and gentleman, before we could actually party, we should let the new king and queen do their first traditional dance."

There's soft applause of encouragement echoing from the guests. A soft, Celtic tune plays out from the speakers on the stage. Actually, that's another thing I left out when I was telling you guys at the beginning of this chapter. During the past two months, Tara and I practiced a traditional royal dance that has been used in their culture for many centuries. I did mess it up a couple of times, yet both of us were patient; mostly Tara and I laughed when I messed up. At the time, I had the song "Can't Dance" from Nick Severt playing in my head because I really didn't know and want to dance. In time, I got the moves down. So, as the song plays out, I stand up and gesture for her to take my hand. She takes it and I lead her onto the dance floor. Once we get there, we sidestep a couple of times with some swaying. As the tune draws on, I spin her around, then repeat.

When the song ends, I tilt her back, letting her almost hang there with her left arm fully outstretched. I bring her back and we end the song with a kiss. Everybody applauds and that gives LED the cue to turn up the actual music, lights, and smoke machines. At that moment, it was the cue for everybody to head toward the buffet and bar.

We party for two hours. By that time, we, Tara and I, along with my friends, move on the stage because during the past two months, my friends and I were able to practice "Alive and True" a couple of times before the wedding preparations got in the way. Thanks to the advanced karaoke invention by the Wolfinoids, practicing the song made it really easy and we feel like we can play it normally. We put on the voice changers, wireless headphones, and settle into our positions. Since it was Tara's idea to play this song, she and I will just sing the song. The rest of my friends will play the instruments. Austin will be playing the violin, Chris will be playing the drums, Hugh will be playing the bass, and Alex will be playing the electric guitar. As they gave the go, I turn on the mic and speak in my own voice.

"Alright, ladies and gentlemen, I would like to give you guys one hell of thanks for being a part of this wedding." A cheer rises out from them. "For this part of this awesome reception, Tara and I, including my friends Hugh, Austin, Chris, and Alex, will be playing a song from a band called Cold Water and this song will really show the love that Tara and I have for one another." I look at her with a smile and she smiles back. "So, without wasting more of your time, here's the song 'Alive and True' by Cold Water."

I turn on the voice changer and so does Tara. I give LED a thumbs up and he hooks up my iPod into the wireless signal transmitter, calibrates the lights to change color, flash, and sway with the rhythm of the song, and finally sets the pause time before and after the song for ten seconds. As the countdown from ten starts, the stage and the area around us quickly go dark. When it reaches zero, we begin playing the song. I start singing the song.

When the song ends, we all dismount the stage, then we are congratulated and complimented by our guests. Again, LED resumes his position and keeps the party going into the night.

CHAPTER THIRTY
Transformation
Location: Reentering into Tara's room
Time: 10:30 PM

AFTER A VERY SUCCESSFUL wedding and reception, Tara and I burst back into her, or should I say, our room, in laughter and full of energy. We dance and horse around a little, just simply enjoying the buzz after the party. Actually, the funny thing about the word "buzz" is we did consume some alcohol. So, yeah, we're a little bit drunk, but our stomachs are full of food.

"Ha, ha! Oh, Nos that was an excellent wedding and I now really enjoy your music," says Tara as she grabs a couple of plain, silver chalices from the same stone shelves above her bed and dunks them into the fountain.

I take a seat on the couch feeling a little dizzy. "Ah, yeah . . . and thank you. Oh man, so this is how it feels when you're drunk." At the same time, I place my head into my hands and lean forward, trying to keep my world from literally spinning. However, I can feel Tara sitting down next to me.

"Here you go, babe, this will clear you right up." She hands one of the goblets over.

I slowly wrap my fingers around it and begin slowly drinking from it. Slowly and surely, the drunkenness begins to slip away. Finishing it, my head is totally clear and as I stand up, the atmosphere suddenly got serious. I look at Tara and her happiness has morphed into sadness. She eyes her goblet, sloshing the remaining water powder mixture within.

"Tara, what's wrong?"

She sniffles, sets down her goblet, and walks away while trying to compose herself by running her hands through her hair. However, it doesn't seem to work and she begins to whimper.

"What is it, Tara?" Now, I'm really concerned because at one moment, she was happy, but now, something is really troubling her.

She soon breaks down into tears, "I don't wanna do it!"

I get up and grab her hand. "Do what? The marriage?"

"No!" She walks away letting more tears fall. "Turning you into one of us! I don't wanna do that!"

Oh. Oh, crap. I guess that time has finally come.

The realization of me being turned into a Wolfinoid and the fear of severe pain that comes with it settles in fast.

Tara looks at me. "Great! I just scared the crap out of you." She continues to cry.

"Why don't you—"

"Because I love your human form! I love you as you are! I don't want to turn you into one of us, but there is absolutely no other way of making you immortal nor numbing you that you won't feel any pain. I find that completely bullshit!"

She grabs the same goblet, throws it against the nearest stone wall, and it shatters. I walk over to her, turn her around, and take both of her hands into mine. Pretty soon, I shed a few tears of fear.

"To tell you the truth, I am scared. But here's the truth."

"What is that?" She begins lighting up.

"At least I ain't that whiney girl from that weird book series, because when you and I first met, I didn't 'throw' myself at you begging you to turn me because I had 'nothing' in my life. When

I met you, you completely turned my life around. Like I said, I was a normal human, an asphalt cowboy going about life with loads of mental barriers in my head. But you, Tara, you've torn them down and brought so much light into my life. I am very thankful for that."

Tara begins laughing, shaking her head which makes me laugh. "Nos, heh. You're so right. When we first got here, I was hearing from the first arrivals, from the girls specifically, about those books and I decided to search them. Once I did, I read about two or three chapters and turned off my tablet because that main character was such a whiney bitch."

We both laugh even harder for a while and during that time, we sit down on the bed. As we look into each other's eyes, the tension returns and it's as extreme like before. To encourage her, I kiss her with passion and love, and I stretch out my right arm. Tara lets out a heavy, quivering sigh, but she knows she has to do it. And I do, too.

"I love you, Will, so much," she says while she strokes my face.

"What's going to happen?"

"The change is going to take at least two days. Once I bite you, you need to remain calm so that the change will not hurt as much. As time goes on, my saliva will enter your heart and start circulating. You'll start feeling cold for a while, then warm, and eventually hot. By that time, your bones will break and morph into our skeletal form. Then a lot of other things."

Okay, okay. I feel like I should've said goodbye to my friends. I think my body won't pull through.

Tara lifts up my head and assures me, "You are going to pull through it. I'll be right here watching over you. Doctor Maverick is on call when I told him about this. Just take a couple of deep breaths."

I do and Tara reaches toward the shelves and retrieves a small medical box. She opens it and inside are a few gnaws and bandages. Later on, she gently grabs my arm and pulls it toward her.

"Are you ready, baby?"

I nod.

She lifts my arm up to her mouth and I start taking deep breaths; she opens her mouth, exposing her teeth; then she slowly sinks her teeth into my arm. I can feel the sharpness of Tara's teeth gently cutting through my skin, nerves, and possibly straight into my veins. My nerves send off signals in my brain to make noises of pain or push her away, but I keep on breathing and ignoring the signals. Looking at her, her lips are wrapped around my skin preventing any blood from dripping, her eyes are closed, and a tear travels down from her right eye. She keeps her teeth in for a minute, gulps a couple of times, and finally releases me. The air stings the teeth mark wounds. Tara swiftly wraps gnaws all around my arm and finally puts on the bandages. Once she completed, she notices some blood about to fall to her bed and she immediately licks them away. Next, she puts away the small medical box, pulls me against her chest to comfort me, and perhaps, restrain me when the pain gets intense.

"Are you part vampire?" I look up at her.

She laughs a little. "Cute, but no. I just did it because the bleeding was kind of major so I had to gulp down some of it."

I lay my head against her chest, remaining calm and continuing to take deep breaths. "And so it begins."

"And so, it begins," says Tara as she holds me tighter.

Hour One

Okay, I can feel her saliva traveling through my arm. The bite is starting to hurt more and I'm a little cold now. I just need to stay calm.

Hour Four

Okay, I'm getting really cold now. Why the fuck does it seem so hard to breathe?

Hour Ten

Oh God! I am so hot! Why am I so fucking hot?

"Tristen," Tara shouts, "He's burning up really fast!"

I feel another hand on my forehead.

"He's doing his best to remain calm. I'll fill the pool with cold water and ice."

"Idiot! Only I can do that!"

"You don't have any knobs?"

"No!"

"Then get on it, your highness."

I hear Tara let a sigh of frustration and disgust.

Hour Fourteen

Snap! Break! Crack! Stretch! Shatter! Repeat.

Oh my fucking God, this fucking hurts! Somebody just shoot me in the fucking head! Somebody take this fucking pain away! I am so fucking hot!

"His heart rate has gone up. He's beginning to panic. His body heat is nearing one-hundred and ten degrees."

"Do you think I don't fucking know that, Tristen! Fuck me, I didn't want to put him through this bullshit!"

Oow! Kill me! Just fucking kill me!

"I'll get him into the pool."

"Get away from my baby! I'll do it!"

I can feel that I'm being picked up. I quiver and shake due to the breaking and morphing of my bones which is so fucking painful. Moments pass, I feel like I've been stripped down, and my skin touches ice-cold water.

"It's all going to be over soon, Will. I promise. I fucking promise."

I kind of register her words, but I still shout in extreme pain.

Hour Twenty

The pain. The misery. The heat. They became too much for me. My body and brain couldn't handle it. I can still feel my heart beating but more like throbbing against my ribcage if I still have one. I gave into the blackness that was surrounding me I don't know how fucking long ago. Everything in my head is dead quiet. I don't have a fucking clue what I look like on the outside or how disgusting the transformation looks like. I must look absolutely horrible and disgusting in Tristen's and Tara's eyes.

CHAPTER THIRTY-ONE
New Body, New Life
Location: No idea
Date: No idea
Time: No idea

THE COGS, KNOBS, AND sensors for my nerves in my head reactivate, yet for the wires to make me talk resume dark. So, I let my nerves come alive. They take their time; interestingly, they reactivate faster than normal. I can feel that I'm a bit warmer than usual. Luckily, it's not as bad like it was who knows how many hours ago. When more nerves come back to life, I can feel that I am possibly taller than usual.

But how can I be so sure?

I focus my nerves on something else. They respond that I am lying on something that is soft and comfortable. While more parts of my brain come back to life, the boom box starts playing. To wake me up even more, the boom box picks and plays the remix version of "Barely Hanging On" by Parking Lincoln, which I find kind of odd, although it does work and I breathe a heavy sigh. What throws me off is that I hear some rustling sound and feel movement. Next, I feel a soft hand coming upon my forehead and combing through my hair. This action continues to reactivate my consciousness.

"Will?" says a female voice. I concentrate on it.

"Will?" It repeats with the tones of hope and encouragement.

"Will, baby?" It finally occurs to me that it's Tara's and I slowly open my eyes. Once I do, she breaks out a huge smile with tears of joy streaming down her face, then she places both of her hands around her mouth.

I should make the attempt to talk.

"T . . . Tara. Tara, it's so good to see you."

She lets out thrills of excitement and talks, "Oh Will, you pulled through! I know you could! My God, you look really good!"

"I guess it worked if she says that."

"Um . . . okay, heh, we're going to take this nice and slow. Just keep your eyes on me." She places both her hands behind my shoulders and gently sits me up, and I keep my eyes on her.

"Alright, touch your nose. Actually, scratch that. Examine your arms and hands."

I look down and examine those pair of limbs. My eyes widen because my skin is no longer tan like a redneck but is covered in black and brown fur. In detail, the base color is black; the pattern of the brown forms tribal tattoo patterns that travel from the shoulders, along with the collar bones, and down to my forearms. Next, I examine my . . . new hands. I still have all five fingers on both hands which is a relief, yet as I look at the base of my fingernails, they look like claws that are not fully exposed—the claws of a canine. Turning them over, my palms remain the same except that there's a shorter and finer fur on them. The curiosity of what I look like now makes me get up a little too fast.

Immediately getting back to my feet, I lose balance within a second. However, Tara immediately grabs my right arm, slowly pulls me back up, and then places one hand on my shoulder and the other on my hip. Next, we begin walking slowly toward the large, walk-in wardrobe. For a moment, Tara makes sure that my stance is perfect, then she walks out for a moment, comes back with a pair of large jeans, and tosses them to me. I look at them in amazement.

Am I really that tall?

I slip them on with some difficulty, yet succeeding, I nod at Tara to reveal the new me.

"Okay, Will, meet the new you." She pulls back one of the doors in the wardrobe that has a complete, tall mirror; the sight scares the shit out of me.

I immediately scramble away from the animal in the mirror because from what I see, it's not Will Young A.K.A. Nos. Tara comes over to calm me down; her reflection shows as she kneels down and places her hands on the head of the strange animal.

"Will, it's you. It's really you."

I look back at the mirror, trying to compose myself. The eyes are brown and wide open. I raise my right arm and the animal mimics. I move onto my knees and crawl toward the mirror in disbelief. The animal still continues the same movements and we both stop. I raise my left hand, point with my index finger, and move it toward the mirror. When the animal's left, index finger and mine make contact, I finally realize that the animal is truly me. I slowly stand up, watching how my Wolfinoid body works. I touch my ears that are now located at the top of my head instead of on the sides and in between them is a mass of loose hair. My entire body is covered in black fur with the brown tribal patterns on my shoulders and upper arms; there are two brown stripes that form into slits as they travel down the center of my eyes; I look down between my legs and right behind me is my actual tail. Finally, I touch my new face feeling that my jaw and nose have been stretched by a couple of inches and that confirms that I do now have the manifestation of the Wolfinoids.

The odd thing is, as Tara comes up behind me, she stretches out her arms to wrap them around my neck. Looking at the differences in our height, instead of being a few feet shorter than her, I am now two inches taller. I raise my eyebrows and move my ears, but they move sideways instead of up and down.

"You look astonishing," says Tara as she rubs her hands up and down my chest.

"What day is it?" I ask, still keeping my eyes on my new reflection.

"It's April 16, 2015. Time, 8:40 AM."

Just like Tara said, the transformation will take roughly two days and it did. My stomach now grumbles and I've never felt this hungry before.

"C'mon, let's get dressed and meet everybody downstairs for breakfast."

I agree with her and we throw on some basic t-shirts and leave the room. However, there's this little nagging feeling that I'm forgetting something. Setting foot into the large, open hallway, I look down and realize I'm not wearing any footwear. I widen my eyes to the sight of my bare, Wolfinoid feet that are shaped like a human but are larger and instead of having human-like toes, I have now the toes of a canine with claws. I pick up one of them to examine the bottom and on the bottom is indeed padded like a wolf's foot with both fur and padding keeping my feet warm, and Tara just laughs by my bewilderment.

Descending down the stairs, my brand-new nose picks up the scents of the food that has been cooked. I can smell every kind of meat, fruit, seasoning, and surprisingly, Tara. I glance at her, inhaling a little more of her scent. Her scent is a combination of two different types of environments: the first one smells like a tropical forest (probably from her home planet) and the second is the smell of the pine from these woods. Within a moment, we reach the bottom and a soft applause comes alive.

Looking around, everybody (mainly from the kingdom and not my friends) is here and standing up from their chairs. Their welcome is a little shocking and for some odd, awkward reason. Cedric and Gothraigh approach me to get a better look. As they get closer, I am literally looking at them straight in the eyes instead of upward like before. Both men cross their arms admiring Tara's work.

"Brother," speaks Gothraigh, "Your daughter did an amazing job."

"I do agree, brother. This man looks far much better in this form than he did as a human."

Wow. Should I take that as a compliment or a complaint?

"Father," Tara hisses her voice, "That hurts my feelings. Do any of you think and know how I felt when he was screaming in pain? I was trying my absolute best to hold back tears. I loved Will's human body. I loved him as he was and I think he enjoyed it when I wrapped almost my entire body around him at night."

I look at her and nod with agreement. I did enjoy the nights when she wrapped herself around me.

"Oh, I am so sorry Tara. I didn't mean—"

"Oh, shut up dad. I am now queen of Sparta."

Now, I can sense that there's a lot of tension in the air and I think I should try to turn this conversation around.

I clear my throat. "So, uh, who's hungry?"

Before long, the tension simmers down and we all sit down at the table. The difference is, when I sat down in my chair the first time, it was against the wall that has the spiral staircase that leads up to our room. Now, Tara and I sit side by side at the head where Cedric and Gothraigh used to sit. This time Cedric, Gothraigh, Zachariah, Trent, Rollo, and Maddox sit on the right side of the table while Cora, Whitney, Crystal, Dawn, Faith, and Lupa sit on the opposite side. This is totally awesome and awkward.

"So," speaks Maddox, "How do you feel being one of us?"

"I'm ah, still adjusting to it."

"Maddox, give the poor man some time to adjust to his new life," says Cora while she winks at me, "For example, look at him, I sense that he's still in some shock. Probably from this morning when he saw his new reflection."

"Plus," speaks Trent, "He is now the new king and there are things he needs to take care of." He takes a sip from his goblet and slightly mutters, "Some *very* important things."

His expression shows that something is indeed important and that Tara and I should definitely be in the know. He transfers the look to Cedric and Gothraigh. They look back at him slightly annoyed, moving their response to Zachariah who shifts his weight in his chair, doing his best to ignore them.

Tara and I look at each other with concern on our faces and turn back toward them. Tara breaks the silence, "Is there something *I* should know and *only* worry about? My husband has been through enough." She looks at Cora for any advice or hints.

Cora tries to put on a brave face and replies, "No, my queen. There is none."

Tara brings back her ears. "Don't you dare lie to me. I can tell that you are."

"No, I'm—" She then gets cut off by Faith.

"Of course, you are! Our enemy has gotten bigger, stronger, and we are doing less to help the humans of this nation!"

"Faith!" Gothraigh slightly shouts, "I. We wanted to keep this low and give Will the time to adjust before we throw all of this on him and Tara!"

Now, I am concerned. "What's going on?"

Gothraigh looks back at me with calmness. "Nothing, your majesty. Everything's fine."

Whitney abruptly stands up. "Everything is not fine, Gothraigh!"

"Hey, guys, can we just start this morning off back on a positive note?" says Maddox feeling uneasy.

"Shut up!" shouts Whitney, Gothraigh, Cora, Faith, and Trent.

The look on Maddox's face makes my blood boil and it even boils more when the argument includes Tara, Gothraigh, and Trent. Both Cora and Lupa remain silent.

"Y'all shut the fuck up!" I abruptly stand up, slamming my Wolfinoid fist onto the table to get their full attention. They stop and immediately look at me, *"Sit. Down. All of you."*

They do. Even Tara sits back down. I look back at her; she is totally surprised by my voice and action. I look back at all of them for a moment and then start taking deep breaths through my nose as I let my head hang.

Great, this is how my first morning of being a Wolfinoid is going to be. I really wanted it to be smooth sailing, but apparently, I have sailed right into the damn hurricane.

I look back up, serious. "Now. One of you is going to tell us the truth right now because I ain't hungry anymore. I am now hungry for information and I don't want any of you to *dare* withhold any detail. I've had enough of that shit when I was going through L.A.C.S.D."

I look directly at Trent and Zachariah, "You two. Both of you are in charge of the military of this kingdom and know the location of the search parties." They look at one another a little horrified. This begins to ruin my patience.

Tara slowly stands back up. "Gentlemen, you tell us right now. That's a direct order from your queen." The tone in her voice sounds like her patience is running out, too.

They keep their mouths shut and their eyes on their plates. I leave my chair, walk over to them, stand between them from behind, and grab their heads while yanking them backward, letting their weight rock their chairs onto the rear legs.

I growl while I talk, "You tell us right now or I'll drag both of you outside and beat the crap out of you for the info."

"Okay, okay!" shouts Zachariah, "The geography of which military force covers and controls has changed a lot, but only in the Great Plains and out toward the West. The surrounding areas here have remained the same."

I look down at my tactical officer and growl at him.

"The surrounding areas have been searched, and we still cover and control them. Any other human that's out there has been taken in by us and by your former species military. The bad news is that any of our search parties who have journeyed into the Great Plains have been slaughtered or rescued by the search parties from Troy."

I let go of them, letting the chairs make a loud thump sound when they slam back onto the carpet while I return to my seat, but I don't sit down. After hearing the news, I look at Lupa; she looks sad and heavily concerned about what's become of her search parties. I look at Tara and nod that she should take this part. She gets my hint and I sit back down.

"What is the status of your search parties, Zachariah and Lupa?" she asks in a concerned voice. Lupa begins to cry and Zachariah walks over to calm her down. The tears, the gasps for air, makes it really hard for Lupa to speak.

Zachariah looks at us with dismal eyes. "From mid-September of last year to about two months ago, we've sent out nearly thirty search parties to cover this part of this very large continent. A mere half or should I say less have returned unscathed. A small portion of the returnees have been seriously injured while the rest have been rescued by the search parties from Troy, which does bring us some relief, but the rest . . . well," he looks at me and continues, "have ended up dead. And that has increased in the past months than before. We, Trent, Rollo, and I have decided to stop sending out search parties because of that factor, including what Trent has told you before."

When Zachariah finishes, his wife bursts out in tears and they excuse themselves. Tara slowly sits back down in complete shock. She leans back in her chair looking dumbfounded as I do the same.

Holy shit. The situation has gotten completely worse in the past three months. Now I know how a new president of this nation feels when he inherits a war that has gotten worse once he is in office.

We all sit in silence. Tara and I were struck by the information. Cora looks terrible at the outcome of this morning. Whitney, Faith, Dawn, and Crystal sit in their chairs and slowly start picking at the delicious food. Maddox is doing the same thing. Trent and Rollo look overwhelmed by the situation feeling terrible about how bad their little war is going between their race and enemy. Finally, Cedric and Gothraigh lean into one another and whisper about the situation discussing plans.

I pull my ears back and shoot a deadly scowl at them, "Mind taking that somewhere *else?*"

They look up a little afraid, excuse themselves from the table, and head down the stairway to the throne room still whispering.

Sigh. What a glorious first morning of being a king.

CHAPTER THIRTY-TWO
Losing Friends and Birthday Celebration
Location: The Throne Room
Date: April 19, 2015
Time: 10:00 AM

"ARE YOU COMPLETELY SURE you want to do this, Will?" Tara asks with reassurance.

"Yes, Tara. I really want to do this. They're probably flying off the handle right now and have been since the last time you and I were together at the wedding."

I keep on pacing the stage where our two thrones sit upon. One is officially mine and the other is Tara's which she's already sitting in. Hours ago, I asked Sean to seek out my friends and bring them here so that they can see what I have become. To put their minds at ease, I'm wearing blue jeans, my camo belt with American and Confederate flags buckled on it, one of my Harley Davidson shirts that have been enlarged to fit me, simple leather bracelets, a simple silver chain necklace, and my enlarged camo hat. Again, the only difference is that I'm not wearing any shoes. Tara is also wearing jeans, a t-shirt that has the kingdom's logo on it on a small scale that covers her heart and a larger size that covers the back, and long feather earrings. The common item that we have on is our wedding/rule of power rings.

"I still find this as a bad idea," she says as she rubs her eyes with her thumb and index finger. "And you being anxious is making me feel anxious."

She does have a point about my anxiety. Why? Because I can sense it. I place my hands on my hips and take in a couple of deep breaths to calm me down. Right after that, I sit down on my own throne and wait. As the minutes pass, there's a loud knock on the door echoing throughout the hall. I look at Tara still on edge.

She rolls her eyes and looks at me. "This was your idea, but I am curious about their reaction." While she says that, she spreads her hand toward the doors. I let a heavy sigh and stand up.

"Enter." My voice booms and this moment feels like déjà vu. I don't need to explain. You guys remember.

The doors open and Sean enters first. Behind them are my friends: Austin, Hugh, Emily, Alice, Alex, and Chris and they seem to be confused. They're wondering why they're summoned here. When they look at me, the wonder of why they are here turns into who is this that summoned them. Sean begins his bow, but I wave my arm to lead them forward. He looks at me confused, yet I still wave my arm to come forward. He shrugs and proceeds.

When they get closer to the stage, I speak, "Let them come around, Sean."

As soon as I spoke, my friends look at one another and whisper.

Sean steps aside and nods his head toward us. "You heard him. Step closer."

They move with caution and stop at the base of the steps. I move down the steps as normal as possible, trying not to be intimidating. The look in their eyes and faces are filled with wonder and fear. My highly sensitive nose picks up both emotions and I rub my jaw with little concern.

Could I be that intimidating? I guess it's time to speak.
"Hey, guys."

Their eyes widen and gasp with realization.

"Nos?" asks Emily. I nod at her question which makes her gasp even more and slowly back away.

"Yeah. Yeah, it's me."

"What the fucking hell did they do to you?" Austin asks in a horrified tone.

I look back at Tara and she seems to quite enjoy this entertainment and nods for me to keep going. Alex sees that and I sense hatred remise from him.

"Did she do this to you?" He points at her.

I nod with agreement and he begins to charge up the stairs, but I grab him. "It was part of the relationship when I got into it. She was looking for a . . . boyfriend/husband to become the next ruler of this kingdom. She didn't like nor love the other Wolfinoids, but when she saw me . . . and when I saw her, we connected. However, for me to be with her and rule with her, I had to be turned into one of them."

"How could you do this to us?" shouts Chris, looking very pissed off.

"Listen, y'all, she didn't want to do it either."

"Oh, shut the fuck up Nos and let me go!" shouts Alex.

I do and he slowly backs away to rejoin the rest.

"Can we try to be friends?" I ask, well, beginning to plead. "C'mon, Hugh, I'm still the same guy on the inside. Just different on the outside."

Hugh lowers his head, crosses arms, breathes through his nose, and looks at me dissatisfied. "You know what, Nos? Fuck no. Just fuck no. Let's get the hell outta here guys."

Then they begin walking away.

"C'mon guys, this is bullshit! It's—"

"Can you just go to hell, Nos, and fucking stay there?" shouts Emily and their walk becomes more like storming out.

Once the doors close, I fall into my throne completely shocked and disowned by my friends—the friends I became tight with at the auto shop when we were in high school; the ones who taught me how to stand up and hold my ground. At this moment, it feels like absolutely none of those things matter.

Tara reaches out to me, trying to touch my arm. "Perhaps it's for the best, Nos."

Right before her fingers reach my arm, I jerk it away. "Shut up, Tara."

I get up and leave in disappointment, sorrow, and mainly, depression. I've never felt this hurt before I was in high school and I hoped that those days would've ended, but man was I completely fucking wrong with that.

As the day progresses, I did forget to mention one thing—today is Cedric's birthday and the celebration is just going to be on a small scale. Being a small scale, it's just us and the royal guards at the party. Anyway, I walk down the halls of this huge castle. Some of the halls only lead one way; some connect rooms and reconnect. The décor, the architecture, remains the same with exposed bricks, curved ceilings, and some paintings. The only difference is the lighting. Some are lit with color-changing torches while others have high-tech L.E.D. lights. Other than that, this castle is just a temporary base. The rest of it must lie on their home planet.

Ha, ha. Temporary base. Kind of like Los Alamos. Find an empty mesa; construct facilities for work, families, and some entertainment. Construct the ever first two most powerful and destructive bombs, then drop them on Japan. After that, destroy buildings, all paperwork, and leave the mesa.

But this is not really Los Alamos; the main purpose of this junior-sized kingdom compared to the actual one is to be a refugee camp for my former kind, while my new kind heads out and attempts to fix their problems hopefully to succeed and leave this region without leaving a trace of evidence. However, the facts that were shown to me and Tara three months ago and were proven exactly three days ago show that it's a losing battle; their enemy is getting stronger by the week if not by the day or the hour. My questions are: where are those strongholds and how many are they?

"Will, there you are!"

I immediately turn around to see Tara jogging down the corridor toward me with relief. The relief that she found me after the . . . I don't know what to call it . . . the argument with my friends? Her reaction definitely shows that she was worried about me and that I needed time to cool off, although the tone of my voice to her recently makes me feel a little terrible.

"How are you feeling?"

"Better, but not so good when I told you to shut up."

She sighs and places her hands on her hips. "Nos, it's okay. You were upset and for me, telling you 'It's for the best' was very stupid. So, I'm the one who should be apologizing."

I accept her apology and we hug on it, then my mind shifts to Cedric's party, "So, what else needs to be set up for the party?"

"Just a few decorations and setting out the food."

On that positive note, Tara head up to the dining hall.

When we get there, we immediately get into action by putting up the remaining decorations on the walls, table, and exposed beams. Soon, we head into the kitchen and the way it's laid out and designed totally resembles the modern kitchen in commercial restaurants. With that said, I'll let you guys visualize it because I don't want to go into the details. Anyway, on one of the stainless-steel tables is the food and we grab them, then set them out on the main table. Within minutes, the delicious food in all shapes and sizes and the cake itself is set out. During that time, the royal guards are stationed at every entry point and secured the place to make sure no accidents or worse things happen during the private party.

A few hours go by. Cedric comes down the stairs, and we get the party going. We, or should I say they, get the party going, singing "Happy Birthday" in their native tongue which I find amusing, and we all start talking with one another. I am curious how old Cedric is. I ask Tara.

She smiles and replies, "Two hundred and twenty-two."

I nearly choke on my food and proceed onto Sean.

He sees me and bows. "My lord, what can I do for you this evening?"

"Nothing, man. But I do have one thing. Your men, both normal and royal, have my permission to not bow at non-serious times."

His eyes widen. "My lord, I'm confused. For years, we've been taught how to bow and do it every time we see the king and queen."

I wrap one arm around him. "Yeah and I respect that, but this is one of the minor changes Tara and I will bring upon this kingdom. I'm just saying you and your men don't need to bow at certain times when the situation is not serious."

"So, is that why you were waving your arm to keep us moving toward you?"

"Yeah, the situation did not involve the kingdom. It was a small matter I just wanted to sort out with my friends."

He gets the idea. "I'll send out the word when I can, sir."

I pat his back and move onto Cedric and Gothraigh who are huddling in one of the corners of the hall, talking in a very quiet tone. As soon as they see me, they cease their conversation.

"Cedric," I start speaking in an upbeat tone, "Happy birthday, sir," while I raise my goblet in celebration.

"Thank you, Will. What can we do for you?"

"I just want to apologize for what—"

Cedric puts up his free hand to make me stop and sighs. "It is our fault to throw all that news onto your plate that morning when you just woke up and you were getting used to your new form. You had the right to make us leave since you are now the king." Once he finishes, he throws out a smile.

"Here, here," says Gothraigh.

Then one of the waiters comes between us and provides a freshly filled goblet to Cedric, but not to me nor Gothraigh. All three of us are confused as we look at the one in Cedric's hand; the goblet is half full and he tries to convince the man he doesn't need a new one. The waiter insists a little more that he should take it, then throws in a reason that it's the same beverage; it's just that he and the staff added a fruity taste to it. We all look at one another in some confusion because all drinks and food were inspected while being prepared before the party could take off. We tell the man about that and he still insists. This is beginning to get on Cedric's nerves and orders the waiter to leave us alone. As the waiter receives the order from his former king and begins to turn away, there's a sudden crashing noise that occurs on the other side of the hall.

Apparently, another waiter accidentally bumped into Crystal making her lose her balance and she grabbed onto something to expel the fall, but she accidentally grabs one of the standing platters that went flying and the contents collided onto her dress, and that pissed her off. For the waiter, the tray he was carrying falls out of his hands and the glass goblets shatter onto the floor. Now, Crystal is shouting at the man and he tries to apologize for the mess. Crystal doesn't want to hear another word about it.

When the incident occurred, Cedric set down his goblet and proceeded to check on the incident but stopped because he took notice that Crystal had the situation under her control. So, he returns to us, picks up his goblet, drinks from it, and we continue on our conversation about the situation that's happening outside these borders. Minutes pass and Cedric begins to look a bit dizzy. I tell the man in good fortune and so does Gothraigh that he had enough to drink. Then Cedric agrees and moves toward the stairs that lead to our chambers. Once he reaches the bottom step, he falls, yet he grabs holds of the banister.

This gets Tara's attention, "Dad, are you okay?"

He turns around, "Hm? Oh yes, daughter, I'm fine. I've just had a little too much to drink." Soon, he pulls himself up the stairway one step at a time.

We continue with the party until a clock somewhere chimes off and we head off to bed realizing it's a quarter past eleven at night.

CHAPTER THIRTY-THREE
Sudden Death
Date: April 20, 2015

I HEAR TARA MOVING around, getting up, and kissing or licking my forehead. Then the door opens and closes, and I fall back to sleep. During the night, I was having an insane, adventurous dream where at one point everything was calm and then *boom*! Chaos breaks out. In this dream, I was still in my human form and I was running with my friends away from the chaos and then immediately, we jump in our modified trucks, kicking up dirt and some mud. After that, we were racing across some desert as the night began to fall, so we had to activate the L.E.D. light bars to brighten up the darkening horizon. During the run, it occurred to me that we were running away from the chaos. The debris cloud filled with all kinds of hazardous material with intense flames was starting to catch up. My friends and I had to ignite the "Nos" tanks in our trucks to gain more speed. When my finger was about to push the glowing lime green button, that is when Tara kind of woke me. So, I try to fall back to sleep, replay that scene, and let it move on, but the scene gets stuck on repeat and I struggle trying to move it forward.

Suddenly, a cry of pain and sorrow combined with a howl echoes through the walls. The howl is so distressful that my eyes shoot wide open and I sit straight up. The pain and sorrow echo again showing that it belongs to Tara. My adrenaline kicks into high gear as I scramble out of our bed toward the doors, throwing them wide open to the hallway. Tara's cries are so loud that it doesn't take time for my new ears to pick up the sound. I turn my head to the noise and the noise itself is coming down the stairway that probably leads to Cedric's chamber. Without wasting another second, I bolt up the steps, skipping three to four steps at a time and as I reach the top, there are several doors that line the walls on my left and right. From the scents, I can tell that those doors lead to the rooms that belong to Gothraigh, Cora, Whitney, Faith, Crystal, and Dawn. Of course, they're already sticking their heads out into the hall looking at the one door that's still open ahead of us. I move slowly, peeking my own head inside and panning my head left to right. It stops as my eyes zero in on Tara who's on her knees, weeping heavily at her father's bedside. The smell and the realization of why she is weeping in such a horrible state strikes and sinks my heart.

Entering the former king's chamber, I do my best to speak, "Tara?"

She turns around, eyes filled and dripping with tears, "Nos!"

She gets up and runs toward me. My arms automatically open to embrace my weeping wife as she collides into my chest, weeping into it.

"He's dead! My father's dead!"

I look at the raised bed where the corpse of Cedric Borin lays still under the covers. I can smell death emanating from his body. The smell of death this fresh, smelling it for the first time, is very disgusting and unwelcoming. Slowly turning around, I see Gothraigh. His eyes are wide open, ears forward, and proceeds into his brother's chamber with caution. Approaching the bed, he stretches out his right arm and places two of his fingers onto the neck waiting for a pulse. Then, he withdraws them while letting out a very heavy sigh and does his best to hold back his tears. Once he looks up, his eyes are filled with sadness and hatred.

"Who did this to my brother?"

I still stand where I am, still embracing my weeping wife. I know his question is a rhetorical one, but I still shrug my shoulders. Then, there's the sound of moving feet. Hustling up the stairway and right into the room is Sean and his men who also heard Tara's cries, and they wait for orders. I look at Gothraigh who looks at me, signaling that I should take this position. I look at Sean and his men who then look at me, waiting. I return my gaze onto Tara who still weeps. The sight of seeing my wife cry angers me and my anger rises more when I look at my deceased father-in-law. The memory of last night immediately plays in my head and gets to the part where one waiter was bugging Cedric to take a fresh goblet. Then, my mind connects the incident where another waiter, perhaps, at the same time, bumps into Crystal causing the mess.

Could those two bastards be partners that planned this stealthy assassination?

Looking back at Tara, then back at Sean, I give out an official order, "I want you guys to break up into two teams. The first one, find those two waiters and bring them to the throne room. While the other, investigate the kitchen of any foul play." They stand there waiting for more. I raise my voice, "We have a murderer on the loose! Chop, chop. Get to work!"

Sean and his men hustle out more than when they came in. Next, I turn my head toward Gothraigh.

"I'm pretty sure you guys have an undertaker. You get him or her to get Cedric ready for his funeral."

At the same time I said funeral, Tara weeps even more. Gothraigh nods and leaves the room. For me, I pick up my wife, leave the room, and carry her back to our room to calm her down.

CHAPTER THIRTY-FOUR
Execution and Wolfinoid Funeral
Location: Throne Room
Date: April 22, 2015
Time: 7:00 AM

TARA AND I SIT on our thrones waiting for the people who were part of the murder of King Borin. The results were true; only two people were involved. Both are male, and in time, they will no longer exist. I say this because we both agreed to do one thing. On my end, I sent out orders for Sean and his men to find them. They succeeded within twenty-four hours and are bringing them here in chains. For Tara's end, she wants to slaughter them after she talked to them or decides to have them slaughtered right away. I've agreed to stay out of her way since she's the primary ruler and whatever happens is by her command. So, yeah, I am not going back on my word. Deal with it.

Anyway, we both sit here and wait. Glancing at her from the corner of my left eye, she is most definitely pissed. On that note, I'm just sitting here, keeping my mouth tightly shut. When another minute passes, the doors burst wide open as Sean and his men somewhat struggle with the two murderers. Within that moment, Tara gets up and walks halfway down the aisle with her hair standing up. Soon, the ice-blue light begins to glow around her form.

She stops. "That's far enough, Sean."

Sean and his men throw them forward and make them kneel at her feet.

"Leave. Now," she orders and the guards turn on their heels and jog out.

Once the doors shut with a loud thud, Tara looks at me with the icy blue fire burning in her eyes. "Nos, come down here, please."

I don't hesitate. I leave my throne and join her with our two captives. She looks back down at them, building her power, intimidating them, which is by far working, and while slowly circling them, growling with the intent to slaughter.

"One of you is going to give me some goddamn, good fucking reasons why you murdered my father." The two captives have fear in their eyes and look at one another. Resuming their silence, Tara sighs, grows out the claws on her right hand, and slashes one of them across the face. "*Answer me right now!*"

The man that got slashed slowly moves back up to his knees and slowly begins to laugh. His laughing increases by strength and sound, making us even more impatient and angrier.

"What's so funny?" She hisses the word "funny" and grabs the laughing man by his head.

"Long live, King Lowsbroth," the man answers.

Looking at these two men, they seem to be brothers. One is younger than the other and I'm standing behind him. I can tell that they're brothers because they have the same black fur, brown eyes, and their feet and hands are white. I clear my throat to get her attention; she looks up in curiosity and I drop my eyes down for a quick second in a gesture that he's the younger brother. Tara gets my message and moves to where I'm standing.

"If you're not going to answer me, then you're just going to watch me tear apart your brother while my husband restrains you."

The man that was laughing ceases and his eyes change from, "I'm the badass and your father deserved to die," to "No. Shit. Please don't hurt him."

This makes her smile. "So, you won't answer one, stupid, single question when I slash the shit out of you. Perhaps, you will change your mind when your brother's life gets immediately put on the *line*." At that moment, Tara lets her hands lightly brush around the younger brother's head and then position them to shatter his neck.

"You wouldn't." He gets up; I counter by shoving him back on the ground. Tara laughs evilly and drops her hands.

Next, she gives him a deadly glare. "Then, tell me *why* you said long live King Lowsbroth?"

"Never," he states.

The glow around Tara gets bright as she focuses her attention on the younger brother. She raises her right hand in a cup form like she's grabbing something, and then snaps it sideways. Simultaneously, there's a loud snap that comes from the younger brother's left leg as the knee cap is suddenly removed from its place and sticks out, yet under the skin in a disgusting form. The younger brother howls in pain as he reaches to cradle it. The older one, well, realizes he's really in deep shit and all of his taunting attitudes fly away from his face and eyes.

"Alright, I'll tell you everything! Just don't hurt him anymore. Please?"

Tara remains serious. "That's more like it."

She swings her right arm toward the doors that lead into the long, entrance hallway and that makes the younger brother go flying at full speed. As he's about to collide with the doors, they swing wide open and immediately shut like a beast's mouth as it swallows the younger brother. I perk my ears forward and raise my eyebrows at such power my wife has. At the same time, I am totally grateful for being on her good side. I do my best to hold back my smile of amazement and as I look at her, she looks back and nods her head sideways meaning that I should step away. I comply.

"Tell me. Everything. *Now!*" Tara snarls at him.

"Okay, okay. It was all me. I did it."

She snarls even louder. Her exposed hair stands up even taller. Her power of light glows even brighter.

"I did it because he was a good, no, a much better Wolfinoid than your father. His ideas and plans for this kingdom were awesome. In addition, I did enjoy the fight between your asshole husband and Gurtruit with his friends. We all did."

The memory of me being in that arena fires off like multiple 12-gauge shotguns and I snap my attention at him, "Come again, asshole?"

The older brother smiles and laughs. His laughter increases with each laugh and Tara loses it all. She places both hands on his open mouth and immediately rips off his jaw. His eyes widen when his nerves send the signal of tremendous pain to his brain, but it only lasts for a few seconds when his life came to an abrupt halt. His blood flows out of the sockets like Niagara Falls where his jaw used to be and pools around his knees. Tara tosses the manipulated jaw somewhere, sticking one hand down the throat and the other up into the skull where it cracks and breaks. With one heave, she rips the head off from the shoulders, tossing it to another end of the room and letting the torso fall flat onto the floor. More blood pools out around the murderer's corpse.

I stand in fear, deciding if I should move, speak, or remain where I stand. Tara lets out a sigh of relief and gratitude that she succeeded at the revenge of her father's murder. She looks at me, taking deep breathes through her nose, calming herself down, and letting her power decrease. I gulp and still remain frozen, yet I am grateful for that bastard deserved it. I really enjoyed being around Cedric and he was a good mentor. But, now . . . he's in a better place.

"C'mon, Will, let's get ready for my father's funeral."

I nod in agreement and I follow her out.

11:00 AM

We both stand with everyone else dressed in black next to a grave that's been dug, reinforced, and lined with navy blue granite slabs. At one end lies the seal that is forged out of gold with an imprinted image of Cedric wearing almost a knight armor set. Instead of holding a shield and sword, he's holding his staff and the kingdom flag as he stands upon the corpses of their enemies in victory while looking forward the horizon that lays before him. Behind him are the imprints of the sun's rays shining around him to further his great triumph on the battles that he fought probably many centuries ago. Around the grave are red roses, in the inner perimeter is the casket crane, and at the other end is a simple, stone Celtic cross that has Cedric's name written in their own language with Roman Numerals of the years and dates of his birth and death. Finally, standing behind the cross is the deacon with a bible in hand that has bookmarks for the verses about the passing of friends and loved ones.

There are a few clouds in the sky, yet the sun shines brightly through them. Some birds chirp away in the trees; for us, we remain silent. More minutes go by until Sean and his men walk toward us in *the* most formal, royal guard wear. Their robes look heavy-based upon the fabric that is used—mainly black yet stripped thinly with the kingdom's colors. Leading the group is Sean; behind him are eight men carrying the casket and behind them is another man carrying the flag of the kingdom. As they approach, they place the casket onto the lowering belts of the crane, then stand at full attention off to one side. The deacon clears his throat and opens his bible. Before he reads the verses for the dead, he declares a small speech.

"We are here to gather today to pay our final respects and say our goodbyes to Cedric Borin. Cedric Borin was, indeed, a great ruler, a great brother, a great husband, and a great father."

Right after the deacon says "great father," Tara bursts out crying. Her tears fall and sweep like a massive flood from heavy rain that has fallen over one of the many valleys and mountains of this nation. She then collides her head onto my chest; I wrap my arms around her, then turn my attention at him with a scowling expression while I shake my head slowly. Gothraigh gets a little unraveled as he sees his niece cry so heavily and also scowls at him, too. The deacon swallows and carries on after knowing his mistake.

"My apologies; King Cedric Borin leaves behind a great kingdom. Nonetheless, his daughter- and son-in-law will carry this kingdom into the future, and his legacy. Now, for the verses from the bible."

He opens the book and begins reading. The minutes fly by as the deacon reads five verses and closes the bible. Sean picks up the cue by walking over and flicking a switch on the crane, which quietly comes alive, cranking the casket where King Cedric Borin lies, down into the ground. Once it reaches the bottom, the straps undo themselves from underneath and Sean goes around the crane and pulls them up. Next, he disassembles the crane system in four easy parts, moves them away from the grave, and rejoins his men. Gothraigh steps up, stretches out his arms, and levitates the metal seal. It hovers a few inches from the ground and then glides over the opening. He then sets it down creating this sealing sound and miraculously, a pile of dirt comes flying out of the woods, completely covering the seal that lays two feet below the surface. So, yeah, Cedric's grave is eight feet deep. Anyway, all the girls weep ranging from tears to gasping for air. For us guys, we just stand in silence as we pay our final respects to a great man by memory.

Then, someone taps me on the shoulder. I look over to see it's Trent with a worried face.

"I know this is really a bad time, but you guys and only you two should follow me to the command center."

I look at my weeping wife in my arms and glower at him, "Why?"

"All I can say, sir, is it somewhat involves you. Again, I need both of you to follow me to the command center. Like right *now*."

The way Trent emphasizes the word "now" sounds really important. I sigh in agreement, do my best to calm down, and encourage Tara to follow us.

She gathers her strength, though before we leave the gravesite, she walks over to the cross, kneels down, kisses it, and whispers, "Goodbye, father."

Tara slowly rejoins us and we follow Trent back to the castle.

CHAPTER THIRTY-FIVE
One Hell of a Surprise
Location: Sparta Command Center
Time: 1:47 PM

WE ENTER THE COMMAND center that lays within the hollowed-out walls of the castle. Its exact location is classified. Sorry, although I can describe what it looks like. It's designed the same way as Maddox's arena except on a much smaller scale. The lighting is done by torches that burn in azure blue which dimly lights up the room. The rest of the lighting comes from the eight advanced glass pane desktops pushed up against the slow, curving wall, and circulate the room. Also, each one is occupied by one royal guard sitting quietly in a comfortable chair with their hoods up. In the center is a large, circular table, and right above it is another circular device that has recess lighting but is programed to display holograms. How do I know this? This is the area where I learned geography and mostly the history of their world. Tara and I enter the com center still following Trent. The atmosphere is tense and I can sense frustration and confusion.

Moving farther in, we take our stand at the table and Trent taps a few keys on the only keypad that activates the hologram computer. Immediately, he looks at the both of us seriously.

"The info that we acquired that was soon to be from our last scout group showed us the most recent update of which fracture covers which region." He taps a few more keys and the hologram of the United States of America forms different colors of shade.

"But that was three months ago. The most recent info that Zachariah and I found weeks ago now shows this nation's geography of each military coverage."

A few more taps and the black shade for the werewolves moves farther west, encroaching onto Colorado and New Mexico yet being thinned out from the south and the north by possibly both military powers. Then, more gray spots and lines begin to appear. On the contrary, the black shade shows up in large blobs in some of the mountain ranges of those two states. Looking back at New Mexico, the location of one of those blobs looks oddly familiar. It is somewhat northwest, off from a few degrees from being directly center of the northern part of the state.

Finally, an atomic bomb or two explode with great force in my head realizing the location of that black blob. My ears draw back and my eyes widen.

"Are. You. Fucking. Kidding. Me?"

"What's wrong, Nos?" Tara asks with concern as she lightly grabs my right arm while I lean onto the table.

"Are you exactly sure that this info is damn as hell, 100% correct?" I ask Trent.

He hangs his head and walks over to one of the royal guards. He taps her on the shoulder and hands him a small tablet that's already on. Then, he walks over to us and hands the tablet to me with dissatisfaction.

"I'm so sorry my lord, but this info is indeed correct before we lost all communications with your former kind's satellites. This is the location where our enemy is producing more, thus gathering strength to take over the Great Plains and perhaps your former homeland." After that, he steps away.

I look at the tablet with a mighty shock, my heart stops, and my hands shake because of the info that my Wolfinoid eyes see before them. Tara looks down, gasps in horror, and relays Trent with the same question, which he answers the same way and tone. The location of the mass production and distribution of their enemy has taken place and over a town that formulated two of the most powerful bombs that mankind has ever seen.

The name of the town and its location sticks in out neon blue font on the screen, "LOS ALAMOS, NEW MEXICO."

I return my gaze, no, I scowl at Trent with anger of the information that we both just received, "Get me Admiral Zachariah Blitz. *Now*!"

"Yes *sir*!" Trent snaps in attention, gives me a salute, and runs out of the room.

CHAPTER THIRTY-SIX
Battle Preparation
Location: Throne Room
Time: 2:05 PM

TRENT AND ZACHARIAH MEET us both in the throne room. We all four stand in silence. The aroma in the air is highly tense. We wait for one or the other to break the silence. I hope it's going to be Tara as she's the primary ruler of this kingdom. However, I know Los Alamos, I am mainly from this world, and I am the one that sent Trent to get Zachariah. So, I should be in charge of this meeting. Yet, as I stated before, this is Tara's say. This is mainly her species' problem, not mine. I was pulled into all of this spontaneously and just taught over the past months. However, their government operates almost the same way as ours, so this is both our problem.

Sigh. I should break this unbearable silence.

I cross my arms and look at my feet while compiling my thoughts, "How many Wolfinoids are in this kingdom's army?"

Zachariah stands perfectly straight and so does Trent with both of their arms crossed behind their backs. Zachariah answers in a serious tone, "Roughly fifteen hundred. On the contrary, that's before this 'situation' got completely out of control. Now, the number is mainly a thousand."

"Nos, is that enough to regain this town called Los Alamos?" Tara asks.

I shake my head while replying, "No, I don't think so. Los Alamos is somewhat a small town, but if our enemy is using the facilities to increase their strength, then we'll probably need backup." Then I look up at Trent and Zachariah and ask, "What's Troy's Wolfinoid military headcount?"

They look at one another, exchanging thoughts through their eyes. Then Trent answers, "Ten thousand, three hundred."

"And the reason being?"

"It's based upon where our kingdoms are located, on the geography that each one has to cover, and the area of cover to remain discrete so that we could avoid conflicts with your former kind's military," Tara replies.

Makes perfect sense.

I walk away and pace the stage where the thrones sit, racking my brain through the history, the geography, and how many tech labs there are. Based upon the areas where average civilians can be and travel are mainly on the roads of Highway 4, the Truck Route/East Jemez Road, the Front Hill/502, and West Jemez Road/501. My guess is that there are probably over thirty tech labs. The majority of them are on private roads that are heavily guarded. Well, not anymore since based upon the map I've seen, Los Alamos has been taken over. Yet, the numbers of military by Troy and Sparta combined may not be enough. Also, there are other black spots in those mountain ranges, so more soldiers would indeed help to fight off and perhaps reclaim those rural areas that have also been taken over by the werewolves.

Again, I rack my brain around the geography, mainly the history, and I have come up with the only, possible solution.

We need more men.

"What's your idea, sir?" Trent asks.

I look at Tara and ask, "Are you completely okay that I take absolute charge of this situation, Tara?"

She joins me, wraps her arms around my shoulders, and smiles, "Yes, I am. For two reasons: first, you sound like you know that settlement very well and second, somebody has to stay here to keep the order in check."

I smile back and kiss her. Then, I look at my two men who control the military. "Put out a recruiting message for any human soldiers retrieved by our search parties if they were cut off from their platoons, and send that same message to Troy in hopes they'll be able to do the same."

They both snap at attention and Zachariah replies, "We'll get right on it, sir." They soon leave us.

I look at Tara, hug her, and say, "May God watch over all of us."

Then I leave her to retrieve my staff from our room because now, I'm too tall for it, and this is part of my battle preparations.

Location: Atticus' Workshop
Time: 3:50 PM

With my short staff in hand, I approach Atticus' workshop with my hood up. I was only outside for the first time in this new form during Cedric's funeral, but that was a private event and it was held on the far opposite end of this camp, away from the business and residential areas. The walk to Atticus' area is almost directly across from the doors to the kingdom, so I had to walk through those areas. I believe a lot of people, both human and Wolfinoid, don't really who I am. Perhaps some do. I don't know.

I continue toward my destination. Looking about, all three tent sectors are deserted except for the left one. Sitting at one of the drawing tables in the drawing tent is Atticus just quietly drawing and perhaps dozing off to sleep. I walk closer and the sounds of my approach make him snap his head up and look at me.

"Oh," he says while adjusting his specs, "Hello there, young man. What can I do for you?"

"It's me, Atticus. Will Young, the young human who made this staff." I bring up my old staff in one hand and show it to him.

He looks at me, then at the staff, and back at me. He gets up to take a better look. I lower my hood to further his investigation.

"Can you say your name again?"

I tell him. At a split second, his eyes widen with realization and reaches for my free hand.

"Will. My God, you look very different. So much has changed in the past months. I guess everything came true."

I nod in agreement, "Yeah. Listen, I need to make a new staff because straight up, I'm too tall for this one and I guess it doesn't respond to me."

He takes it, examines, and nods his head for me to follow. Following him, we head toward the height measures and I take my position. Once finished, we turn our direction to the smelting tent. Once there, I grab the same material as Atticus grabs a longer mold of the same design. Next, I easily feed the long sheet of stainless steel into the smelter and move to the sorcery section. Approaching one of the cauldrons, I follow the same routine and picked the same ingredients. After I slit my hand and poured some blood into the bowl, the same light that I see when Tara got injured appears from the injury, seals it up, and doesn't leave a scar once I wipe the blood away.

Cool.

Stirring the contents around the bowl, the admiral blue liquid glows much brighter than before and I can sense that it's much more powerful. This concerns me. The last time I did this as a human, a shock wave erupted through the cracks of the lid from the smelter, which extinguished the flames from the lanterns and the other smelters.

So, how powerful is the explosion going to be once I pour it into the mold?

"Why should it matter? I need a new staff. I need to have the fighting ability and power to take back that town, let alone other towns that might've been taken over and we might meet the enemy on our way to Troy."

I sigh and take the bowl to the smelter where the stainless steel has already melted and been poured into the mold. Atticus pops open the little hatch at the top, looks at me, and drops his ears. Then, he slowly backs away in caution yet a little pleased.

"I sense that your power has gotten stronger."

I smirk at him and pour the liquid slowly and carefully into the hole. Then, I set the empty bowl aside and prep myself to make one hell of a run. A minute goes by and nothing seems to happen. We look at each other with ease that we might've overestimated my source of power. Soon, we begin laughing in relief. Suddenly, a strong enough breeze comes through and extinguishes the lanterns but not the flames underneath the smelters. Next, the area starts to dim. We look around, confused. I step out from the tarp roof to see if any clouds have come over us, but that proves to be wrong. It's just the atmosphere in the area itself that's becoming darker. Amidst the darkness closing around us, the same ping noise sounds off, followed by the same noise of something like a powerful, electric generator coming to life. Alongside the noise, the same light starts appearing through the crack around the lid and increases its brightness. Our senses truly tell us that a great danger is coming and our hairs stand perfectly straight up, intensifying the moment.

However, both Atticus and I remain standing where we are in fear and awe, just hearing and watching the noise and light grow more intense. Then, finally, reality kicks in and my senses tells me to run, like now.

"Run for it, Atticus!" In swift movement and strength, I run toward him, throw him over my shoulder, and bolt it into the woods.

Getting into the thick trees by several yards, there's a great explosion of blue fire and smoke that goes flying up into the air, sending a mighty shock wave that knocks me off my feet. We roll over to see the great devastation that just took place.

"Will," Atticus speaks in shock, "What have you done?"

"I don't—"

BANG!

The blown-off lid of the smelter slams into the ground a mere two feet away from me, making me freak out, yell, and protect the old man. When our hearts have calmed down, we get up and walk toward the destruction. Getting closer, my jaw drops and eyes widen while I place my hands on top of my head because the smelting tent is blown to bits. Several smelters have been blown into the trees which have torn them down. The different height mold shelves have been cascaded several yards and strewn about. The damage by those and the shockwave has completely leveled the drawing and the sorcery tents, leaving a few remaining bits of the furniture. Covering and surrounding all three sections of the workshop is a black smear mark of where the explosion has taken place, right in the center is the only standing smelter, and laying inside the mold is my new staff.

This is going to put us back a few weeks.

I look at Atticus as he looks at the destruction of his workshop. "Atticus, I am so, so sorry."

He looks at me; I prep for the worse. "What kind of human did your former humans make you into?"

I look back at the destruction, forming one simple answer, and then I look back at him, "The kind that can't confess his true feelings and that he must put a cap on his anger and sadness while pretending that everything is happy in his life because he was a minor learning-disabled person."

I move to the smelter, retrieving my staff, and while I leave the destruction site, I put up my hood, and say to Atticus, "I'll send down a huge crew to reassemble your workshop."

Then, I walk away to my next destination.

Location: Hospital Tent
Time: 4:20 PM

My next stop is the hospital. During my walk from the workshop to here, I turned on my headset and ordered a team of twenty guards to help Atticus rebuild his workshop. After that, I've been mentally kicking my wolf ass for having too much anger, revenge, and justice in my blood system. Still, I have to get this kingdom's army ready for the march to Troy. Without stopping, I pull back the entrance flap that leads into the reception/waiting room area and immediately head over to the desk.

"May I see Dr. Tristen Maverick?"

The receptionist pulls out a tablet and preps herself to write down information, "And what is your name and the state of illness that you're in?"

I clear my throat. "Tell him that it's . . ."

I can't believe I'm gonna say this.

"It's King Will Borin and I would like to speak to him immediately."

She snaps her head up in surprise. I lower my hood so that she could get a better look, "You're . . . you're the human that was—"

I put my hand up. "Yes, yes. I was in here months ago and Doctor Maverick was the man who treated me. And yes, I was the human transformed by your princess, well now, Queen Tara Borin, by one bite of her mouth."

The receptionist dismisses the tablet and grabs for an elegant yet futuristic microphone, "Doctor Maverick, please report to the front desk. I repeat, Doctor Maverick, please report to the front desk." Then she looks at me with a confident smile. "He'll be here shortly, my king."

I nod in thanks and stand by the chairs, waiting. Looking about this place, it looks and feels calmer than before. There are no doctors or nurses hustling about trying to mend a human nor a Wolfinoid back to full health while carrying stacks of paper, probably because the memory drives on the tablets must've been completely full and neither human nor Wolfinoid is being pushed around on beds from one room to the next nor even being rushed in through the entrance. In time, I hear somebody clear his throat and I turn my gaze to see Doctor Tristen Maverick.

I stretch out my right hand to shake his and I smile at him, "Hey there, doc. How's it been?"

He looks back absolutely shocked. He struggles for a moment. To further his investigation, Tristen squints his eyes and approaches me slowly. In a second, he asks for my name and I tell him. Then, his face changes from shock, confusion, to realization and finally shakes my hand.

"Oh, Will! It's so good to see you and you look, heh, mighty well."

"Thanks. Hey, doc, is there somewhere private we could talk? It's very important."

Tristen sees and hears my seriousness and he leads me to his office. As we enter his office, it's nothing fancy; just two solid, simple chairs, a simple desk with some drawers and tablet lying on top of it, a rolling office chair on the other side, and finally some plants. We take our seats and I rub my forehead to ask a serious request from him and his staff.

"Will, what is it?" he asks curiously.

Sigh. "The . . . the situation of . . . trying to fight off or eliminate the enemy is now entirely impossible." Then I turn my gaze upon him. "The werewolves have increased their strength and numbers by pushing farther west into Colorado and New Mexico while in the process of taking over mountain towns in the Rock Mountain Range. One of those towns that they have taken over to increase their strength and numbers is Los Alamos, and Los Alamos is a scientific town that does a lot of experiments and uses nuclear energy. Its first experiment was the gadget, which was the first atomic bomb. The only way to take back that town and perhaps liberate the others is for me and the army of this kingdom to march to Troy, combine forces with their military, and create the final push of capturing the enemy. Before we leave, we need medical supplies."

Tristen crosses his arms, leans back in his chair, and replies, "It's that serious?"

I nod.

He sighs. "How soon are you preparing to leave?"

Thinking back on the explosion that took place at Atticus's workshop and the time to ready the human troops, the timeline automatically pops into my head, "We should leave within a month and half. Or sooner."

"We might be able to come up with the supplies for your long journey to Troy."

My ears perk forward and my tail begins to wag, "So, you might be able to have all of the supplies ready within a month?"

Tristen frowns, "I'm not completely sure. The situation that took place here a few months ago did drain the supply. On the other hand, there might be some stuff left over. How big is your departing group?"

I take a deep breath, "The entire Spartan military. All one thousand men and women."

Tristen sits forward, eyes wide, again. "So it's that fucking serious?"

"I know it seems rushed, but I and the military need to leave before the entire Rockies are taken over. Troy is falling and the entire human population of United States are murdered or turned into them."

He gets up and leaves his office. I follow. I sense a great amount of stress shedding off from him. Tristen marches into the lobby, looking around his facility with his hands on top of his head trying to keep himself together. He spins around a couple of times while taking deep breaths. Then, he brings down his hands and rubs them together, probably formulating his final verdict. When a few more minutes pass in the calm lobby, he looks right at me calm, positive, and serious.

"My lord, I guarantee you that my staff and I will provide you with the medical supplies. This includes not only bandages of all shapes and sizes; we will provide you a good-sized tent along with the necessary equipment. Plus, a few of my staff will come along for the journey to Troy and to Los Ala, Ala . . ."

I place my hands on my hips and shake my head with a smile. "Los Alamos. Thank you so much, Dr. Tristen Maverick."

To end on a positive note, we shake hands and I depart back to the castle.

Location: Lounge Room
Time: 4:45 PM

I let my legs give out as my bottom falls down upon one of the couches in this room. After succeeding from most of the three objectives, the march to Troy is now in motion. Of course, when I get there, I need to give a speech about Los Alamos so that the military of both Troy and Sparta understand what type of territory we will be approaching. This includes the humans that live a mere five hundred miles away from the town and probably don't have a clue about it. While looking around, letting my mind wonder, my eyes fall upon a tablet sitting on one of the tables. I retrieve it, activate it, and relearn about the town.

After an hour or so of jotting down notes, creating simple paragraphs that would form my speech or presentation, I have the entire geography and history written down in pencil. Still, I do my best to cover every little detail of the history though my research is blocked by classified documents and yet again the tablet loses connection with the internet. I sigh in frustration and toss the high-tech, pane of glass to one side of the room, and decide to look over my notes. Within minutes, I hear some people coming down the hallway and as they round the corner, they receive my full attention.

Looking at both Trent Wild and Admiral Zachariah Blitz, they both have disappointment on their faces.

"What's wrong, gentlemen?"

Trent speaks up, "We made flyers and tried to contact Troy to do the same and . . ."

I lean forward with interest, "And?"

Zachariah clears his throat. "And we weren't successful and neither was Troy. Your former kind has all of their men and women operating to fight off our enemy. Our camps are mainly filled with civilians and they are too terrified to help."

I slump back onto the couch. *Great. That's just fucking great.*

"Sir, are you okay from what happened at Atticus' workshop?"

I look at my staff, feeling frustrated about the energy that I have and from the fact that no civilian human is willing to learn any military tactics to take back their homeland. Overall, I am still frustrated from the incident that took place hours ago. I rub my eyes.

"I don't want to talk about it. You may leave."

I hear them leave and I get back to creating my new presentation about Los Alamos to a Wolfinoid military of eleven thousand and three hundred.

Sigh. This is not going to be fun nor easy.

CHAPTER THIRTY-SEVEN
Troy, Here We Come
Location: Western Gate
Date: May 19, 2015
Time: 5:30 AM

MY SPARTA, WOLFINOID ARMY and I stand at the gate that faces west. We have gathered together to make sure everything and everyone is accounted for and are ready to leave. During the checks of having all medical supplies, food, and basically every item that will keep us going until we reach Troy, the departing military men and women are saying their goodbyes to their family and friends. Tara and I stand together, looking around. She is wearing a dress created out of silk that drapes down to her feet with one strap made out of a material dyed in purple that travels over her left shoulder and she has also dyed the tips of her hair in the same color to match the dress. Her jewelry is an elegant necklace studded with diamonds that have the mixture of the colors blue and purple. She has a simple tiara on with the same diamonds and purple feather earrings that hang an inch and a half from her ears. Finally, she's wearing her wedding/ruler ring. For me, I'm wearing dark blue jeans, a mossy oak t-shirt and hat, and a black robe with a single camo print stripe traveling up and down the sleeves with the same design on the side of my jeans. My only weapons are my reflex skills and my staff.

Tara touches my shoulder. "You seem tense."

I let out a sigh, hang my head for a moment, and I look at her. "Yeah, I am. This is my first time leading a large group, especially this size. I'm also a bit on-edge of the dangers that lurk beyond these gates."

"You'll do fine and be great. Besides, you got Trent, Sean, and Maddox tagging along."

I chuckle and shake my head because it's very true. Just a few days prior to this day, I did ask those three men to join me and they were totally ecstatic to join without hesitation or second thoughts. Speaking of which, those guys join us at the gate. All of them look pleased this morning.

"What's the status?" I ask.

Maddox looks at the other two and claps his hands together. "We're all set, sir. Ready to move out at your command."

I take in a deep breath and look at my wife. I look really deep into her eyes, thinking and feeling that this might be the last time I might see her again. To make this moment last longer, I brush that longer bit of hair that covers her left eye behind the ear, wrap my arms around her neck, and bend down to give her one luscious kiss of compassion, love, that I'm really going to miss her. Retrieving my head back, her eyes tell me that she feels the same way about me heading off to war. She takes off my hat and runs her right hand through my hair that I requested to be cut in a Marine style, grabs the back of my skull, and pulls it back to return the goodbye kiss.

"Until I see you again, Tara," I say.

"Until I see you again, Will," replies Tara as she puts my hat back on.

I withdraw my arms and look at my army. I inhale the fresh, spring morning air through my mouth, *"Alright!* Let's move out!"

"You heard your king, move out!" repeats Trent.

A horn sounds off somewhere in the back to further the command to depart.

I lead my army up the hill and just before the path curves into the woods of the Smokey Mountains, I let Sean, Trent, and Maddox lead for a moment as I stop and look back at the outpost kingdom of Sparta. While my eyes pan from left to right, they stop at a group of familiar faces. With my eyes being more advanced than my human eyes, I squint just a little to clear the view; when it does, I see Austin, Alex, Chris, Hugh, Alice, and Emily observing our departure from this safe haven. They look concerned and I can tell that they're looking at me, so I stand at attention, give them a salute, then rejoin my army.

Location: Indiana, Shore of Lake Michigan
Time: 12:45 PM

After running through the fully grown and healthy forests, we've covered well over hundreds of miles within six hours. Approaching the lake shore, I signal the men to slow our pace because some familiar tent-like structure is set up just ten yards away from the beach. Observing the stance of it makes me give out the hand order to halt and squat down. Spending more time scrutinizing the tent, it seems to be abandoned. Its current situation shows it was taken over a while back because the tarps are torn in chunks, just slightly moving in the wind, and the structure is lopsided. I sniff the air a couple of times and no other scent crosses my nose, but still, it could be a trap.

I quietly whisper into the mic, "Do any of you guys smell anything near or around the tent?"

Seconds tick by and I receive quiet a load of replies of "No."

"Okay." Then I turn to my army. "I would like a four-man team to split up, surround, and approach the tent very slowly. Be ready for any sudden attack."

The men and women glance and murmur with one another.

Soon, two men and two women slowly raise their hands to volunteer. I nod and speak to them, "Alright, you four. Be very cautious."

They nod and move toward the tent.

I watch with concern and so does Trent, Maddox, and Sean. The team slowly divides up and surrounds the tent; once in their positions, they move to it with their staffs at the ready. They get closer and closer and next, they peer through the torn gaps, look at one another, and agree. Then, we all receive the all-clear message.

We all move to examine the site making sure that the perimeter is secured. As the five of us gets closer, there's something about this tent that looks oddly familiar. Stepping inside, there's a table that's been overturned, a couple of chairs thrown about, and shards of glass littering the floor. I begin to rub my chin.

"Does this tent look familiar to you, sir?" Sean asks.

I look around a bit more and then answer, "A little bit. Yet, I can't put my finger on it."

I walk toward the table and set it up, then I set up the chairs, two on each side. The feeling about this tent becomes stronger and I sit in one of the chairs while looking at the back wall. In minutes, something begins to take form in my head. I look at Sean and Maddox.

"Can you guys sit in those chairs?" I point at ones across from me. They agree and sit down.

I look at the two, placing my elbows on the table, and folding my hands together. I concentrate on the form inside my head; finally, I ask, "Can you two pretend like you're holding and working on tablets?"

They shrug and do as I asked. Then the memory becomes perfectly clear and I abruptly stand up.

"Fuck," I say, placing my hands on my head and walking out, "Fuck. Fuck. Fuck. Fuck."

"My lord, what is it?" Trent asks.

I still cuss.

I walk toward an area to find the large vessel I traveled on with Ryia A.K.A. Tara, Althalos, Forthwind, and Ulric. Reaching the lake shore, I look around in high hopes.

"Sir what is it? What are you looking for?" Trent anxiously asks.

I turn around to look at him, along with Sean and Maddox who are approaching us. Finally, I answer, "This was the security outpost where Hawkman and his partner evaluated me and gave me the all clear to proceed to Sparta with my search party."

Maddox and Sean cross their arms, shifting their weight from foot to the next and cursing in their native tongue. I turn back to continue my search for that ship. Within seconds, I find it on its side covered by the flourishing vegetation. I nod for Maddox to join me to inspect if the ship is "seaworthy." We walk around and I don't see any cracks or holes in the bottom of the hull and Maddox agrees with me. Next, we leap up and land on the starboard. Maddox walks to the stern as I walk to the bow. During our sweep, he tells me it's all clear and good, and I state the same thing when I reached the bow. How could this ship be brought upon the shore and be rolled onto its port side?

Perhaps by our magic.

I nod to that thought.

"Sir," shouts Trent. I look down to see one of our soldiers standing next to him, "This woman wants to speak with you."

I jump off and join both of them. Observing the soldier, it's a female with black fur except with one white stripe traveling from her nose, up the face, between the eyes, over the head, and down her neck. Her eyes are violet purple that seem to have some impatience in them. Her uniform robe is just like the others representing the colors of Sparta except for the two gold-threaded heads of the symbol sewn onto each sleeve. Finally, her staff is black, yet it has openings to reveal the same color in her eyes as it slightly glows.

"What's your name and your position?"

She does a slight bow. "My Lord Will, I am Zakia Smoke and my position is Second Lieutenant."

"Okay, Zakia, what can I do for you?"

"Sir, I mean, your highness, the men and women, including me, are getting a little impatient. We would like to know what has happened here."

I smile and tell everybody on the communication sunglasses. Then, I give them their next order, "Our next move is by flipping that ship right side up and get it into Lake Michigan. After that, come aboard and we'll sail to a beginning land mass of a peninsula in the state called Wisconsin. I'll instruct you later on."

After that, we all gather around the ship and prep ourselves to move it. We shoulder our staffs, place our hands out, and open it. A loud noise of clanking metal, gears operating upon gears, the grinding sounds of metal rubbing against one another, and the odors of carbon monoxide with burning oil, gas, and diesel whip across our senses. Without missing a beat, we all retreat into the trees and brush, squatting and lying down on the ground while the others climb up into the trees. As the noise of machinery comes closer, smaller noises of a thousand boots or more, and a chatter of small talk and some orders reach our ears, just forty yards away from us, approaching the lake shore, is one of the largest assemblies of the United States Army and Rangers I've ever seen. What I'm about to say to the mic is going to sound so weird, but it seems relevant.

"Nobody and I mean nobody make any damn noises nor move. Remain perfectly still."

My quiet and serious command is understood and we all watch with our muscles locked up and ready to fire to make a run for it if by any chance we are spotted.

The tension increases. We can all sense it from one another. The assembly of U.S. Army and Rangers get closer to the beach and stop. In their possession are forty tanks, fifteen rocket launcher trucks, eighty supply trucks to carry more men, medical supplies, food, and ammunitions, thirty recon vehicles mostly H1 Hummers with heavy artillery fire mounted on the roofs, and several mobile command centers. A lot of men circle and protect their commanders as they ready their fire arms while the commanders look at their maps to decide what their next move should be.

I whisper into the mic again, "Be ready to escape."

The commanders discuss in calm tones but escalate to an argument. One of them climbs a small ladder of one of the mobile command centers and bangs loudly on the door. It opens in seconds and the same man yells at one of the men inside, asking him furiously if the G.P.S. and all other satellite communications are back online. The man replies apologetically and the commander yells in anger, jumps down from the ladder, rips the map from the other commander's hands, and looks at it for a brief second. Finally, he yells once more, crumpling the map in his hands, throwing it onto the ground, and stomping on it. A second later, he yells at the convoy of men and machine to turn and head south. They obey. We do not arise from our position as the last pair of tanks disappear, somewhat, in the trees.

When the noise of the convoy has escaped our ears, we stand up, still looking at their path of direction.

"Damn, that was close," says Zakia.

"Too fucking close to be exact," replies Sean. Trent and Maddox agrees with them.

I sigh with a growl of frustration and annoyance at their dumbass statements with my ears slightly back while clenching my hands really tight.

"Will, what is it?" asks Maddox.

I smack my right hand against my face, slowly pulling it down, growling at bit more at his stupidity, and slowly turning around, "Have you guys already forgotten that I was once a human?"

Their answers stutter in their mouths, and I continue, "It hurts me that I feel like I have betrayed my own kind. I feel more like you, your kind, than mine." I look back at the ship. "Anyway, let's get that into the water and get the hell outta here before the next convoy of U.S. troops come hiking through."

Once again, we position ourselves around the vessel and face our open hands toward it. We concentrate on all our might and we slowly pick up the vessel from the ground and move it over the water. Once there, we flip it right side up and gently lower it into the water.

I throw up my hood and look at my army, "C'mon, y'all, saddle up. We're burning daylight."

I back up slightly into the woods, run at full sprint, then I finally leap up into the air, landing on the main deck safely. Looking back, my army follows and joins me. Once they come aboard, a few pops open the hatches and leaps down the lower decks.

I turn to Maddox, "You're the one who knows all sorceries, so I'm pretty sure you're the one who taught Tara how to move water."

He nods and takes his position at the helm.

Once there, he gives out an order, "Everybody, hang on! This is going to be a bumpy launch."

For those on the main deck, including me, we grab hold of the railing. I hope down below are poles or ropes to hang onto. Immediately, Maddox begins to glow. He stretches out his arms forward with his hands wide open. Next, he grabs the air and throws it behind us, causing the ship to launch forward like a teenager starting to learn how to drive a standard transmission. The ship cuts through the water smoothly as we head north, away from the rampaged security check point.

God, I hope Hawkman and his partner are still alive.

CHAPTER THIRTY-EIGHT

Conflict. Perfect.
Location: Somewhere in Between Minnesota & North Dakota
Date: May 20, 2015
Time: 7:15 PM

AS THE SUN BEGINS to set in the west, I survey the mental state of my men and women army and all of them seem to be exhausted. I survey the geography that we're hiking through and it's all just very dense forest with loads of mosquitos and areas with enough bodies of water. Still, we've hiked over four hundred miles and we need a good area to set up camp.

Pushing onward, we reach a clearing that's somewhat surrounded by very large boulders, mainly pine trees, and nearby is a small lake. I start nodding my head as this spot looks great and gesture my hands toward my supervisors and they too agree. I calmly speak into the mic saying that we'll stop here and make camp for the night. My men and women all sigh with relief and gratitude, and like a steady-flowing stream, they pour into the clearing while sitting down, unshouldering their sacks while others move toward the lake. For me, I holster my staff because I've been using it as a hiking stick, then walk to Trent, Sean, and Maddox who already have set up a small table with a tarp covering it and four lanterns burning. On this small table is the map of the U.S. that has been outlined in different colors to show what the previous coverage of each clan has. The information was taken from the digital map that Trent showed Tara and I, and we decided to draw it out on this map.

Maddox pulls out a compass to aid us while we survey the area and compare it to the map. As minutes go by, we head toward the lake to measure and calculate its location as best as we can.

Within the hour, we discover our location is still in Minnesota, yet on a positive note, we're about twenty miles away from the North Dakota state line. Moreover, our camp is fully set up. There are dozens of large tents, like the one I've camped in months ago, spreading in the circular perimeter with fires to illuminate and cook food; a medical tent has been established, and dozens of somewhat tiki-looking torches have been pegged into the ground to softly light up the lake.

I walk toward the largest tent of the camp because what makes this tent so massive is that it's designed and made for the four of us. Entering the tent, in the main area, is the kitchen and dining area. On one side is our map room and on the far back side is our separate sleeping quarters divided by more tarps. Fully entering our tent, Sean waves at me to join them at the dining fire.

"So, what's the latest?" I ask my officers.

"Nothing new," answers Sean, "It's just been smooth sailing."

I look at Maddox and Trent, and both agree with him. I let out a sigh of relief while my ears perk forward with the good news. At that moment, I take seat next to the fire, watching the meat sizzle in the skillet along with the excellently chopped vegetables. Near the pit are a few plates with fresh fruit. I reach for a banana and munch on it in silence with my advocates as they too keep the silence strong. Still, there are occasional chatters and some music outside our tent, making this night very calm and welcoming.

Being in this current atmosphere really starts making me feel Tara's absence. We've spent so much time in her room. I really enjoyed it and like I told her when I was a human, she's the closest woman I've ever gotten to. And now we're married and we've been through so much. Her absence grows stronger inside me, so strong that I set down my half-eaten fruit back onto the plate. At this moment, my three advocates pick up my vibe.

"Starting to miss Tara?" Maddox asks.

I just nod.

Sean pats my back in comfort.

I look at Maddox. "Are you missing anybody, Maddox?"

He briefly looks up and then back at the fire, lets out sigh while letting his ears droop, and then he answers, "No. I'm just like what you were, mate. I haven't found the right woman yet."

Before I can encourage him with some positive talk, the sensation in the air immediately changes from calmness and laughter to danger and threat. The music outside and other chatter also ceases. The sense of danger and threat arises fast that all four of us immediately stand up. Seconds tick by, then there's a threatening howl in the wind and it wasn't anyone of us in the camp. Suddenly, a male soldier throws open the tarp with fear in his eyes and all around his face.

"My commanders, our enemy is approaching."

"How much time do we have?" Trent asks with concern.

"They're almost right on top of us." And then he immediately leaves.

Shit. It's fucking deja vu all over again.

We all sprint to our sleeping quarters, grab our staffs, and sprint outside. At the same time, I go into commander and chief mode, and ordered, "Alright! Everybody needs to be on the fucking toes for anything that comes our way!"

Not nearly half a second later, our enemy comes through trees with claws and teeth baring.

I grab my staff tightly in my hands and brace myself for an attack because one of those shit heads is sprinting right at me. It leaps right up in the air and comes down upon me with tremendous speed and force that pushes me down to the ground. The werewolf digs its claws into my shoulders, engaging my adrenaline to push it off; it goes flying in the air for a moment, then comes back down to the surface to land onto its back while I scramble onto my feet and leap on top of it. In the process of my leap, I throw down the staff; upon landing, I put my hands deep inside its mouth and with great force and strength, I rip open the mouth. The move kills it in seconds, but I'm not done. I dig my claws of my right hand into the throat and pull down the decapitated jaw, towing the entire thickness of fur and skin while revealing the center bone of the rib cage. I grab the bottom of the torn skin and rip it off. I hold my trophy in the air while howling in victory. Seconds after, I'm knocked down by a couple more, yet I counteract by throwing my arms up behind me to pull them off. I stretch my hand and my staff flies into it. Once the stainless steel touches my skin, the power comes alive with great might. The admiral flame appears around the glass orb and immediately morphs into a spear head. I don't hesitate thrusting the lethal end into the heads of both. The results are the same when the staff is pulled out of their heads; their brains and blood spew out like a high-pressure fountain for about thirty seconds.

Turning my head at the main scene, there's an all-out war at our camp. Every Wolfinoid of my army are fighting in groups to take on a couple of the werewolves; others are fighting them singlehandedly but seem to have it under control. My army have their staffs activated and are throwing all sorts of different colors; at the same time, they're using their claws and mouths to annihilate them. Amidst the chaos and blood spewing everywhere, everything seems to be in slow motion. On the other hand, things return to normal speed as my eyes fall upon Zakia and she's having a lot of trouble dealing with five werewolves. Squinting my eyes to get a better vision, it looks like she's losing the fight and she's bleeding in different places. I immediately sprint toward her in rescue. During the sprint, I holster my staff and increase my speed. Nearing closer to my Second Lieutenant, the same color that glows inside my staff begins to glow around me and I feel much more powerful than before. Focusing onto my destination, everything around seems to blur like in the *Fast and Furious* movies when the guys activate the Nos to go faster and the street lights, signs, buildings, people, and cars begin to blur into one another.

As I'm about ten yards away, I shout, "Drop, Zakia!"

She does.

I fold my right arm across my neck like I'm reaching for my primary weapon, though I'm not. I only flatten my hand, building the intensity in my arm, then I thrust it out, sending out an admiral blue arc blade toward the five werewolves that reaches them in mere seconds and decapitates their heads. Their headless bodies make their knees give out and they collapse to the ground. Reaching Zakia, I slide to a stop and help her up. Examining her over, her battle robe is torn in large sections while some bits of the fabric hang loose. There are multiple lacerations on her face, arms, and legs. Finally, she trembles from the shock she has gone through.

She looks up at me with hope in her eyes, "Th-th-thank you, your highness."

I reassure her with a smile and answer, "Don't mention it. Now, go find cover; you're too injured to fight."

Out of the darkness, another werewolf tries to attack us by jumping into the air and coming down upon us. I suddenly twist around on my heels, throw up my left hand, and strangle the bastard. I tighten my grip around its neck and it begins to struggle for air; I wrap my right hand around his muzzle tightly and cleavage its head off the shoulders, letting the corpse fall down to the ground. I glance back if Zakia is still there. I see her darting away into the trees for cover and joining a few more who are too injured to fight. Seeing them injured makes me angrier, fueling my inner power and making my admiral blue light shine brighter.

Turning my attention to the action, I survey the rest of the battle zone. I can't tell if we're winning or losing, so I scout to see if there's anybody who needs assistance. Near the lake, there's Maddox performing his magic as he thrusts a pack of twelve werewolves into the lake with his staff and setting the lake ablaze. The pack of twelve werewolves howl in excruciating pain until they die when their bodies couldn't anymore take the intensity of pain and shock. Maddox turns away letting the corpses burn and focuses his attacks on the nearest enemy.

Panning my head on the other direction, there's Trent waving his staff in all sorts of directions while casting the light that I did moments ago yet in a golden shade that still decapitates the werewolves' limbs. So, he doesn't need my assistance.

Then I hear a loud snarl and yell coming from somewhere to my far left. My ears pick up the noise and I turn my head toward that direction and as my eyes fall upon the source of the noise, it shows Sean who's shirtless with lacerations on his chest, arms, and head. But he fights on as he unleashes his animal side and mauls down every one of our enemy as he jumps from one thing to the next, sinking his teeth into the neck, and then pulling a decent chunk of skin away that releases every ounce of their blood. There are too many of them. Swiftly, I order my staff to stand perfectly with its butt on the ground and then I remove my cloak and shirt in a violent fashion, letting out a battle cry and joining Sean in the fight. Getting there, I let my animal side take action by tackling down every werewolf and sinking my teeth into their necks so they die in a quick yet painful death.

During this fight, it seems like we're all going to be at this for hours, possibly until the next day or two.

By the next midmorning, the fight has been brought to a close. We all don't know what the time is, but we don't care. Our entire camp has been littered with the dead of our own and our enemy. So much blood, organs, and limbs are strewn about the site. Most of the decapitated limbs belong to our enemy while a few belong to our comrades. Half of the tents, including ours, are torn to shreds. Thank the Lord above that the hospital tent has remained intact while the fight was in action. Now, it's overfilled with our surviving comrades. The sounds of their cries of pain, E.K.G.s beeping loudly, and the doctors and nurses running about delivering equipment and other medical supplies echo from the open tarp entrance. The doctors and nurses hustle out and back to the tent to treat the wounded ones that lay on rickety, collapsible beds that are also strewn about the camp site. The somewhat wounded and non-wounded soldiers aid the medical staff in their procedures to help heal their fallen brothers and sisters. Any other surviving werewolves are immediately murdered by many surviving soldiers and their yelps of pain lasts for a minute as they are slaughtered without mercy.

How am I doing, you may ask? Well, I'm feeling exhausted, overwhelmed, and feeling helpless by the outcome of the fight like I have failed my duty as their king. When the fight ended, I came to rest on a log and once I got near, I've let my knees buckle and my ass slam onto it. I've been sitting here ever since.

The scene has become too much to bear and I let my head fall between my legs and place my hands on top of my head, breathing in and out and trying my best not to fall asleep. Before long, my top three men join me, plopping themselves onto this log and letting out heavy sighs of exhaustion. We sit in silence, listening to the noises I've described earlier.

But you still have a task to do, Nos.

I agree to that thought.

I let another heavy sigh. "What's the latest?"

Sean sighs once more through his nose. "Your highness, the latest is . . ." I bring my head up in some fear. "Fifty are dead. Thirty are severely wounded. The rest have simple wounds and will make a full recovery within two days."

After receiving the information, I rub the back of my neck while feeling a little relieved. I thought for a moment that the news would be a lot worse.

"So, our total is nine hundred and twenty?" Trent asks.

Sean simply nods.

"Sire," Maddox speaks, "Is that enough to still liberate this town called Los Alamos?"

I slap my knees, getting up and taking a few strides away from my high-ranking men while placing my hands on my hips. I observe the massacre that just ended over an hour ago.

Nine hundred and twenty. Not bad, I thought while chewing my bottom lip.

"Sire?" Maddox asks again in concern.

I still look forward, yet I answer, "Perhaps, but I don't really care right now. What I do care about is that we attend to the wounded, bury the dead, try to put back together this camp, and stay here for a few days or so just until the severely wounded are in okay condition to be transported. For now, do as I say, split the survivors into three groups. The first group assists the doctors and nurses, the second is reassembling this camp, and the third is on patrol. I don't want another spontaneous attack." I turn around to look at them seriously and say, "Is that understood?"

"Yes, sir!" all three of them reply in unison.

CHAPTER THIRTY-NINE
Pressing On
Location: Hopefully Halfway Through North Dakota
Time: Noon or Past
Date: May 28, 2015

ANOTHER FLASHES OF LIGHTNING crosses the sky underneath the dark gray clouds, followed by unbearable loud booms of thunder across the open plains of North Dakota while heavy sheets of rain pour down upon us like millions of pennies falling from heaven. We are somewhat cold, but thanks to our fur and battle robes, we're okay. However, we are all drenched by the fast-falling rain. There are dozens of stretches of the severely wounded that are still healing and are yet to be transported. The stretchers are covered by a roof and on both sides to shield and keep the survivors warm and dry. Each one has a team of doctors and nurses walking next to them while monitoring their vitals. Surrounding the doctors and nurses are the remaining soldiers guarding them and are surveying the area for any oncoming attack. Their eyes and ears bounce around from one angle to the next. Finally, on the outskirts of this parade are me, Maddox, Trent, and Sean. Sean covers the head while Maddox covers the right; Trent covers the left and I cover the rear. For the past hours, I've stopped and looked to absolutely make sure that nothing is following us. After the attack that took place a week ago, we've spent the entire time for more preparation, recovery, and reconnaissance.

On this day, when we decided to move out, this storm just rolled in within two hours and has been this way since the past three and a half hours.

Sigh. This sucks.

Still, we press on. We have to get to Troy. We have to combine our military strength in order to abolish and give back L.A.C. to the human race. We have to exterminate our enemy and bring peace to the United States.

What the fuck are you saying, Will? You were a human! You tried your very fucking best to stay out of this bullshit as much as possible because you needed to make a living.

Yes, that is true. Yet, I feel like I was supposed to be this type of creature—to be a Wolfinoid. Maybe that is why I felt a little different and couldn't fit in very well with that society.

"What the fuck? Snap out of it! You need to feel guilty that you've betrayed your original species. You need to feel that joining those three men was the biggest mistake of your life!

No, it wasn't. It was the greatest choice I've ever made. It has brought me an absolutely awesome and unique life. It has brought me love that I thought I've never find. The other shit that has happened was just simply spontaneous; there was no way around it. It was a series of, somewhat, unfortunate events.

Yeah, I agree with that, but you still need to feel a bit guilty that you continued down this path and realize there's no way of coming back.

Yeah, I understand that completely.

No, you don't. You don't see it nor fucking feel it.

Oh, will you shut the hell up? I am really tired having arguments with you. You do realize we've been going at this since we graduated from high school.

No! I won't shut the hell up! Accept what you have done!

No.

Yes!

No!

Yes!

No!

C'mon!

Another loud thunder rings above us, making me slap my head around to end this internal argument.

"Are you alright, sir?" Zakia asks.

The sound of her voice truly brings me back to reality and makes me spin around to look at her. Looking at her, she has loads of concern for me and possibly for something else.

I close my eyes and press my thumb and index finger on the bridge of my nose while answering, "I . . . I. It's just . . . simply nothing. We all have enough to worry about. What's up?"

She lets her head drop down and exhales heavily. "I'm sorry to throw this upon you, sir, but we've just lost another five of the severely wounded."

Well, this day just gets better and better.

I throw up my right fist at the sky as I turn my head to face the falling rain, *"You got one hell of a way to be funny, don't ya!"*

More lightning and thunder spits from the clouds as if a sign that God is laughing or is angry at my statement. Either way, I don't care *at all*.

"What should we do?" Zakia asks with some fear in her voice after seeing and hearing my reaction.

"Like we did last time. Halt, make quick graves, bury them, give small prayers, move on."

Zakia nods her head and jogs to catch up with our moving army. I look back once more to make sure that it's clear. Looking back at the previous direction, it seems that my army has created a fair amount of distance between me and them. I immediately start jogging to catch up with them.

Nearly several hours later after we've buried the dead of our five comrades and packed up the equipment no longer used, we continue with our journey. On a small bright side, the storm decides to come to a close. The clouds depart and dissipate in the sunset sky, revealing the stars of the night that's arriving. We are all exhausted. I pick up my pace to evaluate my soldier's mental and physical states. Easily and carefully snaking my way between each man and woman, they have the same expression on their faces, and their body language is showing it. *Sigh.*

"Alright, halt. Let's rest for a while," I calmly and sweetly say that order into the mic.

Another wave of moans and groans of relief echoes throughout. I just shake my head and proceed to seek out my top three men. As the line begins to break up in small groups, I find them at the "front." We regard one another as we unshoulder our sacks, build a small fire, and discuss our next step.

I look at Trent. "Where are we now?"

Trent looks at me unsatisfactorily, "We don't know, sire." He reaches into the pocket of his cloak and pulls out the map of the U.S. that's completely soaked. "Our only source of navigation is fucking ruined." Then, he throws it into the fire with disgust.

I turn my gaze to Sean and Maddox, and they both have nothing else to say. We all just sit and gaze upon the green and purple burning flames. Within the passing minutes, we all assemble our make-shift tents that survived the last week's attack and begin to settle in for the night. The only noises are the small chatters, cheap food being cooked, the E.K.G.s, and the crickets of the state of North Dakota chirping away in the tall grass. Well, it's mostly the crickets chirping that we hear, but we don't care. It's been a long and miserable hike, plus we don't know if we're still in North Dakota or have finally crossed into Montana.

As the minutes drive on, I softly tell the men and women to be on their own guard as we drift to sleep. Some acknowledge it while others have crashed and are sleeping. Before I say that command, I bid good night to Trent, Maddox, and Sean. Then, I pull the flap of my tent close, extinguish the lantern, and hold my staff tight against my chest as I drift to sleep.

Time: Around Midnight

What feels like I have been asleep for a few minutes, I am suddenly awakened by the rustling of the grass. My eyes open up fast; my ears move sideways if there's any sound of wind. There is wind but only a very light breeze. The noise of the rustling grass is much more urgent that it fully engages my adrenaline, puts my instincts on defense, and makes me snap up, tear off the tarp door, and slam my staff into the ground for the oncoming danger. The light and noise are loud enough to make Sean, Trent, and Maddox appear out of their tents on a haste with their staffs in hand. We scan the horizons, looking east, west, north, and south. The rustling of the grass gets louder and pretty soon, every military man and woman do the same as my top three men have done. Again, we scan the horizons for the oncoming. There's no moon, only stars. The only items giving off light is some of our small burning fires and our staffs. Then, the rustling noise comes up fast behind me.

I abruptly turn around, igniting my full power in my staff and shouting, "Who's there? Show yourself!"

Soon, a silhouette approaches with its hands slightly up. Then, another appears. Then, more. Maddox and some other service members use their sorcery to reignite the fires and illuminate what's coming through the grass. Looking around, the silhouettes' appearances begin to form as they step closer to the fires. The details begin to fill in. In moments, we see cloaks that have the colors of golden yellow and black with their hoods up and staffs holstered. I look at my top three men. All of them lower their staffs and Maddox approaches me with comfort on his face.

"It's alright, sire. It's Judocus Avast, he's the captain of these top men from Troy."

I observe his cloak. On his sleeves are three silver strips with a silver small pole going down the middle, at the top and bottom is one golden halo, and above the pole and stripes is a different wolf head tribal design outlined in a golden color thread on the black fabric. Looking at the Wolfinoid, he seems young, perhaps my age or a little older. His eyes are green while his fur is white. His hair is somewhat spiked, long, and is dyed in the same golden color to match his robe. Turning around, I see hope and happiness from my army as they interact with Judocus' men; some of his men have red, outlined, threaded crosses on their cloaks as they approach the wounded, and bring out their own medical supplies from their gold and black sacks. Observing this scene really calms me down. I decrease the power in my staff. The admiral blue fades away quickly. Swinging my attention back at Judocus, I sigh heavily with apology and embarrassment of my reaction through my nose.

"Forgive me, Captain Judocus. We've had a difficult journey that started on a smooth note but went completely to shit."

Judocus huffs a laugh as he looks away for a brief second and then meets my eyes again. "Apology accepted," he says with a calm, friendly smile. "So, you are King Will Borin of Sparta? The human that captured Tara Borin's heart and she's the Wolfinoid that turned you into one us?"

I nod in agreement and I ask him, "What brought you and your military out here or how did you know that we were here?"

He smirks, "About a hundred miles to the east where your army has come from, we have inserted sensors that activate when any other party passes through."

I think back for a moment and we didn't see any sensors of size or design. So, they must be very well-camouflaged into the surrounding environment. Anyway, my train of thoughts is interrupted when Judocus speaks again.

"By the looks of things, it really looks like you guys need some serious help."

Sean comes over and pats him on the shoulder. "You have no bloody idea, mate."

Judocus begins to walk over me calmly, putting his hands in his pockets while observing the scenery. He ponders as his gaze shift from one area of our camp where his men are interacting with ours to the other area where his men are fully helping our doctors and nurses with the severely wounded. He crosses his arms and looks back at us with curiosity and concern.

"Why are you guys doing *way* out here? This continent is not safe anymore; it's becoming more and more unstable."

Neither Maddox, Trent, nor Sean wants to answer; they all look at me since I'm their king and this is mainly my mission. I look back at Judocus.

"Due to the circumstances of our enemy, we are on our way to your kingdom so that your military and," I glance at my men and women and continue, "what's left of mine can combine forces and march to a town called Los Alamos in a state called New Mexico, which is now our enemy's manufacturing territory. We need to destroy every one of them and liberate that town to bring peace back to this nation."

His eyes widen and nods with agreement. "Well, King Borin, it's a good thing we've brought our camping supplies. We'll stay here for a couple of days and then we will escort your army to Troy and prepare for the battle with King Terrin."

"Sounds like a good plan." And we both shake hands firmly.

CHAPTER FORTY
Entering the Kingdom of Troy
Location: Yellowstone National
Park, Wyoming
Time: 10:45 AM
Date: June 1, 2015

MY ARMY AND AVAST'S Special Forces group casually walk through the beautiful Yellowstone National Park. My breath is absolutely taken away. A few years ago when I was an asphalt cowboy, I stopped here when I was delivering a skate board (flatbed trailer) of used AC/heater systems to an eco-friendly recyclable plant located somewhere in Nebraska, and since the pickup was in Portland, Oregon, the route was leading me through this state. The other two pluses were: I was way ahead on schedule and the equipment was old and used. So, I decided to check out this monument.

Back then, it was literally my first visit at the site, checking out all of the geographical sites and formations. Along the trails, I did notice some packs of elk, deer, and through the trees, a small pack of grey wolves. The most amazing thing was watching them stalk their prey. One of them accidentally snapped a twig, which alerted their prey yet gave them the signal to attack, and the wolves leapt onto their meal, taking down nearly ten. The rest of the elk and deer scamper away since they didn't have the advantage of rescuing their fallen friends. I simply watched in amazement as the pack of wolves drew back and dug into their meat until a mom of a family that I didn't recognize behind me shrieks in horror. Her young son, perhaps five, looks at the scene in front of him with both awe and horror. Within a split second, the mom swept up her child, faced him the opposite direction, and tugged at her husband's arm that they should move. The husband was in a daze since he too was amazed from what was happening before him.

Of course, the mom slapped him back to reality and pulled his arm much harder. He received the message and the family briskly started walking away. I did remember him asking his wife why she had to slap him and the wife replied furiously. I remained where I stood and watch the pack of wolves devour their meal for a few more minutes. After that, I continued my walk. The drawback was that the park has been scorched by a couple of wildfires and the brown, burned scars looked completely out of place. It also made me feel like I was back in Los Alamos, back in those discriminating disability classrooms. *Sigh.* I shook my head to get rid of these thoughts and feelings and keep on walking.

Focusing back on the present, walking through the park now, holy shit, those burned scars are gone and the park looks far much greener than before. With my new ears, I can hear every creature that prowls these woods and I can even smell their scents along with fresh pine and moist air. Journeying down one of the trails, we come to a flight of stairs that has been carved from the cliff face that we have approached. From where we stand, there's only one stone pedestal on the right side of the stairway with a stone bowl that has an ordinary flame burning in it and the pedestal has simple, Celtic writing inscribed into it. Above the first few steps is a large gold and black flag similar to the wolf head design on Avast's and his men's battle robes. The wooden rod that supports the flag is well-sanded and stained while attached to a bronze holder that's iron plated into the cliff face.

Avast and his men stand aside and he nods his head upward, "Up you get."

"What about you, guys?" I ask.

One of his men replies, "We need to return to our original position. Other than that, welcome to Troy."

Avast smiles while nodding in goodbye. They all turn around and begin running back into the forest of Yellowstone National Park. I look back at my men and women, then return my gaze toward the stairway. As far as my eyes could see, there's no railing and the stairway widens and narrows in areas high above with numerous switchbacks. I let a sigh, shrug, and press onwards.

After hours of climbing, we've reached some areas that are large enough for the four of us to stand off to one side to monitor the climb up. Calmly stepping to the unguarded edge and to peer down, my heart begins to race because looking down, I think we've got to be at least a hundred or so feet high up in the air. Don't get me wrong, the view from where we are is spectacular.

Another couple of hours have flown by when we reach one of the largest landings of the stair climb. This time, there's a stairway carved into the cliff face and goes up. Surrounding stairway is an exquisite arch carving with Celtic markings, battle scenes, torches with the flames burning in a gold color to illuminate the large landing, and two black and gold flags lying flat with the rock face yet placed several feet away from the flames. At the crescent part of the arch are large Celtic words that just take me a few minutes to translate.

"The Kingdom of Troy."

Above us, we can smell smoke, food being cooked, chatter, and music being played.

"I guess we've finally reached Troy, sire," says Sean.

I nod in agreement and we all ascend up the final flight of stairs traveling through a tunnel that has more remarkable Celtic carvings and golden-burning flames for the tunnel light.

Coming through the other end, we are greeted by a market and housing community just like the one in Sparta, except that the thick fabric for housing tents are gold and black, with Wolfinoids and humans walking around, purchasing, selling, chatting, playing music, and just having a good time. Looking far ahead, the face of the mountain is now covered in a very dense cloud bank. On this final edge, there is a railing forged out of real gold decorated with roses and vines. At each vertical pole inserted into the rock are torches now with flames that burn green, yellow, purple, white, red, etc. Turning my attention back to the main action, the smell of the food slips across my nose making my stomach growl and I'm pretty sure the rest of my army is hungry and exhausted from the journey. Turning around to give the order to disperse and relax, I get interrupted.

"Excuse me!"

I look at the direction of the voice and here comes two Wolfinoids wearing the same robes as Avast and his men, but this time, they have four silver stripes on their sleeves. "Are you King Will Borin of Sparta married to the powerful yet respected Queen Tara Borin?"

"Yes, I am. And who are you two?" Stretching out my right hand in greeting.

Both Wolfinoids are wearing the same communication devices that we have and the first Wolfinoid speaks into the microphone, "My Lord and Lady Terrin, they have arrived."

Then he looks at me and speaks in urgent voice, "Greetings will happen later, but for now, we need to get you into our castle."

His partner, perhaps a little younger than him, approaches Trent, Sean, and Maddox and asks if he could carry their sacks. The way they look at that young Wolfinoid seems like they know him and gladly hand over their sacks.

"My king, we must move on."

Just by looking at this guy, his eyes really mean that we should get going and I wave my arm for him to lead the way.

Walking up the main street, more men with silver stripes on their robes appear at every intersection, clearing the path for me and my men to somewhat hustle through. Traveling up the street, the mountain that we ascended slowly reappears out of the cloud bank and so does the two towering structures forming out of the mountain side with two opposite walls that come forward at a seventy-five-degree angle, stretching eighty yards, thus standing tall one hundred feet, and then finally being adjoined by the third wall that has the same doors like the ones that lead into the castle of Sparta but on a smaller scale. Getting closer, the walls are more than just walls; they are also a part of the two towers that rise with the mountain. The walls that are a part of this castle have windows ranging in different sizes, shapes, and some have stained glass windows. There are eight levels of windows that evenly align with the windows on the two towers that ascend with the mountain. Approaching the doors, they are in a square frame standing about ten feet high and stretching ten feet long. The doors are a pair, designed to open inward, and are painted gold with black plates and hinges to hold the wood in place.

Two more Wolfinoids firmly stand on each of the doors at attention with their staffs in their right hands. The robes that they wear are identical to the ones that Avast and his men wear; soon, they notice our approach and step forward in front of each door, pushing it open to let us through.

I guess they're not mechanically controlled like the ones back at my kingdom.

We enter a hallway that has a ceiling at the right height for us with torches burning gold; the special wolf guards close the doors behind us as the last men and women enter the hall. Looking about, the stones that assemble this castle are shown on the ceiling, walls, and floor without paintings or any other item to cover them. Plus, I haven't seen a set of doors that leads into their sanctuary.

Journeying forward, we begin to reach the other opening, but this time, there are no doors. We enter into a courtyard that's been conjured to have a warm atmosphere compared to the crisp, nibbling, cold mountain air on the other side. We all lower our hoods, walk upon the lush and thick green grass, observe the pine and oak trees, the uniquely designed fountains, abd the fine stone benches that are strewn about the courtyard whether it be by itself or curving around the bases of the trees. Seeing this, I nod and wave my hand to acknowledge my army to take a seat and unwind. The only people who don't take a seat are me, Maddox, Trent, and Sean. We still follow the same guys that guided us to this castle. Getting closer to the back wall, the same doors appear at the bottom of the two towers, but between the two towers, there's a wooden stage that has two thrones created out of the finest wood with black and gold cushions for the seats and backs. The stage itself only arises by three steps and has awning that covers both thrones. The design is checkered with black and gold with the logo of the kingdom as the top layer.

The first Wolfinoid puts up his hand in gesture that we stop. We do and they kneel down on their right knees in front of the stage just five yards away. We follow their moves and do the same thing. Minutes pass and the door on the left tower opens; stepping through the threshold exits are several special guards' men surrounding the king and queen of Troy. Their clothing is still medieval unlike Tara who combines the old fashion clothing with modern clothing, even throwing in dyed hair and modern jewelry. Both are wearing crowns, their furs are white, their eyes are gold, their jewelry is still medieval, and their formal robes look like they're heavy and thick. When they approach the stage, the special guards stop at a certain distance from the stage; the king and queen stop and stand at the bottom of their stage, looking at us with some confusion and serenity.

The king speaks in a calm voice, "Which one of you is King Will Borin?"

I look at him, still kneeling, and reply, "I am, sir. And you must be King Terrin?"

He smiles, "Yes, that is true, but why are you kneeling? Please, stand up."

We do. King Terrin nods to his wife who lets go of his left arm, then he approaches me with his right hand in gesture to shake mine. We shake each other's hands and he proceeds, "Let me introduce to you my wife Lucia Terrin. Forgive her that she doesn't speak English, but she somewhat understands it."

I nod my head in regards at her and she does the same thing to me. King Terrin continues, "I see you have met Zeke Coal and his partner and brother Armor Coal."

I nod in agreement.

"Come now, let's feast and discuss with one another along with making the battle plans to annihilate our enemy once and for all so that we can return our home planet with ease."

"Well, you lead the way, King Terrin," I respond.

He laughs and we follow him and his wife back to the same door where they pass through to greet us.

CHAPTER FORTY-ONE
Introductions
Location: Banquet Hall
Time: 4:05 PM

SEAN, MADDOX, TRENT, AND I sit down at a large, circular, fancy marble table that has a combination of tiny golden flakes spread all around it. The chairs that we sit are also constructed out of the same marble with cushions for the backs, bottoms, and armrests. Sean is on my left, Maddox on my right, and Trent on his right. On the other side of the table sit King and Queen Terrin and the Coal brothers sit on the king's left side. Behind the king and queen is an open doorway where eight more men and women surge in at a calm pace and fill in the empty seats. All of them are wearing traditional, medieval clothing and jewelry, except one. Interestingly, he looks at Maddox, smiles in a way like he hasn't seen him in a long time, and Maddox returns him the same expression.

"Now," speaks King Terrin with a clap of his hands, "Time for introductions." He looks toward his right at the first male that's sitting at his wife's right side.

"Right, I'm Sargent Dragon Stowaway. It's a mighty pleasure to meet you, King Will Borin. Is it true," he looks around the table and continues, "that you were a human?"

The tone of his voice is deep; he looks like he's in his forties or fifties, and he has his hair cut in a military style yet wearing a traditional medieval robe and underclothing.

The rest look at me in heavy curiosity. *Sigh.* I place my head into my dominant hand, trying to hold back my snappy attitude. "Yes, I was a human and I still feel like one a little bit. Other than that, it's good to meet you."

"I'm Lieutenant Drex Wind and it's a pleasure to meet you, sire."

"I'm Captain Leon Ocean."

"It's also good to meet you gentlemen, especially during these desperate times," I say to them with a confident smile.

"I'm Soren Nightrunner and as you can tell, I'm also the head sorcery teacher here, and I'm Maddox's brother."

I lean forward to look at my head sorcery teacher, give him a crooked smile, and say, "I didn't know you had a brother."

He just shrugs his shoulders and they both lean across the table to bump fists.

Sitting on Armor Coal's left side, the first female speaks, "I'm Second Lieutenant Kate Fire and I hope that you, King Borin, have a plan in place to solve our problem."

I nod at her in agreement.

"I'm Commander Liz Walker and I'm in charge of these two." She points at the last two males with positivity.

"I'm Tactical Officer Hays Rows and this is my partner Second Tactical Officer Damon Noon. Please forgive him, he doesn't speak nor understand English."

Her partner nods his head at me in acknowledgement. When Hays Rows introduced himself, he was attempting to be respectful in his tone of voice, but it was trying to cover up something. When I look at him in the eyes, for those two seconds, they showed incomplete trust. However, the rest were introducing themselves, showed the opposite, and are willing to aid. Anyway, I carry on like none of that happened.

"It's alright, Mr. Hays." I take a moment to look about the table. "I guess that the original kingdom of Troy is much bigger than Sparta back on your home planet?"

The people who introduced themselves burst in small laughter to answer that question.

"Yes, yes," speaks King Terrin, "Now, we all know Trent, Sean, and Maddox very well. But can you tell us about yourself? If you don't mind."

Well, to gain their trust, I should just tell them everything.

I let out a sigh and look about the table one more time, "Where should I start?"

I rack through my mind of where to start. Should I tell them, I don't know, *everything*? This includes the negative, hard shit I had to go through for eight years, or should I just cut and leave that shit out? Maybe I should. I am getting really tired telling the same old, sad, fucking story. I should just tell them the positive things and the others that I like, including the stuff I've learned over the past several months which made me the man/Wolfinoid I am today.

Yeah, I should tell them those things.

So, I start where I was born, going in detail of the town I grew up in, who my relatives are, and what school I went to. Then, I moved to New Mexico and talked about my life there. I try my best to pull out the happy memories from my negative library and most of them are from my elementary school days. Of course, I rarely touched middle school just by saying it was a shit hole. Nonetheless, when I got onto high school, all of the positive memories started pouring out. I travel into more detail of how I received the nickname or I like to call it the street name, Nos. I talk about my friends and the events I participated while attending Los Alamos High and finally, I tell them after I graduated from there that I became a truck driver.

On that topic, I tell them my trucking career. Teaching them the ten code and the trucker language like Smokie means police. By that time, our food is brought out and we are chowing down. I continue with my stories. Furthering into my trucking career is when their problem arrived on our planet and I tell them I tried my best by ignoring the crazy, liberal news.

"Still, your problem grabbed hold of me and I was engulfed by the crazy conflict," I say at that point.

Then my story progresses into my journey back to Wisconsin, which turned out badly as you guys have read beforehand, then it turns into the journey to Sparta which almost ended badly for me, and from there, my traveling struggles increased by the hour. To wrap everything up, I tell them what happened to me while I was in Sparta, how Tara and I hooked up, the conflict that followed me for a couple of weeks, the lessons of how to use my new sorcery powers with my staff and the lessons about their home world, the wedding, the transformation, the death of Cedric Borin, and the events that brought us to Troy after Trent showed Tara and I that Los Alamos is now the werewolves' factory.

"That . . . was . . . some . . . story, mate," says Soren in complete awe as he gawks at me from his chair.

Looking around, everybody else looks at me in silence. I look at King and Queen Terrin and they look at one another. At that moment, Queen Terrin closes her eyes and nods at her husband in way that she might've understood my story and how serious the situation is. King Terrin grabs his goblet and stands up while raising it toward me. Within a moment, we all stand up while grabbing our goblets. Terrin looks at me in a serious, understanding way, then glances around the table at his officers, and finally, our eyes meet again.

"Due to the seriousness of this situation with our enemy and after hearing your stories about you, King Borin, I think it's time that we should not delay any more. Since our race is still new to this planet, I presume you have a presentation ready about the geography of this town called Los Alamos?"

"I do, sir. When and where should it be conducted?"

"In our briefing auditorium. Tonight."

I look around at the table. Looking at the officials of Troy, it seems that I have gained trust and allies ready to hear the plans of the final push to end their conflict. I let a confident smile and say, "Then let's get down to business."

The rest agree while clinking our goblets together.

CHAPTER FORTY-TWO
The Presentation
Location: Briefing Auditorium
Time: 7:45 PM

SO MANY PEOPLE. I think to myself as I gaze upon the humongous, indoor auditorium.

It's designed as an octagon and constructed out of concrete, with walls stretching thirty-five yards from corner to corner; three rows of bright recess lighting following the walls illuminate the area but only in the areas where the walls and ceiling meet. From the ground floor and traveling up is a total of ten rows of benches and at the top rows are entryways centrally located at each of the eight walls. Also, the first row of benches is cushioned and this is where King and Queen Terrin, along with their officials, sit. Anyway, this is where all of the Wolfinoids from my kingdom and Troy's kingdom militaries are pouring in and taking their seats along with some of the civilians from Troy. Down here at the ground floor is the same type of hologram table like the one from Sparta's Command Center, except it's six times bigger. Sean, Trent, Maddox, and I stand at the one control board that operates this huge hologram table or computer, whatever it's called. With that said, these guys are standing with me to support me with my presentation. With my eyes fixated on the entryways, more of Troy's military starts pouring in, and what surprises me is that a good number of humans dressed in combat uniforms file in.

I look at my guys and they look back at me in the same way, surprised.

Trent glances back up at the growing crowd, "It looks like we're going to get some help from your race."

I look back up, "*Yeah, probably.*"

King Terrin rises from his spot and observes the auditorium. Judging from his body language, it looks like he's about to give the order to close off the entryways so that I can or we can perform the presentation. During this time, the auditorium was quiet and had remained quiet as the first Wolfinoids from my and Troy's military started filing in. Yet, as time progressed, it became small chatters, kind of like whispers. More minutes go on and the noise of the chatters increased. Now, the entire auditorium is bustling with voices, talking in English and in Wolfinoid tongues, echoing of the concrete walls, ceiling, benches, and floor.

Captain Leon Ocean rises from his seat and approaches us while pulling out a small, felt bag.

As he gets to us within three feet, he looks at me. "Here." He pulls out a couple of small, wireless microphones. "This will help you sound better during the presentation."

"I think our king has got it from here, Captain Ocean," says Sean in a confident tone as he pats my shoulder.

I take one of the mics and the captain puts the rest away while he returns to his seat. Once he sits down, he nods at his king and Terrin speaks in his own mic. I nervously attach the mic around my ear in one hand while gripping the flash drive of the information I have gathered about Los Alamos tightly in the other.

"Ladies and gentlemen, please take your seats and hold your conversations because the presentation of the town Los Alamos is about to begin." Then he returns to his seat.

I nod at Trent and he activates the table while turning off the lights to let the lights that morph the holograms faintly illuminate the room. Close to the lights of the upper part that operates the table, eight hologram, floating screens appear with a cursor at the ready. He smoothly gestures for the flash drive and I hand it to him. He inserts it and a 3D dialog box appears with one file name on it.

`"Los Alamos."`

He activates it and the hologram lights project a very large, 3D map of the town. I clear my throat while taking huge breaths of air through my nose.

Sean pats my shoulders in confidence, "You got this, mate."

I look at him and he winks at me.

"I got this. I totally got this." Then I activate the mic, "Ladies and gentlemen, thank you for attending this meeting and hearing this presentation."

At the same moment, I hear a light tapping sound and looking up, the cursor moves across the screen, forming the words in the Wolfinoid language. I carry on.

"I am the new king of Sparta, King William Borin, and married to the daughter of Cedric Borin, Tara Borin, who is now the official ruler of that kingdom. Anyway, this situation that you people have been trying to deal with has gotten worse. Your, or should I say, our enemy have taken over this town that's called Los Alamos which is located in the Jemez Mountain Range and the primary reason that they have chosen this location is that it's a nuclear facility. They probably are using the resources to become stronger than us."

A shock of fear and realization went throughout the crowd.

"Here's a brief history lesson. When World War II was on the rise, the United States and its allies were doing their best battling against Nazi Germany and its allies on the European front; when the president of the time thought things couldn't get worse, they do. On December 7, 1941, a naval U.S. harbor based out on the Hawaiian Islands was spontaneously attacked by Japanese naval forces, which brought the entire nation of the U.S. fully into World War II. When three years drag on from battling with the navy of the Japanese Empire, the government here devises a plan to build a weapon of mass destruction that will bring the war with the Japanese to an abrupt end. Two actually. So, the mesas of Jemez Mountain Range were chosen for the secret site to build the gadget A.K.A. the atomic bomb. The first one of its kind."

After saying that, everybody leans in.

"Before this town was called Los Alamos, it was called The Hill for top security reason. Every place where scientists and their family resided, worked, and ate at all had the same address. Everything that the scientists did had to be a secret. As time drew on, those men theorized and developed the first atomic bomb and took it out to the desert of the White Sands far south in the state of New Mexico to test it. On one stormy night, they dropped it and the gadget gave those men the results they calculated months before. So, they build two more and dropped them on the main island of Japan. After that, the goal was to build a top secret facility, design, build, test, and drop the first W.M.D. After that, it is to tear everything down and leave the mesas like nothing was there. However, they stayed and developed the town as it is today.

"Now, moving onto the geography of this town." I look at Trent to ready himself to start tapping certain buttons that display the information. He confirms with a stance and I continue, "This town sits at an elevation of seven thousand and three hundred-twenty feet. It covers ten-point-nine square miles. It's divided by five canyons. Its human population is twelve thousand and nineteen. It has gone through six forest fires; the last two were the Cerro Grande and Las Conchas Fires. In total, they burned 204,293 acres."

With a few more taps on the command screen by Trent, the 3D hologram map shows a shade of bright red spreading across the face of the Jemez Mountains, reaching over the backside while stretching to the southeast and into the outskirts of Los Alamos.

"So, what does that mean?" a voice rings out from the crowd. It throws me off guard and I can't tell if it was a Wolfinoid or a human.

I swivel my head while answering that question, "It means there's not a lot of coverage for a stealth attack during the day. The only two areas with good coverage of trees are Pajarito Ski Hill and the town. In between those places, we are looking at a gap area of nearly ten miles of dead and growing trees that are still saplings."

"How many structures that house the science activity?" This one comes from a female.

I toss the number around in my head, "We're looking at roughly fifty tech sites."

"How could you be so sure?"

Ah ha, this time I was ready for another question; my ears pick up the voice and I turn my head to the direction of that voice. Once I zero in, it's a Wolfinoid, a military one, one from my army.

"Because, there's only a few that sit near public roads. The rest are guarded by men or used to be, with heavy machine guns, high security tech, and no civilians are and weren't allowed in unless they worked for any of those places while carrying proper badges that granted them access."

I look around the auditorium; every Wolfinoid and human are just leaning in interest, but what strikes me a little is that none of them are taking notes on their tablets. I mean, c'mon, this is a serious issue and it should not be taken lightly. This could be our only chance by destroying the enemy once and for all and clean up the mess they caused. Still, I feel like a human a little bit and this current situation doesn't feel right to me.

I can't believe I'll be going with Tara and her race back to her home planet since I'm a Wolfinoid. Shit.

I look back at the crowd, still not taking notes. "Y'all should be taking notes on this. Cause I ain't gonna repeat myself."

After saying that, they all pull out their tablets and start taking notes.

"Do any of you have any more questions?"

"Yeah, I do," speaks Lt. Drex Wind. "How soon should we leave and travel to this destination?"

I walk toward the command console and place my hands on top of the upper frame, gazing at the 3D map of Los Alamos, thinking about the situation and what problems will occur if we don't act fast.

I look back at him seriously. "We leave in two days. At 0800. Sharp." I look at the crowd. "Is that understood?"

A wave of replies saying, "Yes, sir," and "Yes, King Borin," comes out like loud whispers.

"Then y'all dismissed. Get packing."

The auditorium bursts in loud conversations as everybody takes their time to file out of the entrances.

I look at Maddox, Trent, and Sean. "Y'all ready to finally clean up and never have to worry about your mess again?"

Sean looks at the other two and soon, all nod in an excited agreement with large yet serious smiles; and he then looks at me. "Oh your highness, we are so fucking ready."

I smile and nod my head to the doorway that we came through before the presentation began, and say, "Vamonos."

CHAPTER FORTY-THREE
The Real Journey
Location: Exiting Yellowstone
National Park, Heading South
Time: 8:15 AM
Date: June 3, 2015

AT PRECISELY 0800, OUR entire military force exited Troy and for the past fifteen minutes, we've been running, not walking or hiking, at full speed through the park, heading south to our primary destination with determination and revenge in all of our minds. Joining us is Captain Leon Ocean, Soren Nightrunner, both tactical specialists Hays Rows and Damon Noon, and finally Lieutenant Drex Wind running along with me, Trent, Sean, and Maddox at the head of the pack. The sound of our pounding feet creates a very distant, thundering sound like a storm system that's approaching but is still miles away. The sound increases my excitement, my determination, and my revenge to liberate and destroy those shit heads once and for all.

Now, being a Wolfinoid for the past couple of months, my sense of direction was greatly improved and is five times better than the shot that Ulric gave me well over a year ago. Again, the memory of the first battle I encountered with the werewolves with my search party fires off like a shell from a twelve-gage shotgun and that makes me feel terrible.

Goddammit. Why? Why replay that memory?

Sigh.

Those bastards are truly gonna get it. They're really gonna fucking get it!

Anyway, back to my sense of direction, we've covered over ten miles. Yeah, we're that fast.

Man, does this give a whole new meaning to my street name

"Are you doing okay, Sir Borin?" asks Lieutenant Drex Wind.

"Huh? Oh yeah. I'm just determined to obliterate our enemy and a little lost in thought of the meaning of my street name."

He nods in agreement.

"So, what is your plan to attack and reclaim that territory?" asks Hays.

I look at him for a moment and then return my site to the primary direction, "How 'bout we discuss that once we get closer? Other than that, I'm thinking about it."

"Thinking about it?" snaps Hays, "How can you be thinking about it now? You should've thought about some plans way before the presentation of that town!"

Are you fucking kidding me?

I slam my feet into the ground, sliding to a stop while grabbing Hays's arm to stop with me. Maddox, Trent, Sean, Drex, Soren, and Damon also come to a complete stop after sliding a couple of feet, yet it causes a chain reaction for both of our military parties to slow down their pace and come to a stop to see what the problem is.

I glower and growl at Hays for a moment, "It's been years since I've left that town. So, a lot of bullshit has changed!"

He rips his arm away from my grasp, giving me the look that he did receive my answer but chooses to ignore it. "You are the king of Sparta! According to our king, we're supposed to trust you like we've known you for centuries! Well, guess what, I don't trust you.

Ever since we entered through that doorway, my senses told me not to trust you." Then he looks about the rest. "I believe we will be in much better hands if Tara Borin was leading this invasion party and leave this, oh what is that word that starts with a?" He ponders a little and then looks at me with an evil grin.

Oh please, do not call me that.

He continues, "We should've left this autistic idiot to rule Sparta. Actually, scratch that. There should be a pure Wolfinoid we all know well that should rule our allied kingdom."

"You motherfucker!"

I immediately grab his battle robe and throw the asshole to the ground, hard. He struggles, but I stomp on his crotch. He moans in pain. I place one hand over his mouth and use the other to grab one of his ears.

"Now, you shit head, listen to me *real fucking good*. I didn't choose to be one of you. Tara really didn't want to do it either. She told me that she loved the way I was and that none of your kind was suitable. On the night she bit me, she was crying." Then I lower my head closer to his ear, "You guys are still new to this planet. You are still new to the geography. You are still new to the history of the planet and especially of this nation." He struggles, but I hold him down good. "I ain't fucking done yet! She has all the knowledge and practice of being a ruler while I don't. On the other hand, I have knowledge of this nation. I have the knowledge of that town. Tara does not. Do you fucking understand me, Tactical Specialist Hays *Rows?*"

I release him and he stands back up. Hays glowers at me while brushing the dirt and grass off while mumbling under his breath.

This gets Leon's attention and he grabs Hays's robe in one hand. "What the hell did you say to King Will Borin?"

He sighs. "I said, 'He's still not suitable to lead us. He's still an autistic bastard.'"

At that moment, all of my anger spills out like water from the flood gates of the completely opened Hoover Dam and I give that bastard one hell of an under hook by my right fist, clocking him in the chin and sending him flying up in the air a couple of feet backward. He finally makes contact with the ground on his back, creating a loud thud. Immediately, mumbles erupt from both of our military parties. I look at Leon, Drex, and Damon. They stare not at me but at Hays in disbelief. For the asshole, he stumbles around on the ground on his hands and feet while trying to stand back up, yet I just my roll my eyes, groan in slight irritation, and push him back down to the ground. He groans and rolls around while looking heavily dazed. The muttering conversations from our military parties continue in both languages, Wolfinoid and English.

Oh yeah, I did forget to mention that there are U.S. military members joining us. The day before we departed from Troy, they all received the same type of shot that Ulric gave except it's a little more powerful than the one I received last year, so that they could keep up with us. Some are wearing robes that are designed to fit them; others are wearing combat uniform; some are using the original camping back packs while others have the sacks, and some have the military issued firearms while others created their own weapon staffs.

Anyway, Hays loses his daze, stands right back up, and gives me his death stare while rubbing his jaw. I stare back in the same way, letting my inner power to combust on the inside forming the glow around my body. A little later, Hays darts his eyes at Damon.

"Damon, let's go back home."

I look at the guy and he shakes his head quickly side to side. Hays growls in irritation.

Hays repeats himself, "Damon, let's move. Now!"

This time, Damon looks at me for a moment and then back at his boss, again shaking his head. Hays growls and takes one step toward him. I intervene by standing in his way and growling.

"How 'bout you go back to Troy since you don't trust me?"

"No," rings out a voice and I turn to Damon. His expression is strong and courageous, saying no to his superior.

"What?" Hays asks as he slightly snaps his head to one side.

Damon looks to one side, licking his lips, perhaps trying to formulate other English words so that I can hear them. He returns his gaze back to Hays and says, "I . . . trust . . . him," while he points at me, still looking in the same direction. "He's . . . right. You're . . . not."

A smile spreads across my face as I look at him. Leon and Drex pat Damon's back and shoulders in a good and comforting way while speaking to him in their normal language. This makes the corners of Damon's mouth begin to twitch upward, but he tries to contain the serious expression on his face.

Then, Leon looks at Hays and says, "Perhaps *you should* return to Troy. King Borin really knows this continent and especially the town of Los Alamos. Yes, he was a human. On the contrary, that is what makes him an excellent leader to lead us into battle to destroy our enemy. I do agree with you that he doesn't have a strategic plan, but I think he has a lot on his mind." He turns toward my direction. "Is that right?"

I nod while replying, "Yeah, that's indeed correct. Let's just take this journey one county at a time. The closer we get to Los Alamos, a clearer mind I will have to construct strategic plans."

Hays growls and back kicks a chunk of dirt behind him. He lowers his head, "All of you will fail without me." In a quick motion, he snaps his head up to look at *all* of us, "Do you hear me? All of you will fail without me!"

Instantly, he turns on one heel and fully sprints back to Troy. Trent, my tactical officer, approaches me. He looks worried yet confident in my leadership.

He folds his hands behind his back and slips out a crooked smile. "Just take this journey one county at a time?"

I pat his shoulder. "Yeah, let's take this journey one county at a time."

I look up at the sky and the sun is high. It seems to be nearing ten or perhaps past that hour. Angling my head slightly downward to observe the skies to the south, I can see storm clouds brewing miles away from us. I turn my full attention back to our very large battle party. The conversations from both of our militaries have nearly ceased while Damon looks very confident for standing up against his superior. Leon and Drex look at the direction where Hays has taken off with distasteful and good riddance looks. Maddox and Soren talk quietly with one another and their conversations aren't against me, which makes me feel good. Finally, both Trent and Sean look at me for orders.

"Alright, y'all, enough wasting time! Let's keep moving south!"

The same battle horn that blasted when my military and I left Sparta is used again to get the battle group moving. In moments, we all return to our normal running pace, cutting through Wyoming, approaching Colorado.

Let's pray and hope that nothing distracts us, diverts us, or even throws us off guard on this journey.

CHAPTER FORTY-FOUR
Trouble, New Plan, First Attack
Location: San Juan Mountain Range, Colorado
Time: 6:00 PM
Date: June 5, 2015

YES, Y'ALL HAVE READ that title of this chapter correctly. Remember the storm that I told you guys about two days ago? You do remember? Good. No? *Sigh.* You should've started at the beginning. Anyway, yeah, that storm was and still is one hell of a spontaneous thunderstorm and we've been traveling through it for two days. At that time, the terrain has risen up a couple of thousand feet and we've been using it as a cover to avoid the towns and small cities in Wyoming and in Colorado. The best part is that these guys have been using the same power to create a thick fog so that all trees can grow back just like what I've seen in Iowa and in Wyoming. The drawback and the upside are that those towns and cities are very well-protected by the U.S. military. There are blockades of human and machinery which includes tanks, hummers, automatic gates that have three-story tall watch towers with teams of men and women taking positions at very large and powerful machine guns, tall chain link fences with barbed wire at the top surrounding the perimeter, etcetera.

Yet, the blowing rain also creates cover for us. The major drawback is that we're all cold, soaked, and exhausted. Our ways of direction are still our highly tuned senses and our paper maps that we laminated before we took off from Troy. We're not completely sure if the satellites are operational again even though we still carry our communication sunglasses and tablets just in case we could take that chance of powering them up and connecting to the Wi-Fi as a last resort. Again, we hike on, not run. We just hike through the heavy falling rain with the occasional sight of lightning flashing across the sky in huge, long arcs followed by loud claps of thunder.

I step off to the side to evaluate the physical condition of both parties. Coming to a steady halt, the tired feeling in my feet ascends up my legs, making them want to buckle from my own body weight after hiking over two hundred miles under the hard, pouring rain. I pull out my staff, insert it into the soaked ground, and lean my weight against it so that I don't collapse from exhaustion. As both parties press on, my comrades have separated themselves to be mixed into the crowd as they, too, evaluate the condition of the men and women of both races while trudging through this part of the Rocky Mountain Range.

Man. We are trudging.

In moments, Leon, the Nightrunner brothers, Sean, Damon, Drex, and Trent notice my stance and join me. I look at them in the same way as they are looking at me, exhausted. *Sigh.* I look around them to see the back end of the line which is barely visible through the true darkness that is now slowly approaching. The only times I can truly see it is when lightning streaks across the sky for a few seconds. From witnessing those glimpses, all I see are exhausted expressions just as with their body languages. Looking in the direction we are going, the result's the same.

"Sir," speaks Trent. I turn my head in his direction and his expression shows concern. "Perhaps we should make camp and rest for the day."

"I agree with Trent," speaks Leon as he, too, looks concerned.

Looking at the Nightrunner brothers, they both quickly look at one another, turn their heads back at me, and nod with agreement and encouragement. I, too, nod my head due to the circumstances that are clearly presenting themselves on this slow, approaching, and constant storming night. I reach for the mic on my headset, but I am too exhausted to speak. Trent beats me to it as he gives the order to stop and break camp. Quiet cheer of happiness ripples out, well more of a groan, as the two parties dissipate into the thick pine trees, looking for a good area to set up their tents.

Within the hour, we've finally made camp. What held us back was the rain and that made the landscape slippery, muddy, and just hard to pitch up our tents. Yes, some of us do have the power to make it stop raining, but like I stated before, *all* are exhausted from the hike and from the weather. So, now we are drying off, lounging, and preparing for the next time we hike.

In our tent, a Spartan tent which is four times smaller, our cots nearly touch one another. Our cooking supplies and food are pushed up against the rocks that surround the fire pit which illuminates the area along with a few lanterns hanging from the ceiling, and a small wooden collapsible table stands really close to the entrance with three laminated maps on it: the first is the entire U.S., the second is Colorado, and the third is New Mexico. In detail, the map of U.S. is a print-out of the latest information before we lost connection with satellites we rely on to determine which group covers which areas and we don't know if our enemy have increased their strength, thereby changing the boundaries of the U.S. military, Troy and Sparta, and the uninhabited zones. Or, perhaps, they have remained the same. I switch maps to look at the black blobs in Colorado; the areas they're in look so familiar. The drawback of these maps is that they don't have any writing on them neither in English nor in Wolfinoid, which slightly annoys me. To further my investigation, I place the map of New Mexico underneath Colorado, examine the black blob that covers Los Alamos, and move my eyes north. The lines of state roads morph into a mass of small, thinner lines to represent streets of towns and small cities; their names sound off in my head: *"Espanola," "Chama."* Then I move my attention to the Colorado map, analyzing it real good: *"Pagosa Springs."* I let my eyes drift to the west, *"Bayfield . . ."* I stop and look at how close that town is to one of the black blobs.

The blob is a little northwest of Bayfield and as I move my eyes directly north, there's another one that's smaller but is almost directly north of the first one. Within a second, it hits me. The two towns that are covered in black are Durango and Silverton. My eyes widen.

Can that be completely right?

I turn around and look at my men: Trent is just lying on his cot with one arm behind his head while holding a book above his head with the other. The Nightrunner brothers are helping Sean and Damon trying to reconnect with the satellites to establish where we are exactly or trying to connect with communication either with Troy or Sparta to give an update about this march to Los Alamos. Finally, Leon and Drex are out making rounds throughout the camp, checking on the condition of everybody. To let you know guys how big this military party is, both of those men left this tent an hour and a half ago, and haven't return yet. I look back at the other guys still fiddling with their tablets. I let my eyes dart back at the Colorado map for a quick moment and then back at them.

I need to make sure.

I walk over to them, trying to remain calm, but that doesn't work. All four of them stop and look up at me curiously.

Well, this is awkward.

"What's got you on the edge, mate?" Sean asks.

I quickly move my eyes onto one of the tablets that rests upon a large piece of wood looking like a cutting board. It spans from one cot to the next, and there are numerous tools that are built to calibrate the tablet alongside some pieces of folded paper with directions in Wolfinoid tongue. I move my eyes back to Sean.

"How's it coming along?" I ask nervously while rubbing the back of my neck. Looking at the screen, it displays two words in the Wolfinoid language that I can translate to English, "No Connection".

Soren grabs and turns it around in his hands so that he can see the screen correctly. He makes a few taps on the screen while talking at me, "I think we almost got it," then looks he up, "What's wrong?"

I kneel down while rubbing my thumbs together. "I just want to know our exact location."

The men look at one another. The only noises are the small, quiet chatter outside with the crickets chirping and inside our tent, the crackling fire in the pit. Suddenly, the screen goes black, which makes all of our heads snap to the screen. We stare at it with great intensity; less than thirty seconds go by when three little dots appear on the screen, creating a wave motion. They soon morph into two different words, "Acquiring Signal."

Reading those words completely raises our hopes and we can sense it from one another without lifting our eyes from the screen. Immediately, the two words morph into a hollow circle that lights up and sends a wave from its perimeter that expands across the screen, dissipating as it moves and creating a soft ping noise that echoes from the speaker.

Ping. Ping. Ping.

Our excitement builds while our tails begin to move. After a solid minute of seeing the hollow circle, its shockwave, and hearing its noise, the screen goes black again for a few seconds, and then two words appear, "Signal Acquired."

Within a split second, the screen shows a map with a bright orange dot showing our exact location while the names of the towns, cities, national parks and forests, and county names softly appear with great ease.

We all jump up to our feet with great joy, shouting, howling, and high fiving one another. At that moment, both Leon and Drex enters with some confusion.

"What's going on here?" Leon asks.

Soren looks at them and answers with enthusiasm, *"We have connection with the satellites! We now know our exact location!"*

His eyes widen and a smile spreads across his face. "You're kidding?"

Drex quickly strides over to his cot, reaches for his bag, and ruffles through it. He pulls out his communicator sunglasses and activates them. From our perspective, we can only see his eyes slightly dash around in all angles as he gives the commands mentally.

Another minute passes and he answers, "Oh my God, you guys are not kidding." He takes them off and looks at Leon. "They're right, we do have connection with the satellites. This is fantastic news."

"Of course, it is," I reply as I gently take the tablet from Soren and move back toward the table to compare the information.

Once I do, the Nightrunner brothers, Leon, Drex, Sean, and Damon engage in conversation in their native tongue discussing new battle plans and all other sorts, but I'm hardly paying attention while I examine both the tablet and the map of Colorado. Trent moves around the group and approaches the opposite side of the small table, eyeing the same map. When the seconds tick by, my anxiety returns. My fear, my hypothesis, comes true when the two black blobs confirm that they are Silverton and Durango. I make a few taps on the screen that inserts the map of which region is controlled by which party. Within seconds, the blobs appear, yet in a scary way, they connect, creating a signal black line between the towns. Looking at the blue glowing words of the geography of that region, it shows that the werewolves, our enemy, has not only taken over those two towns but also the historical narrow gage rail line that connects them and runs along the Animas River. Also, looking at the bright orange dot that shows our current location, it shows that we're less than twenty miles away from Silverton.

"Shit."

I look up and I see Trent standing perfectly straight with his hands folded behind his back looking at me in a serious way. "What are your orders, sir?"

"We're going to liberate the town of Silverton; use the rail line if needed while we liberate the smaller outposts along the way and liberate the town of Durango. Understand?"

"Understood, sir," Trent replies.

I hastily remove myself from the table and let my ass fall onto my cot. In situations like this one, I like listening to my iPod to calm down and really think about the seriousness of the situation, but as I dig into my jean pockets, I can't find it. I reach for my bag to search for it there, yet the result is the same.

Great, I forgot it. Perfect. Sigh.

The conversation going on beforehand stops and Maddox looks at me with concern. "Sire, are you okay?"

I shake my head saying "No," then I let it hang between my legs, still remaining quiet.

"Why is he so quiet, Trent?"

Trent replies in the same serious tone, "We have two more towns to liberate and we must act fast."

Battle of Silverton
Location: Anvil Mountain near Silverton
Time: 7:30 PM
Date: June 7, 2015

We journey across Anvil Mountain as the sun begins to sink behind the other peaks in the west while casting massive shadows from their tall peaks. According to the GPS on our tablets and our communication devices, we're within four football fields of reaching Silverton. Being at 12,537 feet, a breeze rushes past us, trying to send a chill up our spines, yet our fur and cloaks keep us warm. Some of the human soldiers do shiver, slightly. For the past two days we've rested, we've checked our weapons, practiced our sorcery, studied the geography of Silverton, practiced our hand-to-hand combat if the battle dwindles down to that point, and sent our prayers to God to keep us safe and that there are survivors in that town and no weather interruptions. So far, that prayer has been answered by giving us clear skies. During the twenty-mile trip we've ran, since we're four football fields away, we've just been walking with all of our staffs and firearms locked and loaded in our hands. We've remained quiet, only to hear the whistling of the wind and the chirping of the birds. So far, no threat has approached us, yet. Our eyes scour the trees left to right, up and down, and vice versa. Minutes keep flying by, decreasing our distance to Silverton.

Five more minutes go by and the trees come to an abrupt halt, creating an almost perfect straight border line. The glow of the sun still shines over the other peaks, but darkness has swept throughout the old mining town. We stand in silence on the open face of the mountain looking downward. The stench of our enemy rises up from them and travels across our noses. I for one snarl in the back of my throat and spit out my own snot to the side because of the stench. I shift my staff from right hand to my left, kneel down, and operate the zoom function. There are only a few lights illuminating the houses, businesses, and streets of Silverton. According to my nose, there are more than a few werewolves stalking the streets, yet they are lurking in the dark shadows where no light shines. Speaking of darkness, it has finally reached us as the sun completely disappears behind the mountains, only revealing the stars; no moon arises from the east. I activate the thermal vision and the result confirms it.

There are twenty-five werewolves in total and there are well over a thousand of us. Judging by their body temps, they seem to be normal, not genetically mutated in the slightest way. Ten surround the town, observing the dark horizon for any invaders; some prowl while the others stand in one position. Looking down to the southeast, there are five of them standing on the railroad tracks just doing nothing. Their postures seem to be waiting for something to arrive, but as I move my sight farther down the tracks, I see no head lamp shining or glowing around the trees nor hear a familiar sound of the steam whistle being blown. If something is being delivered, we need to stop it ASAP.

"Ah, crap," says Trent.

"What's up?" I ask.

"Look at their town hall."

Turning my gaze in the same direction, my ears fall against my head. The town hall of Silverton is fully illuminated, but inside are humans, ranging from child to adult, held hostage by five werewolves stalking the halls individually on every level while another five guard the doors on the outside. There are two at the main front doors and one at each fire exit door.

"*Shit.*"

"N-Nos." I look behind me and there's Damon. "What's t-the plan?"

I get up, look about our combined military force, and ask, "Any humans that are excellent snipers?"

I switch thermal to night vision to get a better vision. Mutters erupt from the human military ranks lasting for two minutes. Soon, they start to depart, creating room for a group of ten snipers. Looking at their uniforms, they are from the same SEAL team and by judging their expressions, they really want to kick some ass.

One approaches me, "What do you want us to do, sir?"

I turn back, evaluating the situation, and then a plan pops into my head, "I would like a team of two Wolfinoids to provide cover for each of these men just in case there are any mutated werewolves that lurk on the other peaks that surround us. Snipers, you pick any position that fits your needs, but to reach your destinations in flash, you'll piggy back on one of your two Wolfinoid backups. Do you understand?"

They nod in agreement; I continue my plan of action, "To take out the enemy, eight of you will take ones out that are patrolling the perimeter while the other two take out the ones on the railroad tracks. After that," I look up at the crowd and continue, "I want small battle group of twenty to head down, take the five that guard the town, and do the damnest to draw out the other five so that none of hostages are harmed. Do you understand me?"

A wave of replies come through the speaker of my headset. Immediately, twenty Wolfinoids volunteer to provide cover for each man; quick introductions happen and only last thirty seconds; after that, the SEALs get on their backs and they take off. Some go directly down the mountain from where we're standing while the others take off to the left and right. We all switch night vision back to thermal to observe the attack and remain absolutely fucking quiet as we hear their conversations.

"Railroad team, what's your twenty?"

"We're thirty seconds away from our destination. What's your twenty?"

"This is Rick Axe. We're positioned directly north of town. One hundred and fifty yards away."

"This is Cody Steam. Directly east of the town and we're also one hundred and fifty yards away and ready."

Suddenly, a burst of loud static comes through, destroying our ears. The noise is so intense that we all rip off the devices from our heads and groan with pain. Looking around the darkness with my normal sight, I see a few dashes of light appearing at the bottom of the other peaks and then the same light appearing from the previous stated positions. This concerns me and I immediately put the device back on my head.

"Sniper teams, is everything okay?"

"Yes, sir. The dashes of light that you all saw was us stating that the remaining teams are ready and us confirming it."

Whew.

"Okay, you guys take fire when ready."

With our thermals on, there's a quick flash of light that erupts from the barrels and one by one, the enemy that surrounds the town starts dropping like flies and that also goes for the group of five on the railroad tracks that lay lifeless on the steel rails and wooden planks. A howl erupts from one of the surviving werewolves on patrol but is shot in the head during mid-howl. Still, that gets the attention of the five as they leave the town hall and run to aid their fallen comrades in opposite directions only in a matter of seconds to see that they're all dead. On the other hand, they remain in the shadows and that makes Rick Axe complain.

"Shit. I can't get a clean shot."

The second after he says that, the ten remaining werewolves howl up into the starlit sky with great might.

"That ain't fucking good," says Sean.

We hunt the mountains from the north to the south to the east to the west. Nothing. The ten teams remain silent. Even the crickets become silent. The only sound that we hear is the wind.

Out of the moonless darkness, one of the teams suddenly shout loud and clear throughout the night in fear and pain. Our attention turns to that source of sound and with our glasses still on thermal, we witness one team being brutally attacked by something that just simply tears them apart in seconds. Their dying screams of pain truly alert the other teams. Their reactions, the snipers, mount their guns onto their backs while switching to another firearm which is an assault rifle of some kind that I don't know while the Wolfinoids fire up their staffs, ears straight forward.

One of the Wolfinoid guards shout in distress into the mic, "It's a fucking ambush!"

Suddenly, darker shades of heat reminiscing from their bodies appear right out of thin air and slowly circle each team, ready to tear them to shreds.

"Fuck, they have the ability to be invisible," says one of the Wolfinoids near us.

For the rest of us, especially me, we're in shock and our nerves fry up more when our enemies appear around the town out of thin air. I gulp down my fear, close my eyes tightly, ignite my power around me, and turn my fear into fuel to activate my battle drive. I reopen my eyes, slapping my staff back in my right hand with my left. With the staff in both of my hands, the admiral blue lava lights up in the core, churning in motion while sending the light into the glass orb, which ignites the fire around it, burning in the same color. Still, an increasing number of our enemy appears, possibly up to two hundred. The other Wolfinoids around me do the same thing with staffs, ignite them, and get ready to charge.

I point the top of my staff toward Silverton and yell one basic command loud and clear, *"Charge!"*

I start sprinting down the mountain side at full speed. The entire military party from the combined kingdom along with the saved U.S. military members follow behind me. We all shout with great might; some even shoot off a few rounds of bullets into the air to increase our presence to our enemy. Nearing the bottom, we split into three large groups: the first one swoop to the left to aid the small teams from our force led by Capt. Leon Ocean, Lt. Drex Wind, and Trent while the right does the same thing while being led by Sean and Damon Noon. The center force is led by me and both of the Nightrunner brothers and us charge straight toward Silverton.

Our enemy acknowledges our presence and begins to charge at us at full speed. Their charge increases our pace down the mountain side and also increases our vengeance assault upon them. Within mere minutes, the kinetic energy as we collide with one another with such great force, sends the first one hundred flying up in the air from both sides.

I'm not one of them. Instead, I bend my torso down during the charge, impale one of the werewolves right through his stomach, and thrust the other end through its back. It howls in dying pain lasting a mere minute before dying; still, I charge and impale the glass orb into a tree, throw off the robe behind me, and begin my assault by only using my limbs and jaw. One comes at me; it leaps into the air in a great height and descends down at a sharp angle; the claws on all four of its limbs are fully extended. I extend my arms and hands to grab his open mouth, then I throw it into the ground and break its head apart with my bare hands by tearing his jaw in half, just like Tara did. Blood sprays on me, yet I continue to fight by grabbing my staff from my impaled victim. By twisting both hands around the shaft, it releases a huge wave of light stopping its heart and then bursting into flames in a matter of seconds. After that, I rip out the staff and push forward.

All around me is just pure, fucking chaos. It seems that all the noises of battle shouts, cries of pain, joy of victory, weapon staffs firing off as well as the guns from pistols, semi-automatics, to heavy machine weaponry seem to come together, making my ears completely silent as I dart my eyes across the battlefield of Silverton, scouting for my next victim or if any human or Wolfinoid need any assistance. However, I am blindsided when five werewolves dogpile upon me. Their sheer weight knocks me off my feet and onto the ground, torso first. I struggle to get back up, but they have pinned me down really good.

"What do we have here?" snarls one, technically the closest one to my ear.

"Seems to be the king," says the second one, climbing off from the top of the pile, standing on his feet, and crouching to get a closer look.

Both sound male and I look at the second one straight into the eyes. Their eyes blood with red eye balls and pure black, pupil slits are just filled with hate, blood lust, and intention to just torture and slaughter.

I growl in revenge, but the second werewolf releases an evil grin.

"He smells like he has a mate," the third one says, also a male, and he inhales my fur again with joy. "It's the scent of Tara Borin. Perhaps we should we should interrogate him, then kill him and his wife."

"That's a wonderful idea," says the first one with snarling joy.

Threatening to kill me? Threatening to kill my wife?

I close my eyes and speak softly out loud, "Not on my fucking watch."

Again, I play "Fight It Out" by Quintin Gill in my head, charging my strength and my power to their fullest and tensing up every muscle in my body.

"What was that?" the first one asks in teasing voice.

By the time I set my body on fire, I launch the other four right up into the air engulfed in flames. They scream in pain as they come crashing down to Earth and then they run around like chickens with their heads cut off. I immediately stand right up, still having admiral flames burning around me, then I snap my head to the left to see a modified dually, F-350. I extend my arm forward, snapping my left hand only once and the truck comes to life. Next, I grab the emptiness of air in a way that I'm grabbing the truck; it revs its mighty, modified Powerstroke engine. I turn my head to my burning victims; then I turn my attention at their little leader and smile at him. With one thrust of my arm toward the direction of my victims, the F-350 spins its tires in the dirt for a moment, gains traction, and charges at the werewolves at a full speed while spewing black smoke from its tail pipe. It collides with them in a minute and crashes into one the historical brick buildings while crushing them between the heavy metal and masonry. All that time, I look at their leader who stands in fear and realization that he just made a huge mistake. I stab my staff into the dirt while still playing the same song. With vengeance in my voice, I start singing the lyrics and during this moment, I begin slowly walking toward him, cracking my knuckles. In my amazement, the asshole takes off running in retreat and I fast forward to the chorus.

Immediately, I burst into a full sprint, leaving a trail of my footprints that are on fire in admiral blue flames like from the movies *Ghost Rider* and *Back to the Future*. In mere moments, I catch up to him, then I jump on top of him with my teeth and claws fully extended and suddenly take him down to the ground. I instantly dig my claws on my right hand into his chest to flip him around and with my claws on my left hand, I dig them deep into his neck.

"Threatening to kill me? Threatening to kill my wife? You pick the wrong Wolfinoid to fuck around with, asshole!"

In seconds, I rip open the chest and claw out his organs.

Blood. So much blood. It sprays out as I destroy this werewolf to make sure he doesn't come near nor lay a hand onto my wife! I bite and rip out anything left of the organs, the bones in the ribcage, and spine with my own teeth.

Unexpectedly, I hear familiar noises that make my murderous attack come to an abrupt halt. My ears become their own as they twist side to side, trying to figure where the noises are coming from. The noises echo off the nearby mountains softly. Then, they get increasingly louder.

My ears tell my brain it's a steam whistle sounding off and I can hear the chugging sounds of steam being produced and the sound of the metal wheels rolling along the tracks. Snapping my head to look behind me, there's the beam of light from the headlamp shining brightly through the trees as three steam locomotives, one connected to the other pulling nearly two dozens of train cars behind, come barreling down the tracks. I stand up and simply watch in amazement. My amazement is shattered by someone shouting into the microphone.

"Somebody stop those trains!"

Then another voice answers, "We're already on it."

The dark, moonless sky is lit by three RPG-7 rockets as they fly from the north, the same direction where we charged down from the mountain side, and skew at low altitude with a low thundering noise to their targets. I watch in complete awe.

All three steam engines explode in a massive ball of fire as the flames fly up as if a nuke bomb has been detonated and pieces of steel, large and small, fly away from the wreckage in every direction. More werewolves stumble out from the train cars, but they seem to be the weak ones. My instincts just make me run to the wreckage as well as the other Wolfinoids and humans. I grab my staff in the process and shoot out a large and long powerful bolt of lightning which divides into three branches and destroys the first three train cars while incinerating the disoriented werewolves.

Getting closer to the tracks, more beams of light from the staffs shoot out from their orbs and bullets fly out of their barrels into our enemy. Through my night vision, all I see is our enemy dropping like flies and more blood spewing out from their bodies.

CHAPTER FORTY-FIVE
Reconstruction of Silverton
Date: June 9, 2015
Time: 7:00 PM

THE BATTLE LASTED NEARLY two days, ending around one in the morning, and within that two days, *sigh*, we were able to turn half the town of Silverton into a pile of burning masonry and wood. The mutated werewolves were strong, which made us use extraordinary measures in battle to destroy them and that is why half of the town is destroyed. What about the hostages in the town hall, you ask? They're all safe, just shaken up with some minor injuries like skin lacerations, very easy to heal. The buildings that are destroyed still burn; the smoke mixes with the smell of smoke from the piles of burning dead werewolves. There are thirty of them strewn about the town. We rose victorious although with a combination of both races, nearly a hundred and half were slaughtered so much that we couldn't tell who someone is and their genders. On the other hand, we placed our dead in boxes and bury them with full-honor funerals. In detail, we have one hundred and five humans along with forty-five Wolfinoids. The destruction of the three steam engines and ten historic rail cars still lay among the tracks. Five of them are heavily damaged, while the other ones remain perfectly intact. So yeah, hell was here and still is. The smell of the burning corpses of our enemy still disgusts us; some of the Wolfinoids have used their sorcery to morph an invisible force field around the fires to keep the smell at bay while the others use their power to control the wind so that the smoke can blow the remaining fumes away from Silverton.

We have set up a fully functional hospital tent to tend to the wounded ranging from critical to noncritical conditions. The critical wing, both E.R. and O.R., have the E.K.G. machines that sound off so often that it has created mass rush and panic among the doctors and nurses as they rush from one bed to the next. The sound of the screaming monitors echo so clearly to the nearby towering mountains that everybody can hear it wherever we stand in the town. For security, we've set up a large, oval-like perimeter that has groups of ten spread out with gaps as long as a football field, but I don't think we'll be seeing another ambush anytime soon.

If y'all are wondering what I'm doing, well, I'm just here standing on the tracks right in the middle of the debris field where the three steam engines used to be along with the debris of the ten rail cars I mentioned earlier. With my camo hat pulled down to cover my eyes, I reach into the right pocket of my jeans, pull out a small box containing toothpicks that I found in one of the tourist stores that still stands, insert one of them into my mouth, and begin chewing on it.

I kneel down, still chewing, observing the tracks that follow into the gorge following the Animas River. Aside from hearing the E.K.G.s, I can hear the river gurgling softly away downstream. I know farther down the tracks that the Animas becomes more violent and with its churning rapids, it has claimed so many prospector and civilian lives. Most of the accidents happened during the heyday when the mines are tucked behind the towering, rocky cliffs and tall trees. In my mind, I let the solo guitar play the old western sounds, a man whistling a tune right before the strums come to an end while recreating the sound of the wind, and me trying to place myself during the time when the steam locomotives were the main source of transportation, shipping people and goods across this nation. This narrow gage rail line was the main vein of life connecting the towns of Durango and Silverton so that people, food, and raw material pouring out of the mines can be transported to another steam locomotive that will take them across a much larger distance at a slightly faster pace.

The only question that's on my mind is, *Is Durango still under control from our enemy or is it deserted? If it is still under control, then shit, it's gonna end up ten times worse than Silverton.*

"Grrr." I hang my head and make my right hand into a tight fist.

Looking back at the destruction and what's left of Silverton, I definitely don't want Durango to suffer the same fate. Perhaps, it would be ten times worse since it's a bigger town. I return my gaze back to the tracks entering the towering, narrow gorge. Within a minute, an epiphany strikes me hard.

"Fuck me." I immediately stand up, ripping the toothpick out from my mouth and throwing it down to the ground. "It's gonna be total fucking Armageddon in Los Alamos. Shit!"

I place my hands on top of my head, ripping and kicking up dirt and rocks within the two planks of wood that hold the iron rails together with my bare, right foot.

I glance out from the corner of my eye to look at the security groups and any other non-critically injured human and Wolfinoids that are walking about the town as the sun rises over the peaks, then I swing my head back to the original direction I was looking at. "I don't want to lose anymore fucking, good men and women from either race when we get there and fucking battle there. Fuck you, werewolves."

After saying that, I flip the bird to further express my frustration of reality.

"Hey, boss!" the voice of Maddox makes me jump and I mean literally jump a little bit and makes my head snap toward his direction.

Once I see him, he's jogging toward me while waving his arm. With the expression on his face, it drains the frustration from me and raises my curiosity because he seems to have a happy face as if he discovered something awesome. While I wait for him, I pull out another toothpick and imagine it as a lit cigarette.

As he gets closer, I pop the question while sticking my hands into the pockets of my jeans, "What is it, Maddox?"

Still smiling a little bit, he answers, "Sir, I've got some good news to tell you."

I raise my eyebrows. "Well, I hope it does raise my spirits since we destroyed half of Silverton. I don't wanna destroy Durango when we reach that town." In that sentence, I gesture with my right thumb, pointing down the track.

"Well, you see, that's the good news. Durango is abandoned. There is no presence of werewolves nor U.S. military of the sort."

Well, now, that is good news.

"What about this rail line?" I ask, tapping my foot on the dirt and gravel.

Maddox looks around me for a moment, then looks back with determination but with some slight concern. "Not completely sure."

I hang my head and cross my arms. *"Perfect."*

He then raises his voice in assurance, "But from the results that we received, it shows to be minimal. So, we can take them out easily."

I bring up my head. "Yeah, but what if they are the mutated ones? What if they are more deadly and cunning than the ones we faced two nights ago?"

"To answer that question, Will, you need to see the map for yourself. Just follow me."

I shrug one shoulder and wave my arm for him to lead the way.

We both enter our makeshift command tent and the other guys seem pretty occupied at two tables. The first one is the one that Maddox and I approach with nine tablets connected to one another to form a larger screen so that every geographical mark on the digital map appears and limits the amount of scrolling, zooming, and minimizing. At this table is Damon, Sean, and Trent who are looking at the digital map zoomed out which shows Silverton, the D&S Narrow Gage Rail Line, and Durango. Getting closer, there's a mixture of marigold and sangria purple representing Troy and Sparta covering Silverton and along the rail. Deep in the canyon are small spots and thin lines of black spread so far apart from one another and finally, a huge blob of grey covers the entire town of Durango. Yet, over three hundred miles away are the stars and stripes representing the U.S. military that's slowly encroaching onto the town from the south west. I put one hand into my pockets and rub my mouth with the other, thinking about our current circumstances. I let my eyes wander to the 550, the alternate and faster route to this town from Durango, and there is no shade of any color.

Interesting.

"What's the story with that road?" I ask while I point to it.

Damon snaps his fingers, swipes a part of his screen to reveal a small keyboard, and after a few, basic strokes, a dozen bright, hollow circles appear up and down the road. After that, one line extends for a certain length and opens a dialog box for one picture.

"Completely damaged," he answers in complete confidence.

I lean over the table in awe by the destruction of the 550; every picture that I maximize with one touch of my fingertip shows massive landslides and huge chunks as big as fifty yards completely showing that the road is impassible. Plus, I ain't planning on taking this military group over the treacherous terrain that the prospectors had to face back in late 1800s.

"Then I guess that leaves us with the rail line." Then I change the tone of my voice from optimistic to a mixture of sarcasm and frustration, "But wait a second. Some humans decided to fire a few of RPG-7s that *completely destroyed the steam engines!*" while I shake my arm toward the debris that still lays on the tracks.

"Also, you destroyed a few of those train cars," Trent adds in.

"I! Know! That!"

Then I turn my head toward the other table where Leon, Soren, and Drex seem to have lost concentration on whatever they were looking at. I fixate my eyes at them and instead of seeing more electronics, they're large pieces of paper. I deeply exhale through my mouth to calm down and casually move to that table.

"Ah, yes, that is the other reason why I brought you over here," says Maddox.

I grab one of the large pieces of paper and upon examination, it's a blueprint of a steam engine roundhouse. I set that aside and the next set of blueprints are for a steam locomotive. Lowering it, I look at the guys in calmness and determination.

"Gentlemen, looks like we've got some reconstruction to do."

Date: July 7, 2015
Time: 5:13 PM

"Alright! Fire her up!" I shout the order over the tools that are still grinding, cutting, welding, molding, and riveting the metal on steam engines 235, 106, and 138 in our successful roundhouse and blacksmith building. This is where we are still creating tools and parts for these engines so that they have their chance to operate on the rail line.

Anyway, the reason why I shouted is that we just completed engine 550 and we're about to dump some coal and fire up the boiler. During the past four weeks, everybody has worked so damn hard throughout the days and nights to construct the roundhouse, the blacksmith shop, housing, and a hospital. We've also installed more rails to connect with the existing track, plus we have sent a group of ten guys to inspect as much of the track if there are any damage. To be on the safe side, they only inspected a mile and a half. Why? Because journeying farther into the gorge would put them at risk and I for one am exhausted to lose more humans and Wolfinoids by the claws and jaws of our enemy. The surprising thing during the four weeks we were reconstructing, by the grace of the Almighty, a group of twenty humans or so emerged from one of the mines just outside town along the rail line. At that time, they were all shaken up with fear, famished and dehydrated. Nevertheless, our doctors got them back to their full health. To make the reconstruction easier and faster, some of them knew the blacksmith trade and pitched in to speed up productions, which was nice. The drawback during the four weeks was that we didn't celebrate the fourth of July because we didn't want to draw attention with louder noises. Some of the humans, including my human side that still resides inside me wanted to, yet I had to understand the facts that laid before me. Another reason we didn't celebrate is that most of the Wolfinoids from both Troy and Sparta didn't really understood the celebration. Their minds were and still are set on eliminating the enemy for good.

"Coal's in the boiler! Flame's hot!" shouts a human.

I climb up the ladder that leads into the operating room, yet I hang onto the handles as I watch with enthusiasm another Wolfinoid from our military and a human wearing U.S. Army gear getting the steam engine ready. The Wolfinoid eyes the gauges and fiddles with the knobs while the human pops open the hatch to the firebox and inserts a long wooden pole with a thick flame burning on one end. The Wolfinoid nods at his buddy for a confirmation and the human touches the coal with the flame; he lets fire erupt and flow throughout the coal rocks, and then withdraws the pole.

"Temperature is beginning to rise!" says the Wolfinoid in his Irish accent as he watches the needle of the gauge slowly crawl up.

I shout over the noises still keeping eyes on the same gauge, "Is there somebody dumping water in?"

"Already on it, sir!" replies someone.

Soon, the needle on the water gauge begins to rise. The temp gauge reaches its critical number to boil the water. On the other gauges of the steam pressure, combustion slowly rise but barely; yet, it's still a good sign. The needle for the water gauge stops and the order is given that the water be shut and spigot moved away. Within seconds, the needles on the pressure gauges move faster as they move up clockwise. I lean away from the cabin to see if there's any smoke arising from the stack and sure enough, a thin, transparent cloud of black smoke arises along with some steam dispersing from the cylinders at the head of the locomotive.

"Alright, steam pressure is building up good," says the same Wolfinoid in the cabin.

I look up to see a long, faint, continuous cloud of steam rising from the whistle. I jump off and nod at my fellow Wolfinoid soldier to pull the rope for the whistle. He does it with a smile. A long, heavy, continuous sound of the whistle echoes off the brick walls and the metal rafters that support the heavy shingle roof and makes the production within the roundhouse cease for a moment. Every person of both species looks up and begins applauding. I smile and nod with excitement; I jog up to the doors that are opened slightly and stand in the way of our first, completed steam locomotive. I reach the chain and start pulling on one end, opening up the doors further. As they are completely opened, I wave my left arm to signal the men inside to open up the throttle of the steam engine. They do so and the mighty black beast slowly moves forward into the setting sun over Silverton.

The steam beast continues to roll down its rail line; every time the pistons pumped steam, the cloud of black smoke gets thicker and rises higher in the sky; the metal wheels grind along the rails as the engine moves down to the turntable with me leading it to the contraption. Getting closer, I man the control console and successfully get the turntable operational; I give the guys the thumbs up and wave them on. The steamer and its tinder car get directly in the center of the turntable and I begin moving the device counter clockwise, spinning it one hundred and eighty degrees forming a Y turn and allowing the engine to back up the awaiting train cars that weren't completely destroyed during the battle. On the downside, they did suffer bullet damage and drenched with blood from our fallen enemies. Nevertheless, we were able to restore them to their originality. During the past four weeks, we've constructed several more and followed the blueprints to keep them true.

Anyway, the final supplies of medicine that can handle medical and trauma emergencies, food, and military supplies that include the usual guns and ammo are being loaded into the cars. The current situation is that the U.S. military force that has been with us from Troy have been reduced to a hundred. Among us Wolfinoids, we agreed that half of the military group of fifty humans stay here while they continue to tend to their wounded, hoping for any chance of the actual U.S. military to come from the same direction where we came from. The other fifty joins us on the train ride to set up an outpost in Durango. Overall, both parties of both species agreed that this plan is the best to avoid conflict and more mass casualties.

My God, it still feels weird to call myself a Wolfinoid.

I shake my head at that thought. I lock the turntable in place and observe the engine, beginning to reverse up to the first part of the Y turn where the couplings on the tinder car and first train car could meet. The minutes pass when they get closer until the magical noise of the two couplings contact each other. The loud, chain reaction ripples throughout the air when the momentum of the steam engine and the tinder box push the train cars slightly back, creating the metal bang and groaning down the cars almost to the caboose. Two other humans approach the tinder box and the first train car and begin locking the couplings and attaching the cables from the tinder box to the train car. Within moments, they stand up and signal the Wolfinoid and the human on the engine that everything is set. The human, being the engineer, lets out two quick blows of the whistle.

The remaining Wolfinoids inside the wheelhouse come out with their gear in hand; a few bid goodbyes to some of their human friends who also took the time to pause their work and exchange their final words. I already have my gear on my back and head toward the historic, majestic site. Getting closer, I flip the switch on the Y turn track so that the steam engine, with its cargo, can head straight down its historic rail line toward Durango. Next, I continue to the first train car until Sean steps out of the same car while holding his right hand up against his communication glasses. His face shows a combination of confusion and surprise. He looks up at me, still in the same way. This makes me slow down my pace.

Approaching him, I hear him say, "Alright, I'll bring him over. But remember, he isn't going to be happy to see you." Then he rolls his eyes. "Yeah, yeah, Greenwood out."

"What's up?"

He sighs, placing his hands on his hips. "Just follow me, sire."

In the time I begin to follow him, I morph two signals with my hands to the guys on the engine: the first one in a fist to hold up and the second to wait a moment while raising my index finger in the air. Both men nod in acknowledgement.

We walk two football fields away from our ride and I come to an abrupt halt because forty yards in front of me is Hays Rows. I glower and growl at him. Sean's ears perk up in concern and he spins around on one of his heels, facing his hands toward me in surrender.

"Sire, just hear the man out," he says then morphs his left hand to point his thumb behind him, "Look behind him."

Shifting my focus away from that dumbass who told me I don't have the capabilities to lead this military party, my anger softens a bit when I see Judocus Avast with his Special Forces of men and women. I proceed a little closer to the both of them; however, I shift my gaze back to Hays. Once I'm ten yards away from him, I speak in disgust.

"The fuck you want?"

Hays gulps and slightly looks back to Judocus for verbal back up, but he smirks while waving his hand for him to do all the talking.

"Lord Will Borin, my greatest and deepest apologies for ever doubting your leadership skills and insulting you back in the state called . . ." He rolls his eyes trying to remember its name.

Sigh. "Wyoming!"

"Yes, yes. In Wyoming. When I arrived back in Troy, my king was very outraged to see me and was further outraged when I told him why I returned. So, he clawed the side of my face, smacked, and ordered me to return to you while bringing our Special Forces group and listen to your orders only."

He takes a few steps closer to me. In the dim light from the setting sun, I can see scar marks across the left side of his face where King Terrin struck him. The injuries themselves are still pink. Then I look at Judocus and behind him is his special army and the sheer size makes me curious how many members he has. He smiles like he can read my mind.

"Forty-five in total, sire." He folds his hands behind his back.

"Yes, you see, Captain Avast has brought—"

"You shut the hell up Hays or I'll break your neck and set your corpse on *fire!*"

"Yes, sire," he says in an apologetic tone letting his head hang and folding his hands behind his back.

I let out a heavy sigh to calm down. "What did you guys bring?"

Avast steps aside, waving his arm forward toward Sean and I; twelve groups of four come forward while carrying long, black, narrow cases made out of heavy-duty plastic of some kind. The dimensions of the cases seem to be six feet long, three feet wide, and two feet tall. This rises my curiosity and makes me almost forget that Hays is with us; I kneel down at one of the cases.

"What's in them?" I look up at him while shaking my tail.

Avast answers with flying confidence, "In them are four, thirty-six-inch special designed towers that will activate a shield that will, without a doubt, withhold the radiation from those facilities if by any chance they explode."

"May I see them?"

"Ah, sorry sire. Once we crack open any of these cases, the devices immediately activate and there is no manual off switch."

"So, they're just for one-time use?" Sean asks.

"Yep, these are fresh out of our own tech lab. The only time they deactivate is when there is no radiation in the contamination zone. Nevertheless, instead of taking centuries for the radiation to disappear, it will only take about fifty to sixty years." Avast answers in the same tone.

I stand up smiling, feeling pleased that some things will go right when the shit hits the fan at Los Alamos, which I have no doubt. I look at Hays, getting serious again, and step right up into his personal bubble.

"Are you really going to obey every order that I tell *you??*"

"Yes, my lord."

I look at Avast, his crew, their cases, then at Sean, and back at Hays. "You fuck me over, just fuck me over one time, and I myself will make sure that you no longer exist. *Do you understand me?*"

He gulps and I think to myself, *You damn right, you better gulp.*

I look up at the sky and I can see the stars appearing; I wave my arm giving the command that we have a train to catch and that we've wasted enough time. During our walk back to the train, the whistle sounds off again over the quiet mountains that rise above Silverton in impatience.

CHAPTER FORTY-SIX
Durango Bound
Location: Somewhere Along the
Animas River on the D&S Rail Line
Time: 9:15 PM

ANOTHER MOONLESS NIGHT THRIVES above us and lets the stars of every galaxy shine brightly with ease. All is quiet except the rolling sound of the Animas River itself combined with the noises of steam and smoke being pumped throughout the steam engine making its way down the tracks; all of the train cars click-clack on the rails. We have the headlamp deactivated, but I don't think it's making much of a huge difference.

Overall, just to minimize attention, we travel at a decent speed of ten miles per hour. I lean out one of the windows of the first coach, train car with the night vision activated on my glasses. By doing a one-eighty-degree sweep of my head, everything seems to be clear, for now. I bring my head back inside and make my way down the narrow corridors of the cars slowly and carefully. In the first four, every small bench is occupied by one Wolfinoid that he and she is just leaning against the wall and propping one of the legs onto the rest of the bench for comfort as they gaze out the windows, taking in the historic ride. Others check their sacks and staffs; some pull out smaller, glass pane tables and write on them. Some just do all the things together. Within this time that I told you what these guys are doing, I'm already halfway down the third car. I'm about to reach the rear door when a female Wolfinoid from the military of Troy pauses from her writing, looks up at me, and pops a question.

"You're King Will Borin, correct?"

I turn off the night vision so that the bright, green lights of the mechanism don't sting my eyes because the display of light from the tablet is very bright.

I answer, "Yeah. What can I help you with?"

"You used to be a human, right?" she continues.

"Yeah . . ." I calmly reply, beginning to feel like she is starting to doubt me just like Hays did.

She turns her soft gaze back to the window, looking up at the towering peaks and slipping out a soft smile. "You have a beautiful nation. Aside from what has happened, it's still interesting. It kind of makes me miss our planet. Our home. And this train," she waves her right arm to further express, "has inspired me to write my first novel."

First novel. Nice.

"How far are you?" I ask.

"Oh, I started on the prologue."

"I bid you good luck and happy writing."

She then says thank you and I proceed to the door. As I begin turning the knob, one of my ears sweeps backward to the same Wolfinoid when she speaks very quietly.

"I miss you so much, Nos."

I look back with some surprise for a moment and return my gaze back to my hand on the knob.

How in the hell does she know my street name? The way she said it sounded like she was into me.

I start putting a few things together in my mind, *The animatronics. Tara told me that she used one to be a part of the search party. Is she using one again?*

I slowly turn my gaze toward the same woman. In the dim light of her screen, I can make out that she's slightly looking at me with her eyes half open in a tempting way, licking her lips

No way!

My heart begins to beat so fast in fear and realization like it wants to jump out of my chest. In quick fashion, I thrust the door open, move around it, and immediately shut it behind me while looking forward to the next door. I rub my eyes with one of my hands and try to bring myself back together.

"I must be going crazy. I might be missing Tara that much."

Immediately, I rush through the fourth car occupied with some humans and their new friends and into one of the six observation cars, Avast and his men occupy the first four as they watch the rocky landscape travel by and keep guard of their cases which take up the foot space between the wall facing the benches and the cars. This makes the men sit sideways or prop their feet on top of the railing. All twelve cases occupy the first two observation cars. Avast steadies himself by placing his hands on the back part of one the benches while standing in the main walking aisle. My rush into the car catches his attention.

"What's wrong, sir?" he asks curiously.

I look back, still in small panic. For a moment, I look back and return my attention to him while shaking my head to get rid of the reaction.

"Nothing. Everything's fine. You guys enjoying the ride?"

"You sure? You look like you just saw a ghost."

"I'm fine." I flattened my right hand in his direction to further my answer and look at the Animas River again.

He sighs in a way of saying whatever and answers my question, "Yes, we are enjoying the ride. How old is this rail line?"

I still look at the river. "Well, over a century."

"Fascinating."

We slightly sway with the car as we stand in the aisle for a while. The entire car is quiet.

"May I borrow your tablet?" I ask Avast.

"Hm? Oh yeah, sure." He pulls it out, turns it on, and hands it to me.

I analyze it. The exact same orange dot appears on the screen and is steadily moving south. Zooming out to see the entire railway makes me smile because the entire railway, including Durango, is covered in gray.

"Well, this is going to be an easy train ride."

"Anything new?" Avast asks.

I hand his tablet back to him; he flips it in his hands to see the screen and he too cracks a smile and looks up at me.

"Well, this *is* going to be a truly easy train ride, but do you realize we have to make at least a dozen more trips to have all of our military strength?"

I look around the car and nod my head in agreement while speaking, "Yeah, I agree with you." And I look directly at him. "You've seen my top men?"

He gestures with his left thumb while speaking, "Farther in the back."

I take my time as I move down the walking aisles of the other five gondola train cars and into the other enclosed cars while stepping over equipment to set up for a command post for communications, human fire arms with ammo of all sorts, equipment for medical and trauma emergencies, bags, sacks, weapon staffs, and over chilling feet in the aisles as some Wolfinoids and humans nap in the darkness. In general, the military head count for us Wolfinoids is eleven thousand and two hundred, so making one trip down to Durango isn't enough even though there is a total of twenty train cars hooked up to our only operational steam engine.

Man, this is going to take a while.

After nearly two hours go by, we finally roll into Durango. The driver slows down the train just enough for us to hop out of the train cars in small platoons as it continues down the line to the depot. The time is nearly ten PM and all is quiet. We activate our thermals and our weapons. I steadily sweep my head left to right and back, slowly stepping toward the historical part of downtown Durango and tightening my grip on my staff to ignite its power. So far, I see nothing.

"Train has come to a complete stop. Beginning to sweep the railyard," says Trent in the headphone of my communication glasses.

"Copy that," I reply.

I glance at the GPS display to see numerous green dots moving east and west away from a pink line that represents the train tracks, and the huge cluster begin to move into the railyard. The area I hopped off is behind the Strater Hotel and from my thermal vision, I see no body heat of any kind from any of its levels and the same results appear in the other structures. I deactivate the thermal and ignite the light in my glass, flame orb to illuminate where I am. Our light and presence attract no one's attention.

"Platoons, do you see anything?"

"Nope."

"Nothing."

"All clear."

"Nothing in our sector."

"Same here, it's all clear."

"Likewise."

"Yep, we see nothing."

"We're all clear here and around the railyard."

"I guess the town of Durango is all clear, my lord," Sean speaks as he steps up next to me, looking pleased.

Due to the amount of light that's shining out of the orb on my staff, Durango looks at it absolutely deserted. There's no sign of any activity, except for us. Still, I nod in agreement and move at a normal pace to the door of the Strater Hotel's saloon. Of course, Sean follows in curiosity.

Approaching it, I reach for the screen door and open it with ease. I prop it against my shoulder and reach for the door knob.

"Sire, we should head toward the other station," says Sean.

I look over my shoulder and shoot a crooked smile. "What's the rush? We need to make at least another dozen more trips to have all our numbers."

Right after that, I slowly turn the knob; instead of stopping immediately, it turns ninety degrees and I gently push open the door. The bell above rings but no bartender greets us at the bar to ask what our choice of poison would be. Both Sean and I are not greeted by any host or hostess to be seated at any table nor are we greeted by the saloon music played on a piano. I look around for the light switches and find them right at the frame of the door. One by one, I activate the main lights of the saloon and they come to life with ease.

"Power is still working," says Sean in a surprised tone.

I extinguish the light, holster my staff, and wipe one of my hands across one of the tables, analyzing the thickness of the dust. "Judging the dust, it seems that Durango has been abandoned but not long enough for the power to cease."

With my curiosity settled, I move past Sean, back outside, and begin my walk down to the station. Sean jogs out to catch up with me. From where we are, I can see that some of the military of the human race have also figured out that the power is still active as they have turned on all of the interior and exterior lights of the Durango Train Station.

In moments, Sean and I reach the fine, historical establishment, assist on unloading our supplies, and begin setting up base camp for the humans. During that time, we send the train back up the historical railway to get the rest of our numbers that still wait in Silverton.

After several, almost agonizing hours, the military strength of Spartan and Trojan Wolfinoids is now complete. All eleven thousand and two hundred are accounted. The fifty military humans have fully set up their command post in the depot and the rest of the taken refuge from the Strater Hotel, enjoying the food and booze that lies inside. On the downside, some of our men and women had to bid goodbye to their friends. It is a little heartbreaking to see, but we have a task to complete—liberate Los Alamos and obliterate our enemy.

Looking toward the east, I can see the glow of the sun arising over the hills. I check with my men to see where the actual U.S. military is located and their tablets show that they are getting close but are still far away for us to slip away into the fading night. Seeing this information, I give out the order to move out and the same horn is blown. We sprint away from Durango and our human allies let out two quick final blows of the steam whistle in bidding farewell.

NEW MEXICO

THE BATTLES OF LOS ALAMOS

CHAPTER FORTY-SEVEN
The Battle of Pajarito Ski Hill
Location: Valles of the Caldera
Time: 9:00 AM
Date: July 8, 2015

"MAY I HAVE ALL of your attention please?" I ask softly into the mic as I stand at the head of the laid-out dry lumber for seating that are neatly assorted into three columns.

The left and right are angled at sixty degrees to make a semi-perfect arc with the center one that curves in front of me. Behind me is an eight-foot high, one-hundred-and-fifty-inch screen TV that is constructed out of over a hundred pane, glass tablets connected to create the screen. The mighty pane of glass screen displays only a two-dimensional map of the valley, ski hill, and the town, but do not fear, I can still maneuver the map like Google Earth with my two, Wolfinoid, index fingers. Moving on, ahead of me and spread out behind the three columns of lumber are tents and small campfires randomly placed amongst what is left of the Santa Fe National Forest in the Jemez Mountain region that borders Los Alamos. In that case, we set up this final camp far deep into one of the off-roading trails that my friends and I went to back when we were in high school. No surviving human, which is a little sad, has not stumbled upon it nor has any mutated werewolf, which is a good thing. My simple, soft command then gets the military group's attention.

I briefly look down at the ground, take a deep breath, and look back up. "Can you all take your seats? If you can find one."

They follow as they are commanded. Once every inch of all of the dry lumber is taken, the remaining Wolfinoids stand near the lumber while others find a spot on the ground in front of the very first rows and on the boulders to get a perfect view of the screen. I look to the east, through the trees, and across the Valles of the Caldera to see a pitch, black smoke that lingers almost above the towers on top of the ski hill. The area is so quiet that ever since we arrived, we can faintly hear the blood-curdling cries of human victims that are tortured; perhaps being eaten alive, or are bitten by the werewolves and are suffering from the tremendous pain of the physical transformation. I shiver from the sound and clear my head.

I point in the same direction with authority and determination in my voice. "Over that mountain is our target and possibly the toughest challenge we'll ever face. But first," I turn to the map, zoom it in in our location, swipe to the east toward Pajarito Ski Hill, then make it come to an abrupt halt. The map clearly shows a black blob that covers every acre of the slopes stretching from the top where the communication towers stand down toward the lodge and other buildings that house the equipment used to remove snow. I continue, "We need to liberate and take command of Pajarito Ski Hill before we move into Los Alamos. From there, we can focus our attention on LANL."

Zakia Smoke raises her hand and I acknowledge her, "What does LANL mean?"

"Los Alamos National Laboratory," I reply in a casual tone. The name is no foe to my mind.

Hays briefly raises his hand and asks, "Just to clarify, you told us back at Troy that this is the town that relatively built three atomic bombs to end World War II, thus 'saving' many human lives?"

"Yeah, that's true."

"So, we're going be dealing with a lot of radiation?" asks Soren.

I sigh in agreement, looking at him. "Yes."

Right after that, he and Maddox breaks into a small conversation and start moving to their tent. Perhaps, they can create some sort of a radiation suit on this very short timeframe set before us. Interestingly, Avast notices the brothers just thirty seconds later and joins them; of course, some of his men, about five by the looks of it, also tag along. Their conversation starts in English but turns into their natural tongue. I don't mind. This is just a tactical meeting.

"So," Hays speaks again, disturbing the silence, "what's your plan on reclaiming this ski hill?"

I look about the crowd, all staring at me, waiting for what I have in mind. I look across the valley one more time to view the back side of the hill, then turn my full attention to the map. I tap a few keys that establish blood, red dots resembling our enemy's position across the ski hill. With a few more taps, the giant touchscreen calculates the number of dots; in microseconds, I receive my answer.

"1,980."

Hm. Interesting. But we must not let our guard down. There could be more of the same type of werewolves we encountered back in Silverton.

I lower my camo hat and cross my arms while slightly lowering my head as I return my gaze back to the men and women of this great battle group. "This is my plan. Around midnight, *we'll* make a full charge at the back side of the ski hill. No shouting or screaming." I turn back to the screen, still laying out my plan while drawing lines across it. "As we get closer, we divide into much smaller groups and take out the enemies' small groups to these highly active locations." I draw circles around the clumps of red that seem to be occupying the control houses for the lifts. "After that, a good-sized portion should move toward this structure neighboring this communication tower and obliterate that group." After I draw a circle around that area, I pause for a moment surveying what to do next. Immediately, it comes to me.

"Once we all have secured the top, we should all scout for any survivors stretching from the northwest down to the southeast. Then, we split into two main groups: one stays and watches the top while the second divides and takes these three main slopes down to the lodge and other structures. Just to warn you, the very top of these slopes," I circle them while explaining, "are extremely steep and filled with very loose and sharp rocks. So, watch your footing as best as you can. Finally, as the three groups reach the bottom, clear out every structure in and out, but also be on the watch for any hostages. Finally, when there are no more red dots at any of these structures and our communication glasses show no more thermal imaging of our enemy, we move onto LANL. Overall, after all of this is done, we, as a whole, can return home safely.

Which is going to be unlikely.

"Any questions?"

The crowd begins to mutter in both languages.

"Hold on," says Sean as he steps forward. "You want every Wolfinoid to take charge at this place?" he asks in a clarifying way.

"Yeah, my friend. If there are any more of the same type of werewolves we encountered back in Silverton, I want to minimize spontaneous attacks as much as possible."

He claps his hands together and smiles. "Alright then. Sounds good."

"Anybody else?" I let my eyes wonder, then I look onto Hays' face. "How 'bout you, Tactical Specialist Hays Rows? Do you have *any questions?*"

He steps up and analyzes the map. His partner Damon Noon joins him and does the same thing. Within seconds, he looks at me attempting to hide his fear so that he doesn't piss me off, but I can sense it. Nonetheless, his face does not show a hint of doubt and shakes his head side to side.

For Damon, he looks at me with enthusiasm and says, "We . . . are . . . going . . . to . . . win."

I smile back at him, then I put my hands behind my back while looking at the map. "Yes we are, Damon. Yes, we are."

Then Sean gives the order to dismiss the meeting and rest up for the night that is bound to happen. Hopefully, it would be a short night with high success, not a long one with multiple fatalities dreading onto the next rising sun.

Date: July 9
Time: Midnight

Just as I planned, we sprint across the Caldera in silence. Hours before, we broke camp, packed everything, and went over the plans again; this time, we go in further detail and here we are. When I did the meeting, the weather was clear, warm, and the sun was shining bright. Now, as the hours passed, a moon has begun to bloom. Nonetheless, it's still a fragile crescent in the sky, barely giving light. Incredibly, its fragile light is being blocked by huge, stratus clouds that stretch for miles, only giving the slightest gaps for the light to shine through. Still, it's the perfect cover as we sprint through the darkness.

The terrain begins to rise, but we stay as one large group. I briefly look left and right. Through my night vision, I see that everybody seems heavily determined to finish the job. I sense that they are all on guard, and so am I. Within moments, the terrain continues to rise, becomes rougher, and dead and burnt trees appear, and we just naturally go around them. Moments pass like a blink of an eye and the trees begin to thin out. I mentally turn on my GPS to display where the enemy is specifically located.

I hope everybody has done the same.

Getting closer to the top of the first ridge yet a few football fields away, I give out the order, "Y'all, let's break."

From being a group of eleven thousand and two hundred, we form multiple groups of a hundred spread in every little direction toward the ski hill. Looking at the GPS, the first few werewolves individually approach my group: Maddox's, Sean's, and Drex's. I deactivate the digital map, switch from night to thermal image, pull out the jagged, curved knife I just made, and run right up to the first one, plunging it right into its heart and then into the skull. The others pick up our scent and action, but they are taken down swiftly and we press on. In detail, every werewolf that we come across got stabbing and slashing of our knives, claws, and teeth. Nothing is practically left from our attacks.

The closer we get, the gaps between the several groups spread toward the northwest and to the southeast. My group specifically approaches just off to the right side of the largest communication tower where a certain group of werewolves see us coming and decide to charge right at us. They snarl in hate, hunger, and determination as they claw huge chunks from the ground. We do the same as we begin to let out our natural inner wolf instincts. What I mean by that is, for some reason, we rip off our shirts, toss off our glasses, and snarl back while letting our claws fully grow and baring our fangs. In a matter of seconds, we collide, biting, slashing, and throwing enemies up into the air to disable them as they fall back to the ground. I got one slash at the face, a rip across my right cheek and down to my jaw. I bleed for a few seconds until the same light appears and heals my wound within an instant, just like Tara when Gurtruit whacked her with a shovel. Immediately, I lunge at the fucker, taking it down, digging my claws into its chest, and with some effort, setting its inside on fire. I throw it aside and move onto my next target. Everything has turned into slow motion. Another jumps at me; I buckle in, then spin into a spiral. I grab its head, again sinking my claws into the skin, and with one heave, the head is ripped right off the shoulders.

I kneel on the ground for the landing searching for more; apparently, my group was able to slaughter this group of thirty werewolves within minutes. Time is slow in my point of view. Then, another pack of werewolves charges at us from the southeast. At the trees in my left, my left eye catches glimpses of the other happenings.

There are roots springing from the ground, wrapping around other werewolves on their four limbs and tearing them apart. Bursts of fire erupt from the hands of others as they concentrate their attack on our enemy without burning more trees. Other Wolfinoids do the same thing. There are some Wolfinoids using shockwaves in ways that can destroy more of our enemy, and I can hear the thundering booms when the waves come to life. I continue with my attack against an upcoming group of forty. The ones at the head jump in determination to tackle me down. I counteract by leveling out my right arm, sweeping it across, and creating the same arc of light that I unleashed with my staff. It becomes a sort of a blade as it comes to life and flies up to my next victims so fast that their heads get decapitated and their bodies fall back to the ground lifeless. I do the exact same thing with my left arm and that blade of light travels to the remaining ones, slicing them in half from the hip line.

Time seems to pick up with my pace as I continue to run southeast and into the trees standing healthy at the top of the hill. At this moment, my senses tell me that my group has totally split up to take care of the rest and I am totally alone, but I don't mind. I am determined to clear the top of this mountain. My nostrils flare tremendously as I let my eyes scour for more enemies that are either approaching me or have finally decided to abandon their posts. The terrain begins to slope downward, yet I know I am still on the spine of the ski hill. Again, more enemies try to come and attack me on both sides. This time, I unleash bolts of lightning from my palms like Sith Lord from Star Wars. When the lightning touches them, they explode, letting blood and organs flying, covering the grass, rocks, and trees. Suddenly, my senses speak to me that our enemy has decided to retreat, perhaps into town, and I can see them running away from me.

One by one, with so little effort, I tackle them down, thrusting my dominant right hand into the back of their skulls, ripping out their brain, and throwing it aside. Chase. Tackle. Thrust. Rip out. Throw aside. Repeat.

I am so absorbed at destroying the enemy that I don't realize I am leaving a perfect, clean line of the dead at the spine of the hill that faces the town. I do not also even recognize I am passing the smaller communication towers until I am about to stumble down the steep part of the mountain that has been burned twice by the Cerro Grande Fire and the Las Conchas Fire.

Whoa! Whoa! Stop, Nos! Stop!

I slam my bare feet into the ground to take in the area I am in and realize how far I have traveled from the main battle site. Looking about, my eyes catch some surviving werewolves retreating down the mountain. With one blow of my blood lust and vengeance, I thrust one wide arc from my right arm of the cutting light blade toward those assholes, sending their heads apart from their shoulders and their torsos toward the ground.

"Okay. Okay. Calm the fuck down, Nos. Bring it *all* back in," I speak softly to myself while taking heavy breaths of air seemingly filled with some foul odors, but I still breathe in heavily and use more muscles to inhale all of that air into my lungs and calm down my figurative cylinders.

Gazing down and upon Los Alamos, the sight strikes me horrifically. No lights seem to be alive on North Mesa and Barranca Mesa. The darkness seems to continue down the main road called Diamond until it reaches the odd intersection of Sandia and Orange. Some of the road lights are active on the Orange Street side. Stretching to the east is the Denver Steel housing area and into the classic duplex housing area. The same lighting goes for Sandia but only in spots as it curves and reconnects with Diamond. From the high school to the south, the lights are surly active and become brighter going to Omega Bridge and right into LANL. The street lamps on Central and Trinity are active too, stretching toward the Sandi Cristo Mountains. The greatest drawback is that while my battle rage is going down, the foul odors in the air become stronger, so much that I cover my nose. Then, my ears pick up blood-curling screams of humans being tortured, transformed, or are being eaten alive. The noises are so strong in my ears that I remove my hands from my nose and place both to cover them. The sounds, the orders, and the sight become way too much for me to bear that I begin to retreat back to the spine and the main communication tower.

Within minutes, I reach the rendezvous point. Scattered about are just dead and destroyed werewolves. Seeing the blood, organs, and hell, even their bones strewn about, it almost makes me want to hurl, but I gulp down to keep whatever contents in my stomach. I search the area for any of the top men from Troy or my top men from Sparta. For some reason, I feel anxious for perhaps, they must've gotten real hurt or worse. They could also be possibly somewhere else on the spine.

"Will?"

I immediately turn to the direction of the voice to see Maddox holding my sack and glasses in one hand while holding his staff in the other as it gives light to the area.

"Are you okay?" he asks, looking concerned.

I gently reach for the sack and he simply hands it over. I undo the strap, turn it upside down, dump all of the contents, and rummage through it, searching for a clean t-shirt. I find one, put it on, and begin putting everything back in. However, I can't find my staff. I walk toward the hill that we came up, searching the field. Then I decide to snap my fingers and within moments, I see a blue light source appearing in the grass over fifty yards away. I snap my fingers once more and my staff reacts by flying toward me at a decent speed. I catch it with ease in one of my hands. Looking back at Maddox, he looks worried.

"It's really that bad over there. Isn't it?" he asks still concerned, perhaps wanting to know what my status is.

I inhale more air through my nose and exhale through my mouth while looking back where Los Alamos lies. I return my attention to my head sorcerer to answer his question, "Yeah, it's really that fucking bad over there." I gulp to get my seriousness back up. "What's the status up here?"

Maddox takes a moment to survey the area and replies, "Complete victory with some injuries but nothing really traumatic."

"So, we still have eleven thousand, two hundred?"

"Yeah, sire."

"Alright then." I slightly drill the butt of my staff into the ground. "Moving onto step two."

"You sure? There's not a lot of them down there." He pulls his glass pane iPod and shows me the map. I look at it and it displays that there are only about five of the blood-red dots. "The majority of them retreated down that road when we were halfway done with our attack."

"Yeah? But those ten could be mutated ones."

He bites his lower lip. "Good point, I'll get the next invading party ready soon."

I pat his shoulder and move toward the only rustic, wooden control shack for the ski lift that leads right down the lodge.

Time to get serious again.

Within half an hour, only fifty accompany me; amongst them is Avast and his crew, Sean, and Hays. Right now, we begin rushing down the three ski runs just as I planned. However, during the meeting, I did tell these guys to watch their footing on the loose and sharp rocks. So, we are mainly leaning back to keep our balance while dashing side to side on the ski runs.

In less than fifteen minutes, we reach the bottom. I launch my staff into the air and order it to stay where it's at while it sends out an electronic shockwave to activate all the types of machinery maintaining this recreational area. Like I told Maddox back on the top, there could be mutated werewolves down here and man was I so damn right! Breaking through the trees and through the walls of the structures are five, twelve foot tall, lumbering, and muscular werewolves that every time they take a step, the ground literally shakes.

"Aw *shit!*" Sean shouts into the mic.

"Keep focused!" I continue charging at one of them, igniting myself into a great ball of fire, and launching myself at one of the giant beasts. It counteracts by smacking so hard that I go flying backwards, crashlanding into the dirt several yards away like a fallen meteorite.

The same giant continues to charge at me. It puts its hands together to make a giant fist and brings it down upon me like a falling boulder. I counteract by immediately rolling away fast and thrusting fire from both hands into one of its eyes. It yells in pain and I take the opportunity to climb up its back. Once I reach the head, I begin clawing out its eyes. The beast tries to wipe me off, but my flames are still ignited so that every time its upper limbs make contact, they begin to burn.

Looking about the chaos unfolding before me, the other guys get the idea and try to do the same. Yet, some of Avast's men begin having trouble as they are swatted into the trees. One of them cries for assistance and I activate one of the trucks, a classic tow truck. Finishing clawing out the eyes of the first giant, it finally dies from the immense pain and collapses. On the other hand, I control the truck while moving my dominating arm through the air to maneuver the vehicle toward them. It drives around them while unlatching the tow cable, letting it wrap around the other beast's legs and soon, it brings it down for the other men to finish.

However, I get blindsided when another one grabs me like a rag doll, almost destroying my ribcage. This fucker lifts me higher and higher and it begins opening its mouth and bringing me toward it.

"Oh, hell no!"

As I am about more than a few feet from its mouth, Avast comes down on top of this beast out of nowhere, quickly inserts the top of his staff into one of its eyes, and twists it into two opposite directions. Suddenly, the entire staff begins to glow a bright, fire-red color. Within it, a stream line of vapor is being pulled right from the eye and travels to the butt of the staff. Within seconds, the strength of the mighty hand that has me goes limp. I fall flat on my stomach upon landing on the ground. I try to catch my breath; looking up, the same thing is still happening to the giant.

After two solid minutes, Avast twists his staff back to the same position; the light of his power fades out fast and he jumps down, letting that mutated werewolf collapse with a thundering noise, then Avast comes to aid me.

"What was that?" I breathe heavily through those three words.

"Just getting information, sire," Avast speaks causally.

"Huh?"

Kaboom!

We both turn our attention to witness the final moments of the lodge exploding into a massive great ball of fire and smoke and sending the last two giant, mutated werewolves up in the air, lifeless and cooked by the intense flames. One of Avast's men comes running toward us.

"All enemies have been terminated, sir."

"Good," replies Avast. "Send a message that this area is now clear and ready to be moved in."

He nods and radios the order in Wolfinoid tongue. Looking upon the burning lodge, gasping for air, I try to grasp the reality of how that building just exploded. It makes me breathe even harder. My breaths become louder in my ears that it begins to mute out Avast's voice and makes my vision go blurry. Without delay, the ridges of darkness close in onto my blurry eyesight that I try my very best to keep it at bay, but it becomes heavier by the second.

"I can't . . . hold this . . . darkness back . . . any longer. I'm out."

Then suddenly, I go out like a light but with a beating heart.

CHAPTER FORTY-EIGHT
Battle of LANL
Location: At the Remains of the Lodge
Time: 11:00 AM
Date: July 10, 2015

I WAKE UP IN a daze feeling unsure about my surroundings and completely groggy. My vision is still blurry, yet my hearing begins clearing up. Again, the first sound that my ears pick up is the beeps of the E.K.G.

Odd. How can I be hooked up to the E.K.G. when I am immortal?

Still, with my blurry vision, I move my head around to get my bearings. In the seconds that passed after I opened my eyes, I can tell and feel that I am lying on my back on top of some thick blanket, on the ground, in some white tent, and some sunlight is shining barely through the fabric of the tent. The beeping gets louder in my ears and I turn my head toward the glass monitor and sure enough, my vision instantly clears to make out the perfect details of the increments that are monitoring my vitals. In the middle of my consciousness, something feels like a flimsy plastic, clear and wrapped around my muzzle. Plus, every time I inhale, pure, fresh oxygen flows through my nostrils. With ease, I remove the mask and analyze it in my hands.

Non-rebreather mask.

I look down at my exposed chest to see patches that are sending wireless transmissions to the E.K.G. monitor. With ease, I begin to sit up, but I check myself over to see if I have any serious injuries; within seconds, I'm all clear. Next, I take a couple of deep breaths to see and feel if my ribcage is okay; again, nothing hurts nor stings. So, I fully stand up and look at the monitor.

"I guess we don't need this silly thing anymore." Tara's voice echoes in my head as it plays the first morning memory awaking in her chambers in her care when I was a human.

My heart concurs with my mind as it aches a little bit to remind me that it has been months since the last time I was officially in her presence. Instantly, her form appears in my head: her warm smile, soft voice, calm blue eyes showing compassion and love, and the touch of her warm fur against mine. These things ache my heart even more to a point that I have to place one hand onto the monitor to steady myself while the other grabs tightly onto my chest as I close my eyes to see her fully behind my eyelids.

"We will see her soon." I take breaths and reopen my eyes to see my reflection on the monitor. "We will see her soon. We will see her soon. We will see her *soon.*"

At that moment, the same sentence sounds off again and I follow its command by turning the machine off and removing the transmitters. Looking around the hospital tent, I'm the only one here. I look around the "bed" to find any other clothes and I do find some. On the dot, I put on a t-shirt and my hat; as I'm about to leave the tent, I hear a quiet hissing sound reminding me that the oxygen tank is still active and I quickly shut it off. After that, I step out into the semi-hot sun that's now high over the ski hill.

Lowering the brim of my hat, my breath is instantly taken away from the smoldering site of what is left of the ski lodge. Its hardened ash pillars of what used to be load bearing, wood studs stand above the cooked furniture, cooking appliances, and art decorations. The smell of the chemicals sizzling off from those things rise up in the air and some of it crosses my nose. The smell of death that crossed my nose last night mixes with these other smells, making my stomach churn real hard. It makes me turn my attention down the road that travels east, and I let my head rise to the sky where a thick, black cloud looms over less than ten miles away. I roll my eyes, growl slightly, and turn my head away from the sight.

"Oh, good, he's awake."

I turn my attention from where it came and I find it's Second Lieutenant Zakia Smoke leaning against one of the flaps that seal the doorway on another tent while smirking. Interestingly, this tent is black without any markings representing either one of our kingdoms and even the floormat is black, too. I cock my head to one side and raise my hand in a way to gesture the question, *"What's going on in there?"*

She continues to smirk and waves her head backward so I'd follow her, and I do. Once I step inside, she closes the flap sealing away the sunlight. From the left side of the tent, the only source of light comes from the screen that was once set up before we charged the ski hill. In front of it are a few chairs. On the far-right side of the tent that's faintly illuminated is another fabric wall that slightly reflects the light of the screen almost similar to when a rubber material has water on it. Overall, standing in front of the screen are Hays, Damon, Sean, and Trent, making me curious where the rest of the guys are at. Anyway, both Sean and Trent turn around and are relieved to see their king walking around.

Sean walks up and places his hands on my shoulders. "How are you feeling, my lord?"

I shake my head slightly, sighing, and massaging the bridge of my nose trying to sum up how I feel. However, I can't think clearly because our ultimate goal dominates my mind and I am pretty damn sure that not a lot of us are going to be able to return home. I swallow, shrug off his hands, and approach the digital map while crossing my arms to come up with a strategy on how we should attack.

"My lord? Are you—" Sean asks.

I immediately cut him off, still looking at the map, "What's our enemy head count?"

I look back if anybody in the room approaches the map and taps the large screen a few times to show the red dots. They look at one another; this thins my patience.

"Yo!" I shout while spreading my arms. "How many *fucking* mutated werewolves are we dealing with here?"

Zakia approaches at once and reveals the red dots. I lower my arms, clenching my hands and jaw tight. My eyes widen at seeing that every facility on South Mesa and the facilities that also belong to LANL stretching toward Bandelier National Monument are filled with blood-red dots and they just grow at a steady pace while combining themselves with the others, making them bigger.

Then the digital number appears, "25,560."

I lower my head, trying to keep my fear down. *Fuck. Fucky, fucky, fucky, fuck! Our chances to win have now dwindled down into signal digits. A lot of good men and women are not going to be able to return back to their home planet.*

I look up and straight to Trent. "Where are the Nightrunner brothers?"

"They're on the other side of that wall." He points with his thumb toward that somewhat-rubber fabric.

"Where are the rest of the guys from Troy?"

"They're out surveying the rest of the area and both of our military parties are doing the same. Other than that, we're mainly waiting on your orders." He glances at the map and then back at me, "What are your orders?"

I look at all of them. "Just prep and pray to God."

Right after that, I move toward the rubberish fabric and push it aside. However, it requires some effort because once I get on the other side, there is a glass box, framed in stainless-steel metal and the room itself is lit up with small industrial, pod lights where the wires are exposed. Within the glass box are the Nightrunner brothers surrounded by tables with tablets on them and perhaps two types of machines that could be fabricators. I pound on the glass with the butt of my fist to get their attention, but it doesn't work. I pound harder, yet the same result occurs; so, I angle my head to see the inside of the frame and it shows that the glass is pretty thick, perhaps two inches thick. Something that twinkles opposite from the inner frame catches my eyes. I turn my head to that direction and my eyes zero in on a line that seems to be etched into the glass. I step away, tilting my head at an angle to see what's engraved and soon, the engraved lines take form of a radiation symbol. I look back at the brothers to see them working hard on something on their tablets.

Scanning the room, there is a passageway between the box and the wall of the tent. I follow it down to a doorway which appears to have no handle on the inside and the outside, though there's a keypad to the left side with an intercom system and it mirrors the same design on the other side. Still, my movement to the doorway hasn't grabbed the attention of either one of the brothers. So, I give the intercom system a chance.

"What are you guys working on in there?"

Both of them turn around, surprised, and Maddox also looks, relieved to see me.

"We're creating radiation suits," Soren answers. "We're adding the final touches to the design and we'll construct them from this fabricator." He walks over and pats a machine they call the fabricator.

"How the hell were you guys able to fit all of this in the sacks?"

"You know those teleportation devices?" Maddox asks with a sly smile.

"Yeah."

"Same concept. It all collapses to become very portable." Then, he turns his attention back to his tablet.

The odd thing is, if this container is labeled to be radioactive, why in the hell they're not wearing a radioactive protective suit?

"Don't worry," answers Soren. "Nothing radioactive in here. We just want to keep the area completely free of dust and static."

"Alright then." My mind returns to the main conflict. "How many more days do you need to fully create the radiation suits?"

The brothers look at one another briefly. "Just another three. By the end of the third day, we'll have enough for everyone to wear for the battle," answers Maddox.

I nod in acknowledgement, then I get serious with my tone, "Alright, three days. Because the more time we spend up here, more human lives are destroyed, our enemy gets stronger, and pretty soon, they might perhaps be able to invade us."

"We know," they say in unison and after that, I leave them back to their business. Once I step back to the first room I was in, Hays approaches me hastily looking a little bit annoyed.

"That's it? 'Prep and pray to God' That's your plan?"

Sigh. Shut the hell up.

"Yes, that is my plan," I answer in a slightly annoyed tone as I open the flap of the tent, relower my hat to shade my eyes, and still look forward.

"But, but, that's not good enough. I mean, *sigh*, we, I need a better—"

I immediately grab his mouth and hold it tightly shut as I try to hold back my frustration. "Listen, Hays, I just woke up from nearly being crushed by a mutated, werewolf giant last night. I am shocked by the sheer numbers of our enemy and how much territory they have under their control. Your attitude is not helping me in the slightest, and do you remember what I told you back in Silverton?"

His eyes look off to the side in a way to replay that evening in his head. Then he looks back at me and nods slowly.

"Good. Now, where are our tents?" At that moment, I let go of his mouth so that he can answer.

"It's um, right behind the black one."

I walk pass him while slamming my shoulder into him to establish my authority. I find our tent, walk inside, then I find my bunk with my things on it along with my communicator glasses. Right after that, I make a call to Avast. He answers right away.

"King Borin, nice to hear your voice. What can I help you with?"

"Where are you?"

"At the top on the far east slope, looking down at the town with a few of my men."

"Alright, I'm heading up."

Looking about our new camp, it seems that we have a few of the ski lifts in operation. I head toward the slopes that we charged down from the communication tower where one of the two lifts are in operation. Approaching the men and women who are operating it, they stand up and bow in respect. I wave my hand in a way to say that there's no need for that. One of them calmly protests. I put my hand on his shoulder and tell him to just get the lift going with a smile. He and his guys do it and I ascend on one of the benches to the top. Getting to the top, I am surprised by the patrols that are prowling. Don't get me wrong, it brings me satisfaction that we have this *entire* ski hill area under our surveillance. Anyway, I jog toward Avast's location. Arriving, he and some of his men are definitely surveying the town by taking notes on their tablets and discussing how LANL is laid out. Others are just simply studying it. With me, I am captivated by the invisible darkness that covers the town from Barranca Mesa to South Mesa. Avast has his back turned from me with his arms crossed and a wide stance between his feet. I stand next to him and position most of my weight onto one leg, almost like I'm leaning back, and I cross my arms, too.

"Do you want to know how this happened?" Avast asks.

Actually, now that you bring it up, I don't have a damn clue how the fuck this happened.

I sigh, then reply, "No, I don't. Please elaborate."

"In our solar system, we do have a planet that is absolutely designated to contain our enemies. During one evening, back in the original kingdom of Troy, of course, a few top men from that army were chosen by Terrain to transport our werewolf enemy to that planet. During mid-transport, one of them was able to breakout from its cell quietly, released the others, and tried to take over the spaceship. Those men intervened quickly, yet amongst the chaos, one of those men were thrown hard against the control panel by one of the werewolves, accidentally activating the hyperdrive. When they came out of the hyperspace, the craft was immediately pulled into this planet's gravity and they crash-landed in the state called Montana. We don't know the exact details that occurred, but after days of losing contact with that ship, Sparta received a distress message from one of the men begging to send immediate help."

He lets out a heavy sigh filled with sadness as he hangs his head. Then, he looks up at me with the same expression, spreading his arms. "And here we are. I am so sorry that this had to happen."

I snort, "Don't be. Like we humans say, 'shit happens.' Of course, I'm not a human anymore. However, if this didn't happen, I wouldn't be able to meet Tara. I would've kept on trucking, still living a lonesome life out on the road."

He lowers his arms. "Hm, that's true." He looks back at the town for a moment. "And what are your battle plans as of now?"

"Just prep and pray to God because I know we're going to lose a lot of good men and women to end all of this bullshit. Along with the prepping, we need to design better weapons that will give us a better fighting chance to win because our staffs and sorcery skills won't be enough."

"Now that you mentioned it, your majesty, we, just my special ops group, have set up a workshop where anybody can manufacture better weapons, so I agree with you." He pulls out his staff and examines it as if it had lost its power. "We need better weapons than these and our sorcery."

"Where is it?"

"In area called Camp May. Quite interesting location. Despite . . . well this." He waves his free arm around as he looks upon the burned scar done by the Cerro Grande and Las Conchas fires.

Yeah, I know.

Then I turn around and begin heading back to the same ski lift until . . .

"I'm sorry about that ski lodge. In the middle of the battle last night, a few of my men were luring in some of those giants back inside and as soon as it got close to the kitchen, my men had to blow it up to dispose them."

I turn my head back to him. "Thanks, but I don't give a shit. We're about to destroy Los Alamos, so we're going to lose a lot of buildings." Then I continue walking up the spine. "You should've seen what we did to Silverton before y'all showed up."

Descending down the ski lift, I look toward my left to the little valley where Camp May is located and almost right in the center is the workshop. It looks like the one back in Sparta, yet a little bit bigger and as I zoom in with my glasses, it does seem a lot busier, not just by the smoke billowing out of the stacks but with the amount of people inside. They're Wolfinoids, not humans. When I reach the bottom, I quickly step off and head to the camp. You know I find it a little bit funny now that Camp May is nestled in our own camp, totally covering the entire area. It looks and feels like we have our own little town that perhaps might be invaded and destroyed by the enemy anytime soon. On my walk toward that camp, I notice other people walking in the same direction while a few are relaxing in the tree line with their comrades as they show off their new weapons. My curiosity begins to rise, so I begin jogging to finally see what type of weapons are being developed.

Finally arriving, I slow down back to a walk, taking in the scenery. There's no doubt that this workshop is bigger than the one I used back in Sparta; it has more machinery to develop such weapons. In detail, yes, there are smelters for making staffs along with a machinery that can create flamethrowers, crystal projectile firearms, and so many others that I can't explain because my mind is on severe overload by the sheer wonder of what I see before me. Getting closer, there is a drafting room but much smaller, possibly to accommodate the manufacturing and the sorcery room; on positive note, the entire place is in full swing.

I enter the drafting room and on the wall opposite me, there seems to be an option board with different designs. To put it this way, it's almost like the option board in Party City stores when it's Halloween and they have all different types of costumes to choose from, however with this board, they are weapons. Standing right in front of it with my arms crossed, I analyze my options; looking about this entire workshop, these are the only questions that run through my canine mind.

How in the hell did Avast's men carry all of this? Especially with those smelters? There's absolutely no way for those things to collapse or even be taken apart, then easily reassembled."

Nonetheless, my mind plays back that one particular evening in Silverton where I met Hays and Avast with his men; and his men were carrying those cases.

It is so unless some of the supplies to construct this facility were stored underneath the devices in those cases.

I look around the workshop once more and shake my head slightly in agreement at the thought and I turn my attention back to the board.

"Damn, so many options. What to build? What to build?"

Letting my Wolfinoid eyes browse the board for a few moments, they soon settle onto a peculiar weapon that seems so similar to a weapon from a different era in this planet. I retrieve the identification number and hand it to one of the men that operates the workshop. He immediately hands out the mold for it. With the mold in my hands, I begin to work on my new weapons.

I hope and pray that all of us are ready to finish this problem once and for all.

That thought runs through my head as I set foot into the sorcery room, take a seat at one of the tables, and raise that small blade to cut my skin so that a small pool of my blood can collect in the small bowl in front of me.

Date: July 13, 2015
Time: 9:00 PM

"Is everything ready?" I ask that question as I step up in front of the screen inside the black tent, folding my hands behind my back.

"Yes, everything is," says Trent in an affirming tone as he, too, looks upon the screen.

"Nightrunner brothers, are those suits ready?"

"Yes, they are, my lord," Maddox answers.

"Ocean, Drex, Rows, Noon, and Avast, are your men and women ready?"

"We are waiting on your orders, King Borin."

I'll take that as a yes.

"Greenwood, is our military ready?"

"Just like Avast said, we are waiting on your orders, King Borin."

Alright, this is the final push.

I analyze each sector assigned to each one of us. I read the battle plans over again. "Ocean and Drex, you will take your battalion to Bandelier to liberate the tech labs. Approaching town, traveling along the 501, Trent, Sean, and Zakia, you will lead your battalion into that region with the same tactic. Hays and Damon, you are staying here on the ski hill with hundred men and women keeping it under guard while you coordinate our attacks to our communication glasses. Finally, in the heart of LANL on the South Mesa, Maddox, Soren, Avast and his squad, and I will strike and liberate the primary region. Hopefully, when all of the tech labs and other structures are cleared, we move onto Los Alamos itself to finish the job. Are we clear?"

They all say "yes" in unison. I look about the room one more time. Their expressions assure me that they are ready to fight to the death. I raise my hood on my radiation suit, then I bring up the SCBA mask, latching it into place to the back side of the hood, thus activating the air tank. Finally, I take one more deep breath with my eyes closed and I reopen them. "Gentlemen, it's been an honor knowing and serving along with you."

They nod in agreement and we begin departing from the tent. Stepping outside, our assigned battalions cease their small talk and stand at attention. I touch the side of my hood which connects to my communication glasses, activating the mic. "Listen up. From here on out, we will be divided in order to conquer our enemy. From what you have seen and heard, it must be done. This is the most treacherous part of our journey and it's highly probable that some of us will not to be able to return home." Some of the guys hang their heads.

That was a bad choice of words.

"However, *do not let your guard down and doubt set in!* It is time to bring peace to this nation and to our planet! With that being said, it's been an honor traveling and serving along with you. Now, let's move out!"

"Strong words coming from a guy that was a human a couple of months ago," says Maddox while he cocks his head to one side giving out a comforting smile.

Yeah, no kidding.

Right after that, the four of us begin leading our battalion to the heart of LANL fully geared up to embrace the radiation and the highly mutated werewolves that thrive in its facilities.

Drex Wind's P.O.V.

With the battalion that King Will Borin assigned to us that is closely and quietly following Ocean and I, we approach the sector that is called Bandelier National Monument. There is a little cover for us due to the number of dead trees in areas that have been burned by severe wildfires, yet Will's home planet never ceases to amaze me. On the other hand, I do miss our home kingdom that sits high in the mountains where the air is crisp and fresher than the air quality back in the state called Wyoming. We have done our best to regrow the plant life back in that particular National Park called Yellowstone.

My God, the geography of that place was spectacular to see and study.

Dammit, I need to get my mind back onto the real, daunting task at hand. I activate the thermal imagery on my glasses to scan the scenery. They pick up nothing at all. This worries me. I feel like we're going to engage in the same attack that we encountered back in that, oh what was that little human mountain town called again?

"Are you starting to get the feeling that we might get ambushed? Or go through the same event back in that town called Silverton?" Leon asks with a cautious voice as he, too, scans the horizon for any enemy that might be lurking in the darkness.

"Yes, I am. Are you getting anything?"

"Nothing." Then he quietly speaks into the mic, "Men, be ready."

We all grab and some of us activate our staffs. Interestingly, some have created better weapons from that workshop that Avast and his men set up. To me, I think our usual weapon staffs is powerful enough for us. I mean, we've been using them for centuries.

Then, the speakers in our glasses come alive with Hays' voice, "Wind and Ocean, in your region, the enemy has taken refuge in three of the tech labs directly east of you and are down in the two separate canyons off your left and right. The very first tech lab is about two miles away. The second one seems to be a communication center with a large disk on it and it's about five miles away. The third is also located nine miles away and it's in the canyon off to your left. Proceed with caution, especially in the canyons."

"How many are in the tech labs and canyons?" I ask.

"Can't tell," replies Hays.

"Shit." I turn my attention to our battalion. "Alright, the first one hundred men that stands before us, you go to that communication center." They disperse. "The first five hundred and three hundred of you go down the tech lab in the canyon while the other two hundred go into the canyon off to our right. And finally, the remaining four hundred follow us to the first tech lab."

Moving to our destination, a deeper and louder howl erupts through the night and one of our men shouts in our ears.

"Shit, it's another ambush!"

Immediately, our enemy storms at us with lightning speed, faster than before, and begins their attacks on us. Yet, we hold our ground.

Trent Wild's P.O.V.

With our battalion of three thousand, we cautiously descend the mountain side to our designated sector. Finally reaching one of the ledges that overlook our target area, I raise my fist to halt; we all carefully form a signal line and crouch down the dark. We scan every parking lot, every structure. To sum it all up, Zakia, Sean, and I were all shocked. We all see thermos signatures that ranked high in temps, which clearly indicates that our enemies are highly mutated. I sigh in aggravation and due to our "cover" by the trees, we won't be able to flank and surprise our enemy, increasing my sigh.

Man, those two wildfires our king told us really did one hell of a toll on this mountain.

"Well, this isn't going to be easy, mate," Sean states with the same tone like my sigh.

"What should we do?" Zakia asks.

I look at both, then answer, "I'll ask base." I mentally connect my communication glasses to the radio frequency back on the ski hill, "Base, this is Trent. We're at our sector, what should we do? Are there any weak points?"

"Stand by, Trent."

The voice I hear does not sound like Damon's or Hays', "Who's this? Where's Damon and Hays?"

The same voice replies, "Hays is busy talking to Drex and Damon is analyzing the map and waiting to give Maddox and Soren coordinated attacks in the heart of the beast."

"Well," speaks up Zakia. "That makes perfect sense."

She's right and I hang my head. Not having any clue of how we can attack this area is going to be hard.

"Trent, I hate to tell you this, but your only chance to attack is a full frontal one."

Now, what I say isn't into the mic, "You gotta be fucking kidding me!"

I switch channels and look at our battalion. All of them shake their heads and grumble about our only battle tactic. Then, someone taps me on the shoulder; I turn back around and see Sean smiling as he points to some device on his right wrist.

As I'm about to ask, he makes his right hand into a fist and stretches out his arm toward one of the buildings. Both Zakia and I watch in curiosity as a little two-dimensional circle scope pops up and glows a very faint red color. Sean lays his head down on his outstretched arm, allowing his right eye to align with the scope. He makes no normal movements. He slows down his breathing, keeping his body perfectly still, and then he holds his breath. Another second later, a projectile is fired from the device, making no sound and flying toward one of the structures. When it impacts deep into the masonry of one of the buildings, a little electrical wave shoots out quickly, dissipates, and immediately shuts off all the lights in our sector.

"A little firearm that shoots bullets that can cause an EMP. I built it in the shop that Avast and his men built back at the base."

Switching my thermos to night vision, our enemy becomes greatly confused by the sudden power outage and my senses tell me that they put themselves on alert.

"Shall we attack, mate?" Sean asks.

I look at him, then at Zakia, who then nods that she's ready to fight, and I quickly look back at our battalion also eager to attack. I activate my mic.

"Let's move!"

And we charge down the hill.

Will Young's P.O.V.

The closer we get to the heart of LANL, the higher squawks that our personal Geiger-counters make on our radiation suits. The weapons that I created in the shop that Avast and his men setup back in the heart of Camp May are metal cuffs that surround my wrists and on the posterior of the cuffs are compartments where one blade in each one is hidden, except I altered the blade material. To shake up your memories, do you guys remember the type of knife Tara used on our special Christmas Eve night? Yes? No? Well, if yes, that's good. If no, then just keep on reading. The type of knife she used had a blade that was ice blue and when it came into contact with my clothes, the blade sliced through them like they were butter and made a quiet sizzling sound. That is the type of blade I recreated. After doing some research, I included it into my weapon. The only difference is that with a twist of my wrists, they expand as they appear out of the cuffs and they collapse as I twist my wrists again. All in all, they are now my primary weapon for intense, close combat.

Anyway, the needles in our Geiger-counters travel high on the analog dials. Our radiation suits do protect us from the harmful toxin in our area, but the foul odors slightly seep in and run across our sensitive noses. With that being said, this makes me question the integrity of the suits.

"Guys, are you sure these things are one-hundred percent sealed?"

"Oh, yeah. They are," answers Soren with confidence.

"What's your plan of attack, King Borin?" Avast asks.

I look about the mesas where the heart of LANL spans out. Multiple buildings with perhaps multiple passageways underground are occupied by lots of enemies mutating themselves and torturing a lot of innocent humans. Since we are the bigger battalion, conquering this area will not be super hard. Still, I'm not completely sure where to start; I look at Maddox; he nods and begins talking into his headset in Wolfinoid tongue to contact the base. His eyes move just a few millimeters left and right. He looks at me slightly concerned and tries again. Soon, he releases a sigh of dissatisfaction. The rest of us look at him in concern.

"We," Maddox starts off, finding it hard to form the other words, "We have no contact with base. It's nothing but fucking static."

Oh, that's just fucking great.

"Then what should we do?" Soren asks.

I look back at the heart of the beast, twist my wrists to unleash my blades which glow as they are fully extended, and with determination on my soul and mind, I spill these words, "This is what we are going to do." I raise my blade on the right arm and start handing out orders, "Avast, you and your men, take care of that area that nearly neighbors Bandelier. I'm pretty sure our battle will collide with Leon's and Drex's battle. Soren and Maddox, you two will lead your party to that sector behind Avast's sector. And I," I look toward the complexes that face the Omega Bridge and the rest of Los Alamos and continue, "will take this sector where the complexes nearly neighbors Omega Canyon."

I look at my guys to make sure they understand their designated targets. They do with determination on their faces.

"Alright, let's move out."

With that said, our very large battalion splits up into three major groups like red ants, scattering in an organized way and running toward different locations to destroy the enemy.

Drex's P.O.V.

"They're beginning to surround us!" shouts one soldier.

"No, they're fucking not!" another soldier replies to the other.

Right after that, an explosion goes off at the facility that is used for hazardous fire training. Equipment in all sorts and sizes used by humans fly in every direction, yet I am slowly making progress with my smaller battalion to Tech Lab 33, the one with the very large satellite dish on it. Ocean is with his battalion, making their way down the canyon to the tech lab that lays there; the other is working their way into the national park. Still, we *all* begin to struggle slowly. The mutated werewolves are the same like the ones we've encountered. However, others seem to be faster and have the ability to jump from one place to the next through time and space. Just those guys, Jesus, they're hard to keep track.

"Leon, what's your position?" I hastily asked into the mic.

The second after I ask, a jumper appears right in front of me and knocks me to the ground; as it leaps on top of me, I deflect it with my staff, knocking it to one side, and then I thrust it into its skull. I look around to what is now becoming an utter chaos. Overall, I can't stand in one place; I must continue on running, dodging, and helping my men and women so that they won't be slaughtered. Another explosion happens from the same facility and mighty wails of pain echo throughout the darkness.

"Yeah! Jump from that fuckers!" a different soldier shouts.

"Soldier, what happened??" I ask.

A different one, a female, answers, "We lured some, I don't know how many, into some sort of a pit, litter it with propane tanks, and lit them up."

Right after she says that, I begin to see our battalion move a little faster to our designated location.

"Drex, I'm sorry it has taken me long to answer, but we are slowly inching to the tech lab in this canyon," answers Leon with some confidence.

"Commander Wind, my battalion is nearing completion of clearing Bandelier," says the soldier who leads that battalion.

"How far are you near completion?" I ask.

"About ninety percent."

"Shit," shouts Leon. "We need backup now!"

I'm about to give an order to the soldier in charge of his battalion to hand some reinforcements to Leon, but he cuts me off and reassures me that he's on it. In mere moments, I see a small pack of them coming up from Bandelier, sprinting behind us, and moving down into the next canyon to aid Leon and his battalion. For a moment, I stop fighting and look straight ahead to see our target and according to my glasses, we're just a few miles away.

Trent's P.O.V.

"Why the fuck did King fucking Terrain had to transport the remaining of our enemy by a fucking spaceship to some goddamn planet that doesn't fucking exists?" Sean shouts loud and clear.

He and I, side by side, battle our way through a structure that's used for coordinating rescue operations for natural and domestic disasters in this town, which appears that it completely failed because as we clear room after room, hallway after hallway, we find slaughtered human remains.

"I don't know! Maybe after we fucking survive this, you can ask him!" The second I say that to Sean, I throw a flash grenade into one of the rooms. It explodes, releasing a bright source of light that immediately vaporizes the enemy within.

For an update, we just cleared out the first floor, not by ourselves, and the stairwells that lead to the second floor. The power outage that Sean created from his nifty device really did give us the upper hand to surprise attack our enemy. So far, as our second largest battalion moves onward, it's been slightly smooth sailing. For some strange reason, the majority of werewolves that occupy this area are normal, which all three of us find good yet concerned with the dangers that Leon, Drex, Avast, Soren, Maddox, and Will are facing on their battle grounds.

"Are you boys nearly done clearing out that building?" Zakia shouts in our communicators with some struggle in her voice.

"Almost!!" we reply in unison.

By that time, we push a group into a large gathering room, send a shockwave through our staffs, and that sends them flying through the windows and wall. I quickly look at the small map on my glasses and sure enough, there are still plenty of enemies to fight and destroy. We leave the room and viscously charge our way through the other halls to hunt down our enemy. During this time, we all decided not to communicate back to base camp because there are literally too many werewolves to take off our eyes from in order to construct some sort of strategic plan and win this battle efficiently. Hays continues to give us a heads up from where the enemy is approaching.

"I hope Soren, Maddox, Avast, and Will are having the easiest time like we are experiencing," Sean says.

I reply, "I highly as hell doubt that."

We round a corner and continue obliterating our pain-in-the-ass enemy.

Will's P.O.V.

Sprinting down a corridor at full speed between some buildings with the group of men and women following me, we waste no time slashing, annihilating, and vaporizing our enemy that comes charging at us. From the moment we split up and went our ways to clear out the heart of LANL, we lost radio contact with one another as well as with the base camp. This worries me. Still, my charging raid is working perfectly, especially for me, because the type of materials that I used to fabricate and conjure the blades of my secondary weapon slices through every one of them like butter.

Nearing the end of the corridor is a building that's perfectly adjacent from us and the distance between it and us gets shorter during our sprinting, raiding charge. Approaching the walls of this structure, we all slam our backs against it. We all snap our heads left, right, and left again; it shows us that the area we're in is clear for now. I snap my head upward to analyze the structure that's right against us and from what I can see, it's a large warehouse with one level. At the top is a long and narrow row of windows that possibly circulate the four walls. Towering above it are several stacks that let out plumes of thick smoke and the screams and wails of pain that can easily penetrate through its thin, metal sheet walls.

"We still clear?" I ask my men and women that stand on my left and right sides.

"Yes, we are," replies a female that stands right beside me on my left.

I turn my head to the only door at my right and by the looks of it, it seems to be constructed out of metal, perhaps to keep a fire within, and has a basic door knob. I slide in front of it and bash the bottom of my left foot into the door near the knob, and the door swings wide open in a flash. My smaller battalion moves in fast; as the last one enters, I follow. Within the moment I enter, we are greeted by a catwalk that surrounds a pit equally one level below us and spans the entire size of the structure. In the center of this pit are dozens of cylinder-sized tanks that are mainly fabricated out of glass with a metal top, perhaps the area to enter and exit the tanks, and a metal base to stabilize them. The majority of their height is made of glass and in them is some sort of liquid with werewolves that have multiple hoses connected to their legs, feet, arms, hands, chest, and head; the other ends of the hoses are connected to the top of the tank with a bigger hose that curves over, travels down, and connects to some sort of a box that has windows to peer in. Within that box are multiple test tubes with various weird colors in them. The top of the test tubes are smaller hoses that separate from the main hose line. Looking back at the tank, those exact colors travel through the main hose, down through the separate hoses, and into the werewolves.

Near the tanks are tables that have all sorts of equipment used for chemistry, physics, and biology. On the tables are beakers that have the same, exact colors that lay within the boxes, while others are being made. Generating all of the power to operate the lights and equipment are gas-powered generators surrounding the bases of the smoke stacks that rise up and push through the ceiling of this facility. However, our attention, mine specifically, is brought to the cries and wails of pain coming from the humans that lay on tables on the opposite side of the pit. Their cries of pain and agony prove that they are journeying through the painful experience of being turned into a werewolf. This makes me feel terrible because I am witnessing my former kind go through from what I went through months ago and seeing the transformation is . . . horrifying to see.

I can't believe Tara had to see this. My God, it looks so horrific.

"This must be one of the many mutation houses," states one of the soldiers next to me.

"We gotta stop this and blow this place up to kingdom come," states another.

"They're both right." While saying that thought, I wrap my fingers tightly around the railing on the catwalk that we stand upon.

"Let's get this done and over with."

After saying that into the mic, we descend the steps. A few stands by the door, guarding it just in case our presence is discovered. Reaching the floor of the pit, the others spread out and start placing explosives at the base of the tanks, on the generators, on the boxes that hold the mutating chemicals, and on the tables. I walk over to the humans, knowing that there is absolutely no way of halting or reversing the transformation. Approaching one of the beds, I look down at one; it's a young female and she shows distress, but no physical changes have come upon her. Within a moment, she looks at me with signs of help to stop the transformation.

"Please, help . . . me. Help . . . us. Take . . . this . . . pain . . . away."

From hearing that message, I act like I didn't understand her and begin raising one of my wrist blades slowly above her.

"Please, stop. What are ya doing?" Tears begin to form around her eyes.

I'm sorry. I have to do this. It's the only way.

As my arm gets higher, more tears stream down her cheeks and she begins to panic.

"No!"

Her shriek falters as I release the tension in my arm that brings down the blade and slices her head off. The head rolls away from the table for a moment and I look to see my comrades doing the same thing to the other humans.

"All explosives are ready to go, sir," another soldier speaks to me proudly across the pit from the chemistry tables.

I close my eyes, breathing in and out my nose, trying to forget the action I've just done. Then I reopen them and look around the room. "Alright, clear out, and blow this shit up."

We all go back up the stairs, fast, and burst through the same door while running away from the building we just entered and found out what it's main purpose was. During the process, some of my comrades pull out the detonators and push the little red button that sets off the explosives. In mere microseconds, the building is engulfed in a huge column of fire and smoke.

Date: July 14, 2015
Time: 12:30 PM
Drex's P.O.V.

Leon and I stand outside at Tech Lab 33 feeling a total victory of liberating it. During the fight, we discovered that our enemy has been using it to block our communications to our base camp and was starting to block us from hearing each other. Of course, this made us wonder if Sean, Trent, Zakia, Will, the Nightrunner brothers, Avast and his men were experiencing the same problems. It surprised us that our enemy was trying to make contact to some other planets that we have knowledge of, but I have nothing to worry about because after discovering and being surprised with this, we immediately put a stop to it.

For an update, the other tech lab in the canyon has been liberated and dismantled. The hazardous training facility which you all have read before and the National Park has also been cleared. After being granted all this, victory does come with a price. Both Leon and I don't know how many soldiers we have lost exactly, but for what we know, it's in the mid-hundreds.

"So, what should we do now?" Leon asks.

What kind of stupid question is that?

"Simple, we establish patrols at these two tech labs, a few down in Bandelier, and send the rest to aid the other guys," I answer sternly.

He smirks. "I was being facetious."

I smack my forehead hard and drag my hand down my face in absolute annoyance. I look around to see if any of our surviving comrades, the ones that can still fully move around with no problems, are paying any attention to us. None of them are listening. Then, I grab Leon's arm and tow him toward the large, satellite dish; arriving there, I look around once more. The area remains clear and I smack him across the face.

"What was that for?" he asks.

I growl, "It was for that stupid, facetious question and how you absolutely forgot what happened back in a city on our home planet that very night."

While he's rubbing his face, his eyes widen. "Oh."

"Yeah," I reply, quickly nodding my head. "To tell you the truth, the situation that our king created seems a little relevant to what is happening on this planet."

"What do you mean?"

"Prior to the months that lead up to this, I was doing some research on the American Government and the issue it was dealing with is in the Middle East. During my research, I was shocked to find that a group of people within the U.S. Government created a conflict of a radical group in that region in order to keep the income of war up and running to its maximum capacity. In our situation, that is what our king has done. He loaded the surviving werewolves into that spacecraft and sent it off to a planet that really *does not exist*! Now, here we are, losing more soldiers on the battlefields to a conflict that we actually created along with numerous humans being lost as well."

Leon sighs in agreement, feeling terrible to the hell we brought upon this semi-peaceful planet due to the actions that our stupid, ass king has done.

"How soon do you think Will and Tara Borin will figure this out?"

I place my hands on my hips and look toward the mountains in the east. "Probably soon, once we get back to Kaladria."

"Hey," Sean shouts in our earbuds. "Can we get reinforcements over here or what?"

"Reinforcements are on their way," answers Leon.

After hearing that request, I give out the command to the majority of our battalion to head toward the battlefield where Sean, Trent, and Zakia are still fighting.

Trent's P.O.V.

"Are we starting to get closer to the heart of LANL or not?" I shout into my mic struggling to keep up with my fighting skills.

"Probably," Sean replies. I don't know where he is. "I just been told by Leon that reinforcements are on their way!"

"Well, I hope they come here soon!" Zakia replies in the same tone.

Okay, so here's our current situation. After Sean knocked out the power to all of the buildings in our area, it surely gave us the upper hand; we have successfully cleared out and demolished almost every building. So, at this moment, we are and have been pushing toward those primary facilities. Still, we keep on eliminating them.

Out of nowhere, I am knocked to the ground and I get back on my feet. I see it's Sean as he faces some werewolves that might've thrown him and he collided onto me. He glares at them as they do the same; when they are about to attack, he raises his left wrist that has another contraption on it. In seconds, a little turret gun pops up above his knuckles and begins shooting thousands upon thousands of rounds into them, and he doesn't stop there. He presses his back up against mine and we spin a three-sixty; the little turret gun continues shooting tiny rounds at every werewolf. Suddenly, the little gun stops and collapses back into the wristband. I'm about to ask Sean, but he cuts me off.

"Just give it a moment, mate."

I look around the enemy that surrounds us as they check themselves over what kind of material they were hit with. Once they were done checking themselves, they look back at us and get back into their attack positions. This begins to worry me.

"One more moment," Sean answers a little on edge.

A few near us take their first steps, but something stops them. Their fur begins to stand up; little lightning bolts appear around them, and boom! They explode and a shock wave spreads from the explosions and begins to evaporate the ones around them. The shock wave itself travels for several yards and stops, creating a gigantic, perfectly clear, clean circle around us. I look at him with a smile.

"That was badass."

Sean smiles back, shrugging one shoulder. "Well, I just can't let our king and friend have all the fun and power with electricity."

"This is Robin Hood from the Leon's and Drex's battalion coming in fast and joining you guys in the fight."

We both look to the southwest and see the battalion charging right at us, aiding in our fight.

"Well, it's about damn time!" Zakia shouts with relief.

Sean and I look back at each other, smile, grab our staffs from our holsters, and charge east to keep on pushing the enemy back to the heart of LANL.

Will's P.O.V.

After receiving the news that Leon's and Drex's battalion have captured and liberated their area which includes Tech Lab 33, having communications back online is an absolute blessing. The first voice that I hear is Hays shouting to the Nightrunner brothers.

"You've got enemies coming from the southeast!"

"Well, we know that, but we don't fucking see any of them!" shouts Soren.

"Where are you?" I ask.

"In some building that curves, has blue windows, and has several stories high!" Maddox shouts.

I look to the west and I know exactly which building they are talking about. I don't know its primary purpose, but you can see almost anywhere in Los Alamos. From where my separate, little battalion is, I check where Avast and his men are at. Sure enough, he and his special forces heard the strain of Maddox's voice and have begun moving to his position.

Before we take off, I look around our area. So far, we've blew up several mutating factories and terminated countless humans that were in the middle of their transformation. And man has that been so fucking hard on me.

I really want this battle to be over with already.

I look at one of my comrades. "What's our current situation?"

One of the soldiers analyzes their glasses, looking at the GPS screen for a few moments, and answers, "Our zone is clear. We have the opportunity to move onto Maddox's and Soren's position."

I, too, look at the GPS on my glasses and I see that the Nightrunners' battalion has the building completely covered, perhaps from the top to the bottom. From the north is Avast with his crew getting closer.

"Alright, let's move!"

In minutes, we arrive and witness the last men and women from Avast's crew enter the building. We follow by jumping over the broken pieces of glass and other structure material that litters the floor. The area that we just entered turns out to be the lobby and in the center is a large circular desk. I'm not gonna go into the exact details like I have done before because mainly, we are at war. Anyway, both brothers are there looking and acting very anxious and concerned.

Looking around, it seems that Avast had recently ordered his battalion to help the brothers' battalion keep the building under surveillance and control. I do the same and my battalion spreads out like fireflies. I walk to the desk were Maddox and Soren stand in the center and Avast is simply leaning against the desk with some ease.

"What's the latest?" I ask.

Avast looks at the brothers, hoping that they could start this little meeting. They show that they can't. He sighs and looks at me. "During the night and up to this time, we pretty much have cleared all sectors at ground level, but we've lost numbers as well."

I roll my eyes, *That's just bloody great.*

"But we don't know where or how many more of our enemies there are. I mean, the GPS is not making any sense," Maddox jumps in.

"I've contacted Damon and he doesn't have a clue either," Soren adds.

I ponder and look at the GPS. There are loads of red dots that are accumulating, almost marching in a very straight narrow line. Looking at the color of the dots, they seem to be slightly dimmer than the original that indicate what Sean, Trent, and Zakia are still battling. Looking at the lines of these fainter red dots, they form sharp angles and adjacent lines. And then it hits me.

Oh, shit.

My reaction gets their attention. "What is it, Will?" Maddox asks.

I throw my hands on top of my head. "The tunnels. I completely forgot about the tunnels!"

I turn my eyes toward them. "We gotta get down the fucking basement of this goddamn building, find any blocked off passageways to the secret tunnels, and destroy them!!!!"

"No wonder we couldn't understand the GPS. Those assholes are underground!" shouts Maddox.

All four of us move out, ordering into our mics our battalions to join us as we begin to search for any sign that indicates where the basement is located. Suddenly, there's a burst of explosions sounding like the time machine from *Back to the Future* in our reality all around us. The minor shockwaves knock everybody off their feet, just here on the main floor.

We all twist our heads around to see this brand-new chaos and it turns out to be more werewolves, the mutated ones. This time, they're different.

"What the hell are these things?" I ask, still on an open mic.

"What are you dealing with?" Leon asks.

"These types of werewolves just came out of nowhere! Like they warped from some other dimension."

"Crap. You're dealing with jumpers."

After hearing that message, one appears right out of the air and tries to claw at me. I counteract by slicing its skin with the right blade, letting his stomach and intestines slowly fall out. I roll over, pushing myself back on my feet and looking around. The only thing that stands out straight like a completely huge ass sore is the utter confusion in the chaos that just occurred. Everybody from our smaller battalions is thrown off guard, but we get right back on it as they begin their defenses and offenses.

"The best way," Leon chimes in, "is to fight each one in small groups."

I look about the chaos. "Did you guys hear?" I shout into the mic to our battalions.

By the looks of it, they did.

"We gotta get down to the tunnels!" Avast shouts.

I nod in agreement and we all begin fighting our way through. These jumpers, *sigh,* are starting to slow us down. Every time one appears in front of us, right, or left, we try to attack, but they immediately produce some sort of a tunnel with special effects that I can't even describe, pulling them in so they reappear in microseconds somewhere else and thrusted out forward. Luckily, before this spontaneous ambush occurred, some of our comrades were following us and are giving us a great backup that takes the jumpers by surprise.

Pretty soon, I find the signs that say "Basement Level" with an arrow in it and the passageways start to get narrow, giving us the upper hand of eliminating the jumpers. In time, we find the stairway that leads down to the basement level while our backup destroys the last one. The drawback of navigating these narrow passageways is that we're nearly seven feet high and we're constantly ducking from the lights and exposed pipes. During our descent in the stairway, some of us accidently hit our heads on those things. In the end, we find one of the doorways which turns out to be locked. Again, I kick the thing wide open and we swarm into the basement. The lights are off, so we activate our night vision.

"Alright, guys," I begin to say truly out loud. "Look for any other doors that lead farther down and after that, look for any barricades that could be blocking any entrances to the original tunnels."

We break and begin searching.

"Hey," Maddox says after several minutes into the search, "I think I found one."

We all move to his direction; getting there, he immediately steps off to one side to let us have a peak. I get my chance to see the door. It has a narrow, long window with wire in it, yet on the other side is a stairway that travels down several more feet, stops, and turns directly to the left and goes down deeper. The drawback of this door is that it opens outward, to us, not inward like the last one. When I jiggle the knob, it's firmly locked. Examining the frame of the door, I find a 1 to 0 keypad and since there's no electricity flowing through the wires to give the lights power, there's no way of operating the keypad. Unless . . .

I can pull the same stunt that I did on the ski hill but on a much smaller scale and perhaps crack the code it hides.

"You guys should give me some space. I don't wanna accidentally electric-shock anyone."

They all back away by ten yards while keeping watch just in case. I kneel on my left knee, firmly holding my staff in my left hand and spreading out my fingers gently on my right yet leaving an inch of air between my fingertips and the keypad. Igniting the power in my staff, commencing it to form electricity, blue little arcs appear around the rod and then appear in between my fingers. Tilting my head slightly sideways, the arcs transform into bolts and start licking the pad. I close my eyes and I can see a four-digit box behind my eyelids and the numbers zip by to find the code. Slowly increasing the strength of the lightning bolts, one number stops. Then the second. Soon, the third. And a later on, the fourth. I reopen my eyes to see only the little red light illuminated and immediately, I punch in the code.

"5784."

When the green light comes on, a buzzing noise sounds off for a second or two while some dead bolts recoil from the door. I look back at my comrades as they look back with eagerness.

"Let's do this."

I turn my attention back to the door and turn the knob. Once I pull open the door, a huge wave of our enemy's scent comes right at us. We gag a little while. At the same time, our GM Counters go off the charts. I look back at our battalion and they show that they are ready to fight in extremely tight quarters.

"Vamonos," I say in a confident tone while tilting my head toward the stairs.

Instantly, we begin our descent farther into the ground with great caution knowing that some of us . . . might not make it out alive.

Date: July 15, 2015
Time: 10:00 PM
Trent's P.O.V.

"Warning! Warning! Nuclear reactor in critical condition! All professional personnel must evacuate immediately! Warning! Warning!"

"Let's go, Sean! This place is gonna blow!" I shout over my shoulder, trying to be louder than the intercom voice along with its alarms sounding off as we both run along the catwalk near the reactor that's becoming more unstable by the second.

"I'm right behind ya, mate!"

Every pipe is bursting at its seams, releasing a lot of hot steam and other liquids while the glass that cover the analog measuring dials for their pressure shatter into a million, microscopic pieces, making the both of us shield our faces from the debris. The only good thing is that Zakia isn't with us because under some circumstances with our battalion following us, we tracked down a small pack of normal werewolves as they were retreating to this facility that Sean and I are now escaping from.

Here's what happened a few hours ago. During the chase, we devised a plan to ambush them when they were heading to certain buildings. Anyway, all three of us agreed that Zakia should lead the ambush party and right off the bat, she and her own battalion breaks off, thereby creating a massive arc and a thick fog that I believe Will has told you at the beginning of this book and using the buildings as part for her cover. In minutes, the plan was in full effect and the werewolves didn't even notice the break off. When more minutes went by, I believe Zakia conjured the fog to move far ahead of her and surround the building. Sean and I look at each for a moment and smiled. The enemy did slow down for a bit but kept on running. I look back at our men who also understood the idea as they, too, were ready for the ambush. The closer we got to the building, the thicker the fog became. Yet our enemy was beginning to pick up Zakia's and her comrades' scents. They ran into the fog, the ambush was immediately put into effect, and the enemy howled in surprised horror and again when we entered to finish them off. As the fog was thinning out, we pretty much eliminated the majority of them, except for perhaps ten werewolves that were able to dodge the ambush and successful in retreating to the building.

After discovering that, more reports came through our earbuds that backup is still needed at the heart of LANL, especially in other buildings where the other battalions have found stairways leading to deep underground secret tunnels because what was left of our enemy at that time were down there. So, we told Zakia that she should lead the entire battalion to help the other guys. She did protest, but we stopped her and said that it's only ten werewolves and we can handle it. Zakia rolls her eyes, took off, and we, just Sean and I, entered this building following their scent. During the searching, we discovered that this facility housed a nuclear reactor, putting us on high defense. We spin around slowly, look up and down, side to side, and let our ears constantly do one-eighties.

Minutes passed and the scents left by those ten led us to and past the actual reactor and for some strange reason, down into a room farther in the back of the facility. Once we got into this room, there was skirmish that made us instantly turn around and look at the door where we just came through. We readied our attack positions by winding up the tension in our legs and tightening our hands on our staffs. A second later, there was an explosion that sounded off the warning lights, sirens, and intercom. A few more followed seconds after the first one, creating the feeling that the entire building had shifted. Pretty soon, the place began to crumble. And here we are.

At this moment, we're just beginning our ascent to the third flight of stairs, having a hard time with all sorts of debris flying all over the place. This includes metal plates along with bolts and screws flying off from the ceiling and walls.

"Duck!" Sean yells.

At the moment, I turn around to see him crouching and placing his hands over his head while a piece of metal flies over him and pounds me in the face, knocking up the stairs.

"Trent! Trent! Trent, mate! Can you hear me?"

I shake off the dizziness and only reply with some groans.

"C'mon, mate! We gotta get out of here! Like right fucking now!"

Another explosion happens, causing bigger pieces of metal to take out the supporting poles that hold up the first two flights of stairs. We both panic and use it to fuel our adrenaline, which easily responds by making our legs and arms scramble up the remaining stairs.

"I take that as fucking ambush!" Sean shouts again.

"I don't know and I don't give a fuck! Let's focus on getting the fucking hell outta here!"

In a flash, the remaining polls that are supporting the steps we're still climbing at start to groan due to the amount of heat now building up, making it hard for us to see and breathe. Without delay, we keep on sprinting up.

What feels like an eternity, we finally reach the top and start sprinting across the final catwalk. Again, the metal beneath us groans more like it can't handle the weight of two, male Wolfinoids. While looking forward, I am beginning to see daylight through the door where we came through from the beginning. My hopes begin to rise until I hear a scream and the sound of collapsing metal. I stop instantly and look behind me only to see Sean holding onto the catwalk with the rest of his body dangling above the fire below. I throw my staff to the side and begin to aid my comrade. I grab one of his hands and begin pulling him up. Sean uses his other arm to hoist his body up from the flaming death. Again, the heat from the flames continue to sting my eyes and the gases in the air make it real hard for me to breathe. Overall, I ignore those and keep on pulling my friend up. When half his body is on the catwalk, one of the pipes above us burst, releasing hot water right into my face and making me lose my grip. That incident puts Sean back to his original problem.

When all of the hot water is out of my eyes and face, I look back at Sean and his eyes show that there's nothing more I can do.

"Get outta here, mate!"

"No! I'm not leaving you!"

Then, those same pipes above us begin to break and are nearly collapsing on top of us. He looks up at them and then back at me.

"You need to get out of *here*!"

"I'm not leaving you behind, Sean!" I say while I attempt to grab him, but he uses his might to grab me and pull me in a little closer.

"It's alright, mate. I'll see you on the other side." He then winks and releases me.

The breakage of the pipes brings me back to reality and I immediately back away from them. Shortly after, they finally collapse right onto Sean, letting him fall into the fire below that was waiting for him.

"Fuck," I look around at the chaos, "Fuck, fuck, fuck, fuck, fuck, fuck!"

I scramble onto my feet, face the door, and begin sprinting out at full speed while grabbing my staff with ease. Finally reaching outside, I don't stop; I keep on sprinting to the east.

"Attention everyone!" the voice of Will come to life in my ear. "I want everybody to clear out wherever you are, get your asses across the bridge, and eliminate whatever type of werewolf that lurks in town, *now*!"

I acknowledge the order and head to the bridge.

Will's P.O.V.

After I gave the order to evacuate the heart of LANL and search for any other type of werewolf that lurks in town, I stand here right at the foot of Omega Bridge, watching the swarm of what is left of our military party from both Sparta and Troy. My radiation suit, along with many others during the fights in the secret tunnels, got torn. So, I finished the job by ripping the rest of it off during the fights. This led to have my normal clothes torn up, but I don't give a shit. I do give a shit that every Wolfinoid makes it across this bridge.

"Avast, have you and your crew set up those towers that activate those shields?"

"We're working on that right now."

I decide to climb on top of the railing to get a good vantage point, close up, so I can make sure I ain't missing anybody, including my top officials from Sparta and Troy. Amongst the crowd, I see Leon, Drex, Zakia, both Nightrunner brothers, and Trent, but . . .

"Where's Sean?"

Just as they begin to set foot on the bridge, they all come toward me and I dismount the railing.

"Repot?" I ask in curiosity.

"The two tech labs," Drex begins, "and the national park is successfully cleared out."

I look at Zakia and Trent. Zakia looks proud from what happened, but Trent shows the opposite and he's looking down at the pavement.

"Our sector along the 501 was successful. Any other werewolves would've retreated toward your position, but since you had the largest battalion, I'm pretty sure you handled it well."

I look at Trent to hear his side of the story, but he remains the same, which makes me worry a bit.

"Our sector," Soren begins, "is mostly cleared out. Hopefully, Avast and his men and women can set up those shields up faster to contain them within the exploding buildings."

"Good." I still look at Trent. "Trent? What happened? Where's Sean?"

He lets out a heavy sigh and looks up at me with sad eyes. "Sean is dead. There was a secondary ambush by a group of ten in an actual nuclear reactor building causing the machinery to explode." Then he looks at the other guys while still explaining, "We were almost out until the final catwalk we were on collapsed, almost taking him down. I tried to help and we were almost successful until I got sprayed with hot water so I lose my hold on him and then those same pipes were beginning to break. I tried to pull him up again, but he grabbed me and said, "It's alright. I'll see you on the other side." Right after that, the pipes break, making me duck out of the way and knocking Sean into the fire below us."

The other four gasp in horror at the news. For me, I am totally shocked and horrified that the first guard of Sparta I interacted with is now dead and gone.

Fuck.

"Shield towers are set and ready to go!" says Avast with pride. "We're coming to the bridge right now! Oh crap, there's some werewolves following us!"

I instantly snap my head to the smoldering buildings that stand in the heart of LANL; through the visible heat wave coming from the fires that are burning them, I can see Avast and his crew approaching fast along with some werewolves. The news Trent gave us made me extremely pissed off. I lost a very good Wolfinoid who journeyed with us from Sparta to Los Alamos.

"Soren and Maddox," I speak. They cease their talks with Trent and look at me. "Plant detonators, if you can, on the critical beams that are holding up this bridge."

They look at me in some confusion and I slightly growl while yelling, *"Now!"*

They get right to it and begin descending the cliff that touches the heavy support beams for the bridge.

Next, I look at Leon and Drex. "You two do the same, but," I point directly at the cliff that neighbors the West Road and continue, "place detonators within the earth."

They understood that order and head toward West Road. I look back at Avast and his crew. They are about thirty yards away from the bridge and immediately, Avast holds up some kind of remote, presses down a button, and the towers, wherever they are, activate the shields producing liquid like bubbles that rises several hundred feet into the air. In seconds, they complete surrounding multiple domes that are both connected and separate. In the end, they work their magic by keeping in the fires and the smoke. Now, to take care of their new "friends," I calmly walk past Trent and quietly send out an order on the mic that Avast and his crew should immediately drop to the ground. They do so and I rip out my staff, swing it hard from left to right, and release a bright blue blade of light on fire. It reaches werewolves that are in pursuit and slices off their heads.

"C'mon, everybody cross the bridge now." I grab Trent's shirt and start towing him while running.

Reaching the other end, I look at Avast. "Is there anybody who didn't cross?"

"No," he answers, "I think everybody made it across. Why?"

I run down Diamond Drive toward Los Alamos Medical Center (LAMC) and getting closer, I leap upon the lowest roof with all my might and repeat this process a couple more times until I reach the tip-top roof of the hospital. From here, I am given an excellent vantage point of the burning of LANL and all of Los Alamos that lays in ruins. I slightly outstretch my arm and then slowly open my right hand around my staff; when my fingers get a few centimeters away, my staff begins to hover just a few inches above the roof and I cross my arms in front of my chest, waiting for the fireworks to show the finale.

"Detonators are ready," Drex says.

I look over at the cliff that goes high as West Road journeys down into Omega Canyon when I see both Leon and Drex put a fair amount of distance between them and the blast site. Seconds after, both the Nightrunner brothers appear from below the bridge and do the same thing.

"Detonators are ready," Maddox says.

I smile at both accomplishments.

"Blow up the cliff first."

Right after I said that, a huge cloud of dirt and rock goes flying into the air and crashes down the road, completely making the road impassable almost like the 550 that connects Durango and Silverton. When dust cloud from that explosion dissipates in the breeze, I look back at Omega Bridge. Having all of my attention turned onto the bridge, the tune of a piano from the song called "Lustrous" by Parking Lincoln begins to play in my head.

"Blow up the bridge."

Another series of explosions, much bigger, louder, and destructible, occur underneath the road that travels on it. In seconds, when the sound of detonators has gone off, they are followed by the sound of metal twisting, groaning, and breaking apart along with the crumbling of concrete and asphalt. This leads to a chain reaction, making more buildings within the shields explode in great balls of fire and smoke, sending every type of debris everywhere in its blast zone. From here on out, the battle of LANL concludes.

CHAPTER FORTY-NINE

Battle of Los Alamos High School
Time: Somewhere Around Noon

THE LAST BITS OF flame and smoke arises from what used to be Omega Bridge against the radioactive shields that are operating flawlessly to keep the burning, heavily radioactive buildings contained. I continue to stand here on the roof of LAMC feeling a little bit proud. My communicator glasses buzz with reports that some of our men and women from Sparta and Troy are actually discovering surviving werewolves mainly in the downtown area but are eliminating them in an instant. After such hell we have gone through, we're pretty much thriving on the ultimate high of searching and destroying.

Looking at the destruction of both parties that has taken place in a very short period, the same song continues to play in my head, comforting me and making me feel proud. However, I don't think I should feel the pride of victory for half of Los Alamos, majority of LANL, and its facilities are engulfed in flames and smoke; many human lives are lost as most of them in the middle of transformations had to be terminated. On top of that, we lost a large number of our military men and women who did their fucking best to liberate and shut down that facility.

Sigh. Poor Sean. I'm really going to miss you, man.

Putting my hands in my ripped, torn jeans, I turn around to look at Diamond Drive. My eyes slowly gaze upon the four-lane road and they instantly stop and zero in on a small pack of nearly seven werewolves sprinting up the road, and within a minute, they cross the front lawn of the high school, disappearing behind the main building called A Wing.

"Not on my fucking watch."

I grab my staff that is still hovering in mid-air, holster it into the sleeve on my back, and begin descending from the top roof of LAMC, jumping and landing so smoothly like an assassin. Upon landing on the parking lot, I immediately begin sprinting toward LAHS.

Within a minute, I reach the front lawn, hardly out of breath. I sniff the air and the same foul odor wisps across my nostrils. I inhale it deeply while closing my eyes, clenching my fists, and then reopening my eyes to begin following the trail. Proceeding forward with caution, I step onto the front lawn while unleashing the blades of my secondary weapons that are still strapped firmly to my wrists. Following the scent of my enemies, I step lightly toward the covered outdoor walkway and walk to the light, steep sidewalk that leads the high schoolers from Griffith Gym, to the Cardio Room and Auxiliary Gym, to the weight room, the Theatre Room, then to a room that safely contains the kids that are highly mentally or physically disabled and challenged along with speech impairments. There were a lot of other bullshit that the Special Ed system up here was trying to lay upon me during my I.E.P.s here.

"Fuckers. They're all fuckers."

Right after that is my "favorite" former teacher's room: Chase Tiger. Y'all remember that bitch? Yes? No? If no, let me jog your memories. She's the one who had me taken, tortured, forced to fight to the death where I was supposed to lose, was involved with Marcus Lowsbroth to have Tara killed, and finally, chased down throughout the camp kingdom of Sparta where I banished her ass. Did that help?

I hope it did. Anyway, the trail of the scent leads right into the little room; slowly looking left and then right, it appears that the mental- and self-esteem-destroying prison is vacant. Returning my head outside, I look up at the windows and my eyes zero in on that one particular pane of glass that still has the crack in it. For some reason, I smiled as the memory of that day slightly replays over in my head.

Now, getting back on track, the scent leads through the doors into the adjacent hallway of A Wing that connects to the newer structure. I watch my footing carefully while I step over the million broken pieces of glass sprayed onto the tile floor from the stainless-steel doors and the numerous debris that litter the floor and hang from the ceiling. The hallway is nearly dark and the only natural light from the sun comes through the classroom windows and other doors that look out onto the back courtyard. In the end, it still does its best to illuminate this hallway. The scent pulls me forward, down the hall, yet at the same time I shoot my eyes left, right, and left again to make sure none of those seven werewolves jumps out from any of the classrooms and tries to slaughter me. Moments go by and my heart begins to race, my senses engage, and my pace down this original hallway of A Wing that has been renovated to match the new building is completely slowed down like a snail. Getting closer to the lobby area of the new building, my gut tells me to stop and I do. Off to my left is the entrance to the nurse's office and I am just a few feet away from it. The scent of my enemy becomes great; I slowly step toward the wall, press my back firmly against it, then wind up the tension in my right arm where the blade is strapped to my wrist. With a slight movement of my left wrist, the blade returns to its holster and I begin opening my left hand. The tension in my entire left arm is tight and ready to strike.

And here we go.

"Come on out, asshole!"

It does in a flash, yet I was ready. I immediately grab the skull, sink my claws into it, pull the head back, and thrust my blade into its neck, past the jaw, and straight to the brain. In a second, I recoil my arm and let go of the head to watch the lifeless corpse collapse to the floor.

One down. Six more.

The glass on the floor where I came from shifts as another charges at me, snarling. I smile, engage the left blade to extend, cross my arms like I am about to show the sign of "safe" in a baseball game, and hold my ground. The bastard gets closer and closer, and I perform the arm movement swiftly and deadly as the blade slices through all of the organs and tissues including the spine, spilling blood and body parts to the floor.

Two down. Five more.

Feeling unstoppable, I reveal my presence, "Is there any asshole that wants to take me *on?*"

Of course, there's a brief explosion behind me and I instantly turn around; quickly looking over my new opponent in five seconds, it shows itself as another jumper. Two words come out of my mouth, "Ah, crap."

The jumper immediately grabs me and teleports us to the upper level of A Wing. When we reappear in that hall, it throws me into the drywall that breaks through and I crash into the desks in one of the classrooms that faces west, which overlooks the other two original buildings from the time the high school was built. Anyway, the pain does hurt, but my immortal immune system instantly starts the healing process.

"Our mother would be pleased hearing about your death. She says to us, 'That you gone too far' and I can see why."

The voice of my attacker sounds male, yet I hardly pay attention as I glance out the floor to the ceiling windows and down the corridor between the backside of the auditorium and the original cafeteria. At the other end of that corridor is my place of salvation, the place that gave me the name, respect, friends, and the best of the last four years of public school—the auto shop. Seconds pass and my sixth sense hunches that my opponent stands above me.

"Not enough fight in ya? Well, that's good because I'm going to tear you apart in revenge for killing my other two brothers."

I look back down to the floor and smile. "Heh, unlikely."

I ball up my right hand, make it tight, and finally unleash a mighty right hook onto my opponent. He doesn't see it coming and stumbles backward. I get up instantly, grab him, and throw him hard against the white boards that break under his collision. He regains his ground and charges at me. I rip out my staff, use it like a metal pipe, and whack it against his head. He goes flying toward the windows and breaks through them. Immediately, gravity begins to grab him, then he jumps from where he began falling and teleports himself back into the room; once back in, he instantly pushes me out. I fall nearly forty feet from the second level of the building and land hard on the concrete steps that face the corridor.

The fucker teleports down to my position, howls for a backup, and two more jumpers come to his aid. One of them grabs my leg and throws me down the alley between the two buildings, putting me closer to the shop.

That's right. Get me closer to that place where my powers become superior.

All three surround me with claws fully exposed and teeth ready to dig in, and their legs tighten up to thrust their bodies upon me. I, too, begin tightening up my muscles to unleash my counterattack including my inner power. The majority of my sorcery is channeled to my right foot. A few ticks of the clock go by and they jump. I counter by twisting my torso to the left, unleashing the right leg while conjuring fire out of my foot and smacking them across their faces. Disoriented and setting fur on fire I bolt straight toward the shop.

Two of the five bay doors are open. I sprint right through the center one, passing the only the full car lift, hopping over some metal tables, stopping immediately at the air compressor, and smacking the level on switch for the machine, then the good old air compressor comes to life with ease. I activate it with my staff, then let it hover just an inch above the concrete floor as it brings the other machinery and tools to life.

I wait, cracking my knuckles and letting out a smile. "Now, let the games begin."

Man, it's great being back home. This is home.

Once they smother the small flames from their faces, the first one charges at me vengefully. As he comes closer, I snap my fingers to activate the lift; slowly rising, he leaps over it but slightly trips over the car that's on it. It's just enough for me to simply step to the right. He collides into the cinder block wall and lands on the floor. Without wasting any time, I grab a wad of his fur and drag him over to a large, grinding machine that has two different types of wheels for grinding. I will be explaining this later because the two are coming up fast.

I drop my opponent right by the machine, smack the other two away, and both go flying. One flies to the other end of the shop, collides with the wooden door that locks up the paint storage above Smith's office, then falls back down to the floor. The other does the same thing, only into the cinder block and above the door that leads into the paint booth, and it suffers the same result. They are both disoriented again. With a snap from my right hand, the air hose lines at the bay doors come alive; they wrap themselves around the ankles, wrists, and neck, then drag the two idiots underneath the lift that is now extended high in the air. As I'm about to release the air from that machine, something sinks its claws into one of my legs. I look down and it seems that my first opponent has regain consciousness. I immediately start stomping his face multiple times, causing him to lose grip on my leg. Next, I switch on the machine and hoist him up. His face shows recognition of my plan and tries to fight me off. I push his face slowly and strongly with all of my strength into the metal brush wheel spinning at full speed.

"No! No! No!"

When his head meets the wheel, fur, flesh, then bone fragments begin to fly all over the place; his cries stop fast, well, it's more like smothered out due to the amount of blood that is now raining all over this area of the shop. The mass of his head stops the wheel, making it stutter for a moment like it still wants to move but it immediately breaks off.

Covered in blood, again, I walk on over to where my other two opponents struggle to break free from the air hose lines, yet they fail over and over again. I slowly walk to the lever for the lift, extend the blade from my left wrist, raise it away from the pipes that flow, and release the air pressure from the lift. I lock eyes on my enemies and I can clearly see in it their thoughts of having no chance for escape and that they picked the wrong Wolfinoid to fight. With our eyes still locked onto one another, I slam the blade into the pipes and air is instantly released without hesitation. The lift comes down fast due to the weight of the car and slams right on top of their heads. Ripping the blade from the pipes and retracting it, I calmly walk toward the air compressor and manually pull the lever down to the "off" position. Right after that, I extend my arm, softly opening my hand around my staff to grab it until a familiar voice reigns out from behind me.

"My children! My beautiful children!"

I spin around on one heel, looking at my final opponent as it gasps in horror by the amount of carnage that lays before it.

"How *dare* you kill my children!"

Listening closely, it sounds female, but I'm not sure. Nonetheless, I look around at my victory in the auto shop.

"Well, they were going to kill me. So, I beat 'em to it."

"I'm going to kill you, Will Young!"

"No way."

"Chase Tiger?"

"Nargh!"

I grab my staff tightly and swing it like a bat; it makes contact with Tiger's head with a small explosion and she goes flying back outside. I leap over the same table and become visceral while I do a high-speed walk back outside. I spin my staff around my hands, activate the flame, and shape it like an arrow. In the moments I'm about to thrust the flaming arrow into her skull, she rolls away and knocks out my legs. I collapse onto the pavement. She gets up and lunges at me; I put my staff in front of me to deflect her attack and with one mighty thrust of my arms, she flies into the air. I get up, putting some distance in between us. I still point my flame-shaped arrow at her. She gets back up again and we begin circulating each other.

"On the day I banished you, I hoped that you were going to be slaughtered within the first three days because you were just a mental, self-esteem-destroying bully."

"Well, I almost had you. You were near perfect in my eyes, but then you had come here. To this place! Make friends, stand your ground, become these things that we, well, mostly me, were trying to prevent!"

My eyes widen, "So, y'all were trying make me feel like I was one of those kids locked behind that yellow gate!"

"And now, since you're not and you murdered my kids, I'm going to kill you and your lovely girlfriend."

"That's strange. The last werewolf that said something like that got his fucking ass slaughtered by *me*!"

"Don't you dare use foul language, young man!"

I throw my staff off to one side. Immediately, the flame goes out, but the glass orb does not shatter. "Come suck my country, Wolfinoid cock, you *bitch!*"

Tiger finally charges at me, snarling like every other werewolf I had crossed paths with. I hold my ground, grab her by her wrists, spin her around, and send her flying into the column frames of one of the bay doors. Her back collides with the hard brick and I hear a few of her bones breaking. I use this opportunity to lunge, land on top, and pin her down. I firmly grab one side of her head and deliver a punch after each word.

"Perhaps," *punch.*

"I," *punch.*

"Should've," *punch.*

"Had," *punch.*

"Tara," *punch.*

"And," *punch.*

"Cedric," *punch.*

"Rip," *punch.*

"You," *punch.*

"Apart," *punch.*

"Back," *punch.*

"In," *punch.*

"That," *punch.*

"Arena!" *punch.*

After that last punch from my right fist, I thrust her head into the same concrete bricks and begin walking away.

"You were never made to be this great because you are mentally disabled," Tiger grumbles through her busted face.

"Whatever. Just die, you bitch."

"You will always be an autistic bastard to me! Do you hear me!"

"That fucking does it."

I look around the small parking lot and lying next to a raised, two-step platform lies one of the many already deceased civilians. I walk on over to him and begin looking over his body, or what's left of it. My eyes come upon something glinting off in the sunlight; getting a closer look, in his right hand is a Double Barrel 1911.

"That's an interesting-looking firearm."

I reach down and pick it up; I pull open the chambers and sure enough, there are hollow point bullets inside

"Do you hear me, Will? You'll always be an autistic bastard in my eyes!"

I turn around and begin walking to her, slowly.

"A simple."

Getting closer.

"Lowlife."

And closer.

"Fucked up."

And closer, now raising the gun with my index finger in the trigger house.

"Autistic bast—"

Pow! Pow! Pow! Pow! Pow! Pow!

Twelve hollow point bullets rip through her body, splashing her blood all over the cement floor, onto the desks, up the tower of cinder blocks that frame the first doorway into the bay area, and into Hugh's office. Immediately, I toss the empty firearm aside, although I don't feel quite satisfied with my revenge kill. I grab whatever is left of the body and toss it into the center of the parking lot. With another snap of my fingers, my staff levitates off the ground and stands itself right up. Next, I focus my attention on some broken down cars that lie in the parking lot; stretching out my arm and hand, I make a few levitate for a moment and viciously slam one on top of the other on Tiger's shot corpse. With that done, I bring up my left hand, cup it like my right, and shoot out two solid columns of fire that's blue from both hands igniting those cars.

Literally ceasing fire, just staring at the flames, I feel a lot of mental chains and walls beginning to crumble away from my mind, freeing it more than it was before and increasing my mental and self-esteem statuses.

"Oh, thank God, there you are!"

I calmly look over my left shoulder and here comes Maddox looking totally relieved.

"I've been searching for ages." He looks about the chaos. "What the hell happened here?"

I look back at the flaming pile and calmly respond, "What happened here doesn't matter. It's done, for all I care. Overall, what's the status of our enemies?"

Maddox puts his hand on me, I look at him, and he smiles. "Every one of them is obliterated. Los Alamos is now liberated. Our mission is a success."

"Good," I say in satisfied tone.

"Now, about reconstruct—"

"No," I say firmly. Maddox looks at me slightly puzzled. I sigh. "Look around, man. Los Alamos is a complete disaster zone ravaged by war. The radiation contained by those shields technically own these mesas. We've spent enough time way out here. The mission, our mission, like you said, is complete. I want to go home and be with my wife. I miss Tara so much."

Maddox removes his hand and folds both of them behind his back. "I understand that completely, sire. I'll relay the message to Hays and Damon so that they can transmit it to our kingdoms."

"Good. Let's go home."

I begin to walk toward the sidewalk then run between the auditorium and the original cafeteria; as the grade of the sidewalk increases in height, railings appear, yet I fling myself over with ease and begin crossing the parking lot in front of the auditorium, heading toward the ski hill with my head that I hold up high from this completed mission.

CHAPTER FIFTY

Returning Home with Surprises
and a Hard Choice
Location: West Gate of Sparta
Time: 4:30 PM
Date: July 18, 2015

ON OUR JOURNEY RETURNING home, we took the same route. The Great Plains were still black yet only in certain areas because the U.S. military was making a great comeback and have regained so much territory. Still, we used the high mountains for safe passage. When we were passing Durango and Silverton, both towns are in full swing of life, yet they have become military bases for safety reasons and I don't blame them. The more territory the U.S. military regains, the better chances we can finish off our problem with ease. On the day we arrived at the stairway that leads up to Troy, Avast received a broadcast that they were already packing up and were readying areas for the portals to open up and take them back to their original home. We bid our goodbyes and I shook hands with the top men from Troy who joined us on this daunting and deadly mission. I told Avast, Wind, Ocean, Rows, and Noon that it was an honor serving with them and they said likewise. By that time, Rows and I have become allies and he heavily apologizes for his actions. I forgave him and right after that, they take their men up the stairs to aid the packing. What's interesting is that Soren decides to join us on our journey back to Sparta; I did ask him why and he told me that he misses home and has spent too much time away from his brother. I absolutely did not argue with that and from there on, it was totally smooth sailing. There were no more conflicts.

So, after three smooth days, we arrive exhausted at the West Gate of Sparta. We easily descend the path, passing the large flags that represent the kingdom. It feels strange like it was yesterday that I, by myself, descended this path only half alive but still, I made here with my heart beating. Getting closer to the gate, a horn sounds off from one of the towers and the Wolfinoids inside its perimeter literally stop with whatever they are doing and charge at us, welcoming us back home. Trent, Maddox, Soren, and I stand off to one side and watch as each loved one embraces the opposite in their arms. Some of them collapse onto the ground and heavily kiss; one of them is Zakia throwing her boyfriend or husband onto the ground. Seeing all of this makes me feel happy. Strangely, looking around our little group, my happiness drains a little because when we left, Sean Greenwood was amongst us in travel and fights, but now, he is dead buried in the piping, wiring, and glass now fully contaminated with highly radiated liquids and other substances that are on fire.

I sigh in grief.

"We are all going to miss him, Will," says Maddox as he places his hand on my shoulder in comfort. "Nonetheless, you should go back in and find Tara. Be with your wife, mate."

His encouragement raises my hopes and I calmly enter the kingdom; my eyes begin searching the crowd as they rush past me. Having trouble finding her, my eyes settle upon Gothraigh as he was jogging toward the commotion, but once our eyes meet, they light up and he folds his hands behind his back while briskly walking up to me. Once we get three feet from each other, he kneels down on his right knee while still looking at me with satisfaction.

"Welcome back home, your majesty. I take it that your mission was a success?" he asks, trying to contain his enthusiasm.

I wave my hand for him to stand back up, he does, and I place my right hand on his left shoulder while looking at him straight in the eyes. "Yes. The mission was a success. Have you begin packing up?"

He looks around briefly and back at me. "We've barely started. By the way, this may sound odd, did you know that you forgot your iPod?"

I retrieve my hand and just stick my thumb in the pocket of my jeans. "Yeah, I do know, but that didn't really matter to me. Why you do ask? Where's Tara?"

Gothraigh begins snickering and bursting out laughing while slapping my left shoulder. I am so confused right now. Gothraigh soon tells me through his gasps for air that she's near the gates of the castle and also, I'll be so surprised by her transformation. I thank him for the information, still feeling very confused as he and I go our separate ways.

I start walking up the path toward our castle in the cliff. There are still some people both human and Wolfinoid carrying on their business. When I get closer, my eyes widen, my heart begins to race, and the warm liquid of love flows throughout my body. My legs begin to tremble at the sheer beauty of my wife. Most of all, the chorus of "Cowgirls Set on Earth" by Josh Kage begins playing in my head as I gawk at my wife in amazement.

She wears denim blue jeans with forest camo pattern strips that come down the sides like the pair of pants she wore during her birthday except they are outlined in decorative metal studs. Her belt is made out of leather styled with western patterns and metal studs. The belt buckle seems to be four inches in diameter and shines brightly with the sun reflecting off of it as it has the same wolf head logo of the kingdom on it. Surrounding the circumference are little purple diamonds. The shirt is a button-down plaid with dark purple long sleeves and white where the sleeves roll up past the elbows. Her jewelry for the wrists, necklace, and earrings show royalty combined with the jewelry design of the southwest. Finally, on her head is a tan-felt cowboy hat.

"Oh my God," I speak out loud in amazement.

Tara doesn't seem to notice me as she is engaged in a conversation with some of the royal guards while looking down at her tablet, perhaps discussing the packing and the moving arrangements. One of the guards notices me, taps her on the shoulder, and point her attention at me. Once she sees me, her eyes widen with excitement. She then shoves the tablet into one of the guards' chest and begins slowly walking toward me; soon, it develops into a full run. I brace for impact digging my feet into the ground and spreading my arms to embrace my wife. The speed Tara is traveling at makes her hat fly off. Within seconds, she collides into my chest, making me lose my footing and I collapse onto the ground right to my back. Her lips firmly lock around mine; she sticks her tongue into my mouth and I do the same while wrapping my arms around her and holding her tightly. Tara does the same with her arms. She releases her mouth from mine, letting us gasp for air, and she nibbles my right ear.

"Don't you *dare* go off to war again," she heavily breathes while whispering that message deep into my ear, establishing those words onto my brain.

I whisper back, "Don't worry. I won't. It's done and I'm glad to be back home."

We readjust our heads to look into each other's eyes; looking into Tara's they show relief, happiness, yet also a glint of disappointment. This raises my curiosity.

"Why do you look a little sad? Aren't you glad that I'm back?"

Tara looks to the side for a moment and release a sigh. "This may sound selfish." Then she looks back at me. "I was really hoping for some reason that the town with its chemicals and whatnot would've turned you back into human."

Oh, c'mon Tara? Really?

"You're still kicking your ass about turning me into this?"

"A little," she replies, letting out a sheepish smile.

Sigh. "You do realize that if I went off to war as a human, my chances of surviving would've been extremely limited."

She then rests her head onto my chest. "I know."

We lay on the ground, still embracing each other while listening to the sounds of people rejoicing about their loved ones returning home. It's only a matter of time when the rejoicing turns into tears of mourning for those who perished during the battles of LANL, Pajarito Ski Hill, Silverton, and the first time when we got ambushed.

I'm going to hate that part so much, especially when I have to tell Rollo that his son didn't make it. I'm pretty sure the same thing is happening at Troy.

"Anyway." The suddenness of Tara's voice going high for excitement surprises me a little. "I have a surprise to show you. Well, both Whitney and I."

"What is it?" I ask.

She picks both of us up and grabs her hat. We enter through the doors, down the long hallway in swift motion, and into the throne room. The place still looks the same, yet the chandeliers are off and the only the lights that are on are the ones between the corridors that dimly illuminate the area. We carry on and go up the stairs that lead into the dining hall. Arriving at the top of the stairs, Tara pulls us to the head of the tablet where she and I sat the next morning after my transformation. From this moment, she tries to contain her excitement.

"Do you remember the day you had a fallout with your friends when they saw your new form?"

The memory of that day replays in my head and the voices of my friends echo as they told me to go to hell and fuck off. I still hate that day. It makes feel like I betrayed my original race. Nonetheless, I shake my head to shut it off.

"Yeah. Why do you ask?"

Right after that, Whitney comes around the corner from the upper stairway; she then leans against the wall and folds her arms as she smiles.

"Well, it's good see you, Will, alive and well. How was Los Alamos?"

"A total war zone. What's going on?"

Whitney tilts her head back, still smiling. "Come on down, baby."

Seconds pass until a male Wolfinoid with red fur, light brown eyes, a simple camo print hat, gray shirt, blue jeans with a brown belt, and a cowboy belt buckle comes down the steps, goes around Whitney, and leans against one of the chairs at the other end of the table with his thumbs in his pockets.

"Who's this?" I ask the two ladies, then the red fur Wolfinoid answers.

"S'up, Nos? I'm glad you're back, man."

That voice sounds so familiar.

"Do that sound that I like, baby," Whitney says.

"Yee-yee!" the man replies.

"Oh my God. Chris, is that you?"

He smiles and he begins to approach me; I do the same. Getting closer, I am just absolutely blown away yet confused beyond the one to ten scale.

"When did this happen?"

Chris looks back at Whitney for a moment. They exchange facial and small body gestures, then Chris looks back at me. "About three weeks ago and man it hurt like fucking hell. I thought I was going to die."

"Heh, yeah, I know the feeling." After saying that, I begin skimming the room and I don't see our other friends, unless they have been turned into Wolfinoids, too.

"Where are—"

"They left, Nos," Chris cuts in. "Three days after you left, Hugh, Emily, Alex, Alice, and Austin packed their shit one night and fled to Long Island to be safe in U.S. military hands. During that night, Whitney and I noticed them, tried to stop them, and convinced them that this place is still safe. But they told us they just couldn't take it anymore and took off. Whitney wanted to alert the normal guard, yet I told her to just let them go."

"Shit." I look at Whitney and Tara and they both shake their heads in agreement that Chris is telling the truth. "Fuck. But hold on, what were your circumstances that you had to be turned?"

Whitney comes up, takes Chris' hand into hers, and looks at him. "Hunting accident. His injuries were life threatening."

"How?"

At that time, Chris is also looking at Whitney. "My hunting rifle went off when I was leaning over the barrel, making sure it was straight. The bullet went through my kidney and stomach, creating sepsis."

Ah, I see.

"Anyway," Whitney speaks, breaking her attention from Chris and looking at Tara, "Should we get on packing our things, Tara?"

"Yeah, we should," she replies.

After that, all four of us head up the stairs to the bed chambers.

When Tara and I enter our bedroom, there are several cases that seem to be like hard sided, carry-on bags strewn about the area. I walk over to one and it has the exact proportions as a normal, human carry-on bag. I look about the chamber and I begin to wonder how in the hell are we going to fit all of her stuff into these bags. In her chamber are pillows big and small, blankets thick and thin, clothes and jewelry for the both of us, large pieces of fabric that covers the stalactites, curtains that cover the French doors and the doors that lead into this room, potions and other tools she used on me to heal me twice, cookware, dishes, silverware, pool lounging chairs, bamboo shelf unit with all the towels and lotions, Tara's small entertainment system consisting of her iPod and two speakers, and finally, couches that surround the camp fire pit. Actually, come to think of it, my mind *finally* considers the sheer size and architecture of the entire castle. There's only one question that makes my mind explode a million times over.

How in the fuck were Tara and her kind able to carve, wire, and perhaps insert plumbing only in a matter of a couple of days into this mountain?

"Will, baby, are you okay?"

My expression fires off the question. She calmly takes it in and waves her index finger. "Ah, those two things can be easily explained. You do know how the sacks work since you've been using them over the past year, right?" I nod. "Well, these bags have the same power. Now, for the things that we are packing up, they're gonna be pillows, blankets, our clothes and jewelry, my potions and tools, curtains that cover both doors, fabrics that cover the ceiling, cookware, silverware, my little sound system, and finally, towels and lotions on the bamboo shelf. The things that I did not mention, well, they're all gonna get destroyed by this friendly device that'll definitely cover up our tracks of existence."

How?

Tara walks deep into the wardrobe, pops open a hidden door, and then comes back out rolling an egg-like device that seems to be three feet tall and has two black lines going around the circumference. One is in the center and the other one is near the bottom. Right after that, she touches the top and the egg opens both compartments with ease; the center has an inner column with six circles around its circumference and the lower compartment also has a spine but only houses one device in the shape of an oval. Tara pushes down one of the circles in the center compartment. A blue light shines around briefly and popping out is a little droid that has three joint arms with needle tips, four eyes, and two rotors to make it fly.

"This is a Drill Bug," Tara says. "It has laser cutters that can literally cut through anything, including any type of rock. These are the guys that formed this palace in a matter of days. Of course, there's more than one Drill Bug Carrier Egg that we've used."

She snaps her fingers and the droid flies back into its hold. Next, Tara kneels down at the oval in the lower compartment and does the same action, but when that device pops out, she grabs it, then its three legs extend automatically from the bottom of it and sets it on the ground.

"Now, this is the Destroyer," Tara continues explaining, "It will scan any object and destroy it with one solid blast of its laser. Yet, when it's used in hollow spaces, like this chamber, it will destroy the other objects and replenish the natural rock that was carved. These are the guys who will be definitely covering our tracks once we're back on our home planet."

During the end of that sentence, she pulls out her iPod and reveals a glowing, red button ready to be pushed to activate this droid. Tara just smiles and presses the "Clear" button on to go back to the home screen and the lock button on top to deactivate the screen.

"Now, let's get packing," she says with joy.

I walk closer to the Destroyer and begin analyzing it. Seeing just one, my mind recalls the pool room and its two secret sliding doors.

How in the hell is this going to destroy that place?

"Tara, how is it going to destroy your private pool room?"

"Oh, the doors are open to let the laser analyze that area," she answers as she points with her thumb toward the doors that are indeed open, yet she has her full attention on gathering her potions and tools.

I shrug and grab the nearest bag and begin throwing in some of the blankets from the bed. Once they enter, they immediately disappear.

Their sorcery never ceases to amaze me. I smile and shake my head side to side.

Just several minutes into packing, Tara speaks up, "Hey, before you came here, your original plan was to go to Wisconsin to see if any of your family members survived, right?"

Holy shit! I completely fucking forgot all about that!

"Yeah," I reply, slowly turning my head and seeing a full tablet in her hands ready to go. "Why do you ask?"

She kneels down beside me. "Well, when we got the word that the satellites were coming back, we were able to hack the U.S. military database, thus were able to answer the humans their main question, 'Where is my family?' And from there on out, we've been telling where they are and . . ."

"And what?"

"If they're dead or alive."

Just hearing that phrase makes my heart race and begins to make me panic.

"What are their last names?" Tara asks quickly trying to ease my anxiety.

I quickly tell the last names of my relatives and who is related to who; she taps them down into the computer. While the tablet loads, Tara rubs my shoulder to comfort me. It chimes off and a warm smile spreads across her face.

"Will, they are alive and are safe on the military base in Miami, Florida."

I release a huge sigh of relief and I begin to feel happy, yet reality sets in hard. I look down at my hands, then I get up and look at my reflection in one of the mirrors in my wardrobe. Seeing my Wolfinoid reflection makes me realize that I am no longer a human. There is no way that they'll be able to recognize me even if I try my damn best.

Fuck.

"There is a choice," Tara quietly speaks.

"And what choice is that?" I question in a slightly disgusted tone.

"I can put you down as MIA or KIA. Which one do you want?"

Fucking hell. Are you kidding me? Shit! Sigh. Alright, if I choose KIA, they will sob and mourn for a few days and then move on. If I choose MIA, that'll give them hope, but receiving the news that the search is off only to be confirmed as KIA will hit them harder. Fuck. This is a hard decision.

I close my eyes and toss those abbreviations around my head, debating, visualizing, and trying to predict which outcome will hurt the least.

After thinking about it for five minutes, I reopen my eyes. "Tara. Put me down as," I turn around, look at her seriously, and continue, "K. I. A."

She nods, does it, and powers down the tablet. She gets up, walks to me, loosely wraps her arms around my neck, and kisses me.

"Why?" she asks.

I glance at the bed, replaying the day I awoke there, in her presence, then I look back at her, smiling a little. "Because I died and went to heaven when I open my eyes and saw you. You're the angel that saved me."

This time, she kisses me more and deeply until there's a knock at the door. We both turn our attention to it. Soren enters looking serious yet a little apologetic, too.

"Sorry to interrupt, but we need to do a debrief meeting, like, now," Soren says.

Tara and I look at one another and follow Soren out of the door and down the stairs.

CHAPTER FIFTY-ONE
The Debrief Meeting
Location: Maddox's arena
Time: 7:00 PM

WHEN SOREN, TARA, AND I enter Maddox's arena, the lights are already dimmed to allow a hologram map of Los Alamos shine bright and clear. The tech that creates the map are the same spheres that were used during my training session and looking around, there is a multiple amount of the Destroyer droids lined up against the wall in the arena and in the hidden garage. Bringing you guys back to the actual matter, joining us is Admiral Zachariah Blitz, Lupa Blitz, Rollo Greenwood, Maddox, Trent, Gothraigh, and Cora Stone. They all wait patiently for the three of us and judging the atmosphere, this is going to be quick and straightforward.

"So," speaks Zachariah, "I hear that you were victorious?"

"Yes, we were," I firmly state.

"What is the causality count?" asks Gothraigh.

I exchange looks with Soren, Maddox, and Trent, then I turn my attention to the map. "In total, three thousand and forty-six. That includes causalities of the battles that we encountered before."

The news I gave them gets everybody shaken and horrified.

"What happened during those battles?" Lupa asks.

I look at the same guys and Trent gestures that I should say the rest. "Okay." I clap hands and rewind all of the battles that happened before, "When we left, just our army, a few days into our journey, we were ambushed, lost few lives, yet succeeded. Trudging through the northern states, heading west through a major thunderstorm, we lost more lives and those were the ones that were severely injured in the battle beforehand. After we were rescued and escorted by Avast and his men, we got to Troy safely. The meeting with King Terrin and the presentation about Los Alamos went smoothly. Right after that, we did have military support from a large number of humans who were with the U.S. military that were rescued and brought to Troy. Anyway, back to the battles, moving south, we had to liberate two more towns in Colorado, which were Silverton and Durango. Both are historic mining towns. So, when we approached Silverton, we thought there wasn't a large number of werewolves, but boy were we so fucking wrong about that."

"I sent a small team of human, American snipers to take out the guards, but when one missed his target and the other werewolves found their comrades dead, they sent out a howl for backup. Again, we were fucking ambushed; this time by mutated ones that have the ability to turn invisible. The battle only lasted a night. Again, there were more fatalities from service members from our army and Troy's along with the U.S. military men and women, but again, we rose victorious. We rebuilt Silverton and used the historic rail line to get down to Durango. Luckily, there were no enemies camping out along the rail line nor any in Durango. Once we entered New Mexico, we took on the ski hill. That time, no fatalities occurred and we made it as our base camp. After that, it was LANL and to summarize it up, that's where *the bloodiest*, shittiest, and toughest battles took place. Overall, it was just one big ass slaughterhouse. However, y'all can see that we won and every mutated werewolf *and*_human in mid-transformation was eliminated."

My other top officials just gawk at me.

"And what about my son?" Rollo asks.

"*Oh God.*"

"Mr. Greenwood, I am very sorry—"

"No," he says.

"I am very sorry to report—" I try to continue.

"No! No!"

"Report that amongst the three thousand and forty-six, your son, Sean—"

"No! No! No! No! No! No!"

"Sean, he didn't make it! I am very, very sorry!"

"No!" Rollo collapses onto his knees, wailing and shedding huge tears, "How dare you let my son die. How dare *you!*"

He begins charging at me, but Gothraigh, Trent, and both Nightrunner brothers intervene, thrusting him down to the floor, holding him back, and begin dragging him out of the arena. Rollo continues wailing while all four guys trudge him up the stairs. We all stand in silence. On my end, I let my head hang.

"So," Cora speaks up, "It was that bad in Los Alamos."

I look up at her briefly to answer, "Yep."

Then I turn around and head for the stairs, still letting my head hang. Stepping onto the first step and placing my hand onto the banister, I can feel Tara approaching me.

"Where are you going, Will?"

Still letting my head hang, I let out a heavy sigh. "A walk in the woods to clear my mind and enjoy, possibly, my last night on my home planet."

I, too, trudge up the stairs and the wails and cries from Rollo echo in the halls, and that puts me in a more depressed mood.

I really want to have this shit end right now.

CHAPTER FIFTY-TWO

Packing up and Final Night on Earth
Location: Outside, in the Camp of Sparta
Time: 2:15 PM
Date: July 9, 2015

THE SERMON THAT WE had was basically . . . dreadful. We mourned for the deaths of the fallen men and women from the Spartan army. The speech from the deacon was short yet straightforward and powerful. When he concluded, we all bowed our heads, prayed for safe travels for the souls that are now traveling to heaven and we, the entire congregation, sat in silence for *hours* in respect. Everybody wore black. As hours passed, the deacon broke the silence and projected the speech of how we became victorious and that we will be returning home. Hearing that makes me feel really sad, yet the entire Wolfinoid congregation rejoiced. My sadness did catch Tara's attention.

When the sermon ended at noon, we all filed out, changed from our black clothes, and continued packing up. Aside from that, we royalists met in the throne room after lunch, which was delicious, and received confirming news from Maddox and Soren from an intel that their home planet will send several teleportation portals to different locations just to make the move easier. I ask them when will they appear and Soren happily replied that they'll be here at one in the morning sharp. The news strikes me harder. I felt more devastated that my time on planet Earth, my time living in the United States of America, is coming to a faster close. Immediately, I left the room swiftly and went outside.

At this time, I slowly walk around the camp and everywhere I look, everybody is in an enthusiastic hustle of dismantling their homes and shops. I walk over to the hospital and standing outside, conducting the packing, is Doctor Tristen Maverick. Seeing him boosts my spirits a little and I walk over to him.

"Seems like you got everything under control," I say to him while I stick my hands into my blue jean pockets.

"Ah!" Tristen shouts, struggling to grasp and preventing the tablet from falling onto the ground. "Jesus." He looks at me and a smile comes alive on his face. "Will, it's good to see you. Yeah, uh, we do have everything under control here. So far, it's been smooth sailing." He turns back to his tablet, which seems to have a checklist on it.

"Is there anything I can help you guys with?"

Tristen reassures me, "Hm? No, no, not at all. Like I said, we got this."

I nod in agreement and watch as the other doctors and nurses remove some of the tarp walls, making it easier to remove the beds and other lifesaving equipment. I watch a team of doctors bringing out beds, then one of them kneels down and presses a button that makes the beds fold up into an easy, hand-held cube with dimensions around a foot all around. I turn my head and some of the nurses have brought out other lifesaving equipment, presses a button, and they too collapse to make themselves easier to pack.

Wow.

"I didn't know that you guys were *this* advanced in technology," I say in amazement.

"Oh, we are. Just in the healthcare sector. Anywhere else, well, it's been a struggle."

"Why?"

Tristen looks at me. "Cedric, God rest his soul, was very strong on tradition and so is Gothraigh. They both say and agree that it's best to keep our medieval, Celtic culture alive so that we don't lose the heritage that our ancestors created, but Tara's mother is different. She supports the new technology and so does Tara." He looks back at what is going on and continues, "I have no doubt that after Tara receives the official throne, Sparta would be immediately brought into the twenty-second century."

He's right. Come to think of it. The clothes that Tara, her mom, Soren, and Maddox wear are modern and the clothes that Gothraigh, Cedric, Cora, and the other guys, aside from Tara's friends, their clothes are very traditional.

Hold on! Slam the breaks on the eighteen-wheeler! Twenty-second century?

"Y'all are in the twenty-second century?"

This surprises him. "Yeah. What century is your planet in?"

"Twenty-first."

"Wow. That makes sense to me, especially when I saw your iPod with you on the very first day you were brought here."

I look about the camp, which appears nearly halfway packed up. "Yeah, no shit."

"Is there anywhere you need to be, your majesty?" Tristen asks.

I shake my head while I answer, "Naw, not really. Listen, Doctor Maverick, if you and I don't see each other once we get back to your home planet, I thank you deeply for healing me, well, practically bringing me back to life, and showing me around."

He smiles, "Hey, I'm a doctor. It's what I do. You take it easy, my king."

"Yeah, you too."

I continue my journey around the camp. I begin to pass the workshop where I made my staffs. Analyzing how those men are taking it apart, it only seems to be the tent itself that house the drawing, the smelters, and the sorcery sectors. The smelters, moldings for the staffs, tables for the sorcery bowls and equipment, and the drawing tables along with their high chairs don't seem to have the capability to collapse; so, I guess a portal to their home planet will open here.

Aside from that, last night, on my walk in the woods, I found a small mountain of boulders on this one particular hill. I climbed it and at the top is a large, flat surface big enough for two people to comfortably sit on cross-legged, look over the trees, and survey the camp. I sat there last night, overlooking the camp for hours, replaying my entire life through my head, connecting all of the events that happened and how in the hell they lead me to this place, even including how in the hell they have turned me into a Wolfinoid. I didn't return to my wife until, maybe, three in the morning. I couldn't sleep last night.

I begin following my own scent and footprints. In minutes, I find the same rock formation. I climb it with ease again, sit myself upon the top, and overlook the camp.

Time: 6:00 PM

"There you are." The sound of Tara's voice breaks me out of my daydreaming and reminiscence. For some reason, the sound of the birds turning into the sounds of the crickets put me in a very deep trance and lets my mind forget about time. I turn around to see her climbing up, smiling that she found me, and has one of her arms holding a basket. She sits down beside me, removes my hat, and strokes her fingers through my hair.

"Are you okay?"

The sadness and the realization officially break through, knowing that in several hours, I'll be moving to a new home millions of light years away from here. I begin to nibble my lower lip.

"What's wrong, Will?" she asks concerned.

I sniffle, "No Tara, I'm not alright. Actually, I'm not very comfortable with any of this." Tears begin forming in my eyes and I let them fall. "I . . . I'm going to be moving light years away to a new planet similar to Earth. I am totally . . . shocked. I didn't even mentally prepare myself for this! I was born here." I spread my arm above the trees, above the camp. "I was born in the United States of America and it's the only place I know because I grew up here! I'm really going to miss my human family and my human friends. I do feel like I really died. And this . . . this feels like heaven. It doesn't feel like I'm in the U.S. anymore. I'm really going to miss this place."

I place my face into my hands and sob so much like I'm at a funeral for someone that I knew so closely. That person is *me*.

"Oh, Nos." Tara begins to deeply rub my back to comfort me. "Shh, shh. It's going to be okay. I know that this is a really hard transition on you, but look at the bright side, your friend Chris is coming with us. Of course, he's going through the same emotions as you are."

I sob harder, gasping for air.

"Hey, hey, hey! Shhh, shhh . . . You two are really going to love our planet, Kaladria. It's very majestic in all sorts of beauty. The geography of the land is very unique. Do you remember that mural in the pool room?"

I shake my head saying "Yes" while my head still lays in my hands.

"Like I told you months ago, the original kingdom of Sparta neighbors a tropical beach and the architecture is to let the outdoors come in. What's interesting is that Whitney and I found out that you two have the same taste in music and almost have the same artists on your mobile devices."

Her rubs on my back start to get to me and I begin to calm down; I begin wiping away my tears and taking in deep breaths of air.

"What do ya mean by that?"

"Oh, you two will find out."

Time passes and the pressure of Tara's hands on my back really calms me down, yet they let my mind wander again to the events here. One of them is when we buried Cedric. I carefully set the tone of my voice to properly ask the right question in the right words.

"Did you." I gulp, hoping for the best. "Have you told your mom about—"

"Yes," she answers calmly like she was expecting that question, "I told her over a month ago and she did sob, and that was hard for me to watch. After that, she really begged for me to return home. To tell you the truth, no offense, Nos, I am totally ready to get back home. Your planet's air . . . it's not so . . . clean and crisp as it is on Kaladria."

I smile, "Heh, none taken." Then my eyes zoom in on the basket. "What's in there?"

"Huh? Oh, yes, um, heh, it's our dinner that I prepared. Nothing real fancy, just some sandwiches, fruit, and veggies."

That sounds good enough for me.

Tara brings the basket into her lap, opens it, and we just dig in. The temperature tonight is at comfortable level. Though we both have fur to keep us warm, we are both wearing jeans and t-shirts. I return my camo hat back to my head and Tara did her hair the same way when I saw her in the hospital. On a much more positive note, we both look at the trees and we can see several fires burning to give light as the final tents are brought down, packed up, and celebrations flourish throughout the grounds. We can clearly hear the people singing and playing instruments. We mainly turn our attention to the stars shining so clear and bright. Looking at them has me remembering my lessons when I was converting from being a blue-collared man to a man of royalty and learning about their planet. I realized they failed to mention which star constellation their planet is in.

"Hey, Tara?"

"Yeah, Nos."

I continue to look up at the stars to ask my question, "Which star constellation is your home planet in?"

She scoots in closer to me, lays her head against mine, and stretches out her right arm with her index finger pointing straight up in front of my eyes. I let my eyes follow her hand as she points and outlines three particular stars that are indeed the brightest and are almost exactly aligned with one another. My eyes widen and my mouth opens. She laughs and kisses my head.

"Our home is in the solar system on the star to the left."

"You're from Orion's Belt?" I ask in amazement.

"Mm-hm." Her answer makes her sound like a child as she quietly chews away, looking very pleased, eyes closed.

"Wow."

After that, I take another bite of my sandwich, still looking up at Orion's Belt.

Location: Tara's Chambers
Time: 1:00 AM
Date: July 20, 2015

With the Destructor droid set up and ready and our large carry-on bags also stacked neatly, Tara and I hold hands as we wait in her former bedchamber for a portal to magically appear in front of us, allowing us to easily walk onto Kaladria from Earth. At this moment, I am no longer discouraged nor afraid of what lies ahead me. In fact, I am very excited. I feel like I am officially starting all over again literally on a new world.

I squeeze Tara's hand like a young, anxious child who's about to enter the zoo for the first time while his parents pay for the admissions. She smiles in a way that she's glad to see me in this state. Most of the chamber is dark. Only a few torches are burning in their natural colors that dimly light the room. The atmosphere feels cold, empty, non-friendly, and almost threatening, completely opposite from what it was before.

I really wanna get outta here.

My excitement increases and so do my heartbeat and anxiety. Tara squeezes my hand back and laughs.

"Any moment, baby," she says in a tone that she, too, is happy and ready to return home.

Suddenly, a bright, small dot appears out of thin air in front us and hovers six feet off the ground, then two lines expand both sides from the dot and stretch to about six feet. Right after that, they form both halves of a circle in seconds, completing the portal.

Through the liquid screen is a limestone patio stretching about ten feet ahead and spreading ten feet wide. At the edge ahead of us are two large limestone bowls that have fires burning in a great mass. Off to the left, there is a tropical forest that slowly morphs into a mountainous forest. In the middle is a city that looks like and possibly represents Plato's story of Atlantis. Off to the right is an ocean with the sun shining brightly in the sky. Ahead of the city is a mountain and nestled in the trees is a large structure that seems to be constructed out of the same material as the patio in front of us. I don't know. Returning my head to the forest, there's an accumulation of levels forming a complex, yet the interesting building itself seems to be closer to the patio.

Tara lets go of my hand and uses her enthusiasm to grab and thrust the bags through the portal like they mean nothing to her. After she throws the last one, she begins to step through it, though she stops midway, turns around to look at me, and stretches out the same hand I was holding onto. Her face and eyes coax me to take her hand and pull me through.

"Come, Will," she speaks in a sexy, pleasurable, coaxing tone. "Take my hand and live with me in peace and happiness on planet Kaladria, your new home."

I raise my arm and begin stretching out my hand to take hers.

CHAPTER FIFTY-THREE

A New Life and a Coronation
Location: Outskirts of the
Royal Palace of Sparta
Time: 2:45 PM
Date: Unknown

ONCE OUR HANDS TOUCH each other and intertwine, Tara gently pulls me forward. My feet move smoothly, one in front of the other. The space between me and the portal is only two strides. I keep my eyes locked onto hers and in microseconds, my right leg rises, steps through, bring my body along with it, then my left. I am instantly greeted by the warm and humid tropical air along with a breeze that's coming off from the ocean; and the air like Tara said is fresher than the air on Earth. Looking from the patio, I am totally captivated by the scenery. It's absolutely beautiful; at the same time, my mind starts playing "Go Out with You" by Brian Mountain.

I smile and let that song play out, making me feel more welcomed.

Anyway, Tara continues to guide me a few strides away from the portal because on the side where we came through is the actual device that sent the receiving portal. Looking at the actual structure of the machine, the portal immediately disappears, turning the machine power down. It does not collapse into a tiny, circumference box for easy transport.

Tara releases my hand from hers, fishes out her iPod from her pockets, and activates the Destructor's app which brings up a live screen of a camera that shows us the vacated cavern. Below the visual screen, the red button appears and begins to glow red, ready to activate the droid. Before Tara pushes it, she moves her finger to the visual screen and moves it left to right, giving a full three-hundred-and-sixty-degree view of the cavern. All that is left are the doors that lead into the large hallway, doors to her balcony, hollowed-out rock shelves for her potions and equipment, a sunken, cold looking, hard rock oval used be the bed, couches that sit near an empty, cold fire pit, and the three torches that are still burning. Tara then leaves the camera looking at the torches, puts her index finger behind her iPod, and hovers her thumb over the button.

For some reason, regret of coming here starts building up in my soul and I nudge her to do it so that this feeling will go away as fast as it appeared.

Tara nods and begins quietly counting down, "Three. Two. One."

As her thumb taps the button, a bright flash of red light shoots out from the camera's point of view, arcs out very fast, and once the red light touches the wall, the visual screen immediately turns into a black screen, indicating that the signal has been lost. Tara hits the home button, deactivates the screen, and pockets the iPod away. For me, when I saw the black screen, the regret immediately retreats and never shows its bitchy, ass face again.

"How do you feel, Will?" she asks.

I breathe a sigh of relief. "Much better. Thank you."

"Good," she answers in a perky tone. "Now, let me introduce you to my mother and show you around our real palace."

After saying that, she begins bounding the stairs that lead to a walkway hovering above the tropical trees, then etching itself into a hillside, thus forming the rest of the walkway that leads to, I would assume, the real palace of the Wolfinoid kingdom of Sparta. Interestingly, reality brings my attention back to the bags that Tara chucked through.

"Tara," I slightly shout at her concerned, "What about the bags!" At the same time, I gesture my arms to them.

Midway down, Tara stops and shouts back in enthusiasm, "Don't worry about them! I'll send some servants to pick them up!" Then, she turns her attention to the sky as she touches down the walkway, throwing her arms up and skipping down it. "It's so good to be back home!"

I throw my hands up "whatever" and quickly and safely descend the stairs; reaching the walkway, I begin to jog to catch up with my highly enthused wife. She takes notice, slows down, and we reconnect our hands to enjoy the rest of our walk.

Continuing down the walk, with a width of ten feet, the walls that are pushing the soil away only rise three feet without an indication of any light source. However, when we round a corner after walking a hundred yards, the masonry slowly changes from limestone to all-white quartz, directing to the palace. With every step we take, the palace gets bigger, the details begin to show, and the feeling like I am at a resort begins to rise.

After walking one hundred yards, we enter a very large courtyard that seems to be as wide as a football field, although it seems to be eighty yards in length. Its floor is in a checkered pattern with tiles measuring up to four feet by four feet. The tiles that contrast from the white quartz are clear like glass and looking down at one right under my feet, there seems to be a plenty of little dots that are clear and facing upward.

Those have got to be LED lights.

Looking around at the far edges of the courtyard, there are two above-ground gardens that form barriers like fences and they house all sorts of tropical plants, especially full-grown palm trees. Plus, they cover the entire length of the courtyard without break or gap in between the walls. Turning my attention back to the palace, there are two waterfalls that border a stairway leading up and into it, which would be Tara's home and my new home.

The overall architecture of the palace is very modern with flat roofs. The balconies have stainless-steel railings with glass as the wall, and there are even panes of glass tall and wide in between the columns that support the roof and the other levels above. All in all, I was expecting something different; perhaps, a castle that's constructed out of stone that has been dug out of a quarry nearby or like the castles I have seen in fairy tale movies and in reality on planet Earth. Perhaps, it's kind of like the castles from the camps of Troy and Sparta. Other than that, it's beautiful.

"That's some palace you got, Tara."

She doesn't respond. I look at her and her expression shows astonishment and disbelief.

"Tara?" I ask in concern, "Are you okay?"

"Yeah, it's just—"

Her voice gets cut off by the sound of bagpipes that blast in front of us. My head snaps back in their direction and what I see are ten royal guards, five on each side of the stairway at the top in the front entrance of the palace, blasting the instruments, and behind them are two large banners resembling the kingdom that unroll from the ceiling of the first roof and cover up the first set of windows. Tara lets go of my hand again and begins to walk slowly across the courtyard like she is blown away from what she sees, which I find a little odd.

Then the bagpipes cease and someone from the royal guard speaks, "Please stand at attention for Athena Borin; queen of Sparta!"

At the same time, I shrug and begin to follow Tara toward the stairway. Halfway across the courtyard, a Wolfinoid female with brown fur like Tara's and dressed in superb silk with colors that softly combine white, blue, and purple, appears at the top of the stairs and begins to descend. She is wearing a two-piece with a long skirt that softly waves in the breeze and the top covers the chest and shoulders, exposing her arms and stomach. Her hair is designed to be long in the front, covering half her face, short on the sides, and on the back. The tips of her hair are dyed in azure blue. Her jewelry is simple with light-brown leather bracelets and small silver chains around her wrists. The necklace is also a silver chain and what hangs from it is a silver wolf head that symbols the kingdom with a purple diamond eye. Finally, her earrings are nothing really fancy. They're just white feathers with a blue trim and are connected by simple leather strings to the studs in the ears. To top it all off, bestowed on her head is a tiara decorated in diamonds that are clear and purple.

As Queen Athena Borin gets halfway down, a welcoming smile comes alive and she increases her descent speed. Tara begins to run toward her mom with a smile and tears of joy fall from her eyes.

"Mom! Mom!" Tara shouts in glee.

I . . . well . . . for some reason, my shy human side kicks in and I stop to watch both mother and daughter spread their arms to embrace each other. Once Queen Borin reaches the bottom, she takes the impact of her daughter. Tears of relief and joy also form and fall from her closed eyes.

"Tara, my sweet daughter. My wild child, welcome back home. I miss your father dearly, but I am glad you are finally home."

They both sway like the breeze. No other noises are made except from the sound of the waterfalls beside the stairway, the breeze through the trees, the ocean, and the birds that sound like seagulls flying overhead. I stand perfectly straight up and fold my hands behind my back. A few more seconds pass when Queen Borin spots me and I gulp in anxiety.

"Tara," she asks in pure curiosity. "Is that?"

Tara looks back at me. "Oh!" Then she pulls away from her mother. "Mom, that's Will, my husband from Earth."

"Are you serious?" Athena asks in a surprised tone.

I immediately kneel on my right knee and bow my head in respect.

"I'll introduce you to him," Tara says.

Silence.

Someone gasps in awe, perhaps Athena. "Are you sure?"

More silence. Then footsteps come my way. A hand gently tilts my head up. I look into the eyes of Queen Borin and they show gentleness and greetings. I'm curious of what she sees; perhaps anxiety.

"Why are you kneeling?" she speaks in a soothing tone just like her daughter and smiles. "Please, arise. You are part of the family."

I do, keeping my eyes on her, yet I keep my mouth shut in respect.

She looks at Tara. "Tara, did your husband lose the ability to speak? Again?"

Tara laughs a little, steps over to me, and rubs my shoulders to ease my anxiety. I gulp to ease it down.

"Yes, your highness. I can speak." I stretch out my right hand toward her. "I am Will Young, well, Will Borin, the human that you chatted to awhile back. It's really good to finally meet you."

She laughs, hugs me, and kisses my left cheek. "Still has the human country boy charm. I like it. Ha, well likewise. Plus, like I said, we're family and you can call me Athena." Then, she looks at Tara and says, "You did pick an excellent man." She sighs. "But, it would've been great to meet you in your human form."

And here we go again.

"Well, Athena, if I stayed human, I would've been slaughtered during the journey to Los Alamos in eliminating our enemy."

By that time, we begin up the stairs.

"Yes, I am beginning to hear a word about it. But, Will, please forgive us for giving your world our problem."

"Mom, there is no need for it," Tara reassures.

"She's right. There is a phrase that we Americans say when things just go bad," I reply.

"And what is that?"

I smile, "Shit happens."

Athena bursts out laughing. "Oh, Will, I'm really, really starting to like you."

Tara and I look at each other briefly, then back at Athena and reply in unison, "Well, that's good."

At that moment, we reach the top. Athena questions about our bags and Tara answers that they're at the portal. Athena simply orders the same men that played the bagpipes to retrieve them and take them up to her daughter's room. They bow while saying yes, head down the steps, and went across the courtyard. We continue our way into the palace and my mind gets blown by the sheer modern designs. Looking at Tara, she has the same expression as I do, but I don't know why.

"Mom, you really redid the palace."

By the sound of her voice, I'm thinking that Athena hired a very large crew to operate a swarm of Drill Bugs and Destructor droids to destroy the former palace and build this one.

Athena laughs, "Oh yes I did. Your father was very tight with traditions. I still loved him, God rest his soul, but you and I along with the Nightrunner brothers and our people could see the real value of modern technology. So, when you all were away, I took advantage at the time."

And so, she did. There are multiple recess lightings in the ceilings, modern-looking furniture, balconies above and below us with stainless-steel pipes that hold panes of glass in, and the same type of railing that travels along the other stairways and up to the other floors above us. Only two go down to the lower level. To somewhat take up some of the space, there are many pots with the same plants filled with fruits on them, ready to be picked and eaten.

"So, Will," Athena's voice brings me back to reality, "What was your occupation before, well, all of that series of unfortunate events happened?"

"Mom, seriously!"

I pat Tara's shoulder. "I was a truck driver for a few years after I graduated from high school. Before that, I was working at our local golf course." I fold my hand onto her shoulder. "If it wasn't for your mess, I wouldn't be able to meet your daughter because I was walking on an empty street that's a road of hopelessness and broken dreams. However, your daughter," I look at her and continue, "breathed new life into me."

Tara raises her hand, lowers my head, kisses my lips, and quotes from our wedding song softly. We both look at Athena and she looks down at the floor ashamed and apologizes. We both forgive her and continue following her deep into the palace. From there on out, we climb a few stairways, perhaps leading into the family's private quarters. Athena now carefully chooses her words to question about my former human life. I do my best to leave out most of the negative crap about my life and I easily summarize it up after five questions. At that moment, we enter an area where there are more walls that divide rooms on the highest floor of the palace. When we reached the top of the final stairway, the interior design of the walls, floors, interior decoration, and furniture change in color and texture. To start things off, the white tile floor becomes carpet dyed in macaroon. The walls are changed from concrete and painted white covered in granola-colored wood panels that are installed horizontally. The chairs, tables, and shelves change from being white and black to brown, cinnamon, and walnut; these colors make this area feel warmer and homier.

Athena leads us into a lounge room with the same colors. Right off our left is a mini wet bar, a counter pushed up against the wall with a mirror and glass shelves that hold different kinds of alcohol. In the middle of the room, there are two lounge couches with a coffee table in the middle. Ahead of us are floors and ceilings made out of a single pane of glass that stretch the entire length of the room. Behind one of the couches on the far-left side of the room is a stereo system. Anyway, when Athena enters the room, she waves her arm to gesture to take any spot that we like, then she turns her attention to a touch screen panel and lowers one of the electric bars, activating the tent in the glass and starting to reduce the sunlight coming through the window.

Looking out, I get the best view of the city of Sparta. I walk over to the window and right below me, I am greeted with a stadium built out of the same kind of granite forming an upward V shape. Down in the center of the V-shape arena is a long and narrow walkway and rising from it on both sides are multiple stairways with stands I assume are where the citizens can sit. Now, looking directly down below me is another walkway, but it seems to be higher than the first and it spreads out, creating some sort of a stage and on that stage are two rows with individual chairs and one row higher than the first one. Perhaps, that is where the members of royalty sit, but for what?

"That's for coronations," speaks Athena.

I turn my head to look at her and she is comfortably leaning onto one of the arms of the couch opposite from Tara as she stirs whatever type of clear alcohol in her glass. "Speaking of coronations . . ." She flicks her eyes toward Tara and Tara begins to moan.

"Ugh, mom," she begins with, leaning her weight onto one of the arms of the couch that she sits on while rubbing her eyes. "Do we really need to do an official one on that scale? I have been declared queen ever since our wedding."

Athena removes her tiara and places it on the coffee table while she sighs. "Yes, I know. But that was on a couple of different circumstances. You are now back home and we still must carry on that tradition even though, heh, I changed the majority of it." She waves her free hand around the room, gesturing to the entire palace.

I walk over to the mini bar to see what kind of alcohol is available; just looking over my options, they are all Wolfinoid drinks and my taste buds don't know any of them. So, I just grab a pint-sized glass, fill a quarter of it with ice, and just pour cold water from the faucet.

"Will, what's your opinion?" Athena asks.

"Hm?"

"What's your opinion on another coronation?"

I look at both of them, then turn my eyes to look out of the window to the beautiful blue sea that gently smacks the sandy shore line neighboring the city.

"Oh, mom don't bring him into this."

Another coronation?

I toss that question around my head and replay our wedding through my mind. Recounting the events, I know Tara and I repeated the words from the deacon, slipped on the rings, and the deacon announced to the crowd that we were husband and wife and the new king and queen of this kingdom. However, I actually think about what really happens during a coronation. I don't know the exact details. Comparing the two, they seem to be different.

Athena is right, what happened back on Earth was on different circumstances. They, or we, were at war. Our relationship before we got married . . . happened spontaneously."

I take another drink of my water while still looking out the window. "Athena, you're right. We need to do an official coronation." Then I look at Tara and say, "I'm sorry, babe, but what happened wasn't an official one. It's just like in the U.S. There's an official ceremony to inaugurate the president of the United States. They don't immediately become president right after they win the Electoral College/popular vote during the official voting day, which was like our wedding, in some aspect."

"I rest my case," Athena says in a pleasing tone.

Tara looks at me, then at her mom and back at me, and closes her eyes in annoyance. "Oh, fine. But let's make it quick. I would like to throw a party later tonight."

"Don't worry, my wild child. I'll make sure to make it as quick as possible."

It's on.

Location: Coronation Arena
Time: 4:15 PM

With the day still hot and humid, Tara and I stand at the entrance from the palace that leads to the stage of the arena in a heavy clothing material of the medieval, Celtic, traditional robes, and they are so unbearable to wear. I mean, if it was winter, like it was back on Earth, this wouldn't be a problem. Plus, we're not the only ones suffering in these clothes. In front of us is Athena who is about to give her speech and strapped to her side is a ceremonial sword. Behind us is Chris and Whitney, Soren and Crystal, Maddox and Faith, Dawn, Cora, and finally Gothraigh bringing up the rear. Cora and Gothraigh seem to be comfortable and they both shake their heads at us as we groan about our discomfort. Anyway, Athena breathes in and out to build up her confidence. Then, she steps out and walks up to a live mic that's dead center on the stage. Once she reaches the mic, the stands are filled from the bottom to the top with the citizens of Sparta and they cheer. She raises both her arms in command to settle down and they do.

"Citizens of Sparta, as you well know, it has been centuries since we had a coronation. You also well know that we have won the war against our enemy and they have been completely wiped off from the face of the universe."

The crowd roars triumphantly as cannons at the top of the stands fire out large pieces of purple confetti. Again, Athena raises her arms for silence.

"My citizens, as you can see, my husband and your king, Cedric, is not standing beside me delivering this speech to you. But, let's not allow that to sadden this beautiful day that our daughter, Tara, becomes your new queen and ruler." The crowd cheers again. Athena talks over them, "And ruling beside her is her husband Will, who once was human, yet is now one of us. Do not let that mislead you for I see he has great intentions for this city."

In reality, I actually do, but I will let Tara do most of the ruling business.

Anyway, that is our que to step out and walk onto the stage. While so, the roaring of the crowd is more powerful, yet we all remain serious. Tara and I approach and stop like five feet away from her mom. At the same time, the other guys take their seats in the chairs behind us. Athena turns around and puts her right hand on the sword, ready to pull it out; before she does, she asks both of us to kneel. And we do.

"In all of the lands of Sparta," Athena begins as she draws out the sword, raising the blade into the air, "I, Queen Athena Borin, dub you, my daughter, as Queen Tara Borin, the new ruler of our great city." She then taps the blade once on both of Tara's shoulders. She then steps to one side, in front of me, and raises the blade back up. "I, Queen Athena Borin, dub you, my son-in-law, as King Will Borin. The new assistant ruler of our great city." She taps the blade once on both of my shoulders.

"Arise," Athena orders and we do while she inserts the sword back into its holster and takes her seat next to Gothraigh.

I stand behind Tara, placing my hands behind my back while she takes her position at the mic. "My citizens of Sparta, it is such a great honor to be dubbed your new queen. It is a bit sad that my father is not here to witness this event, but I am sure he is seeing this from heaven with our ancestors. On a positive note, it is spectacular to be back home in the original city of Sparta, back on my home planet Kaladria, because I nearly spent a year on the planet called Earth while my father and King Terrin, king of Troy, was trying to solve our problem that surged and caused a major havoc across the nation called the United States of America. My time there wasn't a complete waste since it's there I met a charming human, a young man with a country boy side called Will Young. Of course, due to our laws, he had to be turned into one of us, as you can see behind me."

Curious conversations spread but a few turn out cheers and applause. I see that the people who are cheering are the same ones I met back at the basecamp of Sparta.

"Speaking about laws and tradition, my citizens, you all have known that some of us here in the royal family are strict about them and want to keep on following them. For example, our clothes, but since I am now your new queen, it is truly time to bring this great city into the twenty-second century. That also includes the advancement of technology, transport, and clothing."

Right after that, me and everybody else who were starting to feel we were suffocating in these robes take them off and reveal our modern clothes. Also, once the heavy garments fall off our bodies, we are greeted by the humid air that feels cool, even though it's ninety-five degrees Fahrenheit with seventy percent of humidity. The majority of the crowd gasps in awe and perhaps fear while a small portion celebrates as they too release the buttons, zippers, and snaps of the garments relieving the same clothes that we are wearing.

Tara smiles, "Heh, now with that said and out of the way, I say it's time to turn this traditional coronation into a party with a kickass concert that will be mainly performed by my awesome husband along with his friend Chris October. Joining them will be me, Whitney, Dawn, Faith, and Crystal. LED will be our tech guy for lights and sound. Anybody here can join if they want to. This coronation is now over."

The crowd stand up on their feet, cheering, applauding, and whistling; the cannons fire off three more times with the same confetti softly covering the arena due to the breeze. At the same time, royal guard members standing right below the stage start playing another celebration tune from their bagpipes. Tara turns to us and waves her hands that we should make a circle like the ones you see during football and soccer games.

When we do, she raises her voice only to us so that we can hear, "Now, how 'bout we get this party really going?"

We all nod in agreement and start heading back inside; Chris taps my shoulder and puts his mouth next to my ear, "What songs are we going play, Nos?"

"I don't know. We'll just go with the flow."

At the same time, I look over my shoulder at the beach and mentally pick the first song that will totally match the geography of the land.

CHAPTER FIFTY-FOUR
Concert
Location: The Beach
Time: 6:00 PM

THE SUN BEGINS TO set over the ocean while we do an equipment check, mostly tuning them so that they sound right. Yes, we are going to use the same devices that make us sound legit. Yes, it's cheating, but guess what? Y'all ain't here to stop us. Nonetheless, LED does make sure that the lights, sounds, and other components are working properly. The area that we are in is on the largest part of the beach on the northern rim of the city, right next to the mountain. There are some areas covered in boulders, but behind the sandy shore is a grass-covered field that's flat and big as a football field's length and then slowly goes upward about fifty feet. Closer to the stage are three towers. Each has two large, stadium lights for the field and in between the lights are cameras that face toward the stage to project our performances on large screens for the crowd that sit far away on the hill. Around the perimeter of the field are several bars because according to LED, *a lot* of Wolfinoids are going to show up; at this time, only a few hundred are on the lawn and it's only been nearly two hours ago when the coronation concluded. Also, it's the summer season and Tara told Chris and me that the sun doesn't fully set behind the ocean around twenty hundred hours. So, we have loads of time to discuss what songs to play and from what genre while making sure that the lights along with the other effects are calculated perfectly at certain points of the songs.

Now, the stage sits on the beach with a concrete foundation that spans forty feet into the ocean with breaker rocks surrounding it and in width, it spans one hundred feet. The stage itself rises six feet from the ground and only has two sets of stairs on both ends of the stage that are exits and entrances. Like any other human concert, we have security to guard the entire length of the stage at ground level without barriers that's going to hold back the crowd. However, we don't mind. Like I said before, there are cameras that will show us live on large screens that are just two very big panes of glass and they are secured to heavy-duty chromed trusses that stand twenty feet high and have cross members that hold the lights, speakers, and other components for the show. As of now, we only have normal lights on to illuminate the stage and the mics are off.

"Alright, guys," LED sounds pleased with himself while patting the side of the screen that controls the effects on the stage. "Everything is set and ready to go? My lord?"

"Yeah, man?" I answer while sitting on a stool, tuning one of the electric guitars.

"What song are we going to play first?"

I look out to the ocean for a moment and smile as the title of the first song arises in my mind.

"Oh, boy, Nos, what song do ya have in your head?" Chris asks as he, too, is sitting on a stool tuning a bass.

I look at him and say, "What Tara told me was right. You and I almost have the same artists on our iPods."

"And what does that mean?" HE asks.

I look at the other guys and ordered, "The first song we're gonna play is 'Rum and Girls' by Brian Mountain."

"Why that song?" Crystal asks as she leans over her electronic keyboard.

"Because, it's a tropical song with a tropical tune based in a tropical environment." When I get to the words "tropical environment," I spread my arm around the stage to show that we're in a tropical environment.

"Oh, I like that one," Tara says with a smile as she sits behind the drum set and spins one of the drum sticks in her fingers. "And I think it's a good choice. Let's do it."

"Yeah, but there's a problem. It's eighteen hundred and ten and the sun hasn't completely set. Plus, the field isn't entirely filled up," Whitney explains.

She does have a good point.

"What other songs should we play?" Dawn asks.

I set aside the guitar and pull out my iPod and begin browsing, mentally playing the songs in my head that I have heard before, and checking which ones will smoothly after the previous ones.

After a while, this is the best answer I can come up for Dawn's question, "I don't know? We'll just go with the flow. Whatever we play, the crowd is still going to enjoy the show."

"But what about the sun?" Whitney points out, "I think the show will be better when it's dark."

I look up from the iPod and checked out the sun's position. It hovers casually over the horizon, and I turn my attention to our crowd; people are still entering the field and situating themselves in their desired spots to have a good view of us.

Then I return my gaze to the guys. "We'll start the show around twenty hundred hours."

Everybody nods in agreement and then LED answers, "Alright, then, I'll get the timer set up."

Time: 8:00 PM

Once the timer on the screens reaches zero, they shudder as they change from being a black screen with bright-orange-colored numbers to crystal clear HD pictures revealing us. Some stage lights are dim while others change colors. The stadium lights are turned off, and the crowd begins to cheer and whistle. I step up to my mic as the bracelets begin moving our hands to strike the very first chords.

When the song ended, I swing my guitar to my back, deactivate the voice changer, and speak into the mic with enthusiasm.

"Y'all enjoyed that song?"

The crowd cheers again. I look around me and everybody on stage smiles at their audience and I, too, smile to the positive vibe rising up tonight.

"Does anyone of you guys enjoy digital rock music?"

Everybody in the crowd looks a bit confused yet curious of what's coming next.

"Yo, LED." I point to his direction as he stands off to my left side on the stage in front of his control panel; I power down my guitar. "Let's do New Canyon by Parking Lincoln."

He gives me the thumbs up and turns off the main lights as we change our positions. I'll be the lead singer, Whitney on the drum set, Dawn on the turntables and other devices, Chris on the electric guitar, and Tara on the bass. Then, we give him the thumbs up and soon, LED activates the smoke machines and lasers as that song begins to play; within those few moments, I reactivate the voice changer and remove the microphone from its holster.

The crowd goes crazier when that song came to an end. In the middle of the excitement, Tara surprises me as she grabs one of my arms, and slightly pulls me toward LED. She raises her voice just loud enough for me to hear.

"How 'bout we do this song next?" She nicely gestures for the man to move out the way and she begins scrolling through my iPod library on the larger screen of the control panel. She finally finds the artist she's looking for, taps the icon, and looks through the songs by that artist. Later, she finds the one she's looking for and points at it.

"Florida Queen-Crescenting Wave."

I nod in agreement. She smiles.

"I want you to play the electric guitar."

I smile, "No problem, babe."

We switch positions again. I situate myself on a stool next to the mic that Tara is going to use. Whitney does the same thing except her stool is next to the drum set that Chris is going to play and she's going to play the acoustic guitar. Finally, Dawn situates herself on a stool behind me and is going to play the base. Again, we give LED the thumbs up.

When we finished, LED comes around from his stand with a mic at the ready. "Wow, those songs, just wow, Will." Then, he turns his attention to the audience. "You know, some of you guys that were with us back on planet Earth and joined us for our queen's birthday party and our Christmas Eve party have been asking me, 'When is Will and his friends going to replay those songs?' And I've been wondering about that, too."

Some parts of the crowd cheers and applauses LED for saying that. He continues.

"Well, I see that this is the great time to replay those songs."

Tara and I look at one another for a moment. She turns off her voice changer, and speaks into her mic, "And what songs do my great people want to hear again?"

Just to give you guys a heads up, the answers come from small groups from our left to right in this order.

The far-left side, "'Trust is Back' by Diamond Back!"

The left side, "No, 'Screw the Law' by the Duramaxes!"

The center, "Better, your wedding song, 'Alive and True' by Cold Water!"

The right side, "Do 'Oh Man' by Josh Black!"

The far-right side, "Even better, 'Rockin' in the Woods' by Quintin Gill!"

I stand back up and place my mouth next to Tara's mic, "How 'bout we play them all?"

The crowd goes absolutely nuts. With that said, this how we ordered the playlist: we start off with "Alive and True," then play

"Trust Is Back." Next is "Screw the Law." Right after that is "Oh Man," and finally, we play "Rockin' in the Woods." In between those songs, we changed our positions on the stage while turning off and on different instruments to play the songs. When we concluded playing the final song, our audience shout out one, simple demand.

"one more song! One more song! One more song! One more song!"

I turn to look at the guys and I ask, "What are your suggestions?" since I was the lead singer for the last one and still have the acoustic guitar in front of me.

All of them shrug their shoulders and give me the expression that they don't know what to pick.

I look at my good old high school friend, "Chris, do you have any suggestions? Since you and I were human."

He shrugs one shoulder. "I don't know, Nos. I've been having a badass time."

I look about the stage and my eyes stop on Tara as she bites her lower lip and looks down. The expression on her face shows that she is in deep thought, remembering something. At the same time, I remember Gothraigh told me that she got a hold of my iPod and the majority of the library is occupied by country music, influencing her to bring out her cowgirl side, especially on the day I returned, well, home.

What song is she trying to remember?

Soon, her eyes shoot up to us, light up, and she snaps her fingers. She quickly looks at me with a smile and then pulls out some scratch paper, a pen, and writes on it. Then she gets up from the drum set and shows me her little message in her beautiful handwriting.

"'You Don't Understand' by Quintin Gill."

I look up. "You sure?"

She nods quickly.

"Alright then, let's play 'You Don't Understand' by Quintin Gill."

We all agreed and we rearrange, but this time, Chris is on base, Tara is back on the drums, Dawn is on the keyboard, Whitney is on the acoustic guitar, and I'm back on the electric guitar. This time, we move the drum set to the front while setting a stool beside it for me to be next to my Wolfinoid cowgirl. Once that's done, Tara walks over to the right side of the stage and opens up a box. In moments, she pulls out the same cowboy hat I saw her wear on the day I returned and places it on her head. She then pulls out a solid straw similar from what I had when I was an asphalt cowboy. Coming back to sit down behind the set, she leans over while removing my camo hat and replaces it with a cowboy. She leans back while admiring the small transformation. I smile while huffing a laugh and returning my gaze back to our audience. Within moments, we get ourselves situated in our last, playing positions, and both Tara and I nod to our D.J. Our man gets the pause time ready before we play and programs the song in his control panel. Right after that, he gives us a thumbs up. Immediately, Tara starts banging the drums for the opening of "You Don't Understand" by Quintin Gill and I immediately follow in with a few guitar chords.

As always when the song ended, the crowd goes wild again. The main lights on the stage come alive again and Tara speaks into the mic I've handed to her, "Thank you so much for coming out and enjoying the show. We're going to turn in and you have a great night."

The crowd cheers again, begins departing the field, and the stadium lights come back on; we all stand up and walk straight to the front edge of the stage and bow. Interestingly, one of the guards standing by the stage gets their queen's attention. She bends down to hear a message from him. I cock my head to the side and Tara nods slowly as the message from the guard is whispered into her ear. She looks back at me, then back at the guard, and thanks him for the message.

Tara puts the mic aside on top of one of the speakers that sit on the floor of the stage and takes both of my hands into hers. The look in her eyes suggest that she is very pleased by the news that she received.

"Is there something I need to know?"

She glances down at her hands as they slowly massage mine, "Yeah there is." She looks back at me and continues, "But you need to follow me into the forest because it is mainly about you. It's something you're really going to love and thank me for."

What?

Tara laughs and begins to tow me to the steps on the far-right side of the stage. My curiosity and confusion slowly begin to rise.

CHAPTER FIFTY-FIVE
My Official Welcome Home Present
Location: Deep in the Spartan Woods
Time: 9:00 PM

TARA AND I WALK through a narrow gap between the extremely tall pine and maple trees, holding hands, still enjoying the vibe from the concert, laughing, and just enjoying the light breeze that blows through the trees around us. The night is moonless, yet the stars shine so brightly in the Kaladrian sky, perhaps brighter than the ones that surround the Earth. Our eyes have fully adjusted to the darkness and lighting our way are hundreds upon hundreds of fireflies that twinkle softly at different heights. All in all, this environment feels to me so magical, almost like a fairy tale. And I love it. To top this beautiful area off, Tara guides me up a nice easy slope and right next to us, perhaps just a few feet into the woods, is a brook that softly gurgles downhill. I am curious where Tara is taking me.

We still walk side by side, hand in hand, enjoying the night.

"Is there something on your mind, Will?" Tara asks.

"Yeah, there is. Where are you taking me? Actually, what was that message that the guard gave you?"

She stops us, comes in front of me, and lowers my head to kiss me, "It's a surprise gift and you'll definitely love it."

After that, we continue.

Later on, a soft glow of light outlines through the trees.

Tara stops us. "We're here," she whispers with a smile.

She lets go of my hand, pulls up one of the leggings of her jeans, and unwraps a piece of fabric from her ankle. Next, she comes behind me, holding the fabric in her hands.

"Close your eyes," she commands.

"Why? What's over there?" I ask in curiosity.

"Just close your eyes, babe."

I quickly throw up my hands for moment like "okay, whatever" and I close my eyes. I can feel the fabric being draped in front of my eyes and a knot being created on the back of my head. Tara secures it tightly, laughing, enjoying the moment. I laugh too but in slight confusion of what's happening.

"Can you see anything?"

Just darkness.

"Nope, nothing," I assure her.

"Good," Tara happily replies and starts pushing me forward.

This totally feels like when we had sex the first time.

"Are we going to have sex again?"

"Hm, maybe. It just depends after you see your surprise gift."

We keep on moving forward. Pretty soon, the slope evens out, but that doesn't stop Tara as she continues pushing me forward. After several strides, she tells me to stop, then says we're finally here and tells me that I can remove the cloth from her eyes. Once I do, I am completely blown away from what stands in front of me.

In front of me is a log cabin. Its beautiful design has three flat walls, one on the far left of the house and two (one of them facing us) on the sides. On the far-right side, it's shaped like the tip of an arrow, mainly pointing toward a large body of water that's twenty yards away and dimly lit by the electrical lights that illuminate the cabin on the inside and outside. There is a deck that wraps around the entire cabin with small lights at each corner and three little stairways that are four steps high; one in front of us lead up to the original front door and two in front of the arrow head. The cabin only has two levels, along with large windows, especially near the front, that clearly show the ground floor and the second floor.

Tara kisses one of my cheeks. "Happy late birthday, Will."

"What?" I look at her.

She smiles, "Your birthday was on June third, correct?"

"Yeah," I answer in disbelief.

When she mentioned, it I think back to what was happening on that day and I'm reminded that we were out to war, so I didn't really care about it. Looking back at my welcome home and birthday present, I am totally grateful that Tara put this together.

"Would like to step inside?" she asks.

"Yeah, sure."

I open the door and enter the foyer, which immediately opens right into the kitchen that smoothly flows into the dining and living room area. The pieces of furniture and decor in the dining and living room area are Western Mountaineer. On the center wall, against the point of the arrow in the living room, are chimney and fireplace that's constructed out of huge, smooth river rocks, and hanging upon two hooks that's been drilled in the mortar is the American flag. I walk into the living room, getting a closer look to make sure I'm not hallucinating. Looking around the cabin and taking it all in, I stand near the fireplace, looking at the kitchen. Off to its right is a short hallway that leads to another room and above the kitchen is a loft where a king-sized bed along with other pieces of furniture resides and continues the Western Mountaineer style. I return my attention to my wife as she leans against the stairway that leads up to the loft with a pleasing smile on her face and arms crossed.

"What's—" I begin to ask.

"Down that hall is a recreation room with a foosball table, a billiard table, and a simple dart board. Overall, do you like it, Will?"

I let my eyes wander all over the place, then I look back at her. "Again, this is my late surprise birthday gift?"

"Yep."

I walk back to her, placing both hands on her shoulders. "Like it? I love it. But how . . ."

Tara puts one of her hands on my face. "Remember that day you and I spent time together so that can we know each other better?"

I nod.

"Remember what I was doing something on my tablet?"

I nod again.

"Before the satellites went out, I sent a message back here to have a crew build you this place to make you feel more welcomed at home and remember where you came from."

I kiss my wife softly with gratitude and I move my mouth to her ear, "Let's go to bed, baby."

She kisses me back and agrees; then, we start turning off the lights on the main level and when we get to the loft, we turn off the ceiling lights, only leaving the lamps on that sit on each night stand beside the bed. All the times, Tara was the one to lower me into her bed before we went to sleep. This time, I lower her onto my new bed and we kiss once more.

"Welcome home, Will," she says quietly.

"It's good to be home," I reply back in the same tone and I turn off the lamps.

THE END